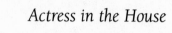

*Actress in the House*

# Actress in the House

*a novel*

Joseph McElroy

THE OVERLOOK PRESS
Woodstock & New York

ACKNOWLEDGMENTS

To Gilbert Girion, Nick Pappas, and Robert Walsh, thanks for reading this
book in an earlier form and helping with criticism as well as praise.


First published in the United States in 2003 by
The Overlook Press, Peter Mayer Publishers, Inc.
Woodstock & New York

WOODSTOCK:
One Overlook Drive
Woodstock, NY 12498
www.overlookpress.com
[for individual orders, bulk and special sales, contact our Woodstock office]

NEW YORK:
141 Wooster Street
New York, NY 10012

The author wishes to thank Alfred A. Knopf (Publishers) Inc. for permission to quote,
on p. 134, lines from "Turning Point" by Rainer Maria Rilke, translated by William H. Gass
in *Reading Rilke*, 1999; and for permission to quote, on p. 59, lines from *Elia Kazan: A Life*
by Elia Kazan, 1988; and Penquin Books Ltd. for permission to quote, on p. 402,
lines from Homer's *The Odyssey*, translated by E.V. Rieu, 1946.

∞ The paper used in this book meets the requirements for paper
permanence as described in the ANSI Z39.48-1992 standard.

Library of Congress Cataloging-in-Publication Data

McElroy, Joseph.
Actress in the house : a novel / Joseph McElroy
p. cm.
1. Actresses—Fiction. 2. New York (N.Y.)—Fiction. I. Title.
PS3563.A293 A64 2003    813'.54—dc21    2002034555

*Book design and type formatting by Bernard Schleifer*
Printed in the United States of America
ISBN 1-58567-350-1
FIRST EDITION
1 3 5 7 9 8 6 4 2

# Contents

# FIRST NIGHT

## 1

A SHOCK, THAT'S ALL IT WAS, IN THE DARKENED HOUSE. THE GIRL struck by her partner very hard. It had staggered her, it was over the line, you wondered how she was standing. Her partner had clapped her one to the side of her face with the full flat of his hand, and it had swung her right around toward the audience, almost knocked her off the stage, and she was hurt. The man in the eighth row from his angle hadn't seen it coming; but neither had she seen it you could almost believe, the actress herself. Something wrong up there. He was stunned and amazed, he was honestly thrilled, not stunned at all.

A sound from the house, a gasp, a groan, almost a word. You could probably understand her partner's reaction, what she'd sprung on him, meddling in his home life. God, a small disaster in his life. The actor's arm coming up out of nowhere so quick it wasn't acting. It was over the line, assault, a desire to rid the place of her—her not-to-be-denied voice, her face. But he can't. At one blow it all goes to pieces. A blow like that. It says it all. But what? It all comes together. The man in the eighth row could be up there with her.

Anger recoiled through him, protest condensed and was gone. He'd been miles away yet following the action. The woman next to him whispered, "I knew it." *What* did she know? What did Helen know? He smelled her scent leaning up against him now reminding him of whatever she can. He had forgotten she was there and why he was here. His last name whispered is all the years she's known him. "Daley?" It's quite some whisper. "What did you say, 'He *can't*'?"

Daley hadn't said a thing.

"Can't do what?" The whisper threatened to be chatty. When up there on stage the actress stood in some danger. Who was she to get clobbered like that? She acted like her hands were tied. The actor had smashed her, wiped her right off the stage, but he couldn't do it. She wouldn't fall out into the audience. Who did she think she was?

Across his brow fell a lock of lank, black hair, his potato-picking broad face virile with obligation and a pride pale and nearly purpose-less. *Mm-hmm*, something of a killer.

Somebody snorted, incredibly. The big fellow directly in front of Helen and Daley. His head lolled from side to side, but he wasn't try-ing to see; he could see perfectly. The actress was hurt. She was slow now. You could tell, her gaze held in place by sheer damage control, looking out into the house. Daley wanted to remind her of the chair upstage behind her. She looked his way, he thought.

"*What?*" came Helen's whisper. He had exhaled deeply.

The actor spoke. "Yeah, *I* did that. Glad I could."

It was a little off, dumb. "Get outa here," the actress said. She tried to smile. Because she cared almost. The planes of her face were young and worn. She was twenty-three, maybe less. Her voice, her shoul-ders. She took a deep breath and kind of looked into the house—at Daley, it seemed—and absorbed him, her way of thinking. *I'm fine*, her eyes said. Was the shock look acting? Daley knew a little about con-cussion. Her ears must be ringing with brother love, and he thought she should sit down in that chair a few feet behind her. The chair upstage of her that she'd *been* sitting in. It actually sparkled off its legs or the horizontal slat along the seat, couldn't tell, and lifted a little. She had been sitting in it a minute ago, leaning forward, her buttocks alert on the seat, and Daley thought the chair, now empty, lifted an inch or two off the stage, as much as your average pretentious chair, or a star on a summer night budging slightly in the sky.

What did Daley know? No more than the next pretentious fool. Concussion.

"Well?" the actress said. The actor seemed to be thinking it over. He was a little short on talent, that was all. Some hell that caught up with the two of them. The audience didn't know what to do. Hard to put your finger on. The actor said something. You could hardly hear him. It helped, it was kind of convincing and bitter, and a murmur from the audience at this spread into restlessness against him like another silence. They got it. A young unmarried crowd in this down-town house quick to pick up what they recognized.

The blow had silenced her, yet not really. It had spun her around and aimed her, her ears were ringing, Daley knew. Concussion, com-motion in the eye, retina displaced. He'd had it explained to him once, a dozen retina X-rays for a litigation. No matter what she'd done the blow was extreme, the stroke to the cheekbone the broth-er'd given her, the side of her head. She'd told on him. Had she tor-pedoed the marriage?

She'd taken the blow. That was what she had done. It hadn't bounced off. She'd absorbed it, Daley thought. He liked her for a sec-ond for this. Why you were here. She makes them stop and take notice. Loudspeaker voice came out of nowhere from time to time soft and strangely informative, hers, just like a voice on the phone and everything stops for twenty, thirty seconds, and it's *her*, Daley knew it at once, it gets inside you, some personal history rerunning now, the kind of thing they would do in the theater, he guessed. If she would only go sit down again in that chair. Is she giving her partner one more chance at her? Anybody who'd let you do that to them. She was looking this way now. It was the shock in the eyes, canny, seeing narrowly but everything; a smile of disquiet above the landscape of audience that was not a smile, thank God.

She had had experience of this, it came to him. She was wiped out, fragile more than you'd have thought (all bets off), thriving on it, determined, foolishly voluptuous, a learning curve in herself, and she was looking this way now, free, edgy, blonde, frizzier, panting a little at this distance, her chest and belly. He'd been taken aback. *Siddown*, Daley said to her with his eyes, for it was in his direction she stared as if she knew him. His eyeballs tickled and the darkness of the house receded upon the lantern of the stage, Daley shoulder to shoulder with Helen, people in the row behind whispering.

*Sit down*, he thought. The actress brought her hand up. A pink place grew where she had been smacked. A tiny darkness at the nostril, snot, a crack, a trickle, she smeared it over her lip and its blood color came up under the lights, honest blood. Daley's sight felt physical, peeled. To be up there. (*Was* it him she marked with her look, or a pillar? Or this guy in front of Daley and Helen who couldn't control his head. The big fellow who made the rude sound again.) The young woman's mouth parted, stricken, electric, the cheeks gained resolve. She held up her finger. "Look," she said.

Helen leaned against Daley. "Think she bleeds every night?"

*Please*. He lifted a hand in the dark. He couldn't believe she'd said it. She'd had to.

The whisper came again, "How do they *do* that?"

As if faking blood were some technical thing a man knew about, ask him. "It's not *how*," he murmured; "it's . . ."

"I remember it," the actor said. The words surprised the actress. Her blood? Her finger?

"That's right you remember, and you'll be sorry," the actress said. ("Oh *yes*," Helen breathed.)

"Why did you ever come back?" The actor said his line, but he felt careless of her, the blood leaking, accidental.

"God," Helen breathed. Daley felt her body next to him relax, they were a little mad at each other and he saw them once upon a time taking a bath together.

Would the loudspeakers break in again with the voice-over that had several times already halted the action? A weightless authority in it. You had to like it. What had been was turned into Now. She herself did it. "Have I seen her before?" Helen asked.

"*You* might have," Daley said, for he had truthfully not seen the young woman before.

"That voice." Helen was the one who knew about these things; she was the one who got the tickets as a rule, but this time he'd had a little surprise for her. She was tired. People had been talking about this play, she'd told him when he picked her up. Really? Mm-hmm. Well he hadn't known about the play. He hadn't? she asked. Then how . . . ? —as if something had tipped her off. They were leaving the lobby of her building.

A cab had pulled over. Daley had stepped into the street. Helen was tired, for her. He smelled her wholeness. He held her hand in the cab. She asked what had been going on. San Francisco had been awful, she'd wanted to tell him upstairs, tried to now, leaned against him, couldn't think who to be—she looked at her watch, was he glad she was home? He'd been to hear some jazz Monday. Over by the river. Remember that old drummer?

*And you didn't know anything about the play?*

The young actress looked this way. She had to key on anything, a face, a cast-iron column in this former warehouse. She's nothing like the newspaper photo outside. She's holding on, she's navigating. But something *was* up to Daley. *Is this,* her hand said, *all he can do to me?* Her lip, her cheek said it, absorbing like a terrific blow untold causes of things, telling him, only him. The chair upstage definitely budged then, lifted a little. Like a person *in* it. It was the light. And the girl glanced behind her, but her hands were tied, you felt—she made you feel it.

"Daley?" he heard beside him. He rested his hand on Helen's thigh, spread his thumb snugly. "Daley," the whisper came at him again, and he turned and looked at her, and the aisle just beyond her. Years condensing into this man who happened to be sitting in this seat off to the actress's left in light shed from the stage, from the two people up there. Her new readiness, her shoulders her hips unprotected, subtle, rich. She wouldn't know him from some other spectral face out in the house, would she? Into the expectancy of this place came a haranguing voice from outside in the street: "You know it," the voice bawled, and a truck, directly offstage in the wing it was so close, tumbled by as if it would fall apart; and out in the city an ambulance speeding north, Daley was sure—a fire truck. Somebody had goofed on the acoustics in renovating the building. "Daley," Helen whispered. The big man in front of them heard. He was superior, head swaying, not drunk, half undone, young but. Dumb? No. Wasn't the actress in some danger? Daley took his hand away from Helen's leg.

The stage went dark. The houselights had come up, like a lowering of the light, the stage now drab and equal. We've landed. The chair on stage sparkled no more. A halfway mediocre show if we were talking about the play itself, in a downtown twelve-dollar-a-seat house.

"Was she looking right at us, or what?" Helen opened her program.

"She had to look someplace."

"That's right, she did." Helen was about to read from the little computer printout.

Slipping out of her shirt, slumped in a straight chair in the dressing room, her legs out, her shoulders pale, holding Kleenex to her nose or a cold red Coke can, the actress—who would go to her? The guy had wanted to kill her. She was telling *him* something. The actor had burned his bridges. What was it? He had crossed the line. Fuck her, he could just break her neck.

"She's in trouble," Daley said.

"Yeah," Helen said for some reason and laid her head on his shoulder a moment.

"You haven't slept in a bed since the night before last," Daley said; they'd had a little difference of opinion before the play began and it was probably over now. "What person in your position takes the red-eye?" In Helen it was no bad thing to get two or three jobs done at a time. Daley had only the deepest respect for her. He knew her, though she was sometimes misunderstood.

Working all night on a plane, Helen with the aisle, of course.

"From the red-eye to the bathtub to the office," he said. He felt her chuckle.

"That's it."

"The mirror steamed flat," he added.

"That nice message on my machine. That was nice."

"*Mm-hmm.*"

"It was great that you got the tickets. People are talking about it."

Glad to be back from the Coast, walking in the door at seven-thirty this morning, jabbing her answering machine, her thoughts collecting. Helen just in toto, the whole package. Working her way back across the continent. Clock hands racing the arc of dark land, yet paused by the breadth of the continent. Daley was familiar with the pale patch of a mountain out the window like a delta. A string of highway visible even at night like snow with a single light here and there. He could be with Helen.

A woman behind them said, "You could see it coming a block away." "Not me," said Daley over his shoulder. Helen elbowed him. A man said, "She had it coming." There'd been a feeling in the house like a test of friendship. "I didn't see it coming," Daley said, "and I don't think she did." "Oh she must have," said Helen. "She didn't and she did," said Daley. "You sound . . . ," said Helen against his shoulder, pushing him, but didn't mean it; he wanted to tell her. The actress was in trouble but he had known that.

"I must say they worked the voice-over for all it was worth," Helen said.

"Those were the letters to the brother," Daley said.

"It was what she was *thinking*."

"No, it was letters she wrote him from Nepal."

"It was what she was thinking," said Helen.

"That too," Daley said.

Never *really* hear these voice-over words in the darkened house that came from everywhere and nowhere, passing, stopping everything, they made the people freeze onstage, a voice (an authority) close like a beloved on the phone; amplified but from the outset unmistakably the woman. Coming from the house. Borderline embarrassing, Daley thought, a voice-over. A voice that knew something. That's why you're here, Daley thought. Dominant, unbearably dear, proof against anything that voice, even the blow. The odd story took shape. A young American, an adventure she had come back from. Better she should never have come back, though not really. Kid sister comes home from abroad to find her brother's life in Connecticut something of a mess. Nothing you couldn't live with, but something here, options, and she's in the middle of it somehow after three years in the Peace Corps or two there and one in Nepal, not clear. Her doing partly, you get a feeling; or her way of reminding you. He asked for it though. "She's at the center of it all," Daley said, sounding a little important. (An outsider, it came to him.)

"The brother wanted her back but then he didn't," said Helen.

"Well."

"The audience liked it. That's what it's all about," said Helen.

"I don't know," said Daley.

"What do you mean, you don't know? 'Becca Lang,'" Helen read.

"That's her," said Daley.

"It is? Well, she's got two lines of bio, what's the matter with her?"

"Maybe she—"

"Whereas the brother's got . . . twelve. And look at the bartender from the first scene. *Why* does she need only two lines?" said Helen.

"Read them," Daley said.

"Hiding her light under a bushel. Who does she think she is?" said Helen, "'. . . studied philosophy in Canada. She is preparing a one-woman—'" Helen glanced at Daley—"'theater piece.'" The big young man in front of them made that sound again, his head rolled—a mouth fart. Just another person who knew better than the rest of us. Or weak necked, or it was a vestige of athletics, some habit of breathing.

"Another remarkable woman," Daley said.

"Undoubtedly," Helen said.

People were muted, getting up.

"Who had hemophilia," Helen said, "Richard Burton?—I think that's right." Daley looked at her lips, she at his. The action would resume, the actress, hardly more than a girl, the young woman, set apart, alone, close to the others by virtue of her travels, her superior experience. It was thrilling to see the girl get slugged—it was dramatic, it was even weirdly cool, up-front; in the movies next thing she'd be spread-eagled on a quilt. They could fake the blow to the face.

"Still, it's got something," the woman behind them said; "but what?"

"The blonde," said the man.

His wife laughed harshly. "We should go to Nepal."

"She must have said something to him just before they went on," said Helen.

The woman who took tickets, answered the phone, did everything, came out onto the stage. It was her moment, but it wasn't. She got hold of the two straight chairs with her strong hands and carried them off like a scale. She moved her lips, talking to herself, an attitude in her eye. People depended on her.

"They're moving this uptown," Helen said.

"This?" said the woman.

Helen gave Daley a look. In the cab she had told him all about this play that *he* was taking *her* to. "Well, they're not moving yet," Daley said, watching for Becca, wondering how you got backstage—

something was about to happen, it came to him. The big young man in front of them who had laughed when the actress got hit made that sound again with his mouth, his head rolled.

"Full house on a Wednesday," Helen said in a way she had of speaking to everyone.

"Small theater," Daley said. "These are house seats they sold you," said Helen. It sounded like he'd been fleeced for a second when these were just the tickets they'd had. Yet she was grateful, and now she wondered what would happen.

"House seats," the woman said; "you know someone?"

"The girl said they were," said Helen. She didn't really want to talk to the people behind them.

Daley said that he hadn't known a thing about the play.

The guy in front of them made that sound again, his head rolled. "But they're moving up*town*," said Helen, "that's what I hear. It's closing down Saturday, or maybe it's a week from Saturday. What is it?" she said. The woman now coming out on stage with a glass bowl of apples and oranges might have been alone in the theater. She was tall and half formed and believed in her job and was in New York wherever she was from. But she was the person Daley and Helen had had words about in the dark just as the play was starting. Helen had believed the girl was from Rome with quite beautiful features, her cheekbones molded upward, her eyes wide apart, her mouth immature, yet from her bearing who could tell what she would say? She set the bowl down and clenched her hands. What had happened?

"There's your woman from Rome or wherever," Daley said.

"It was you she made the fist at." Helen wasn't including the people behind them: "You see that giant ring on her hand?"

"It's a silver ring," said the man behind them.

"More like a steel part," Daley said. "That's right," Helen said; "when she found our tickets I said, 'Look at that ring,' and she made a fist: 'If I could unload it on someone,' she said, that's what she said, she was looking for someone to un*load* it on." Helen twisted around. The man said, "I'll take it."

"It wasn't quite like that," Daley said.

The wife made a sound: "What *really* happened?" She touched

Daley's shoulder, good mother, dark little terrorist who knew Daley knew something, as if it mattered.

The big guy in front lifted himself out of his seat. He peered around at Daley and Helen, this baleful figure, puffy about the eyes, looming. "So you thought she was looking at you."

"Not only—" Helen began. The young man erupted coughing terribly, or laughing, whatever it was, saliva flying—he badly wanted a cigarette. His shirt half open wanted it, the suit he'd been in all day, his yellow tie down and twisted around showing the label, his great chin wanted it containing his history if you read it at the brink.

"You *laughed*?" said Daley, "when she got hit?"

"Laughed? Coulda taken a swipe at her myself," the young man said humbly.

"You and the actor."

"Oh she's askin' for it."

"Not *you*." Daley had his hand on the seat in front.

"Speak for yourself." The young man getting out of the row into the aisle cleared his throat. Daley laughed; it was not a good moment. "That's the Peace Corps for you," the other said, and erupted coughing.

"What *about* the Peace Corps?" Daley slid forward, Helen's hand on his arm; "don't tell me about the Peace Corps." Helen's hand turned Peace Corps into whatever: "He can't do with*out* her," Daley said, "where would he be without her in the play I mean?"

"Connecticut, that's where he'd be," said the big fellow. He was turning away.

"They're like this," Daley crossed two fingers. People listened. "You know it," said the other seriously; "they're the same blood 'n' all that. She can take a beating, say that for her, and come back at you with you don't know what." He was big and overweight, impressive, a fool sort of for one so young, and able to burst out laughing. "But she's got the crooks"— coughing consuming and terrible and hopeless and confident rose in this man again, behind it that laughter, from the chest breaking upward into his head, crashing out of him canny, quite grand, good, helpless before his life—"got the crooks running—" again his thought halted by hacking laughter, hoarse, ready-to-hawk-it-out-on-the-floor laughter insolent and knowing, yet not above you; not a loner really, a little-brother type, no future to speak of except a future out there suddenly—jabbing at or uppercutting or smashing whatever—no, awash with material it came to Daley (the lawyer sizer-upper), swimming in it.

"Crooks," he said.

"Well. You know. The guys running the show."

"What guys?" Daley asked.

"You're in for a long night, brother," said the young man.

"It's half over," Daley said.

"Less," said the other, "much less," his eyes in the meat of his face a joke, something about him.

"*You* came back," Helen said, joining in. If she only wouldn't.

The man made a face, he was funny, didn't care, he sniffed deeply, squeezing his cheek up to open one arched nostril. "The evening becomes the night," he said like a fool and set off up the aisle, which was built in long steps; "she was lookin' at *you* all right even if she didn't—"

"*What* crooks?" Daley said and got up.

"—even if she didn't know it," he heard the retreating figure say. "Lookin' for trouble, prob'ly find it . . . *both* of ya."

"*What* crooks?" Daley called after him, and thought he heard, as Helen squeezed his hand, "Got it all figured out."

"He's bluffing," Helen said. "He's . . ."

A couple now squeezing past Daley. Daley caught a man's eye several rows back and did not give ground, it was stupid, a man holding a big hat, a New York or Colorado face that looked familiar toward the center sitting with a boy. The boy was freckled and dignified. It wasn't his boy, it came to Daley. Helen squeezed Daley's hand.

"He'll be back."

"He took his coat with him," said Daley.

"Good, he won't be in front of us. It's raining."

Daley stepped over Helen, through her scent, her humor and mature intimacy, her understanding eyes; and he thought she might get up. He was standing in the aisle.

She was making up just a little after the words they'd had as the lights went down. "He knows someone," she said; "I thought you handled him."

"He *knows* someone?"

A small child lay against the woman behind them like a confession, in a red sweater and pink overalls, out of place. Four years old it came to Daley. "School night?" he said to the woman.

"Where you goin'?" the woman said. The child was getting ready to cry or to go back to sleep, didn't know what time it was.

"Never saw 'm before," Daley said.

A question waited between them. Helen let his hand go, she held him there in the aisle, his old friend, and he saw what would happen and was already there too soon to understand it, and he nearly told her he knew the actress, though this would not have been especially true, one business call, and it would still not have been clear why they were here. From Helen a neighborly radiance looking darkly up at him in Daley's experience unavailable to women under forty. He prided himself on Helen. Paying such attention to him or some side of him. He hadn't finished with her over the nosebleed remark. He counted on Helen's staying put; she didn't care much for intermission. She had a skirt on.

"Doesn't even know I'm here," Daley said then.

"*Who* doesn't?" Helen said after him.

"Exactly," he heard the woman behind them say. The dressing room, the street, he could do what he liked. Whatever he was about to do, get a breath, knock on a dressing room door, he and Helen were equals, old whatever-they-were.

The bearish young man's shoulders, the manners of the shaggy, combed hair, the quick-witted overweightness, the sprightly step and tender feet, the visionary back, the fairly well-brought-up insolence of that act of his, all passed out of sight, leaving in Daley's eye the girl insulted, stunned in a dressing room, wanton, courting some risk, the dressing room door and what could happen behind it at the hands of a partner, business as usual unshocking. To his right as he made his way up the aisle, the man and the boy were getting up out of their seats. And Daley wondered where he had seen the man. He was holding a hat. It was pretty big, an outdoor hat, and on one side the brim was folded up against the crown and snapped in place. The man with the boy with the freckles. The man had gotten up, not the boy. The man even nodded and Daley had seen him in a bar somewhere or someone Daley knew knew him. Why did you bring a hat like that to the theater?

The man was at the aisle as Daley came even with the row. "Good," Daley said, "that blood was real enough."

"We hope so," the man said.

"It should travel well."

"You mean . . . ?" The man had a narrow, aimlike instinct about you or it was business, he had a tan and some experience that he was a trader in what he didn't deserve. Daley could just have shared with him Helen on the subject of the bleeding. She didn't know what she was saying dismissing the blood trickling from the young woman's nose; why did she do that? He knew why. She knew why. Name it. Not jealousy, not love; just why he was here, which was why she was. The big fellow gone up the aisle, people in the way, Daley said over his shoulder, "Maybe not much longer." He didn't like the man. He could sense the man let in someone else in front of him out of an aisle; it wasn't politeness so much as this place, but he felt the man's attention close behind him. "I mean, it's up to her," Daley said, and knew the man had something to do with her.

"Hey wait a minute." The man with the hat's voice pursued Daley, who now heard him speak to, it must have been, the boy.

What was desolate? Nothing much. Is it foretold by your life that happened one night but given like a thing to be absorbed later? The blow absorbed by the young actress stayed with Daley. He had been right up there with her. That was all. Ahead of himself, an advance guard. Filling up with chance and what drained away and came back, past blown away to return almost. She had absorbed it, yet what you saw gave back the blow. It blew her into the future away from him. She was an actor in her own behalf.

And who is to say where these things or blows are borne? An old curiosity, not blood spattered on a Kleenex or whatever he would find happening in the dressing room—and maybe he could not curve back (for where was the door to backstage) but just maybe keep going through the lobby and into the street. She's nothing like the newspaper photo outside. Helen would save his coat, not do anything dramatic or forsaken, even as she forgave him this evening, forgave his prevailing *good* manners. The last thing he wanted to do, pursue this; you knew what would happen. But why did he see it in the vanished broad back of the obnoxious, knowledgeable young guy out there in the lobby by now—your own house in old New York visited with hungry performers freeloading, young, looking for a place, opening doors, using the phone? Experience, the lawyer's clock ticking. And a pesky phone call that had prompted him to track down this place will put him on the spot out here in the aisle. You would like to be completely used, no problem. Client privilege to be sure sometimes keeping events themselves clear of each other but tonight preparing not prudence but the *last* thing Daley wanted to do, hearing tonight over the speakers large and softly the voice he'd heard over the phone a couple of days ago that had made him scratch his head like a city crow and think he would do something, he didn't know what.

# 2

"IT'S YOU," EXCLAIMED THIS NAMELESS VOICE, THIS PERSON UNKNOWN to Daley—did she have the wrong number? Who did she think she was?—a city nearness all it was, some small danger over the phone: "You have someone with you—?" said the voice, the half question getting in there before you could; presumptuous, something distinctly irritating here, warm, familiar, inflected with the ghost of an accent, maybe Irish, Daley thought, not quite American but.

"Well," he said. For the client, leaning rakishly and stoically on his rolled umbrella, had eased himself up out of his chair as if he had heard the voice in the receiver, and Daley covering the phone said it wasn't who he'd been expecting.

"Another time," the departing client said over his shoulder, this long-legged, hunched stork of a man Sid Knox, it was something to see him.

"No, wait," Daley said, reaching his hand out toward Sid Knox, he wanted to tell him what the person had just said, but Sid was out of here and Daley, the phone in his hand, really had what he needed on a yellow pad in front of him. A first-time client but a musician Daley knew well and would hear this very evening, a drummer whose work he had known for years. Here, though, he was a first-time client with a nasty little ill-advised litigation against a hotel chain. Self-absorbed, opinionated, wanting (in Daley's opinion) some fresh, country air or he would die, taking his thoughts with him now into the outer office—his philosophy really—this rare banger, improvisor with the crash-and-ride cymbals, the snares and high hat, two old-style heavy bass drums and three tom-toms around him, inimitable, leaving the particulars of his case on Daley's legal pad, one of two pads on the red blotter, a book to one side, this woman on the phone he'd thought was someone else doing a voice job on him, evidently young.

Daley with one ear heard his assistant welcoming Sid Knox into the outer office. "Strange," Daley thought he heard, and then Sid was gone, tall, stooped, crabby, interesting man who was having hip problems and life problems, but had an uncanny ear it came to Daley. While the woman on the phone, who had said *Wait* also, was doing whatever she was doing, speaking of her apartment. He was not taking her case whatever it was. She had said, "Wait—?" with that half question again, she was speaking of her apartment, and Daley was aware of things scrawled on the yellow pad in front of him, "hotel," "agent," "Helen" (with concentric doodles around it). And numbers to call. A breach of contract he had all but decided to farm out to a building construction insurance firm. And an accident case. The midtown number stared at him of the client whose call he'd been expecting, Lotta, whose entire history had come to him in a moment, come and gone—an importer you could call her, who had brought out a memoir. Some trouble about it his assistant, Donna, had gathered from two or three calls Friday and today: he had the book in his hand and he remembered two figures on a beach—a seashore—and birds and a plane up there hardly moving, he thought. And when the present call had come unintercepted this time, Daley had picked up assuming it was Lotta, with whom he had not spoken in upward of a year or more, but it was this young woman.

She had his name from a Mr. van Diamond, who had recommended Daley and recommended him highly. The name meant nothing, or almost nothing, but Daley didn't like it. It seemed partly familiar, but that was New York. The last name *van Diamond* was what she had said. Daley took his stocking feet off the desk and leaned forward on his elbows. She spoke well, with a slight accent, not Irish really, not English but Anglo-Saxon and sort of New World civilized. First acquaintance over the phone. How you are to be used. Daley was used to that. Responsibilities that you might grasp as yours too. Your lot. How to use one another. What better than to be fully used? it occurred to Daley observing how the pigeons and a single brown dove outside his high office window twitched their heads this way and that to get a better view of whatever they were looking at along the stony parapet or out beyond it. He consulted his watch.

Her voice was close as close could be. She was asking for it, and Daley, the phone against his ear, felt her relief, or wonder, some complaint. "It's you," she had said. There's a jolt coming, he thought, a small one, it's in here somewhere.

She so wanted Daley to take her case. Her flattery expressed hope somehow for both of them; it was premature. Some feminine faith in him that came with inklings of its opposite, a feminine lack of it. Housing case, he thought.

"What's it about?" he said.

"About!"

"Yes."

"They're trying to throw me out of here."

She was being sued for eviction?

"That's it. They say I don't live here."

And *did* she? Well, she thought she did. "I mean, of course I do."

Daley wasn't a housing lawyer, he could give her a couple of *names.* Good people.

"But it's you I called." The woman lowered her voice. "I know you could handle this."

How did she know that?

"How do I know that?" she said.

The phone against his ear, *Wait*, he said, he would give her the name of someone who . . . *Look out*, he thought, against the current of her talk, her not exactly pleading, her something or other, the drama of her, her

mouth and attitude that needed a little friendly correcting; she was riding for a fall, she thought she could just pull this off. He disliked her for
a second almost *because* she had been sued for eviction; or her tone, the
warmth, a not-too-expert voice job she was doing on him. Was he being
used, and did it matter?

Daley had experienced all manner of clients over the phone. And
would-be clients picking his brain with the meter off. And sometimes
certain people suddenly at home with him or agreeably at odds with
whom he meandered into unexpected conversations that were too
rich to be going anywhere. Some encounter. How it had gone. What
it was like. What people do together, what you've seen recently, the
whole package, the kind of food you eat, the brand of filter you purify
your water with, your sacrifices, your parents and all they have to
answer for wherever they've retired to or expired.

Of her own life, however, this person on the phone hardly spoke.
Was it possible? It was what it was and not justice, but business. The
old stationary telephone lends itself (like the later around-the-house
portables) to distance *and* intimacy and all the nerve-tuned intervals
tedious, sensitive, stupid, pathetic, abusive in between. In the office
Daley was not so much someone who may have nothing to say himself or lies in wait for you to say something damning but one of those
listeners able to be nothing much at a given moment—and so pick up
what's there and have it. Good, too, at getting off the phone with a
little help from his assistant.

The caller late Monday afternoon was no client, and was not
going to be if Daley could help it. "Just say yes," he heard at the other
end of the line.

"No, of *course* I'm not going to just say yes," Daley replied; "it's out
of the question."

"The question? What is the question?" It wasn't humor exactly.
Out his high window the pigeons—one had the cloudy juvenile mark
at the base of its beak—had been joined on the parapet by a long-
tailed brown dove, November-plump but out of place, it occurred to
Daley. The blue pigeons out the window would roost on any ledge,
but for the dove this was high, not to mention late in the year. Daley
watched an unusually small helicopter pass near the Metropolitan

Life tower. A personal chopper that he thought he recognized.

And where did they think she did live? he asked.

Oh she'd been away—four, five, six months at a time, working.

Which was it?

Though not recently, she stressed, again with this slight huskiness of long acquaintance. Working, he said. Research really, was the reply; and now they were saying it wasn't her residence.

"Your primary residence," Daley said.

"That's it!" said the woman, he had hit on the phrase. Daley couldn't tell how old she was; she was young. "This is not just eviction. This is a primary residence case."

"That's it," the woman said as if they were in this together.

"I'm not your man."

"You're not my man," she said.

"What?" Daley said.

"You heard me."

"You need a specialist."

She made a sound. "They say that about—"

"Everything. I know."

Years of paper the tenant had to come up with, so the landlord could make *his* case, bank statements, tax returns, voter registration, discovery of documents, everything. Good one to stay away from, primary residence. A loser, he had heard. November outside. A risk for the defendant. The lawyers always get paid. "Well, what *is* your specialty?"

Daley ignored this. "The papers have to be—"

"Papers?"

"They have to be answered"—she made him mad—"whoever represents you."

"They served them weeks ago." A faint sound of derision, this unknown woman, or girl. He was not sorry for her, an irritating sinew, some obstinate scar of faith, the voice grown-up—Canadian, distinctly Canadian in the accent, that Anglo-Irish roundness, though not this heavy sell, which was not Canadian. What did she mean, weeks? Months, he heard her say half to herself; *years.*

"Not years," Daley said. It gave her pause.

"Well, weeks. You know what I'm saying." (She sounded New

York.) No, she'd been to court twice already not counting post-ponements.

"So you've *got* someone."

"Oh, he was ready to settle."

Daley nodded. She named a lawyer.

"Because I'm a woman and the case is a loser *he* thinks; and we can't have that." She felt Daley's flash of doubt. "You might think I had a husband and a child at another address, my *real* home or something," she said. "I know someone who was in that bind."

"Oh that would do it," Daley said, her firmness like a touch on his arm.

So they'd gone to trial . . . he took down the attorney's name . . . when *was* this?—"No, hang on," he stopped himself. He stood up and caught Donna's practiced eye in the outer office. ("It's no secret" the voice said in the phone receiver.) Donna was returning the women's room key with its attached penguin to the middle drawer of her desk and absorbing *him*, and now she watched him, her dyed hair brilliant, lipstick darker, a real girl Friday, a woman he admired who lived in Queens.

"We can talk about it," said the voice on the end of the line. Daley actually laughed; it was outrageous, unruly. A shadow across the phone line of this getting-personal voice and now silence of hers was his own shadow, this slowdown like long time, your will in question; she's uncomfortably dramatic. "What are you doing right now," she said, "are you looking out the window?"— as if she were sitting in her underwear at her end.

"No, hang on," he said, thinking *van Diamond*, the afternoon clearing itself or its mind, its useless loot, with approaching darkness. "It's been a day."

"Ah," the young woman said.

It had been a day. He was going to go hear some music at Waters, rare Monday-night appearance of a bass player's trio. Waters with the glass blacked out and threatening to lose their lease. Daley knew the people who came there, the women and the men, and the bass player who weirdly didn't play Manhattan much and the drummer Sid Knox, a client now.

And now this woman who wanted Daley to represent her in an

eviction suit was already telling him things he wasn't interested in hearing, the sublet, threats, a roommate—*room*mate's not illegal, he got in, they'll put her on the stand of course. She got off a low laugh, contemptuous and sexy. She volunteered information he hadn't asked for and it came out sounding like questions. She wasn't afraid of the risk.

"This came out of nowhere?" he said.

"Out of nowhere? It never comes out of nowhere." That voice again. "But I was in shock," she said lightly. Young but grown, Canadian educated—they had a better system there. Rent's paid up? Daley heard himself asking. Well, they weren't accepting her checks.

Had she deposited them? Not really. A Puerto Rican gentleman who'd knocked on her door and served the papers, he was a dream. It was what you made it. She'd asked him in for coffee, he almost didn't know what to do.

And the lease? Oh, an inherited sublet—the young woman sounded slick like an out-of-towner—hers by agreement though the owner threatened to go back on it, he and his *associates* she thought they were called would like to do something to her (she was saying something moderately wacko or bloody, or about to, and he didn't like her). But her not living there was what it was about.

"Because you've been away," Daley said. A few months at a time. Recently? Not too. "Doing research," Daley said, he didn't think much of research and didn't know what *he* was "doing" at this end of— trouble. Yes, that was it. And what did she do?

She was an actress.

Ah. Here studying.

She was amused at this, he could almost see her mouth, her nostrils, a little furious, warm, severe, a brunette with hair tightly combed back from the forehead. "Research," you said. Back home. What did she do to make ends meet? (For a second, he imagined she said *Fuck*.) Oh she was working at the moment. Good.

"Downtown." It had a ring to it.

Oh in the *theater*.

She didn't think much longer, was all she said, half ignoring him. The show must be closing, he thought, if there even was a show. Time to hang up.

"It's partly up to you," he said.

"That's it," she said as if he had said something.

"It is?"

"That's what it's all about, thank God," she said, apart from him and proud.

"You are . . . ?" he said. She told him her name and he wrote it down. It was Becca Lang. Did that mean he was taking the case? Nope.

She named her discharged lawyer again.

The attorney's name on Daley's yellow pad, a face came to him, let's see, ruddy, myopic face-flesh and a first name that didn't go with him: not that he knew the man, not a memory at all. What, then? A sweet, mealy scent of cardamom seeds, a flat cell phone molded against the shaven, plucked-looking jaw and cordovan unexpectedly nontassel loafers pacing a hall of the civil court building—that definite. And a bow tie. Sometimes a lawyer would wear a bow if the judge did, though Daley could not see the judge. Daley knew in the most objective, unstartled way that he would meet the attorney soon notwithstanding the lack of need, when a phone call and a fax would suffice to get the transfer of case documents moving. He knew his picture of the man would turn out pretty accurate. Daley wasn't getting out of this yet.

Now, the man who'd *gotten* her the place *knew* the landlord?— Daley went on.

Oh he was the last person. She couldn't ask him, she wouldn't.

"He won't put in a word?"

Silence reached out to Daley from her end of the line.

And the person who'd given her this number . . .

Oh she didn't know him. She didn't really know Mr. van Diamond. (Van?) Other people seemed to know him, or he knew them, she thought. He might be in real estate. Just came back from . . . Arizona, she thought, her voice asking if . . . And he'd given her Daley's home number as well.

"Can't place him," Daley said, not reacting. And she didn't know his first name? She knew he had not reacted. No, a voice on the telephone.

Daley felt it from a time of first names; whatever it was, it chilled him a little. An era that like all these eras lately didn't end. Like this call. Not just in zero space but in time, he was sure. "I guess you weren't on that footing. How old-fashioned."

"Oh he has a hacienda. He said the place was mine anytime I wanted. He raises buffalo, buffalo coming back." She made a sound. "He meant it. One of these awful men who means it, but . . ."

The first name, Daley thought, that was the one.

"He has a house here."

"It doesn't matter."

"It doesn't matter," she repeated. "He said you had a gift, he couldn't take that away from you."

"Like to see him try."

"A touch," said the voice.

"People say things."

"People you wouldn't have anything to do with." She was so close he could see her; she was dark, she was lying, she looked up to him for some reason.

"No way to shop for a lawyer," Daley said, and she laughed, relieved.

"The gift wasn't a gift for the law, I felt." They laughed.

"So why call me?"

"He said you were a good listener."

"How would he know?"

"Good audience was what he said."

"Quite the authority."

"Yes."

"People you wouldn't have anything to do with?" said Daley.

"Borderline people, they have good advice. Like our sleazy life," said Becca Lang.

"A whole life has advice?" said Daley. Wasn't it un-Canadian, that thought or sentiment, whatever advice *life* could give. He liked her for it. "I have a gift for work—for managing my time. It's getting on for five," Daley said. Extending the phone arm's length, he told her to hang on, she understood he (he brought the phone back) he wasn't *taking* the case?

"I understand?" she said.

The next court date might have to be put off, he told her. It was the third week of November. She remembered it. Sure, but could she give him the attorney's name? She gave it, though Daley put up his hand. She said the phone number again. "Just to coordinate things," Daley said.

"You do know him," the woman said. She got younger.

"Certainly not," said Daley.

"He must have—diabetes. Of course: all the signs. I picked up this huge leather salesman's case he carries. I said, What is *this*? It was during a recess and he tried to be arch, like your father or somebody. It was full of water. I picked it up and listened. Plus his files. He sets it down and he's a new man for a while. Do you know he goes through bottle after bottle of distilled if you can believe it water out of his briefcase in front of the judge?"

"What did he want to settle for?" Daley asked patiently.

"I'm talking about some man's briefcase and water supply, and it's a jolt—"

Why was it a jolt? Daley slipped in.

"—because it's my *life* I've been *thinking* about. Five thousand dollars. That's why I fired him. He's a plaintiff lawyer if you ask me."

"You fired him?"

"Him and the seeds he chewed from his pocket—"

"I can see his bow tie," Daley said, freed somehow, "his red face and—"

"Oh, you know him." No, Daley did not. "The bow *tie* . . . you . . ."

"No, hang on," he said.

"And an Indian restaurant he smells like," said the voice, "and his business cologne, his thirteen children, his three wives, his red face, taking them all to *Cats* on Saturday afternoon, the musical that touched a generation," the voice said. "*Family*," the voice said.

"Gotta support your habit."

She thought *he* meant Family, and laughed; he felt her eyes on him. She said, "*He* knew what they were up to."

What was that?

"They want to *do* something—to me, but you'll—"

"No, I don't think so."

"You'll find out about that."

"No, I don't . . ."

"Push me."

"I can see that."

"But do something to me."The caller's voice was barely audible.

"Get your green card pulled?"

Silence at the end of the line.

Cardamom seeds, thought Daley, how *about* that? You could just see the guy. "Hey, *I* like Indian cooking," he said.

"I know you do," she sighed.

"Now that I've *said* it."

Still, she knew something; it was inevitable. People you met here in the city, they would always know at least one thing, no matter what, and she had gotten around in the few months she'd been here. (Daley didn't take the bait—who *they* were and what they wanted to do to her: evict her? An employer could probably get her green card pulled.)

"Used to be that gifted people frequented Indian restaurants— gifted *Americans*," she said; "*your* gift, now . . ."

"I have a gift for work," Daley said (*toil* came to him); "it's getting on for five." He just couldn't squeeze it in— this.

"I know you do, so do I."The voice wound its instinct about his, a never-prove-it-in-court, unprincipled female, secret violence you could say acquiring a signal, somewhere on target, and she was not close and only a voice for a second—how she used the phone. "I didn't mean *that* gift."

"That's *it*, though," Daley said.

"Not what *I* hear," was the reply.

He didn't ask *what*, then—or *where* did you hear it? She must mean what the recommender had said. She was a little wild, sharp and politely covert, probably not at all awful, pushy in the extreme though you could bug her: for Daley knew her, her type, yet had never quite run into it. A gift for toil, he thought; who could argue with that? And foresight, gut intuition, the burden of it, and for expe- rience it came to him (from *her*), for trouble once upon a time, and so on.

"You were a giver, that's what he said I think."

"This . . . ?"

"Un-hunh. A fool I think he said."

He and the girl laughed together. "A compelling recommendation." Daley wondered what he was a giver of.

"*I* thought so. Experience, I think he said—a little wild, I think he—"

"*Me?*"

"We're of the same blood, you know," the voice confided.

Daley was chilled by it, but she didn't mean much. It was boring; he'd heard it. Did women say it? A Russian woman had said it once to him. *Of the same blood.*

"This is a chance," she said.

"I'm afraid I don't gamble with other people's . . ." Donna watched from the outer office, her desk drawer open.

"You're a daredevil really," the woman said into his silence, "all you've seen, all you've done, you've done dangerous things . . . I know someone who bungee jumps and threw her knee out falling, and a boy who power glides on the Hudson River."

A chance to take on a loser, Daley thought. Donna's hair, its color, her glossed lips, Daley checked his watch, her figure humorous, upright, handsome.

"Someone listening," the woman said at the other end. How did she know?

"She's leaving," Daley said.

"She's a Roman Catholic. She doesn't lean on you."

"How'd you know that?"

"Just guessing. You're high up. What do you see up there? But I know you've . . . worked," the woman said. "I know *you* feel that." She seemed to laugh. Wasn't she something. "Over the years I mean. But *this* . . ."

This case? Years of his toil immaterial to something; to experience.

"And you had an employment agency I understand," the voice husky now. Was he being deposed?

"You what?"

"Or did I get it wrong?"

"No, *wait* a second," Daley wondering if this was about a job. He was not really hearing things before she said them, but—*the same blood.*

She was deaf to his words whoever she was. The case was a loser, but the case isn't the thing. This came to him like foresight we don't quite experience alone, this sensible fool Daley suffering this caller who has envisioned him as a fool with an office on a high floor. Maybe fool wasn't so bad. How she had found him—this man who had turned her on to Daley and who could not take the gift *away* from him. It came to Daley that the man's *first* name (whatever it was) had been the name he was known by. Friend of a friend. Praise from an enemy was always possible.

"Just say yes," the woman said.

"I'll just say no."

"You've already done that. You would know how to question those stupid people. Could I come and see you at least? Just talk . . ."

"What would be the point?" Daley heard himself being somebody.

"We'd *see*," she said. "You'll be sorry," she said.

She was half his age *and* Canadian, the will of an educated Canadian woman; why this persistence? "I'll be sorry," he repeated.

"You see?" she said.

He knew Donna was watching behind him. "And the person who gave you my number is in real estate?"

"Maybe not really."

"And threats you said?"

"What threats?" was the reply.

"The usual?" said Daley, now supplying her with *her* account. "The person who recommended me threatened you?"

"Oh he would never do that. But he did recommend you. That's no secret. Probably a crook. But he said . . . he said you were a fool, I think that was what he said, that was just part of what he said I think."

Daley could just take her by the shoulders and shake her. He looked for the birds in the air outside. His heart was damning her to hell. A person unpleasant came through, who would do a voice job on you, you picked it up like the breath of a total stranger, over the city phone right from the get-go. (*It's you*, she'd said when he'd picked up; she took these leaps without looking.)

Daley didn't want any part of it though he wouldn't tell her like that. She was a wee bit disturbed. It was a close call. "Let's see," he said, "the man who got you the place in the first place and won't help you now but you won't ask him . . ." Daley started over. "The guy who gave you this *number* knows him?" Daley heard rock music bust out behind her like a radio and then heard it drop to a beat; someone had flipped it down. Was she communicating with her roommate? Her bare legs extended from her chair.

The *employment* agency, Daley for some reason wanted to say to her, was quite separate and was about phased out.

"Please," she said then, "just a few minutes of your . . ."

"For old time's sake," Daley said dryly.

"That's what *he* said. He had these vile cufflinks."

"Well, I'm not a housing lawyer." Daley ignored what the other man had said, its possible falseness.

He heard Donna say good night. She looked at him. He smelled her as the outer door shut—he was glad she was gone—and contemplated his yellow pads and the phone number of his always difficult client Lotta who had been drawing some flak the last few months it seemed for this book he still had in his hand that she had apparently written that Daley would be expected to know word for word.

"Just a few *min*utes," said the voice in his ear.

"At the end of the week maybe," he said into the phone; he might squeeze her in then if that was any good.

She was distantly sobbing, or chuckling maybe. More of the same. "Oh I knew you would." Daley heard coughing at her end, a scuffle of feet, a man sounding like a dog, who then somewhere in the distance spoke to her.

"What threats?" Daley asked, "what threats did you mean?"

"Nothing I can't handle, I'll have to let you go," she said softly. "Safety net never materializes unless you . . ."

She was the limit. Yet something he wanted to tell her, well that's it, it's all obvious.

He knew she would call back. Thursday afternoon he would say. Around this time, the mineral, flat light of November casting into relief the windy faces of the buildings from his window, broomstick weather and helicopter terrain, he had recognized a news channel's chopper and then an executive commuter swinging across from one river to the other. *Of the same blood.* Did women say it? It was scrawled on his red blotter. What was it in his shoes his feet felt for and found? The onset of a time Daley marked as the late 1970s when people might meet you and say only their first name, take both of yours and give back your first, like young brokers pitching you over the phone, or California Christians, or heavy hitters at lunch. Men did it, he'd once thought, and an understanding of decades was somewhere in Daley fore and aft, history in a small way, materials that stayed somewhat raw, his geometry teacher who took him sailing on Lake Erie with her daughter. Out the window the dove on the ledge scratched its head (he'd never noticed) not directly but from around behind its wing (like a sparrow!). It dropped down off the ledge only to fly up a moment later to alight, feeling perhaps the building give as it was built to do in the wind, but no more taking wing because of that than a tree in the park should know its stirring branch or falling leaf or its roots or water pushed upward through its veins or inner paths or pulled from the top or, Daley understood, pumped by a series of jumps called "hearts" along that mysterious vertical way. The brown dove had dropped away onto the air, someplace else to go, or a falcon near.

Daley picked up the newspaper, the largely unfamiliar theater page. What did he know? Downtown, she'd said; let's see. He knew her name. It occurred to him that he needed a different newspaper to identify the place where she was "working," some play he wouldn't know the name of, and he heard the key in the door of the outer office. He heard the dim, limpid communication of birds on the ledge. Donna by her desk contemplated him. "Forget something?"

"Remembered."

"You were absorbed in your work."

"In yours."

Donna had something to say, Daley realized. He patted the phone.

"*What* 'threats'?" Donna said.

Daley looked at her.

"You said you would 'be sorry.'"

"*She* said I'd be and I was agreeing." Daley scrolled down the unfamiliar theater listings; a name, a title, a word here and there registered.

"Did she want a job or a lawyer?"

"A lawyer."

"She asked about the agency."

"She had heard of it, you're right. But how?"

Donna lingered, a mature woman who knew him all the better for not quite knowing him.

"You're right," he said.

"Why did you pick up?" she said.

"I thought it was . . ."

Was he about to ask her something? When he didn't, she slid her drawer shut. It was full of stuff. "Well, good you didn't encourage her."

"*You* heard what I said."

"I could almost hear *her*."

"Hardly," said Daley.

"She sounded determined." Donna paused at the door.

"No reason to."

"You're right."

Daley had a sensation of relief threaded with end-of-the-day lust. You learn things of necessity by accident. "What do you mean, I'm right?"

"You work hard," Donna said; "that's what I mean."

"Cufflinks," said Daley.

Donna at the door. "You don't wear cufflinks."

"You're right."

"Mr. Knox, he wears cufflinks."

"So he does." A question, a wrinkle of knowledge between them. Daley said he was going to hear some music tonight, and it sounded like he was saying he was on his own for a few days, which this woman who had worked for him ten years going on eleven and lived with her brother in Queens happened of course to know, and the moment passed, knowledge they shared if they could put it together, harness it, talk about it.

Donna sees a man standing over a newspaper spread open who has so far as she can tell declined to take the case. She is thinking, Women. It is past and future about Daley she is surely thinking at this moment, foreseeing what has happened in the past. A challenge there for Daley, the yawp of a gull circling back toward the river, some hidden cost or jolt coming (no more than that), like justice we discharge from memory if possible together.

Remember to call Lotta, said Donna leaving.

What was it?

Somebody bothering her, Donna thought.

Bothering her?

That's what it sounded like.

At the grocery his next-door neighbor Isabel was speaking Spanish with the old man; his grandson had been mugged in the playground Sunday night. Daley found another paper they apparently weren't charging for anymore in this city and leafed quickly to the theater listings but he was here and he closed the paper and folded it. Isabel was buying charcoal briquets in November and milk and orange juice, and Daley was about to invite himself (just kidding) into her adjoining backyard for supper. But he was going to hear some music later on.

She didn't wait for Daley, oddly. End of the day meant a story for one another, if you meet. He asked Arcadio if his rent was going up. He had an orange bandanna around his head. "*Ni pincha ni corta.*" He had no say.

In the squad car at the corner, the partners, a man and behind the wheel a woman, were sipping coffee and reading the newspaper. A large potted plant behind the grill brushed the ceiling. Daley turned into his block and Isabel changed her mind and waited for him. She was irritated. "He could have got his throat cut," she said.

"Never. It's not what they do," Daley said.

"Well you know all about it," Isabel said.

They didn't look at each other. Daley wanted to ask about the boys but tonight it was like asking them about school, though why not?

A bike came up the wrong way, an Asian housepainter they knew.

Isabel was angry about something. Daley said, "But what was that kid doing in the playground at eleven?" Isabel said it was not the point. Daley looked up at her house and one of the boys darted tall-ly across a lighted third-floor window and darted back. All the things Wheelock and Bear might be doing up there.

Isabel called to Daley from her areaway. "I had some seepage in the cellar last week. I suppose you didn't."

No, Daley was okay. He let himself in the basement door. Isabel was going to landscape her yard. She had a contractor's license and all the work she could handle now.

He spread the newspaper out on the kitchen table. The three dark floors above him of his own house, he read through the listings. *Blood* in two titles came to him. A hunch. Before he went out again, he phoned one theater and got lucky with the second. A foreign woman at the other end of the line, young: "Yeah she's in it."

"I understand not for long."

"What?" said the woman. Two house seats left he could have. *House* seats? He remembered. Good, fine. Pick them up no later than ten to eight . . . okay? the voice asked.

So that was how, still resisting the voice of someone named Becca Lang saying, "It's you," Daley reserved tickets for Wednesday, though you could always bag it when the time came.

# 3

THE NEPAL PART'S LIKE TRAVEL, A LEGENDARY VACATION GROWING ON you, an American trip, a vision coming from a legendary place. But fairly silly so you wondered what you're doing in a renovated warehouse basically. The answer was the blonde up there. Surprising, when the *phone* voice Daley could have sworn had sounded brunette, edgy but mellow, husky and tired, then silent for a moment, she might have gone away, a speaking voice rangy as her free stride across the stage, secretly hopeful. If voice correlates with hair color. Pigment follicles up above the brain, damped or excited, causing (we understand) the cords below to vibrate. People largely what they are, were it not for each other.

Let's see, sister and brother close as could be till he had married and she had gone away to a Peace Corps job in Africa. Each day something.

Later she'd landed in Kathmandu. There she had undergone a transforming spiritual experience. Fair enough. A born-again foundling the feeling. Was this the Peace Corps too? Still barely three years out of college, she taught English language to the folk of that high valley while working six days a week for a farmer. Wise old Sherpa who would like her to lay off his grandson, go back to America.

They do what they like in the theater and should, with their lights and sets, their entrances and unaccountable exits, their sound system guilty of one or two fogged tweets so far for this voice-over that now and then stops everything.

"Each day we work. Then we walk miles and miles. It's not the roof of the world, there is no roof. But I have to tell you it's where I want to be. I'm getting there." The voice too compelling. You know who it is, but do you? Because it's dark, as you hear people say now.

They use what they've got, to tell about the brother and sister. And the brother's redhead wife and the others—in one scene three of them, in the next four, then later just the blonde and the brother. She makes him stumble over his words; he's attached to her. Well, she's a loose gun, and what good can come of her coming home? The brother in Connecticut thought she oughta come home. Why was not clear. Devoted to his boat, why is the brother so pale? Nothing of the immediate or foreseeable future gets by him unnoticed. Rereading Sister's letters, he was angered frankly by their faith, their irresponsible calm, their sheer geography. Her distance. From what she really *knew*—to hear him tell his girl Friday. It was in *her* ear he spilled these thoughts. He and she have a history going.

So has he with his wife. Each starts a story-of-the-day to the other. He at first prevailed, talked faster, a virtual bullying she recognized and processed; but she slowed him with a look and temporarily prevailed by suspense and sheer gender. This couple enjoyed just hanging together in their farmhouse in the Hartford area, she with her red hair. His story was something irregular and uneasy going on at work: an independent idea man and industrial designer, it seemed, he had a contract with a noise abatement firm, was that it? The noise-cancellation technology you had heard of in the early 1990s though here in the play not much explained yet mysteriously clear: a counterwave propagator—unless you were mistaken—that erased oncoming wavelengths and with them all kinds of noise we could do without. Husband heard somebody outside in the yard. The wife stopped him from going to the door, she had her story she wanted him to hear at the end of the day. Hers by contrast was of two mere kids, one with a skateboard carried like a book, who'd knocked on the door from the garage into the kitchen who didn't look too great, grimy backpacks, gaunt, hungry-eyed, whom after feeding she had hired to look into the foundations of this hundred-year-old house the overall structure of which they seemed to have analyzed.

Presently the husband's story of a problem at work is allowed to continue as if now it might have some traction. Now (for it happens all the time), he had allegedly come up with technology belonging to another company at a moment when that company was going under. He had stolen it, *they* said—telling *him* what was his life! Whereas it was as simple as the bullfrogs he and his summer interns had studied who seemed to croak through their ears because of membranes that twanged key frequencies yet would prove the springboard and gold mine for a fortune waiting to be scored.

Well, he might be needing a lawyer. A good one. His wife understood. In spite of everything, they both understood, interrupting each other, hanging out, knowing more than was possible in this still very brief scene; telling each other things you knew they *knew*. For instance that he had optioned an upturn in the market that was a sure thing; that some visiting football players had shot up the neighborhood last weekend, joined apparently by several Brazilian soccer players. But mainly that he had visited his sister last year in the high valley of Kathmandu and been introduced to her boyfriend, saffron skinned, basically dark skinned (not *Negro*), the grandson of this Sherpa farmer, "digger-in-the-earth," in their tongue. Why was it always the Sherpas? Here at least they were not just assaults upon the Mountain. They danced for Buddha apparently in a happy, big room.

What had the wife just said was between her and her husband? A sense of humor. Thank God for that.

The sister was the thing.

The letters would join the action from time to time; they came in like the horizon of Everest, and stopped it. Her breath amplified all through this converted warehouse tonight, how many people here know her? You knew who the voice was early, it had to be the blonde. "We cooked these beans he grows called *pul-se* in a pot with no handle over a pine fire that smelled like home. A trip we took. In the night we opened our eyes under the moon, and there, a hundred miles away, was the Mountain. Nearness and distance, and thought" —the actress seemed to add spontaneously—"ready to erupt like lava, like your life. You know where *I'm* coming from, my dear." It is her brother she addresses. The letters put you there. The woman surrounded time with her voice and you felt the scar on your arm tingle.

Well, she wasn't in Nepal now. The play began when she got home, bringing with her eerily this voice-over you might have thought had been packed in her luggage. She was with her brother and the others now, the fluid, vulnerable sinew of the sister just come home. (What was it one had against Connecticut, where was the space for all those farmhouse-style homes when you looked at the map?) She's right here with them, the folks on stage.

Three years Sister's been gone, almost doesn't want to know what she's missed, though you feel it was nothing, a phase, American. The brother and his surprising red-haired wife. The dark secretary woman, his girl Friday, she's a distant cousin of course, and has done some things; it's her lookout what she gets into, she can't help her own seductive sound, like a smell or languid, witty movements when she's a workaholic (just happens to be), never noisy like the redhead but is just as big. Also a man who so far only bartends in a place. But went to college with the brother, seems like donkeys' years ago. Yet got wind of professional improprieties his old buddy is liable for though he would never divulge them—a frat brother once and always. Will someone go to the authorities?

It was a mess now but you were *in* it, you got it. On stage the blonde had a stride from the hips, the buttocks (our Sister). Quick, free of fear, slightly awkwardly poised. Too free, was that it? You'd like to shake her sometimes. Home from living abroad, she offers her hand, a hug in greeting. Daley's found jobs for friends' kids like this, the so-so story going on, entangling, irritatingly not quite bold, but what had the brother's business dealings to do with it, his perhaps impropriety? He had thought up a generator and a focusing filter that listened to and propagated frequency at the same time, enabling the system to cancel out industrial noise, like a time switch; Daley happened to know about it—a small-cap stock somewhere for the unwary or if you had the savings to blow. The technology only seemed arcane, like the energy we would never possess or warps never completely accessed to visit other galaxies.

Sister's lips heard in Connecticut as voice-over clear from Kathmandu you figure, who was it she already long ago forgave . . . too long ago? It was the brother. "Please, this I know about. Spread out under the sky, I may never come back. I think I may have a spirit. I forgive you." It had to be the brother. Good of her. Is she running things from a distance? But she's been summoned stateside by something, drawn back home. From one angle it might be the redhead who's running things. The blonde curiously you have seen the likes of and could give a miss.

Till each voice-over's done, her own lips still, until the players come back to life who were transfixed, caught bare-handed, on the stateside, pretty furnitureless stage, hearing almost themselves. This breathy, love-at-first-sound voice-over memory of good works in the Kathmandu area fifty or a hundred miles east, includes even you a grown man twice her age, remembers you. Lips, you could feel them parting over the loudspeaker, the voice-over account had kicked in half a dozen times during the first half, here it started again, the mouth clicking moistly, lapping, uncanny: these people aren't really frozen by the voice, but paused.

You felt like shaking her. This loose talk about reincarnation. Perfectly good idea abused by loose thinking. Dalai Lama's rumored plans for retirement—decided against reincarnation, doesn't want the Chinese-Communist-appointed Lama to . . . to take in his spirit? No, that wasn't it.

The actress hesitated like making it up sometimes, you felt. You so knew that voice, older than the thing before us. "The old man in the valley thinks I'm using Christian magic. He abuses me to his family. He would like to turn me into something else and export me. It's how he sees things. He has a gift, to be sure. I'm not afraid. I'm afraid I'm past it. What magic am I using on his grandson who has an unusual glow around him? No magic about it, no miracle, it can be explained."

The letters had vanished. From his desk at the office. Only the Secretary would have taken them. Tail wagging the dog. But here it is, *the same blood:* "My friend thinks we are of the same blood." "So what do you say to that, my dear?" She addresses her brother, who we already know is accused of being a white-collar crook in Connecticut.

Sister's a blonde, a little frizzy or electric, a style. You didn't *know* what she would do. She was asking for it. She asked for nothing.

Everybody's on hold again a few minutes later, voice-over alert, cast stopped in their tracks: "I might never come back, I'm nothing," the recorded voice bears steadfastly across the wastes of present time. "Events have controlled me. I forgive you—almost." Daley has seen this kind of thing before, this promise, this destiny manifest in, well, just someone's will to speak. Voice-over halts everything on stage, it suspends the audience almost, it's you it turns to; the actors go dumb, the materials of the story drift closer. Isn't there a child prostitution market there too in Nepal, perhaps seasonal? Daley may be mixing it up with Taipei. She is something to take in if she doesn't absorb you like nothing. God! Give her the benefit of the doubt. As if you didn't. Take her or leave her, *and* her play. "We left the tent in its bag and slept together on the hillside high above the river. You see Everest a hundred miles away. It dwarfs the moon."

We've seen something like this. An old story, a legend, a commercial perhaps, history rerun, though it will pass. A little vague. It's sex, or getting away from it. They do this sort of thing.

He hugged and kissed his sister when he got her alone, ate her up, took a long look, her memory, her mouth, her eyes; it was from his lips she learned the news: he has been having a thing with someone. A businesslike affair, a business associate as it happened; well, a sailing friend. A longtime woman friend. Hell, someone his sister used to know!

The indefatigable girl Friday, who was friendly also with his wife, with the bartender, with everyone, though a workaholic and a love. These things meandering nowhere constantly leave Sister standing alone—no more than that.

She becomes recognizable as the one blown up in the newspaper photo outside on the street, outside this palpable warehouse, this "re-novation." And because she is before you on a stage you can track the story and still be miles away. The voice Monday saying your name over the office phone, like the voice here in the darkened house tonight ample, husky, prevailing. Canadian, though, and in unpredictable things not hip. A sometime singer, the vocal cords rosy, dark, a tone of a lady not quite used to being winning yet she had been adored by someone; there was light in the voice. Older on the phone, she was routinely wise—it came through; and trouble. No problem.

We were all better off in Nepal, even if the sister was the only one there. And not there anymore, having come home to her fool of a brother though to America with its potential for error, blood, and repetition.

It was her voice that was out there. "I want to show you this yel-low-painted shelter we found up the mountain," the woman's voice came over the speakers, a traveler so near: a letter that's been (we guess) read and reread, but by whom?—"built of hand-notched saplings. How I didn't need you. How we used each other . . . I could just stay in this high valley full of hope. It comes to meet you." The place a prism drawing prediction out of an incomplete past.

Exposed by distance, by her foreign jobs, which the family don't want to hear about (which is cool), or America's potential for . . . for relativity, for how it strikes *you*, or your relatively dimensionless iner-tia waiting for input if not history—when now here alone stateside she pays her sister-in-law a visit one morning, and that resident red-head produces one of the Nepal letters from a psychic cookie jar in the kitchen closet, a surprise prop. So this is where the letters to her brother wound up thinks the far-flung traveler home from Nepal, as her sister-in-law quotes verbatim from them while still leafing through pages looking *for* this passage, reads now from a longhand page anyone can read if they want (she has it in her hand), and then tells our returned globe girdler a few home truths: that she ought to get herself a man to look after: bird can't fly on one wing—Get with the program, girl—blunt, light, local, the everyday offensive unit.

Whereupon the other tells her sister-in-law no matter how red-headed that she should look to her own man—

*Por qué* retorts the hostess!

—if she expects to keep him, completes the thought.

The blonde tells her sister-in-law what's going on. Just tells.

Then there was little left to say (over coffee). How do you top that? Turn it into something, make something of your*self* is all we would do. Where the letters from abroad told you through all that work you'd done, the brother-sister love got turned into later life, a spiritual impression, landscape. But what could she do to improve if not transform the current event? Go alert the brother.

So she went and just told him what she'd done, he was the one she had to tell, and he just reacted, striking her, and if she seemed physically shocked she wasn't knocked into the middle of next week or the arms of rows one through eight. Falling, falling. Though struck now and ever after. Though also before, because you should have seen it coming if you allow for the unforeseen, it's what you're out for, it's you if you're lucky.

# 4

AN EARTHQUAKE HAD PASSED LARGELY UNNOTICED ACROSS Manhattan Island in the middle of the night, and a client phoned Daley within the hour asking if she could sue for the cost of two priceless figurines that had tipped off a shelf during the temblor, which she had it on good authority emanated from Connecticut. Daley knew that he too must have felt it or its aftershock. And for a second, waking prophetic in the darkness of his house near the North River, not alone in those days, he had recalled a woman's cry, a kid's, a man's, surprised and simultaneous and terrible, a dream probably, a foretelling like the phone going and you wake up to no phone: yet it does ring then, but with a nutty scent close by, sweaty warm skin. This ring was real all right. He might still not have believed it listening to the woman's voice and her news with the bed-table light on.

Yet somewhere in the power of uncertain sleep Daley had known the windy shake of windowpane, some ripple of displacement or a change in the materials around him. The winds of an eighteen-wheeler blowing by you on the interstate. A Hudson River Line express train that close, except no such train passed this far downtown. Reality come and gone along the cemented bricks that Daley had been meaning to repoint.

Who would you sue? he had asked his caller, knowing what she was capable of, and he gave the legal name for what had apparently occurred, and expressed his sympathy for loss. The angry pause at the other end promised further talk; he was handling her and she didn't like it, it was like saying to a woman, I'll call you, but he did not descend to her level.

His wife not on the other side of the bed, doubtless settled in the kitchen reading, eating an orange, he wished his client good night, "Good night, Lotta," though she was not satisfied, and who knew what she'd do? Certainly not call another lawyer at this lunatic hour. And her first words when he hadn't been registering came back: the good news, an earthquake; the bad, the damage. It would take an M5 or M6 to make art objects fall off a shelf, Daley seemed to recall. A considerable quake—bells ring, sleepers awake. And this tremor from Connecticut or Westchester whatever its course along four or five east–west or north–south fault lines could hardly have exceeded a feeble M2. Yet he would sooner believe a person than—than what?

It was three-ten on the face of the old alarm clock, and Daley put in a call to Seattle to his brother where it was just past twelve, a South Pacific freighter weighing anchor in the old harbor—he saw it as clearly as the mountains near to the east—and the big block of Alaska, which they both knew spread out northwest, a boat ride away. He needed to ask his brother Wolf a question that had not quite formed itself, framing and reframing in the night from materials of the day; until the materials actually from various times crystallized as the phone rang at the Seattle end into (for he loved his brother, who worried him and interested him unfailingly for they really went back) a rather ordinary question as to the stability of a bonding unit used in the now aborted construction of a waste plant in Michigan that a client of Daley's had subcontracted.

Wolf was something of an authority on explosive concussions of the man-made kind. It was part of the package, his work as a structural engineer and troubleshooter. Trouble taking a shot at *him*, he had absorbed shock waves nearly lethal from a ship that blew up in a Japanese harbor while he was engaged in underwater repair analysis a hundred yards away. Chaotic like being in a war, was how he described it, it was what it was. Just experience, his older brother had thought. Wolf had in fact been turned down for military service years before because of a childhood dirt-bike injury sustained in South Euclid, in collision with the contents of a moving van on the sidewalk extending into the street, chairs flying up into the air, the older brother following, resigned to what he had foreseen (despite the city ordinance against the noise of dirt bikes, forget the bikes themselves). Yet he could tell the Osaka story to his Korean friend Sook, the explosive side of it (so to speak), who knew the city and knew Daley well. Sook was a lawyer and an old friend and because they ran along the bike path by the river early in the morning they talked several times a week.

That brother.

Well, yes.

Trouble is looking for him.

Sook, like many other Koreans, knew Osaka, the university, and he could easily picture what Daley had told him. The harbor bay. The hospital where Wolf had been recuperating from injuries sustained in the explosion. The sunlit waters where he had gotten himself blown out of the water, the bay suddenly silent. Wolf blown clear of the water it was said. Daley and Sook actually had a laugh about state-of-the-art explosives that could blow you to kingdom come but were nontoxic (!); they burned off into $CO_2$ and nitrogen. Also *shock*-insensitive it says here, that is you couldn't set them off like a mine or some of those old shells launched from the West Point artillery grounds only to wind up in the turf of that sculpture park next door unexploded. But they did a job on Wolf. Inconveniencing incidentally Daley and his wife, who'd been traveling a couple thousand miles to the west in India! And this wasn't only about Wolf landing in the hospital but about the Daleys and vehicles. His brother still recuperating, pretty deaf, having gone barefoot, paper slippers, unlaced sneakers in and out of a semiprivate room for days, said get him outa here. Well, what happened now could have been foreseen by anyone who knew Wolf or could be bothered to predict it even at a 120 rented kilometers an hour on a seemingly sunny afternoon east of the hospital. Behind you Osaka, behind you slightly higher on the passenger's seat of the bike your brother, you can feel him still half deaf behind you on the stepped, double saddle, fingers curled into the steel grips, rented helmet, matching black boots and jeans for the first time in ten days. What had Daley's brother thought he was doing yelling up at a trucker, Get over, asshole, on a foreign four-lane intercity? *You're* the operator of the *bike*. But what is it Wolf's saying, what is Wolf's basic body vocabulary eloquently now instructing the Jap trucker to do and how to do it who wouldn't get over and let them pass? The older brother in charge of the road but blind to what his brother's doing behind him. Or what vectors that survivor's body long unfit though subtly for military duty traced toward future convergence with the homegrown six-wheeler that had been all over the road as Daley had come up behind, with a slight sway, warp, or shimmy un-Japanese and imperfect in the suspension or shocks Daley was certain.

So what did the trucker do?

Wolf yelled something up at him, and the driver—this blue-goggled roadman—gave these alien bikers on a red Honda 650 ('79, one of the best-ever vintages) a mustached Jap grin. Daley, his arms straight out never squeezing the handlebars of the rented bike harder than he would a tennis racket, scythe, pistol, shovel, paddle, found in the corner of his eye a dark, *flapping* rhythm, and as he glanced over all but found it in his face, a hard, peeled-off arc of tread whipping over to take revenge. What was it that Wolf yelled? It was Wolf whatever it was. Daley's brother. What about the tread? Slapped Daley's helmet missed his face by an eyelash.

He's got a bomb inside him, Sook had said, and not the first time. Sook understood.

Wolf had made a name for himself in materials (you could be happy for him); also in the design of extremely slender hydroelectric dam intake towers that would nonetheless absorb not only the compressive charge of water but seismic events as well. Called in to help rebuild a bridge and a viaduct in eastern Turkey, he had absorbed what geology he needed for that job. But rock layers, the ages, faults, the earth, hot plates, the vectors there below, spelled responsibility he would as soon delegate or leave to a higher supervisory power, like meditating the future or getting another degree. He knew his fault lines along the Pacific Rim and discounted the volcanic past of the Cascades where he and his family had settled. Would Rainier blow one day? How dead was Mount Saint Helens? No deer walked there; bare trunks lay drawn in masses of orderly lines like the end beyond anything you could call a bomb or a mistake. He had visited the huge broken cone on a professional backcountry permit thanks to a geographer he had struck up an acquaintance with. At the lip you could see the ancient fume below suspending in a cloudy solution debris the scale of which you could not estimate. Thank God Wolf had not been encouraged to haul his wings to the top—with help he was good at getting. He figured you should pick up a killer lift if you took a chance and dropped off the rim on a hang glider. His older brother trusted water not air. The drop into Saint Helens laughable, and likewise then the expected thermal from the middle of the earth spiraling skyward. A thing to do, an act.

Wolf had a touch with reinforced concrete and steel, and arcane polymer compounds he had dared to coat and line blocks of basic materials with. He thought up another way of insulating marine cable. He had worked on dams in the Northwest and Asia, and in South America after his Peace Corps adventure; had an instinct for angles of pressure shock where clear water overflows a spillway to fall a thousand feet down upon the toe of the spillway and burst upward in a boil or what is called a "jump." Wolf could eyeball a maximum load for a steel alloy shackle, he could pack the pin with washers to keep the shackle from slipping off center when the legs could open letting one end of a load of steel reinforcement rods, say, break free and javelin down upon workmen a hundred feet below.

He could handle things, he knew the design of miles of coolant pipes without which Hoover couldn't have been built, had actually studied the subsidiary wing dam built above the primary vast simple-gravity structure of Grand Coulee, and he could think for himself. Though he was not a thinker. Though he could bother anyone, for some engagement had been denied him, and his brother knew what it was, or anyway had been there to protect him occasionally.

Wolf did not experience doubt, even of people he offended, and probably lacked freedom because of it. Thought gives you freedom to doubt what is doubtful. Wolf made big things so they stood firm. Yet some disorder attended his life. Wolf wanted no overall responsibility for a team or long-term job. Clever and a worker, but socially feckless and blunt. Just as their father, year after year, had foreseen. "Shoulder the sky, lads," said the smoky bass voice overbearing even its own words, whatever they meant half hidden by history and perhaps patriotic habit needing an update, God knew, from quoting President Eisenhower or his secretary of state that Korean peace would be a travesty if all it did was release Communist forces to fight elsewhere and why would they want to fight where we had dropped almost eight million gallons of napalm (on North Korea, that is) during the first three months of that war; yet hadn't Wolf shouldered the sky—hadn't he "done that"? His older brother, only a New York lawyer, had phoned Wolf to alert him to new work on the effect of vibration and shake pattern on Wolf's favorite materials, which for some reason Wolf hadn't known about. Wolf would take physical risks himself as long as he was being paid; he would invent some.

Wolf had not regained full hearing on the right side after the harbor accident, which reached out in all directions in advance of its own sound so the concerned older brother summoned from a traveling vacation in India could practically recall those concentric effects in a form of causes converging on a center from a kind of space in sequence. Yet a year after injuring his arm, the nerves in the shoulder capsule in fact, he had recovered its use mysteriously during the night a month before another accident to end all accidents: Many Mouth suspension bridge. It was a story for others to tell. The buckling and rolling undulation of that span had flung him two hundred feet off into a terrific Southeast Asian river riding a twisted length of steel glimpsed on videocam footage aimed everywhere and nowhere. Yet it left him only sore, excited, well exercised, ideas for projects streaming from him for the next forty-eight hours following a dramatic swim. An explorer his brother saw him as (but get in, get out), who didn't take the long view except with regard to his lawyer brother in New York whose interest in science was greater than his albeit layman's mishmash—in, for instance, the effect of ultraviolet rays on the chemistry of basic ice compounds found everywhere in space—and whose foresight was unmatched except by his highly uncertain (or delayed) application of it to his own life. Wolf, on the other hand, needed to be protected from himself, didn't he? And that was where Daley came in if he could.

Wolf would tread on moving lava—we speak not of lava beds through flowed rivers harnessed by his favorite dams but live lava; he walked a steel I-beam five hundred feet above the street; would troubleshoot like any union construction worker ("specialist," they were called now). But he deferred to his older brother as the real risk taker. It was curious and partly unclear.

This night of the quake emanating from Connecticut Wolf doubted that Manhattan *had* experienced an earthquake, mini temblor, whatever Bill's client had been yammering about, and Daley, who loved his brother and his brother's family, felt impatience stir in him like anger or even understanding here in his dark house, the house itself uneasy, for once upon a time Daley had thought to redesign the inside of it. On the phone Wolf's family boxer was coughing, having a slow but sure heart attack over time. But Wolf, as it happened, had something to broach with his New York brother who'd rung *him* across three thousand miles, saved him a couple of bucks (for Wolf, so free where he went and how long it could take, treated money as what others would lay out). "Must've read my mind."

"There's more of it around but less that's worth reading."

"Hey, it's late there," said Daley's brother.

It was a job in Australia, this odd night, a project huge in itself yet for Wolf little more than a Band-Aid quick-fix consulting trip, just one of their emergencies, "whatever *I* am in this" ("Trouble," said the older brother, hearing something in Wolf's words). Brother Bill must come along. A week at the outside. "Associate consultant." Right. "Legal arm." Wolf would pick up his expenses.

"Handler," Daley said.

"*You're* the one," Wolf laughed. What was Daley not getting, or was it right here in his house, some sound accompanying his voice over the phone?

In the older brother alone if not absolutely in a dark city house, a pang of hope and warning visited Daley and was gone yet nearby, a half thought. Some original reason why he'd phoned Wolf. An act whose causes had been long absorbed in its onset—now lost in the ensuing conversation.

It was only after these two very late calls that Daley had discovered his wife's absence from the house. For he had found his robe, remembering they had a guest tonight, a sort of business contact of his wife Della's staying in the south bedroom, and he had descended to the first floor and then the basement kitchen, come back upstairs to the third floor and even knocked on the door to the loft space where his wife worked.

She wasn't home. She was out walking. Not unheard of at this hour. This time a decision of some magnitude she was making, a career move— strange to say the least—the details of which Daley would hear eventually though he thought she had been discussing them already with friends.

Possibly with their overnight visitor from abroad. Dutch, Daley thought, but something else. Connected to a bank, he had evidently on a previous trip six months and more ago been taken with Della's per- formance and the company she was a lead dancer in, and she hoped to gain support for the company through this Austro-Israeli group he trav- eled for. Then he had something more concrete for Della's company in August. Resourceful, Daley could tell, frank. A man forthcoming in their brief encounter when Della brought him in just before midnight. An international commuter who would know friends you hadn't seen in years, long-lost people in Paris, Rome, Vienna, Jerusalem. It was exhilarating for a moment, and a little silly. (His own organic rhythm instinctively passed jet lag by, outwitted it; he took catnaps, he said, that was all he needed supposedly.) Long limbed, not particularly strong looking, yet he was in shape in some oiled, interior tempo of his own.

Voluble but suddenly tired (or cautious, armored) from his trip, though a banker with a credit card surely, the man had blown into JFK from India without a place to stay and this was why on the night of the earthquake at three-fifteen in the morning he lay flat out in bed in the south-side room sound asleep, lightly snoring with moonlight in his face from the garden. Daley put it out of his mind. The phone like an alarm rang in the other room and for a moment Daley thought this stark naked figure's eyes were open a slit like a glimpse to come. Passing back through the hall and the dark stairwell, Daley recalled that his bank was known apparently for its agronomy research grants and its astute corporate art collection. Daley picked up the receiver and sat on the bed. It was his client Lotta again.

"What were you doing on the phone?"

Talking.

"At this hour?"

"What is it?" Daley asked. "I was talking with my brother."

"Didn't know you had one."

"What is it?"

"He must live far away."

It was the middle of the night outside and Della had better be home soon. Why did he let her go like this? It was a way of caring. Yet Daley had been attacked during an early-morning run not three months ago, and why would his wife's late-night peripatetic (was the word) head clearing be less perilous? He listened for the front door, to make it open—and for steps; listened to the stone itself, the walk, the steps up to the outer vestibule door—while Lotta—what was it in her woman's voice, in the entrails of the phone itself? Something foolish, terrible, dangerously silly. No, *original*, poor thing.

Could she run something by him? (It was a phrase people were using, and Daley had become aware of it.)

Shoot.

No pressure; just your quick reaction. "*Why* couldn't we sue Connecticut?"

Come on—her "we" brought back some down-the-drain dream residue from the moment the phone had rung.

Where the quake had originated? she explained.

How deep did Connecticut go? Daley had replied gently. He almost didn't believe it. He was hard to surprise but it was late.

"Or the *builders*," Lotta went on—oh she couldn't sleep, it was her chemistry, she didn't eat properly, she didn't exercise, she told him. You wouldn't know it, he thought —couldn't *they* be sued? The developers who had thrown up this sixty-story condo tower where she was housed on only the third floor, tiles peeling off the bathroom ceiling and grouting dividing the week she'd moved in.

Was it the hour? Some vein in the night of hysteria, of *depth* there, of being badly used, some buildup of circumstance? She was almost an unholy mess. It wasn't the money value it came to Daley. It was the figurines. Some darkness she cleaved to. Lotta—a German name given her by her mother, a German name, a childhood friend's name in suburban Maryland.

Daley was used to people expecting to be saved money and trouble. Who got his home number. That night in the early 1980s, however— late '81 it might have been, Helen would know because Daley had met her soon afterward and regaled her with earthquake night—a sound had betrayed Lotta, or them both. It was her life she meant, her home against his, time mixed and gone—it stayed with Daley, alone in the dark house with a sound-asleep visitor taken in by Della who herself was out for one of her walks, very late, along the North River, though he knew at that moment that her hand was aiming her key at the lock of the front door. "I'm afraid I'll have to let you go," Daley had said, his gentle signature trademark.

"You're letting *me* go?" the woman said. A passion there, an authority meaningless like most. He heard the front door slip shut downstairs. "Come on, Daley."

A wrong done to Lotta that could not be fathomed during this second call punctuated with a silence from her now that Daley could honor with "'Fraid *so*, Lotta. B'bye."

The phone is where you are for the moment; in your chest and brain where you live and are found. It should be mind over matter. Your voice potentially free and named; an action. You can move if you will or be trapped. People know something, vessels whoever they are, whatever they sound like or think it is they have to say, the person at the end of the line knows something and it's that that you listen for. It kept Daley there at times. But you don't like this person or know she's stupid or limited, or the phone contact is physical and chaotic.

His bare feet on the carpet, the phone under the bed-table lamp beige, he heard his wife ascending the stairs, soft, barefoot. "Hi," he said toward the doorway. So he was up. She had shaken out her hair. He knew what she would smell like. He would tell her about the earthquake, and his client, a woman living alone and in business, an unthinkable action she's proposed to bring. And Wolf's trip.

He heard Della reach the landing, her feet, her body whispering, and go and pause at the south bedroom, the guest room. Now she came this way. He was not the cleverest of lawyers, not an attack dog, though in anything he undertook Daley would have come through, as Helen had told him, he recalled exactly when. Honestly it was some betrayed strain, indifferent in him, or unshakable or waiting, not the visible attention he gave to his clients and, now, on that night of the elusive Connecticut quake, to his wife who was determined to retire from dance.

If she would only tell him about it. She had shaken out her hair on the way upstairs, he knew. Her olive skin warm from her walk, her strong unadorned fingers, her spirit canceling whatever around her, happy, wretched, Della in essence, smart, she knew how to stop at the threshold, thinking. *Hello*, she could say as if he were a genius, the one person in the world, yet it had a humor to it unsettling with some wanton abrupt search in her eyes upon him so he didn't know what next except it was up to him.

"It's been a busy night." In reply she pointed toward the hall. No, nothing had been heard from the guest. Della gave him the dearest, private smile, it was as good as the story of what was going on; and Daley told her about the call, the earthquake, took its measure, the curious damage to the art objects, while she pulled off her blue jeans, and he spoke of the Seattle call and Wolf's trip, it might be *the* thing about marriage, this talk now. He was telling her yet again about Wolf. He had smelled her, a sour energy on the surface of his wife, it carried him away, home happiness, almost nut-sweet, green pistachio oil, a faintly (to be truthful) sweet steam from her, skunklike, not unpleasant. Her nightgown on over her underpants, coming near she sat on the bed, the thick new mattress, next to him, and he planted his hand behind her. Her shoulder on his, a scent of hot clams, or a scent of welder's burn full, though, and flowering as Asian cattle they'd seen licking their lips before the monsoon, her back then tender as a lotus fiber. She was changing jobs—"careers"—and was not talking about it much. How it had started he hardly knew.

So Wolf was flying out to a site in southeastern Australia for a week and wanted him along, he explained. A week, max. Yeah, another dam (Della shook her head in awe, who didn't like Wolf much), a pretty big one, in the model stage, yet apparently half begun and he suspected farther along than that, and there was trouble with the hydraulic tests. They would see. Della cocked an ear. The model spillway anyway didn't test out. It was the intake towers. The gates and actual draft tubes you could tell were okay, but some *materials* function affecting flow channels and load test Wolf had refused to fathom over the phone with the engineers at that end. Daley had pointed out to Wolf that Wolf just wanted to go basically. His wife Roma knew this. She was used to it. A week away. But she was a West Coast person. Yes, it was true, basically, that he just wanted to go. A month before Christmas. The *children* didn't like the idea much, but had not too keen a sense of time, it was like noise they didn't have the code of so it canceled out, and like the little girl on the screen in *2001*—did Daley remember? his brother asked—they would miss their dad and could think of presents they'd like to see brought back from Down Under but were absorbed in what they were doing and in not knowing even the near future. It was drizzly November in Seattle, but very warm in Wagga Wagga. Daley didn't see how he could do it.

"You have to go," said Della.

Daley made a gesture with his hands. It meant the office. Not *this* client? Della didn't even name Lotta. The earthquake? No, that wasn't a case even; though . . .

"Wagga Wagga." His wife's voice, droll and passing, a frontier, something terrible at that moment too. She had met an old dancer friend on her walk. He had let her have it about quitting. They passed two tall kids carrying a ladder and a toolbox. She let him have it. They were jogging—it was a run not a walk. *Earth*quake? They hadn't felt a thing.

Their earthquake Wolf had shown little interest in tonight (like Della), this negligible Northeast Corridor disturbance weighing in along apparently an east–west axis (where the Daleys' house abutted other houses), whereas the front facing north and the back looking out upon the garden behind the house were the exposed sides. "You know Wolf."

"I'm not his handler," his wife said. Well, Daley was hardly that —Exactly, his wife said—and nobody was going to keep Wolf from getting hurt, Daley added. But his wife didn't need to be reminded of their vacation Wolf had interrupted, the Osaka harbor explosion, not really anything unexpected (though by that standard, what was unexpected?). He had often feared for his brother. You suffered whatever it was and put it behind you eventually. Risks running into years, and not only phone calls and cables but letters, always from somebody working with Wolf, sometimes a carbon, once the original specially to the big brother though Daley didn't get it for weeks from a girl when Wolf was working for A.I.D. in South America, about twenty then in '69 or '70 and restless down there—yet what this Algerian woman in her unpredictable and vivid English had described was Wolf showing fishermen how to rig a sail on a huge canoe, whipping about for fun among dolphin, rays, tuna, shipping water surrounded by topes and hammerheads until the mast cracked; waves breaking out along the shore to the north; the singers passing the aguardiente extolling these Volunteers of Peace (Daley hadn't thought there could be any Algerians in the Peace Corps at this time), the boat making in to shore, the surf a rising and falling horizon.

And over the years, injuries.

"Think of midtown going." Della looked into his eyes as if he would know what to do.

"Bricks knee-deep in the streets, but. Its vibration liquifying the earth," he said. Columbus Circle splits open, there's water down there, a sea at the crack, canal water with little waves humping like wave humps in charged gases ringing the earth, Daley had heard from old acquaintances from the 1970s who were ready to publish the research, it was about motion like if you shook a rug—Della had come up with that one; it wasn't hers, she said. Della was a risk taker too, but cleanly, with a vegetarian's squeamishness. She was the uncanny one though maybe it was a joint venture. She had come a long way tonight, miles, a walk along West Street, and she was aroused he could see in how her bare thighs below her nightgown flattened on the bed—the succession of neighborhoods, river lights moving, and she had come home in a promising mood, for being out when she had a houseguest whom he didn't know was kind of emphatic. The houseguest knew her apparently well enough to bring up her career plan, the agency plan. (It was a generous initiative, if strange for an artist—like a sculptor or anyone in her thirties applying to med school, which would have seemed less strange.) He had no quarrel with the employment agency, yet he saw the rough material of it—the hardworking morning–afternoon push or drift or devotion of it (what non-artists mean by work). He put it out of his head, what would come of it—death there it almost came to him, he wanted to be supportive, and it wasn't as if she were doing high dives off a cliff in Mexico. They would see, and he would see what would be expected of him. She was blonding her hair in a stripe. She loved him actually but did not want to hear his mind spreadsheeting her project, her agency, prudence itself imagining creative people like actors needing day jobs, night jobs. When he himself had this . . . this . . . *quality.*

He lived with her. Looking ahead to when things would change a little. They lived in the present; they had even been told so by an admirer. "I married a man of law," she said to her friends. It was an unlikely pretrial deposition she had made him describe that had won her—her heart, her hand, he had a gift. Something quite out of *her* world, he didn't make all that much of it. His prudence and durability joined with her original moody gift. She had a thing for Daley. Hadn't it been like that on the earthquake night? For she heard his cozy, hushed report of these middle-of-the-night phone calls sitting with him. Australia so close to Christmas? "You should go; you'll be sorry if you don't."

"You could come."

"He wants you. He wants to talk to you."

"That's it." He heard distinctly the sound of his brother saying words he had never said except in spirit, and Daley could just almost make them out, they were momentary and they were about . . . he knew what they were about.

His wife leaning against him, yet erect, trying to understand about the action against Connecticut. "Maybe she's right," said Della; "it would be unprecedented." They laughed softly. "Connecticut," Della said. He agreed. "Her way of being in the world," Della said; it was a thing Della said. "I think she's been abused."

"By her lawyer at three in the morning," said Daley.

"No, she's over the line, she's abusing you, why does she do that?"

Well, it was not client-lawyer, Daley thought. "Not as if you're easily swayable. But she knew what she was doing," Della went on; "no, she didn't, but she was doing *something*." He could throttle her but not over the phone. And she was his client, but are you a client if there is no job? She had shown him a side of herself. The night had insight itself, he wanted to tell his wife, but.

He described Lotta's life, a number of things about her, while he listened for a sound in the hall. She was a connoisseur who half despised her business—no: who listened to people's small talk and despised that. She was disturbing was what she was at times. He couldn't come up with the words, yet while he tried—this *waiting-like-a-thing* (he couldn't quite say it) that Lotta did though active and a talker—Della said, "Exactly." An old-fashioned or class reply everyone was beginning to use in the very early 1980s.

She leaned against him. "You have other gifts besides saying the right thing." These people he told her about—when he himself had this . . . this . . . *quality*. He didn't ask her what it was. If *he* didn't know. Probably never learn what it was.

He described Lotta's life. He knew her. She was sinuous or big boned for a person underlyingly nervy (and mercantile), and in a way grasping, for somebody so . . . Della found the fold of his robe—what was he doing with it on anyway?—she ran her hand up and pressed her hand against his chest, she might have thought he'd had something with Lotta. He had to kiss Della's palm, beings apart, her odor of irritation and talent, he'd been thinking really of her. Yet if she imagined no inferiors or superiors, she had no real partner in her new—he sometimes thought unhinged—undertakings on behalf of equality. Daley heard the street, a tree, or something in the hall; but it was the woman's underlying presence, his shoulders and now his arms bare. She gave him that little push and he fell back across the bed, this night of the earthquake, eyelids dropping, the chill of the night room new upon his chest and belly, for he and Della fell back with dead aim. He sighed like a word, her fingers on him, a hand on his arm running up and down a long silky ridge of scar from wrist almost to elbow. She breathed over him and he breathed back, a saving lilt humorously swelling to hold this hour of the night. Oh the ones who've been pushed around in a former life they are the unbelievable ones trying harder, was one of her incomplete ideas that grew on him. The secret power of *private* life too. He would get up and close the door. She was talking to him and he stayed put. Residue of dream upon him, some *we* again, hopefully down the drain.

She would come to bed in the middle of the night wet as if she'd been with someone. Had she? Was it the walk, her thighs, her thoughts? And slippery as Marilyn Monroe was said to constantly be, according to the famous director's autobiography Helen had quoted in outrage to Daley—"with a behind like a nigger"—Helen shook her head, it made Daley remember his wife. And in those earlier days Daley, high sometimes on life, would foresee Della, in some sentimental abuse of their relationship, pregnant; abuse of Della's calling and profession, a dance of dark-haired women gravid, that somebody made up, some choreographer in residence. That momentary make-a-baby thinking thrown into the swirl actually only stirred him. Like *How are you?* or *What happened?* or *Could we take a walk?* spoken by a serious woman in such a way that everything fell away leaving the question itself.

But now came his wife's voice, her torso reacting in the sound she made, harsh, startled. *"Ruley,"* her houseguest standing in the doorway, droll, transatlantic; and Daley had known that his gift would come to him years, damn them all, a dozen years from now, this former life.

How did he know? From experience. Borne out of that moment, though, back into what hasn't happened yet. He would know what the gift had been all along and that he'd had it all along—had caused it, not entirely his, this gift. A gift for the law? A proof against any threat or trivial emergency or shock. Or he had spent what there was of his life the way you would call up and recall an evening that might not even have happened yet (or, like danger to his wife, brother, nieces, some client, someone falling away, hadn't been saved from happening); and years later when his situation was different would experience in its fell familiarity the midweek evening when he pursued like a fool onto the sidewalk outside one of the new downtown warehouse theaters someone he couldn't quite flesh out (though offered to help him find a job), when, a moment before, Daley had set off meaning to go backstage to find a young actress—they often (the women) seemed to call themselves "performing artist" or, according to Helen, "actor" now—this Canadian woman who needed not his legal help at all, he persisted in being sure, but his presence— his personal voice-over. When you've heard one you find you've heard others, addressing you at length or so low you froze—not unequal to it but plunged in the midst of your own unknown gift you've made too little of or too much of, its alleged existence, which is probably just rerunning events, not from guilt long ago buried or from the not-guilt of extreme clarity, but to take a good look at what's going on behind you in the so-to-speak vehicle that you're driving. Belly of the beast speaking when you listen, if you yourself are not it. Hearing it a long way off when maybe it's only acoustical- ly modulated way down but extremely close by. Saw through it by lis- tening, and determined to go the distance to see if it was true what you had seen both back and ahead to, a prudent businessman taking a little time off, being grasped though (fair enough) by the whole pic- ture, that other Wednesday night years earlier of the alleged earth- quake actually buried twenty-some pages back in next morning's newspaper in an item out of Colorado.

He sat up like a slingshot. "Ruley" what? For his wife had betrayed, to his ear, that it was not she and her *hus*band who'd been interrupted but some other way around distant as your constitution you lived through and felt the warmth and luck of and never saw except in the statistical proof of it and in your secret (kept to your- self) of surviving other people and occasionally recalling down the drain the dregs of a dream and its free-falling *we*, and the eyes of a stranger not missing a thing, you imagine, the room, the ceiling molding, the placement of the telephone, out the window the tree luminously plain and leafless in the light of the streetlamp, Della's body seen through her nightgown, the bare torso of the host down to the raw-looking wound-scar along his arm, no more than that.

# 5

AT THE GREAT RIVER SEARCHING THE CANYON FOR HIS BROTHER, Daley had thought it was the Beatles he was hearing. Up there among the steely escarpments, the coppery, zigzag stripes of strata, iron stained, taking off their own material and kind of violently it developed—interrupting themselves up there somewhere among beds of sedimentary and, Daley realized, volcanic deposit that touched for an instant a motion in him, alternatives yet to occur—nothing to write home about.

It was not quite the Beatles. The boom box cut out in the middle of "Ob-la-di, Ob-la-da," and Daley could hear arguing voices, their anger itself up there among the outcroppings and dwarf juniper was it?—and boulders they called "gibbers" poised to tip. Then he recognized the voice of the site engineer and the foreman for sure (sounding pissed off) and maybe the black man, a rhythm, a collection of sounds, twangs not quite an accent that marked the speech Australian or American whatever the words, even the meaning. "Delivery," he heard *Wolf* say, and "bedrock," quite patiently explaining, infuriatingly perhaps, for Wolf could get his head handed to him; and "time" and "middle-*third*." It was Wolf but they were seventy, eighty feet up. Somewhere a chain saw jabbed its snout into the distance, getting there. They would chop Wolf up in pieces, these people, Daley knew it would happen one day.

Soon after dawn they'd been driven out from town in a company van. Wolf was breezy and objective. It was the rubber and lead oxide model's ability to test load shifts—that was the disagreement in the smoky van. Wolf himself was the issue, though the disagreement with their hosts, which began to sound a little unpleasant, was about materials, extending then into the soft earth they had used for another model. "Diatomaceous" —it was an algal earth, Daley recalled. Wolf pushed his hosts. The hazards of concrete bonding and anchoring into the particular bedrock of the site. Did they know what they were doing with this nearly outdated reinforced concrete? Wolf courted it, his brother thought, silent in the speeding van, an event extended grossly without clear meaning until it will go to pieces if the point of it doesn't emerge. Wolf let it out like a horse's dick, an architect's corbeled extension beyond what can be supported. The discussion lapsed from Aborigines, their rights, the state's here and back home, states' rights—what was Wolf getting at? Wolf made that chuckling sound in his throat. "Ask my brother, if you don't believe me. He'll stay out of this as long as he can," Wolf said; "I'm at his beck and call if he only knew it." They happened to pass a fresh upland field, sheep standing among stones, four drooping trees like trees Daley had seen in Peru perhaps, southern California, someplace, with black scale in the upper bark building its infection. Pepper trees, he thought. (Daley was here and no place else in early-morning light. You wanted to stop at a farm, buy some cheese, at that hour hug the farmer's daughter to tell the truth.) Farther along a gutted carcass hung on a post, a sheep. A boy sat on a barrelly and piebald pony that didn't want to move. At the corner of a pond, a black swan turned and glided along the bank. Sometimes Daley could strangle Wolf. A tiny bird on a fence post with a speckled rump should have been a brown wren but was missing the sharp, up-pointed tail. Daley thought he heard a woodpecker knocking. What was it? The men in the van smoked. The drive took an hour; Daley staring out the window saw what would happen. Wolf told of a chopper pilot he'd flown up to Hue with who had a Confederate arm patch. Daley loved brother responsibility, yet it was a loyalty job like a dying parent, you must be there and nowhere else. He was as irritated as could be, though—if only for the moment. What was it? Palpable, material; his time; but material of *him* sliding out and glomming into someplace else, material of himself, just an early-morning dream existing in advance of yourself. Besides bodyguarding (frankly) his brother, he had his own things to do. What were they? Not law. Law wasn't it, here twelve thousand miles out by way of Seattle, Hawaii, Central Pacific Basin, Fiji (those magnificent curved roofs thatched), and the International Date Line adding a day going west, and all he could think of was that Wolf had been turned down for the draft and neglected to mention it.

Construction had begun on the dam. Unwisely, Wolf was pretty

sure. When Wolf had pointed this out last night the wiry little engineer Young asked the black engineer something Daley didn't pick up.
It was the accent or another lingo. Patience in short supply. You
didn't tell them their business, least of all the economics. Yet they
feared Wolf. Why they'd gotten him out here. He shook his head. A
side rampart begun where intake towers high up would be built out
like suspended concrete skyscrapers. The big man with the ginger hair
down over his ears and on his arms and chest like an orangutan,
named Boothroyd, hadn't said much about work already begun when
he had Wolf on the line in Seattle. Why hadn't Wolf demanded to
know exactly where they were? Boothroyd's deep-planted eyes were
small and blue and understanding and he was angry. Daley took a
walk along the river. The others disappeared. Now Daley heard them
high up.

Daley caught sight of them way high. On the far shore of the river
December cast into steep shade a stretch of escarpment, while on this
side was the precarious vantage of observation the group had reached
in their ascent. Wolf looked down and saw his brother, a wonderful
distance Daley felt it to be, the open, first-strike, probably stupid attitude in his brother's contentious squint against the light. Wolf sig-
naled him with his whole arm to get up there in a hurry, and Daley
heard the voices rise and fall. Together he and Wolf went only so far.
Over on the far shore of the great river a quarter mile and more away
stood a blond woman. He would like to have a word with her about
anything, he felt the future reach out to her, while Wolf on this side
might do something, you didn't know. Daley heard the knock of a
woodpecker across the water, like a quick rattle in your stomach; it
was still early, but there were no woodpeckers in Australia.

A mirror-slick scarp—Daley picked his way beside it a hundred
feet above the river now. Glancing down at the glitter seemed to prepare him for what might happen. The current swung and cut across
the orange glare. Wolf hadn't told them a thing they didn't know
already, Young said, but since he was here . . . "We got you out here
from Seattle?" Surrounded by these people up here as if their eager-
ness for answers were really to dump him off the cramped footway at
the brink of a sheer drop, knock him into next week.

Well, Wolf had been explaining the angular risks in the scheme—that the shifting sideways loads "full *and* empty, right?" upon the upstream face of the dam as planned might move the thrust line beyond the middle third and crack the concrete. What happens when water gets inside a crack like that? It exerts—

"—a vertical lifting force five tons per square foot at a depth of a hundred feet," interrupted Boothroyd.

Crack widens, dam *tips*, Wolf shrugged. They knew this. Their impatience burgeoning in their thick shoulders, the two big guys and the black man, and the curious tensile narrowness of the bald little one, Young. The American fella they got here to tell them what they already . . . They were all at loggerheads. The black man said that Wolf was a hard case.

The river muscular below them. "I told you"—Wolf pointed upstream along the canyon wall—"if you build up from over there, setting your rods into the rock could be too hard, you might blow a hole you couldn't . . . Don't ask me how I know" (he read the faces). Daley felt that Wolf dared these guys. "It's your Commonwealth concrete."

"What would you use?" Boothroyd said.

"They're working on it. They're a year, two years, away from . . ." Wolf saw something. "You could get cracks two-thirds of the way up when you're all done." Daley saw the river and thought he shouldn't have come. He and Wolf had known what would happen, and their closeness stalled a thought. Daley had work of his own to do, and why Commonwealth?—it didn't mean much anymore. The queen was what she was, which was about it.

Wolf bumped his brother. "You're thinking forty-eight hours ago I was home in New York talking to Wolf in the middle of the night."

"Not to mention I left a stranger holding down the fort with Della," said Daley, staring across the river.

"You New Yorkers," said Wolf.

"Not really," said Daley.

"I got hell myself," said Wolf; "but my wife . . ."

"Yeah," said Daley.

"Coulda done all this in one trunk call," Boothroyd said. Wolf's name almost had done it. "You're the one," Boothroyd had said grudgingly. They had in common an Italian rigger Wolf had once dined with in Amsterdam. A force secretly out of control like the future but transferred to the identity or name of a person, as if being well known made self-evident the old land bridge between personality and work that might emerge.

And materials science in the 1970s and early '80s, or its expectations, had given Wolf among other consultants in America and at either end of Asia an authority way beyond what they'd actually done. A raw, contagious publicity at a certain level like any other. Yet the seeming aura was deserved. It was in what was coming. The smart materials that would act on their own in thicknesses too thin to much measure—in coatings like a glaze. Virtually plan ahead. Because built into the chips was Time measured in advance yet heading into the true bends of its thought.

The brothers located two of the new mountain bikes. Not on the market. Shocked for all-terrain performance. Wolf and Bill went out and covered sixty miles one late afternoon, got back at midnight. Messages from Seattle and from Boothroyd who had hoped to have dinner with Wolf. And New York: just wondering when Daley was getting home. "They need you for some consulting work?" Wolf joked. What was the last name of this Ruley? Daley wondered, doubting an Austro-Israeli bank for a moment, then believing it.

Violence almost put things in perspective the fifth and last day. The situation would get worse before it didn't get better. "You're supposed to be the one." The black engineer lowered his voice, his hand on the counter gripped a little blue glass of rum from an unlabeled bottle. Some sort of very long farm shed Daley remembered later, a mile from the river, its structure simple but with dark little storage annexes, and it was operated as an irregular-hours place by the company. Late-1940s swing was playing off a tape deck, clarinet, and vibes, a drummer Daley instantly knew. Wolf had been describing a job east of L.A., a masonry fiasco. Concrete split out in three places but you couldn't see it—polymer insulation left off the pipes. Not on the level of Australian work, mind you (did he mean "up to" or "as embarrassing"?). Wolf was good on the subject of wasted work.

A crew guy in orange jeans with a long scar from Adam's apple to earlobe that lipped out dark yet raw stood next to them as Wolf concluded his account. "My brother will now tell you of an earthquake in New York."

The black man persisted, "You were mixed up in the Many Mouth Bridge trouble."

"I ain't God," Wolf said, he talked down a little, he sounded a little off, and he eyed the crewman in the orange jeans who had a wild head of blond, fuzzy kinks, what was he doing with that hair? The little bald wiry one Young looked none too happy, would give back as good as he got and not in kind. Where was Boothroyd? "They said you should have been killed," the black man said. He was more open about whatever rankled here than an American black man at that foreman level of management would have been. Daley was the one who explained: the span had bent like a musical saw blade. "You saw the footage, that piece of steel he was riding like one of those arcade games."

"Were you there?" Young said.

"At Many Mouth?"

What did it matter? You could see it better on the tape.

"What's yih line 'a work?" Young asked Daley.

"He's not afraid 'a nothin'," Wolf said, "he's the crazy one. Birdman. Chopper pilot."

Daley shook his head. "Not really true."

"He'll cure what ails ya." Wolf wouldn't shut up.

"No, I'm a lawyer."

"A demon of depositions," said Wolf—"know what that is?" If Wolf wouldn't talk down. "Going diving in the Black Sea, how 'bout that?" The crewman tossed off his pint like the threatening distance between them.

"Since you mention that paht a the weuld," the black man began, the interesting one in the group who'd worked the manganese mines and really bored into the history of things, "now, the trouble in Turkey? The blast we heard—"

"The blast came out of the quake an hour later," said Wolf, "if you want to know. And I fixed it. It's what got us here; ask B.R." (This was Boothroyd.)

"But the viaduct?" said Young.

"The viaduct just happened," said Wolf.

"Whilst you were someplace else?" said the crewman. He had a quick, outsider laugh.

"So where you s'posed to be at this pawnt'n tahm?" said the crewman.

"They gave it to the Kurds," Young said, ignoring the crewman, "because they didn't know who to blame it on."

"Some dissident," said Wolf. He was alerted and blank.

"That's what they said." Young seemed to watch Daley and Wolf, who turned a visionary eye on Young.

"Man, all that concrete flying, trusses forget about it, steel burning like a covered bridge in Bangor. Cost you an arm and a leg," said Wolf. The brothers laughed. Daley couldn't see a thing but what was right here, something about to fall. "You needed a little earthquake in New York New *York* to get *you* out here."

"No," said Daley.

"I was gonna phone you in the morning."

"Australia," said Daley.

"You *wanted* to come out here," said Wolf. "His wife's a dancer."

Crewman stood his glass on the counter, a pint, but delicately flared, tumbler. "Vietnam?"

Wolf looked at Daley. "Did you hear me?" said the man to Wolf.

"Little construction job," Wolf said then.

"When was thet, pray tell?"

"What is this?" Wolf said.

"Little construction job," said the crewman.

Wolf looked at him quizzical as hell. "Had to see for myself. You guys screw up, you can't fix it on the phone. Jes' kidding." Wolf indicated Daley. "Takin' a trip with my big brother, my handler. Knows his rocks, you'd be surprised." Wolf turned to the crewman, who had put his heavy hand on Wolf's shoulder. "Knows more geology than I do and he's only a . . ." Wolf eased out from under, but the hand—swollen knuckled and burned dark by outside work—gripped his shoulder and with the other hand reached instinctively for the beer glass. "You *need* to get away," said Wolf and patted the crewman's cheek.

"Rhodes," said the wiry bald man Young.

"You needed to get away, eh?" Rhodes said, moving Wolf now, and

Wolf cuffed the hand away and the tumbler, which was empty, got swept off the counter. Rhodes shoved him lightly in the chest and Wolf light as the simplest answer backhanded him on the cheek and Daley reached between.

Where was Young?

Men around the room called out. Rhodes's hand came to his side as Daley gripped the man's wrist with his other hand to destroy it. Rhodes made a sound but didn't care; Daley had a grip not throttling not steering but going nowhere. Rhodes's free hand whacked Daley in the back of the head. Daley could have worked on him methodically from the wrist up. It did not make you better, or relieved of doubt, or clearer or more or less anything (except that Daley knew there was a knife someplace), nor confident in your mortality though he felt an old scar along his forearm prickle (and not that old)—or sure of anything but that his brother, who always called him the risk taker, said things people didn't need to hear. Rhodes, his bluish cheeks drawn darker than sunburn, held his wrist close to his face. The finer framing bones of the wrist looked different. Daley felt some impact of why he'd come—the foreseeable future as you would put it to a client, get some distance on it in the light of Australia, which he and his wife had seen already but let Della handle her immediate professional fate without him around for a few days, a prickly question; yet why seemed this a foregone future in some light of the yet-to-happen slow past: Daley not only prudent but physically a little viciously strong (or ready, prescient, unshockable)—picking up the curved pieces of Rhodes's glass off the floor. A south*east* Australia this time where Ruley his wife's business acquaintance had loaned his bank group's money for the purchase of experimental irrigation grids and somehow sold the Australians the grids himself: "Lucky ya gotcha thumper along," one of the onlookers had said, "we'd have a friendly casualty"—serve Wolf by protecting him from injury—or from legal action should he do violence to Rhodes; somehow getting Wolf and himself out of the bar (to forestall what Wolf was capable of saying, of volunteering with regard to *him*), Daley had looked back to see come up out of that long tool pocket in the jeans trouser a clean blade, it looked like an old six-inch Mackerel Tracker if Daley could have seen the handle, and Daley had looked down and felt the sting in the palm of his hand, which was bleeding. No blood in the bar but some curious damage to an Australian wrist.

A girl waited at the filling station staring into the distance, listening to the Beatles. There were coops and there were birds walking around in the distance. She pointed out the mountains. The men asked where the skydiving was, it was near here; and the open-cut gold operation, how did they . . . ? The blond girl didn't speak till she was done pumping. She carried a small pistol in a suede holster. She was a kid, she had breasts, she might be fourteen, she might be *twelve* nowadays, she was in charge. That's right, it was the Residents, they sorta take off the Beatles. The mountains weren't really blue, it was all the eucalyptus trees, it did something to the light, she said, the oil evaporating through the leaves out there. Her uncle made stained glass in Toronto—around there—an artist, he'd done a church in Syracuse and Banff—where was that from New York City? He was coming out here again someday soon for the light. And the cricket, he was an off bowler, he could give you some useful innings. The girl's eyes looked at you fondly when she talked about her uncle. Were Wolf and Daley stopping in *Canberra*? They should see the museum, she said, her voice husky, nice. "That's an American city," Wolf said. The girl walked away to make change—she was more beautiful from the back—"the capital planned by an American from scratch."

"A Wright protégé," said Daley.

"Yeah, well they hated it, what he did, vegetarian teetotaler, Griffin." Wolf shook his head.

"See the museum," the girl said when she came back, "see the artwork, some of *your* guys there—see Australia." She was something reincarnate.

They all went behind a shed and she showed them a champion turkey with one leg. A great silver-bronze sixty-six-pound turkey a quarter wild pecking at grain with wings that could still carry him across the garden still if not bank him into the old stunted fig tree, but what she had to show Daley was what you heard when you put your ear near the lower edge of his wing and listened to his gizzard—for it was Daley she meant with a curious (what was it?) farsightedness beyond her years: a grinding and grating going on in there, believe it or not gravel, pebbles, glass, sometimes bits of machinery a bolt or sliver of cog at large between the two long muscular walls and the leathery ridges and lining of the animal's gizzard, that act like teeth in flesh-eating birds to crush the food and day by day mill all these things into particles almost dust-fine, the girl was telling him intelligently, softly, while bent over he listened to the turkey, his eyes vaguely on the girl's tummy and, not amazed but grateful, Daley had told her almost in a whisper what he knew about quartz and other crystal insertions, crystalloblastic insertions, where through metamorphic mix any of the minerals may be found inserted in any other. Maybe so, but it was pride in this old turkey she would take care of until he was done, letting you listen, a champion that could have defended himself against anyone; against who knows (Daley thought) what X-ray beam defracted by atoms of its innards. The girl, though, was the remarkable one, for she wanted you to see what her bird could do—the shrapnel he could process, even perhaps absorb, which Daley didn't believe. She wanted these American guys, or Daley, with whom she felt good, to understand. "What'd ya do to ya ahm?" She ran her fingers over the gristly scar.

"A New York mistake." Daley was listening to the turkey. The turkey had had enough. Look out not to get pecked. A turkey. Daley and the girl, some habitually unfolding will-like digestion. Yet the girl through the turkey shared a promise that asked to be saved at the moment of leave taking, a joint vision with the girl if she developed someday, no more; or a consequence of his and perhaps her knowledge that there was no future vision, no actual future, just as there was a running down of life and a throwing forth of it into action.

"See you in a few yihs," the girl said. Daley said he'd be there. "A few lahftahms," the girl said. If she needed a roof over her head, Daley added; the words came out forward, okay though.

"Every man for himself in that jungle," said Wolf.

"He lives in Seattle," said Daley.

They took a look at her. "Your eyes," Wolf said; "the color."

But Daley had seen what his brother meant: like a sea captain's blue-green bottle glass, and like the iridescence of starling feathers as your angle changes, or for an instant at a distance the wild fraction of this huge turkey along the shingled layers of throat plumage and the wings' structure of covert roofing. Color aside, her eyes were very slightly, in fact beautifully, walleyed like someone with a long view, a very intelligent someone to come. Wolf's older girl—or, years previous, Daley explained as if it was color, a rather famous *flight* attendant—"That's the ticket," the girl said, she was a mature fourteen, anything to get airborne eastward. The girl patted her holster. They got back into the car. Wait, she wrote her name and address on the back of a garage business card and took it around to the driver's side. That was it. "I'll wrahtcha a lahn." Daley dug out his card.

They were on the way out past the turkey's tree when they heard a shot. Some rodent caught running between burrows. "Take her home with us," Wolf said; "just kidding."

"Five years she'll be eighteen if she's lucky," said Daley.

"Think of her now," Wolf said, "putting your ear into her little belly. Just reading your mind." The blond girl wasn't spending her life introducing you to the insides of champion turkeys. She had thoughts. If not the best of plans. What spirit.

They turned off at the mine and it was blacktop for a mile before they came to a cement-block building. A ravine opened below them and beyond it the hill and the cut. The brothers talking in the car, Wolf stared out the windshield, said he thought the mine was a loser, what was the mine in Perth? Coolgardie, said his brother but that was a gold rush, 1890, this is 1980s. 'Eighty-two. They saw the sky out the windshield, discussed the thermals, countries to live in.

Older bro had overdone it. (Tell him about it.) Hadn't known that Rhodes, eternally a construction worker, had been a member of the small SEATO force embarked for neighboring Vietnam '69, '70, Australia the next to last of the free dominoes likely to fall before America did.

Though had Wolf known?

Well, he thought he might have, it came up with the black foreman up the canyon wall. Grabbing the wrist was what it was. The dam-in-progress they had flown Wolf out for, and he had told the truth his way, it had about preceded him, a hunch, theirs *and* his, known for his raw grasp, what you're in for; for surviving natural disaster, human error, pick both, and bring along a handler.

They wheeled and set off again. The driver sees it all. Several gray birds swung by low in a flat fore-and-aft orbit around the car, with featherless patches about the head, good singers, and again there was a woodpecker knocking, though Daley believed there were no woodpeckers in Australia and if it was mimicry when did those sociable honey eaters (he thought) meet a woodpecker to do an impression like that? The driver channels the car and every detail of the road and the air through the open window and his own emptiness and the adolescent girl's card with his phone number on it into what his brother is saying, the passenger, his Washington State driver's license revoked for the time being and hardly seeing the road (Daley is certain). What does Wolf see?

"You're a wild man. You're something, Bill." They laughed with understanding and inanely like brothers, like fools, and life swung past in great detail, swimming a river, fighting it, slugging each other in somebody's rec room, up in the air at cliff's edge, Della and Daley aborting their north India trip before they ever got to Nepal and—and a woman who had flown Resupply the India route ("Oh yeah!" from Wolf the civilian remembering her), for the older brother had thought he would introduce this lady to him. It was after the civilian construction job Wolf had had no particular business to be on and he was pretty mad at him at the time. It was a standing joke who she was looking at—you couldn't quite tell ("Maybe all of us," Daley suggested) —though *they* were the joke (*sitting*)—her courage and angular beauty bearing them all across—and rumored to be able to fly herself ("Like this guy," Wolf had said of his older brother in his presence once years ago long before Daley was licensed). Until one night part of the landing gear jammed without instrument warning, they had heard, and the plane spun on the tarmac and broke in half and the walleyed woman was gone. Hey, it wasn't adventure Wolf wanted in his marriage when he had eventually made his move. And the turkey girl and her entrails and plotting her future more the older brother's recollection, what have you: cut off however in the knowledge that, though he was Wolf's brother, Daley from that afternoon did not quite understand Wolf. "You could strangle her," Wolf said. Surely he didn't mean the blond kid at the filling station.

They were going back a day early, Daley to watch TV with his young nieces, in his lap in Seattle after we hope taking them for a helicopter ride to Tacoma and back, maybe solo, if he can persuade an old Boeing buddy. Through the bandage his cut palm stung against the wheel. The pinched nerve in Wolf's back was acting up. Australians don't *do* this. They don't go in for knife fights, Daley said off the top of his head. "See how Young handled it?" said Wolf; "don't make me laugh. They've worked together."

"Building," said Daley. Wolf said Rhodes could use a little killing. Daley said he would not have let it . . . get out of hand. Unless it happened, said his brother. "A veteran, remember," Daley said.

Here was when his brother, abrasive to the last, popped the question: "What're you doing with Della?" All the way Down Under for that. Right then Daley had feared for her across those leagues of sea and land, fresh water giving way to salt, as space tells time to fall through us or us to do the falling.

What did Wolf mean? Getting beyond himself on the way to Sydney; you had to think he cared and he was a loose-gun brother, gifted and could actually take care of himself; but did he? Did he care? He'd always had strange potentials.

But all this way for this exchange?

Daley acted happy. "Doing with her? Oh sometimes I could . . ."

Wolf lit up a cigarette. "Strangle her!" they both said, and Daley laughed and Wolf coughed. Well, she'd been a little deluded of late. Of late? the brother exhaled smoke into the car though the window was open. Occupationally. But she would land on her feet probably.

That gifted woman? And the weeklong houseguest who was harmless. Yet here in the driver's seat anchored to the wheel, looking for Princes Highway but it was a hundred miles too soon, and wondering what it would take to go up west a thousand miles and more and see if they had a helicopter to pass over the Aboriginal sandstone formation in the Northern Territories that Wolf himself had pointed out on a map, a vast rock but there was no time; yet what would it take to pass over it so slowly they would not be moving, to hover a hundred feet above that place, what was bound to come didn't need to be said or thought, and wasn't prudent but could be distant if you lived. It was in there already in what you did, how you acted. The blond girl's heart and what lay on either side mingled with the turkey's insides and he would sentimentally ponder them for days for their hope, specific knowledge, and prediction, and he felt her finger on his arm, that was all, a case of call waiting. She had his address, the petrol station girl, the turkey girl, recalling from somewhere the gift of—he was touched by it—joint foresight, a looking ahead that improved if there was intimacy, teamwork. "Maybe she won't," he had said to his fellow strangler, who was looking out the side window.

"Land on her feet? Oh you're way ahead of me," Wolf said, blowing a trail of smoke out the left side of his mouth. He was thinking about Rhodes's war, Daley was as certain as Wolf was that a person is a mobile container and you can get things from anyone and like other, cruder dangers he realized he would gravitate toward embarrassing people and who could tell who remained to be seen?

# 6

"I'M CONCERNED FOR HER," DALEY SAID TRYING TO ESCAPE THE NICE couple in the lobby; "it was over the line."

"You think . . . ?" said the woman.

"He creamed her."

"Oh I bet they're just friends," the woman said, "I mean—"

"She is what she is," said her boyfriend, a kid in a black outfit, black baseball cap.

"Well *that* doesn't . . ." She appealed to Daley, who had backed into the heavy glass street door and was leaning on it. Someone else needed to get out. The boyfriend took hold of his girlfriend's shoulders from behind and slipped his fingers down across her collarbone.

Daley found himself on the sidewalk.

Peering out into the street, the big young man who'd been sitting in front of Daley and Helen peered into the street. He dropped his lighter into his raincoat pocket, calling it a night. This insolent, opinionated, curiously polite if borderline trashy spirit who squinted at him, waiting. "Can't seem to get away from you, slugger."

"You took your coat," Daley said. He felt her struggling in the dressing room, face a little broken, a spray of blood, table with a pinched Kleenex, between the actress and her partner hardly a sound.

"Would of taken a swipe at her, wouldn't you?" said the other.

Daley shook his head like an old obstacle. It was the cigarette, the smoke in the young man's chest. A weird equality he conferred on you. The fellow had this look on his face, contempt, depth, visited now with a storm of coughing. "There's something going on," Daley said.

"There always —" the smoker got out, half choking, "always is," he forced the sounds, his broad body bending.

"Between them I mean," Daley said.

"Oh this instant."

Daley looked around. A few people had been smart enough to come out of the jammed-up lobby-vestibule going the opposite direction from the man in the hat he was sure was the producer. On the sidewalk stood the easel with the blown-up review and the picture that had amazed him getting out of the cab (not startled him at all, just amazed him) of someone in the play pointing, or shaking her finger, a fair-haired actress with an imperfect nose he now knew to be Becca Lang, her lips flared, speaking some line—but Helen, as he reached for the tickets, had reminded him to get a receipt from the driver.

Hunched over, the young man absorbed and alone sucked his cigarette almost into flame and snapped it into the street with his fingertip and thumb. Across the street great, stiff bent triangles of cable rose from a freight-car-sized Dumpster. Smoker reached for his handkerchief, exhaling through nose and mouth.

"You'd have taken a swing at her?" Daley said.

"Missed my chance," said the other, he liked Daley, he could care less.

"No discipline," Daley said.

The young man liked it. "Well I do what I want," he said; "that ain't so easy." Daley took out his wallet. "Get out now," the fellow said.

He had been an athlete and let himself go. If he'd grow a big beard, you could see him decked out on a Harley. A *swimmer*, though, it came to Daley like part of a résumé he would see what he could do about, that was it. Burly, connected, or curiously buoyant or blessed even now though not for long, he would kill himself, you could see him plowing through an Olympic pool over the middle distance. Daley offered him a card and asked the familiar question Helen said was socially crude, "What do you do?"

The man blew his nose. His eyes cleared. "I'm probably between jobs."

"Sounds like I could help you," Daley said. The young man blew air. A performer in there too, maybe that was it. Not surprised at Daley. Bothering him. What was it this options trader (let's say) with a habit, snorting his amusement in his seat in front of Helen and Daley, knew? Daley explained that he had an agency, and he was a lawyer, that was what he was, but he had the agency, full service, but corporate placement you know.

The young man took his card. "What I had in mind was C.E.O.," he said. They laughed differently. Step by step, hey, Daley said. He practiced law; the agency . . .

"Just what are you saying?"

He had a qualified assistant in the office, a woman who did the simulated interview prepping, at least for the next month or so, what they're going to ask you, that kind of thing. He had kept the agency going, the two operations under one roof, one umbrella, for some years now.

The other man hated Daley for a second, the one looking backward, the other ahead, yet there was help here for each. "Just what are you saying? Wearing two hats?" He lifted his elbow, tilted his head to see his gold watch on his turned wrist; it was quite commanding, a countdown.

"We don't really *know* what's going to—"

"You better," the large young man said and gestured toward the lobby.

"—happen with the economy," Daley said.

"The economy," said the young man, "the economy. You're doin' fine."

"Oh, I'm ready to unload it but—"

"Why don't you *down*load it," said the other—and bowed over in a fit of coughing like his last.

"The agency," Daley said.

"That's what I said," said the other.

"There's something about it," Daley said, waiting, "but it's —"

"*You're* gonna do something," said the other; "I heard you get it when the lights went down."

Daley started to explain.

"I *know*, I *know*," said the young man, "I heard the whole thing."The woman taking tickets? Daley persisted. From Rome? The person Daley was with always knew that sort of thing. "I *know*."The *stage* manager. "I know."

"A ring on her hand," Daley said.

"That's right. Stay clear of the ring on her fist, but you always— you always"—the speaker was coughing and took a moment—"you always knew that." A woman who had been phoning at the corner rejoined her friends. A couple of women reading the review seemed to hear a signal. They were holding hands.

"I thought, She's not a Roman."

"And the lady you're with is not your wife," said the young man.

"Oh *she's* long gone," Daley said. A poor remark, something about it.

"I know what you mean," said the other.

"It's more than *I* know," Daley said, recalling he didn't know what, his wife, her habit of being right—a gift—and a film producer he had met through Helen who said his second or third wife's name was a dirty word, but this young man understood Daley's wife was *dead* and gone.

"Long gone—it can happen just like that. You've inspired me," said the young man; "what was her name? I see you've . . ."

"What?"

"Done everything. "

"Her name?"The question was not unkind. "Della was her name."

"Not much of a name," said the young man, "I mean for her." It was embarrassing, even very slightly, for the young man.

"It's a good name," Daley said.

"Hey, in itself," said the other; "but it's country, it's west of here."

"North."

"Okay, north."

"What do you mean I inspired you?" said Daley.

"I'll give things a name," the young man said.

"Things?"

"I can do that." He was at the curb. "What'd she die of?"

It stopped Daley as if the guy had no right to know, no right in the world. "Della? Lung."

"Nothing special?" said the other.

"Nothing special. Fibroids like a farmer or . . . not cancer."

The yellow tie, coat over arm, asking nothing. "Your friend, she had something to tell you."

"She always has."

"She just got home."

"What about it?" said Daley.

"Well, you know what's going to happen, but you want to see it again anyway. You, I mean." The fellow's clothes weren't an actor's but he had some dumb instinct about the blonde; it was in his massive size somewhere. *Helen* had said he knew someone.

"The agency was Della's. We kept it going."

"That was good of you." The young man's eyes widened, it was good of him. "That was what she did?"

"Her second career."

"What was her first?" The young man had abandoned his tone.

"She was a dancer. It's done okay."

"We wouldn't expect anything less." That tone again. "She started an employment agency and she was a dancer? Well, that figures."

Daley wondered if he had a name, a name came to Daley and he looked around at the sidewalk emptying. The man in the Anzac hat (that was the name) regarded them from behind the glass door and turned away. "It didn't figure."

The big guy had stepped off the curb but now he held up Daley's card. "I'll drop by tomorrow." He opened his wallet and came back and handed *Daley* a card. "Token of my self-esteem," he muttered. A good sign. Financial-district type. He seemed abstracted.

"I was only concerned about her," Daley said.

"Not up to you," said the other not unkindly. "She'll never wind up on the street. She's knocked around, in Canada even," he said over his shoulder, raising his hand like a more experienced man, but an equal. "You were just worried about her, she's something." The wheezing laugh, braylike, challenged the street now sounding past the Dumpster and toward the river.

"Not leaving?"

"Oh it carries you away," said the other, who it occurred to Daley would not be sitting in front of them. A hinge. Each had seen the other.

"How many times can you get hit like that?" Daley called. Leander was committed to the glimmering street—that was his name on the card—Daley had guessed half of it, *I'm Andy*: banker-boy not obliged to lean over to tie contingency loafers; not junior litigator. Not this swimmer, never slim, with a small, bizarre gift he carried around somehow, it put you in mind of scavengers on the piers at dawn when Daley took his run—except that Leander on the prowl did not collect things he could sell. He could go take a jump in the river.

The couple with the child came out. It was raining. The woman pointed at the easel photo. "So I was wrong, it was a shitty idea," she said.

"You weren't *wrong*," said the man, the little girl awake on his shoulder. "It was just an idea."

Standing near a streetlamp was a figure he would have sworn was the actress. A stage door round the corner? She looked around this way and that or she saw what she aimed to see. Then she was gone.

"They'll never move this uptown," the man said.

His wife looked at Daley: "Now you be nice."

At this distance of many blocks the smell of the North River slid into Daley's nostrils. Daley did not think Hudson this far down but the river, the harbor. The ethylene and monoxide and spilled soda and beer, the burn of trash, or weld, the tunnel ventilators along the West Side, even the street tar smell approaching the piers asked of him nothing more than to be part of it with its Gotham history and wide sound (though he had not been really to sea in decades), and with its immediate future instinct in his body and routine quick as a city developer's thought containing, lodged somewhere in those structures that would rampart the rivers and lay esplanades and plazas, inhabitants for whom in his prudent imagination he had a haunting knack: for where they'd be in ten years or days, where they wanted to be, or what be part of. Even a knack to gut and fill a modest warehouse like this one with a little profit. For these creative people who did something else during the day. But more the piers were what came to him active and waiting in decay obscure as a slashing in an alley, but more the waterside acrid salt compound of wood and marine flesh, the driving current he had felt swimming across the river on his birthday on a dare a dozen years ago and the chop of the thick waves and sour hawser rope and flaking hull paint and the settled restoring smell of winch grease, rusted shots of chain and in the early mornings an opiate of clarity, a scent of material, bales of packing: your own house left behind in the visionary chill of dawn when Daley took his run along the esplanade to the Battery and back (in company or not), a tugboat beside an oil barge bound south to the harbor, materials drifting near the rocks at the end of the night, unimaginable rafts of bleached and sludge-imbued timber scavenged by the unhoused and by artists he'd seen for years there at dawn who must be unaware of him, though a Port Authority cop in his white patrol car knew Daley; the city heaved and hummed and sighed like gravel and ground glass in the gizzard of a giant turkey that had once been parked up against Daley's ear, right against the feathers, the night river washed among the piers blocks away from where Daley stood for a moment free in the evening outside the renovated warehouse theater, the high-ceilinged ground floor surmounted by five more levels held up by piers at street level clad by simple pillars squarely decorative with diamond-shaped insets and at the top of one instead of a capital a stone sunflower (terra-cotta?) on a bed of leaves. Leander departing had held up his hand to slow a truck that Daley recognized, a demolition and trash-carting service. It was funny, unruly, and it made him mad, this man not in condition, but of a navigating portliness and command unusual for twenty-seven or twenty-eight. Spoiled, authority-ridden near-juvenile in a suit Daley recognized, who had a fallback discretion superior to what was stalling him in his life, and beyond spilling whatever he had to spill about this evening—which he had decided not to—he wasn't the braggart lowering over Helen and Daley minutes ago. Leander knew Becca, it came to Daley, and was well out of it. In the lone lighted lobby the stage manager leaned against the wall addressing a pay phone Daley hadn't noticed and would almost say hadn't been there before. She held the receiver now in two fingers away from her—you knew someone was still there talking—and she dropped it delicately and exactly and desolately onto the hook and seemed to look out into the street to see if he was alone, where he paused by the easel. Daley thought he would go listen to some Japanese jazz tonight whether Helen wanted to or not.

The moment of the play caught in this photo of Becca had not yet happened. She was indigestible if you were a dragon. She was real in her promises and with a skeleton about her ready for anything, intellectual, not entirely finished with you ever. The actor knew her voice but the face is what you show the other person and you might want to go for it, fair enough. Toss a drink at it, stare it down, or just look away. What the sister had done to the brother, why would she go and mess up his life like that?

The actor almost hadn't meant to hit his partner such a whack. But he would take it. You took sides with this curious-looking woman who hadn't deserved to be hit like that if you recalled how the story unfolded, slender though sweetly, femalely broad in the hips, future wide open like an explosion to look at, pliant and capable. But the brother—hell, he had told her he was making it with this person she had once known, and she had gone and told his wife, her more or less unknown sister-in-law. You could feel for the brother, he was what he was. Not the actor, who was tough to like, ominous as a heavy, unearthed brick.

What was ending?

# 7

HE CAME UP THE THREE STEPS AND RECOGNIZED THE BOY BEFORE HIM looking down into the theater, the rows of seats, the exposed light boxes overhead. The boy stood here at the back eleven or twelve years old in a sweater. He'd been with the man in the big hat you might easily think you recognized. Daley whispered to him, What did he think? The boy looked around, his cheeks and forehead in the dusk dense with freckles. Helen down there in her aisle seat twisted around and saw him. Daley asked the boy if he liked it back here, and the lights dimmed. "Decided to stand?" Daley said.

"No," said the boy.

Helen twisted around again, the people behind her gone.

"I didn't want to sit . . ." the boy said.

"Well, there's certainly standing room."

The boy was looking at him in the dusk. "You know him?" the boy said.

"Who you're with? Oh"——he recalled the man. "He's not your father," Daley said without thinking.

The boy looked at him; the boy was being used, but for what exactly?

"I thought I knew him." Daley shrugged.

"He owns a whole theater," the boy whispered; "he's a producer. He's going to make a movie, but not here."

The word *producer* explained everything, it was a story, it bore down on you and things were attached to it. "What're you doing standing?" Daley whispered back.

"My mother's in it," the boy said.

"Not the one who got slapped?"

"*No*." The boy grinned and, shaking hands with Daley, dropped his program and picked it up.

"You've seen the play before."

The boy turned his deep attention to the stage. In his eye there shone the flame of a volcano. The house dark now, the lights came up on the brother and his wife, the red-haired actress, who was telling a story to her husband as if nothing had happened. She was looking at the back of the house Daley was certain where her son was standing.

Helen uncrossed her legs and turned them knowingly to let in Daley in the dark; he felt her fingers on him. The people on stage were just standing there comfortably. Weren't these two people supposed to be dealing with what the sister had told the sister-in-law that had precipitated the blow at the end of Act One, the brother-sister thing, the blood? There was a table and a bowl of apples and oranges.

"I had this incredible . . ." Helen whispered, ". . . during the interval." Daley remembered why he was here. "I had this incredible . . . thing," Helen whispered; "I *felt* you still"—it was true, Helen murmuring *Hello* in the kitchen, surprised, the clock above them—"and I knew I shouldn't have taken this trip"—her whisper came out harsh, she meant the West Coast—"but it's over." She indicated the seat in front, "Get whatchoo wanted?"

"I'll tell you," he whispered. But it wasn't true, it wasn't necessary, and the plate of apples and oranges on the table on stage had still the woman's hands on it, for something had happened. Leander wasn't jumping into the river, thank God, but Daley was close as if he needed help to see Leander. Daley was sick at heart. Behind a backstage dressing room door the blond girl calling for assistance, splayed, half naked, rolling away from blows, from feet, a silent plate of fruit, seeing him when he couldn't help her, an odor of the docks he had in his nostrils still. Footsteps could be heard somewhere backstage.

He was right about some of this, and the city with all its greatness held out no hope for him. Gone into the night streets the man whose card Daley had on him, Leander, a middle-class drug user at a guess, who said the evening wasn't even half over, a swimmer you would have sworn— you saw those very large hands on a piano keyboard, fingers sinking in. Daley knew this as well as he knew anything, not that it mattered, Daley angry with himself, waiting. The audience was who the actors pretend aren't there. It *had* been Becca minutes ago at the corner. The layout of the place, entrances, space, and so forth gripped him.

What had become of her in the dressing room? Was she bleeding? He couldn't wait for what was to come, the next fool scene, ominous, it came to him that it was all about you but remotely. He did not know why he was here. Daley had talked to Helen in restaurants, in her kitchen, on a hilltop, on a porch, on the plane, he had talked to her in bed, swimming, in a boat, every other day at least on the phone. The actress's voice was with them now, voice-over describing spooning *pul-se* out of the pot over the fire, and the mountain comfortable a hundred miles off—with them—belonging to them like an

American mountain that wouldn't go away. This loose talk about rein-carnation.

The woman entered now, and she was fresh as if something heavy had slipped away or she had woken at dawn and found something inside her from her sleep, a force, for she was the sister, composed and light. The husband and wife—the wife could slit the sister-in-law's throat and was big enough to do it. Daley waited for her to find him, the man in the eighth row, and recognized her as the person outside a few minutes ago.

"Nice he's not in front of us," Helen whispered and took Daley's hand in the dark.

"He'd seen it before."

"Why?" Helen asked.

Daley disengaged his hand and thumbed the empty seats behind them: "How you can bring a kid to this?" He looked around and the boy was gone at the back.

"They couldn't get a sitter," Helen whispered.

"A baby," said Daley.

This play was moving uptown, if you believed it. The husband and wife and sister and secretary and the others, and a new figure, a hood-lum child who had begged at the wife's door in Connecticut! Business lurked here, too, improprieties the fraternity brother bartender who had not made much of his life knew about. The noise-cancellation technology. Make a killing canceling factory noise with this counter-force device killing not only air traffic over the neighborhood but even general ambience—time, waste, abuse of gifts, any *blow* (it came to Daley like some future of this routine thing he was looking at) that on the other hand we can live with if we let it settle in time as if we're history or make something of it, which is the American way. Daley was desolate and didn't not keep the story straight though people around him were absorbed by it.

This wasn't it, though. You guessed they'd had their hooks into each other, had a thing sometime, brother and *sister*. Daley felt Helen's hand very close as the minutes passed. The woman's voice over the phone had said she *didn't think much longer*. Did she mean working, or working downtown?

The blond actress up there with her brother. "We're of the same blood," she had said. Back in the house, somebody laughed, a minority vote, nervous display. You felt like shaking her. She had forgotten Daley. For, closing in on whatever, she had a big speech; when the brother's *marriage* had seemed the thing, not exactly sweeping you away but grown-up and inconclusive.

Yet she found Daley then, or the pillar off to one side. He was certain she was looking his way. The husband and wife had lived through the crisis brought on them by the returned traveler.

Wife offstage, the last word was Sister's, not seeing Daley now. Such lonely nerve or poise visible in the actress, she searched the audience like talus at the base of a (Himalayan) cliff, city streets, the particular pavements that from inside this improvised postindustrial place you heard tapped and scuffed from time to time or would trudge home along tonight. You could try to bore through her face with your eyes. She was quite alone up there with the brother, the strange miles she logged, the Dark Continent, the spirit of Kathmandu, more deeply memorable than a glossy brochure all of it for the moment, a remarkable young woman. It *is* after all moving uptown, this play: Who's doing it? She came around to Daley then, she could do what she liked with her eyes, shaking her finger on this Wednesday night as in the newspaper photo, and Daley heard Helen breathing next to him, quick and shallow, he knew her, he could smell her, they hadn't had dinner, she was moved. *We're of the same blood* you heard still. Anything you wanted to hear said, you could hear it.

# 8

BECCA COULD HAVE SAID MORE. DALEY WAS UNREADY. GRIMLY ENGROSSED, desolately concentrated as much in what was to come as in someone who sat down at his table Monday night in the middle of a set or in this would-be actress in a twelve-dollar-a-seat downtown house.

Would he take her case after all? The sense was in him, some law to be dragged out of the theater onto the sidewalk at ten o'clock, the emptying hell of give-and-take, the noise of others striving to just be there, the bartender who had his moment or two, one good speech, these damn *things* people got into, brothers and sisters, the drift and plunge, the next level (but downward). This young person still in danger. And Daley was uncomfortably aware of Helen's trip and his observance of her return, he knew her backbone up and down, and her shoulders, and how she toweled herself beginning with her hair, her hands up wrapping her hair, gently stretching, raising her breasts. And then they were out in the street and he was terrible, he knew.

"*You* could use a trip—I'd love to go with you, but . . ." She took his arm. "Remember how we met?" Daley did. He knew to the syllable what Helen would say next. (Was that knowing someone?) They had walked two whole blocks not quite ready to flag a cab.

"You should go see Wolf." Wolf and his family she meant; Wolf, though. Yet she didn't. It was her damn jarring instinct tonight. Helen had known Wolf like other people of Daley's at a distance through Wolf's adventures and injuries, his far-flung consultancies, his actual concussions, and joked that his brother Bill was his right arm.

"You didn't think she was bleeding," Daley said. They had walked three blocks and he was losing time.

"Lay off," Helen said. He wanted to talk with her as you do with a wife, an old friend, someone blessedly your age, while at the same time he figured how to dispose of her for the night, which had begun with her finishing getting dressed.

"Oh it was blood, I guess." Helen found his hand, she was thoughtful like the stone arches, columned commercial spaces, these cast-iron fronts. The air damp with the prospect of escape.

"Damn right it was blood." He looked back and someone familiar silhouetted by the light of a streetlamp was coming up the block, his raincoat open; it was the bartender. Old storage lofts, the vacant greatness of warerooms, the nineteenth-century aroma of use, the spirit smell of varnish retreating into inventories commodious and available once upon a time though stored secret as turn-of-the-twentieth-century employment practices.

"Oh it was the story," Helen was saying; "the wife will love him, she won't *see* him the same way ever again, that's all, he didn't need to find himself. Oh my."

"It was the brother and *sister*," Daley said.

"Oh *that*." Helen waved at a cab, what did the drivers think they were doing not stopping? "What do we look like?"

"Did we see the same play?" said Daley.

"'Fraid so."

The *writer* had held the marriage together by *concentrating* on it, Helen was explaining. "She was on a talk show, you know. She's right out there. She can write. She's been everywhere, she met her ex on a 707."

"She did what?"

"But she was never in Nepal," Helen said. Daley said she could have fooled him. "You never were either," said Helen.

He heard the steps coming up. "It isn't *that* good." Daley caught Helen's eye.

"Still," she said.

"It isn't."

"You were thinking of your brother, I know," she said.

"I was?"

"When you took him up on the Peace Corps."

"Maybe I was."

"I thought you would like the story," Helen said as if she had gotten the tickets. "Something happen?" she asked. A woman's question.

"Hey you mix a convincing drink," Daley turned, for they had been overtaken by the actor who had played the bartender.

"Hey yeah." This spare, judicious young man, stopping reluctantly, but his eyes widened darkly and glittered and he didn't really look at Daley. Helen complimented him and took out a little vial of tiny white breath-saver pellets and a couple of them bounced into the gutter and were lost and the actor smiled and said he was going to lose his job, he had a fifteen-minute walk and was late. He hadn't changed out of his white shirt and black pants.

"Memorable performance," Daley said.

"Aw. . ." said the young man.

"Bartender knows things he's not telling."

"Small part," said the actor, "but . . ."

"Long bio," said Daley. Helen touched his arm.

"That's nothing," the actor said; "my stepmother used to lock me in a broom closet—just like my acting teacher, would you believe it?—somebody should . . ." he slapped himself on the stomach. Helen stepped into the street.

"Now, the blonde's bio," said Daley.

"Yeah, well," said the actor.

"Two lines," said Daley.

"She challenges you," said the actor.

"She earned her knocks," Daley said.

"I could strangle you," Helen said softly.

A second cab pulled over, at the wheel a very old man, in a fez, not the turban and the trimmed Sikh beard lately so common but a patriarch's bush.

"San Francisco was awful. I wanted to tell you about Tom," said Helen. She reached for the door handle.

"I want to hear," said Daley—he would hear all about it but not tonight, the young musician she had helped to come to the States when he was only a boy, and the client who was also why she'd gone, a novelty sundial and its market; Helen didn't take on just anything.

"Gotta roll," the actor said.

"You're moving uptown," Daley said.

"Oh I don't know," said the actor. He raised a hand.

"Something happen?" Daley said. "She took a hit there."

"He was at her tonight," the actor said, "she had something extra."

"Something happen?"

"She feeds off the audience," the actor said.

"You really remember her," said Daley.

"You should see it again," said Helen, "see if she bleeds."

"What am I doing standing here talking?" said Daley.

"Exactly," said the bartender.

"Is it true she's added lines to the play?" Helen asked.

Well not much but that's what it was all about in a way, the actor waited, on instinct. "The story itself," he said.

Daley tried the door. Helen took hold of the handle. She was thinking he had fucked her in her kitchen tonight, after all these years, and what was that all about, what had he been thinking of? She was serious, but grown-up, momentarily fixed upon the door handle, her eyes shut, her trench-coat collar coming up over her dark, fluffed hair. Daley should have asked about Tom if there was time, the boy was now a man, once a musician on a street corner, Prince Edward Island, his eyes half closed, whom Helen had sponsored, he'd been dead set on California.

The driver succeeded in releasing the door. Daley gave Helen a hug with one arm. "I knew it," she said.

Twisting around, the driver in the whites of his eyes waited for Daley, seeing him, offering scorn or curiously electing him, Daley given a gift of cruelty, a license, an appointment, just a recent immigrant tired and late-night secretly from the angle of his ways scornful of these folk.

"You knew her in a past life," Helen said getting in.

Daley was in a cruel hurry. Helen was usually right, he thought, yet with no real right to be. Helen left the evening of a long day open, her knee intuitive and shining. Skirt halfway up her thigh sitting forward to speak to the driver, she reached for the door. It was something not going home with Helen after her trip, after the kitchen, she felt him still. The window rolled down, she liked the air, the aisle. He slept deeply when he stayed with her. Not even a sweet dream of peace. It was a fact. Her particular vintage. She was telling the driver again.

"Something happen?" she said out the window. A woman's question freeing you to explain yourself.

"After all these years I . . ." he said.

"Call me tomorrow."

"I might be dropping the agency," he sort of finished his thought. Not what Helen wanted to hear. She asked the actor where he was going, and moved herself over and then her legs. The actor looked at Daley, who felt a business card in his pocket.

"You're right," the actor said, "those that will bleed, let them." He had on a good pair of olive-yellow high work shoes. The door slammed shut, the actor leaning forward to speak to the old man. Helen vanished from Daley's life for the night.

It was raining just a little like an old danger small and quickening, nothing you couldn't handle, invited and recommended as a fool. Was that the recommender with what history you could probably easily find the right name for, or was it the caller herself who had both Daley's numbers?

The theater in the sheen of the light rain had passed like a transparency into the gray-green commercial facades, with one trace of motion that Daley could feel somewhere when he reached the block again. The easel placard advertising the play had just been taken in off the sidewalk, he was certain, the blown-up review, the shot of Becca, that eerie finger wanding at the brother, you now knew. A single headlight all over the place of a northbound cab hitting a pothole or two potholes caught a person crossing against the red light.

# 9

THE ACTOR WAS IN HIS SHORTS BRUSHING HIS TEETH HARD AND FAST. He did not acknowledge Daley. He had worked on his arms and had gotten out what he had put in. A scrunched-up Kleenex had opened ever so slightly on the dressing table and revealed splotches of scarlet in the folds. Becca's skirt hung tossed on the back of a chair. This dressing room was the right one after all.

The actor aimed a dollop down the drain. He snatched his pants up off the deck and his wallet fell out and he caught it and turned away bobbing his head at Daley. A garment on the floor Daley recognized; hardly anything to it, Helen had one. Daley heard women's voices far away. The actor was in his black jeans and fingering the bills in his billfold. Daley asked if this was Becca Lang's dressing room?

"No this is not Becca Lang's dressing room"—the actor toed the underwear out of his way—"it's easy to lose sight of that fact." His name was Barry. A very large pair of black running shoes lined up near the wall were certainly the bartender's. This was the men's dressing room. Daley had tried another door across the hall. "You must have missed her," said Barry.

"You know, you really smashed her," Daley said.

"Yeah," said the actor softly.

"It wasn't just the play."

Barry wore a big signet ring that clearly meant a lot to him, an ugly silver and black and blue skull; his hands had done hard work.

"You could of broken her nose."

"It's already broken. It gets in your way. Am I right?"

Daley shook his head.

"Fuck her nose. *Fuck* it, I say," said the actor, with great reserve. Barry had his pea coat on. "Look, we're professionals," he said.

"'Cause you gave her one hell of a wallop," Daley said.

"And *you* are . . .?" said the other.

Daley shook his head.

"Right," said Barry.

"It wasn't just the play," Daley said; he realized how he sounded. "I mean, it was interesting; it was a relief."

"You in the business?" Barry didn't quite leave. Daley said he was beginning to wonder. "The two of you, you go back a ways. She had it coming mind you," Daley said.

"Hey," Barry said.

"She was very good," said Daley.

"She's quitting, what's the difference? How'd you get in here anyway? Don't answer."

How the door from the lobby bypassed the stage and led here along a hall Daley could hardly tell. Admitted to the lobby without the slightest surprise by the Italian woman who was on the pay phone Daley had not noticed before, he had passed freely through the door she had indicated bearing the yellow poster for a movie Daley remembered, it was from perhaps his boyhood moviegoing days, his brother Wolf would remember, it was a coming-attractions poster, the slightly ajar door itself absorbing him however, a jogged passage and then a dark little stairway that smelled of disinfectant and camphor that Daley recalled from somewhere, a lacquer factory or an explosives plant, not fresh here but strongly, understatedly, functionally of a time before the building had been renovated. Not the only route backstage but a particular one and so Daley didn't see any point in being confused. The Italian girl had let him in but ignored him as if she had put a spin upon his passing presence or he was of an inner circle or she secretly trusted he was an assassin or could complicate things, let it happen, whatever. She was a tall comrade. "I'm unloading on you," she had said into the receiver. Her sound was bitter and specific, a little foreign, New York. "He doesn't care," she had said into the phone, a little glum and sexual. She'd looked at her watch, muttered something and had to hold the receiver away from her ear for a second and she smiled and her eyes connected with Daley you might have thought, her life in her eyes, her tact—and remembering him she pointed to the door he hadn't taken at intermission and turned away affectionately. "In one ear and out the other," she had said with a strong accent and turned to indicate the door again; she was discussing a guy. (She had recognized Daley: *It was you who called*, she'd looked at Daley absently, it was what she had said when Daley and Helen had arrived at the door tonight, and she had made a fist at Daley, and there was that heavy ring on her hand like a silver brass knuckle right under your nose.) "That *ring* . . ." Helen had said when they were sitting down, "she's looking to unload it on someone, I'm sure of it." There had been people waiting, the lights dimming a little. The ring was done. The woman was tired of it. You're from *Rome*, Helen had said, in that way of hers. The woman only smiled, but when Helen found their seats and they sat down in the dark Helen was sure of it, Daley had said something that put her off, thinking the ticket-taker didn't mind being taken for a Roman.

Daley described to Barry the young woman alone in the lighted lobby. How she'd looked out into the night, how she'd left the phone dangling when she came to let him in and waved him right through.

"That's it," said the actor, "I can see it. You don't own the place?"

"She made a joke I think."

"Clara Jane?" the actor said, content for a second, then "What am I standing here?"

"Not that I know Italian."

"She can speak it all the time. She's a different person." The actor felt his hip pocket. "She was on the phone?"

"Talking to somebody," Daley said.

"She's got a motherfucker of a loft," said Barry. "She's also got a father back in Parma."

"You may need it," Daley said. He indicated the room, and Barry looked around him. "She gone for the night?"

"She had a date." Barry made a face. "He left early." Daley saw Leander crossing the street though there was no street. Barry paused in the doorway. "You didn't see her?"

And Leander was long gone, and it was experience, no more, and a sadness broke over Daley in this drab room of all that he was able to see. "When you smashed her—" he began.

"You liked that?" said the actor.

"When you hit her . . ." Daley began again.

"Fuck her, she doesn't care," Barry said. "What did you say?" said Daley.

A mean sparkle in his eye, Barry rocked on the threshold. "Helluvan actress. She plays to you. Nobody can teach you that. No experience like hell." He was serious. "Gotta run," he said, quite friendly. He could club someone with two hands.

"Where's it coming from then?" Daley said, because the actor had left the room.

"That's her *scene*," said Daley.

Barry leaned into the room, his hands on the door frame. "Turned down an interview last week. I said what's a matter with you?"

"What did she say?"

"That educated face of hers. Why do I think I'm not telling you anything?" Barry was gone. Daley had heard voices elsewhere in the building. Was it the theater? The work of a warehouse continuing somewhere. A generation and a half ago storage and light industry; now these actors.

Daley took up the Kleenex. The blood absorbed into it was bright. From a small purple pad he tore off a sheet with phone numbers on it. From experience, trivial possibly, it came to him that Barry was Becca's roommate. (In these things Daley was always right.) It would be her place and her eviction notice, her problem. He heard someone in the hall.

# 10

THE SECRETARY WAS LEANING AGAINST THE DOOR THAT BARRY HAD knocked on. Seeing the man leaving the other dressing room she pulled herself together. It was in her eyes still and her washed cheeks, she'd been crying, she was mad. You could take her anywhere. She was big and her hand on the strap of her bag was long and delicate. "I know," she said. Daley came up to her. It was Inga or Ingrid; Daley remembered names. He heard voices down the narrow, ill-lit hall. "You're doing something else right now, I know," said the Secretary. Daley said he'd enjoyed her work tonight and was assuming she had not lost her job in spite of the affair with the Brother. Ingrid embraced him, he smelled water and towel and material. It was only thank-you, a hug where you don't want to look the other person in the face. She smiled. "You don't know what goes on. We don't know from one night to the next. We thought it had a chance. It's all incredibly dumb how they do things" —her eyes on his now. "You've got to go, I know. You've come a long way. You didn't find who you were looking for." Daley asked what was the best way out and this tall, gracefully awkward young person laughed—"Thanks," was what she said.

"What're you going to do?" said Daley.

"Oh go back to work; I've got three hundred more monoprints to make for a hotel. I'm a painter." And no, she added, she apparently at the end of the play had not been losing her position as Secretary because of her affair with the cousin. "Oh they change it every other night, who knows?"—the young woman didn't really mean it—"It's a success but he still may not move it uptown, it depends, he's such a wonderful man *I* think. I think he's rich, but maybe he's broke." She took Daley's hand. A passage appeared, and at its end a familiar-seeming opening that must be the stage, like another room. Here Ingrid seemed to change her mind. She hugged him and thanked him for something, her wide eyes glowing with tears, she remembered to give him a little push into the passage.

Two plastic milk crates full of things hung on a partition. Daley found himself in the wing. The actors could take their props on the way on, the plastic cocktail shaker, letters in envelopes, a rock the Sister had acquired in Africa (though it was flecked with tiny diamond-sharp twinkles of mica when he took it in his hand that Daley thought you'd be likely to find in India, Canada, or Westchester, but not Africa); a white long-billed yachting cap flattened under two oranges, a soft toy of the Secretary's—a wallaby it looked like—and a gold compact that she had flipped open when the Brother had demanded to know what had become of the letters from the Sister in Nepal. Daley saw the stage. The stage was as good a way to get out of here as any. A long room or part of one out there; you had to hand it to them, he had almost forgotten Becca Lang who after all would come to him in some form. Too bad the Secretary, too bad she was gone, she was a warm person and silly. Upset by the red-haired Wife, it came to Daley, who must have been changing with her in the other dressing room, the mother of the freckled boy. Daley turned back toward the wing not expecting to see Ingrid, but she was waiting there at the end of the passage. She grinned.

"It looks so easy to walk out there," he called.

"I doubt not you deserve it," she called like a speech; "wait." She was at his side. Lighted from the far wing by a single hanging bulb, the stage was theirs. Women's voices lifted and confided somewhere out there, with news for each other, surely done for the night and going away or pausing in the lobby. The sultry Italian. The Brother's Wife (if so, the boy who had shaken hands and dropped his program, he wouldn't go home alone).

Hey, ramps of seats, those were what you wanted. He liked those women—where the hell were they?—their sounds not gone after all; two voices off there in the lobby, maybe three; under the same roof anyhow. Above him black light boxes hung angled, the warehouse sprinklered for some reason—legal—renovated. Daley was nearly content after all with what he'd done with his evening, his life. "That's what it's all about," Daley said aloud. "*That's* what it's all about," he said. You let your hands be, you had the chance to just stand facing the audience.

"Hey," said the young woman softly. She took his hand and let it go. "You deserve it, whatever you're up to," she said.

"'I forgive you almost, we left the tent in the stuff sack and slept on the ground, the mountainside,' wasn't that it?" Daley said.

"Maybe you're in the business."

"I was looking for Becca."

"Yes of course you were. Oh, you're someone."

"I thought she was going to get herself . . ."

Ingrid was at the steps at the corner of the stage. "She might make it yet." Now she was halfway up the ramp in the dusky house, she had put Daley behind her, she was gone.

Who was this wonderful man of a producer? Ingrid disappeared.

Daley said some words word for word from the voice-over, "'I have loved you more than I should.'" The Sister had needed to get home to the States, she needed to get back into the scrap. It was her continent. Wherever she went stateside, it didn't need to be Connecticut.

Steps tapped and whispered and passed away and he turned with them like the space of the building, a blueprint he would be glad to read if given the chance, the steps of one person somewhere sounded some length and breadth known to them. The stage did not make you want to go on a trip; you wanted to stay here. From the lobby came a laugh free and raucous. Women adopted it lately (the last few years, in Daley's opinion, though Helen would make a face, while Donna, of a different class, would think about it), a crazy laugh (*haggish, unleashed*, it described itself to Daley), letting go they pretended, high—*Let's laugh, girlfriend!*— beauty crashing through sounding new and blunt. Why didn't they get on home? It was the Wife, the Sister-in-law, coarse and mature, holding forth, healthy redhead Sister-in-law coming into focus, forceful of person, sporting, and at home; what people called warm, the laugh for when she'd skinned her man alive after the voice-over had frozen them and they were lovers at some level. And Barry was there called up by her voice.

Two in from the aisle on the left was the armrest he'd leaned his elbow on, the seat in front of it so empty you had to wonder why the big fellow had come back to see a play he didn't think much of. Becca was the draw. Because he didn't have much to say good of her and had to say it. "That's what it's all about," Daley said not loudly at all, some stage release lifted his body with nothing at stake and there was more to it, like somebody hearing.

Daley, the play touched him here on stage. Not a *good* play but the audience took to it, down here in this part of town. Love but not love, marriage and family but your life comes first, Daley couldn't quite express it, the brother's petty corruption marginally dreaming a way of being. Of *being in the world*, Helen had said.

The women's voices weren't gone after all, people falling silent out there just as they did close up. The Secretary's poignant, unwise grip on things. A man's stupid voice—into it poured the others. It was Barry, a sink of talk—young people, and the Italian woman, then Barry absolute and delayed (she liked him)—he would say anything, she imagined. Then Ingrid again and the Wife's reply sounding like the freckled boy was not there with her though he had to be unless the man—the producer—he'd sat with had taken him home—a school night. But her voice didn't stay put, and who knows what a parent shares? And Becca, more than silent, was gone. Barry came through: he had some purpose for the balance of the evening. One voice leaving now ushered silence into these seats. Near the wing steps developed, then Daley didn't hear them.

"Bahrry," the hard, present voice of the Italian woman struck through the building, a metallic, singing noise, a person, a team.

When she had seen Daley on the sidewalk, he had mimed, *They still here?* From the street the lobby was a little stage; a phone he had not noticed. She'd come to him to let him in, a young person, her breasts brisk with responsibility, sighting past him. She'd bent her head, a member of the family, returning to the receiver dangling on a silver cord from the pay box.

Let her come now and throw him out. In the other wing to his left, a bulb burned into the night. Galactic, a seventy-five-watt high up drew dust. Lines came to him. Steps passed back and around again, hanging fire or scooped up by the end of things, yet heard out there in front again where the voices had been happy or contentious. "'If the world is inside you,'" Daley said the voice-over words out loud a little flat, or the voice-over needed a dark, amplified source, "'you can love it and still be one.'"

One what? These seats out front found you out, they were beginning to see him. "'What will I have there? I come home, as you asked.'" He'd absorbed some of the voice-over, he must have, he tried them back almost word for word. "'But you are there and a whole continent.'" Daley reached up toward the black light boxes and stretched back, was *he* doing it? A spasm of relief, eyes and jobs, young folks, full employment. Up to him, though. Tell him about it. He let go and the house narrowed brownly into a path of raked seats, for there was somebody here.

Daley had company.

# 11

"EXCUSE ME," SAID A WOMAN IN THE EMPTY HOUSE, "HELL*O*?" HE PEERED and blinked, he knew her, her hair obscurely pale like the almost eyeless face. The voice not at all obscure in the dusk, he felt the edge of it, interface from phone, stage, now a back seat of this place. "Nice up there," she said, it was nobody but his would-be client, the woman on the phone, Becca Lang.

"This place . . ." Daley inspected the beams shyly.

"You were doing something," Becca Lang said.

"I doubt it."

"Sometimes it comes to you," she said, "it doesn't matter."

"Was that you walking around? Because I thought you were behind me," Daley said.

"Somebody was looking for me."

"Did they find you?"

The young woman made a sound, surely she had an ear for voices. "Oh, you made me feel happy." She stretched in the dusk. "No problem." The girl was absolutely there. "What were you doing?" She had been with him already it felt like, watching or listening. "Yes, what were you doing just now? I know what you were doing. A dive?"

"Just a stretch."

"No, I heard you talking. It was a relief seeing you there; isn't that dumb?"

He agreed warily. He trusted her about as much as he belonged up here. Didn't she know it was him? he thought. On the gray Masonite underfoot dark spots appeared. "This old place"—Daley spread his hands—"they did nice work. A nice renovation."

"Looking to buy?"

"*That's* it." It was how she saw him. Age, clothes, watchful look, some experience.

"I don't think it's for sale. Our producer bought it and fixed it up and didn't even know he was going into the theater. A warehouse."

"No, I was directed here by that young lady who played the Secretary, Ingrid I believe? I don't know what she had in mind; I was leaving. I am still."

"She sent you here?"

"No, she was quite lovely and sad, I think—"

"Say no more."

"She must have told you."

"No, I was out on the sidewalk. Lately they don't tell me anything. Which is okay." She sounded doubtful, acute. She believed in the Sister at least. Daley could tell. From Nepal the Sister had come home. She loved her Brother and her country—the two together, you saw.

"But I know what you were doing when I came in, I'm always right."

Daley said he was interested in what they'd done here, he looked around, guessed he was a closet architect circumstances had never quite . . .

"Come on, you were doing a dive, don't try to tell me you weren't." He said he wouldn't then.

Daley had just been stretching, noting the rafters, their age, the amplitude and trapezoidal structure of the renovation or maybe it was the warehouse. Yet she had given him an idea and he would take credit for this closeness with her, as they got down to business, he suspected. He made a sound, which she liked.

"Do you know what a half gainer is?"

He thought she shook her head, objective back there, a bit charming.

He showed her. You went and jumped on the end of the board and

you went up like this, he explained, like a figurehead carried forward—only you arched back—"like this"—Daley reached and lost
sight of her— "like a *back* dive—"

"But toward the board?"

"Right; the trick is—"

"It's not a trick, it's—"

"—is which way you're going." Now he could only describe. "I
can't show this I can only . . ."

The actress beamed at him, nodding. "It's going to be a close call,"
she said; "it's quite beautiful, it's what *I* could just do."

"Well. But what is it that you"—he had had a thought and tried to
save it—"that you want to participate in?"

She came down the aisle a ways. A leather knapsack hung from her
shoulder, in it the little undershirt he was certain. "Think I could learn?"

"That's different," Daley said. She sat down again, her legs
sprawled apart, her jeans threadbare at one knee. She had worn a
skirt on stage. She had been hit.

"You could crack your head," she said.

"Oh not me," Daley said.

"Oh not you."

Why did she irritate him? It was the Monday phone call all over
again.

"I'm not a pool person," Daley said.

"You swim *real* water."

"That's right. I think we've met," he said.

"If you're not sure, let's forget about it," the girl said sharply. "You
swim the ocean? The Great Lakes?"

"Just a river now and then. A sea." His slight eloquence sounded
like he was with this person who had just spoken like a woman reject-
ing any line you might try.

"What sea?"

"The Black Sea," he admitted; "not clear across or anything."

"But you've done it. You know about it," the girl said.

"It doesn't always work out."

"The Black Sea. Imagine that. A hundred and fifty miles across to
Yalta, isn't it?"

It was something like that. It was a moment that passed for Daley like information, but of what? A mood or depth that passed nearby, her more than her education, experience not geography. What did she mean?

"Give you something to say, *you* could do this," the young woman said.

"You can just stand here too," said Daley. She said his hands were amazingly experienced. He said he wasn't doing anything with them. You must feel that, she said, though he didn't understand.

Her arms on the seat in front, the young woman hadn't recognized the sound of him. She gave a short laugh, woman's madness, contempt coming from her chest, but she didn't know it was Daley. The seats in front held all that Daley had absorbed. That was all. She liked him. She was out for herself.

She was out of her seat again. He tried to see her face where she'd been hit. "God"—he glanced at his watch though it was hidden under his cuff—"why am I standing here?"

"No water in the pool," said the young woman looking right up at him now, her suede jacket open on a T-shirt. "Hell of a coach you'd make. Maybe you could recommend one."

Daley liked it.

"You do know one," said the young woman.

It was quite a coincidence. It was Ruley Duymens, Daley realized. She was persistent, but a woman not his type. Didn't need to know who she was talking to. Which was nice. "This guy was very busy with things. I mean he now that I think of it seemed busier than maybe he was, but secretly he actually was busy. And *didn't* seem that busy."

"I know him, oh don't I," said Becca, sounding Canadian.

"He had time for you," said Daley; "and time to do you."

"*Man*," that hip frustrated note but not quite on; it was the Canadian maybe: "landlady, producer, my super, my accountant, my personal trainer, my personal insurer, my banker, my this my that, my deposition, my divorce"—she was making it up, she was at the corner of the stage—"and they all know each other."

"A sort of banker," Daley added. He was uneasy. "You haven't been *divorced*."

"Not me."

The evening was over for Daley. He must identify himself. He had no idea yet why she was here if she hadn't figured out he was her phone lawyer. Unless she recalled him out front. SAIGON, VIETNAM, her T-shirt said. Daley went along the apron peering at the Masonite, but it was the person below him who hovered, the same who'd phoned the office, been clobbered tonight, and night after night came back to do that scene. He bent down to look. She reached to finger Daley's raincoat where it brushed the floor, and she listened.

A woman listening. Voices somewhere didn't come from the lobby now. Two people back behind the stage, it seemed. Becca went away from Daley.

Daley bent down and ran his fingers over spots you could just feel. They were blood. It was to do something, because he needed to leave.

The voices were gone in the interior of the building. Was *she* going? She came back where Daley squatted. He ran his fingers over the spots. They were almost smooth or sanded flat like varnish before another coat.

There at the foot of the steps this woman—thinking or hoping or auditioning for all you knew—became equal right before his eyes to what was going to happen. It was all he could make of the slightly awkward way she stood or the eyes that found you.

"Good this diving coach has references."

"Everyone does."

Daley squatted and felt the blood spots and smelled her, her face close by waiting for him, softer than the lights had made her on stage, promiscuous, the chin less historical, faint odor of orange and cigarette and flesh. She touched the skirt of his raincoat on the floor. She had acted on this stage. Walked on it. It was a place of work. Was it a lawyer she was after?

"It's a little boring," the woman said; "what are we waiting for?" she said, the quiet of two people alone in the house, chatter absorbed in the overall experience of the building, summoned here, workplace warehousing the potential that kept you here, what you happened to say. "You are someone," she said. Maybe legal representation wasn't it. It must be almost eleven and he was going to go. So she had knocked around. What had she been through? Daley was gone outa here. What did she know, what had she done? He was old enough to guess that, or he was a New Yorker. "I have an hour, if you'd like to have a drink. You *are* someone," she frowned, it seemed she would tell him. "Why are you even here?" she said.

Daley said he'd been one act too late, he'd started to come back at the intermission. "I came back because I thought you were in trouble. Just a thought I had. I thought you were going to get hurt. I didn't know."

"How bizarre—you came backstage because you thought I was in trouble?" She made a sound. She still didn't know him.

"I was an act too late," he said.

"How dear," she murmured, he could hear her. It didn't sound right. Maybe it did. "And you were looking to come to my assistance back-stage?" Becca said, older again for a moment, amiable as a woman can be, identifying him, sounding not quite American. "With a couple of Band-Aids and a Tampax?"

"It was when you got hit."

"You liked it. *Barry* said, but I didn't believe him."

"I should introduce myself," Daley said.

The woman before him blinked. She clapped her hands. "Oh Mr. *Daley*, what're *you* doing here?" What a clap it was, how it came back from all corners bringing the whole place with it solid to his ears, encompassing some common old process, walls, pillars, dry goods and storage, some old oil or methyl of wide, wooden stairs, work, tall unwasteful windows, twine, use, but a thought he was having.

# 12

"I KNEW IT," SHE CRIED, BELOW HIM. "I thought you did."

"No, I didn't." Daley didn't believe it.

"So that was *you*." She thumbed the seats behind her, he hated how she did it. "When I came out after the interval, I saw you, you came in late." She shook her finger at him.

"Only then?"

"Oh you were quite exposed." They laughed. She stopped and listened. She must have seen clear across from the wing the space formerly occupied by the big fellow Leander in front of Helen and Daley. And the people with the child? And others Daley recalled almost to life.

"I ran into this boy at the back, he didn't want to go back to his seat—"

"He's not afraid of anyone—"

"—obvious why."

"I could take him to my heart, I could pet him."

"The Wife's son? With a faceful of freckles in the dark."

"You'll see what he makes of all this one day."

"He dropped his program." Daley remembered the narrow handshake.

"You'll see what he makes of all this one day."

"It was the man he'd been sitting with, with the big hat."

"Of course. It's his money. He's been showing up."

It came to Daley that the producer would infiltrate the cast in an athletic, unpredictable in-the-house-tonight. His name was Beck. It was in the program.

"I knew you'd come," said the young woman looking up at him.

"You knew more than I. I was looking for the exit."

"You knew more than I," said the woman below him, "but not much longer." What could she mean? It gave him a start, that she wouldn't know more than he much *longer*, words he'd heard before from her.

"You were having a look-see," she said, "I wouldn't take that away from you. You were doing your homework."

"I do that at the office."

"See you there then," she said. She was at the corner of the stage by the steps, sort of blocking them.

"This will do," he said and felt exit like coincidence combining things once free and clear.

Daley always knew things. Becca and Barry probably roommates, Becca turning down the TV when she was on the phone (how did he know that?) Clara really liking Barry, Barry liking her car (how did Daley know that?)

"*That's* why you came. You were with someone who didn't know. How did you manage it?"

Daley made a fist and shook it like a fool. (Helen's efficient kitchen was what he thought of, the chair between table and fridge holding the both of them, the view through into the living room, how when she had needed to tell him about San Francisco and the young musician she had helped for years who treated her poorly, Daley didn't wait, he wasn't even sure how they'd managed it.)

"You're a smart girl," Daley heard the word as he said it.

"I would never take that away from you that you came to see me," she said.

"*You* take something away from *me?*" Take what away?—the very words of the man who'd sent her in the first place.

"What?" she laughed.

"Ruley!" he punched his palm. "That's who gave you my number."

"Van Diamond?" In Becca's face, an imprint, something wrong with what she'd originally told him.

"Duy-*mens*, Ruley Duymens, forget the *van*."

"Oh let him have it," the voice of a longtime equal, with other things to do, blond but not extremely blond, hanging out. Words familiar again, you get to a certain age.

"The name is Duymens: D-u-y-m-e-n-s. Dutch. Stay away from him."

"He helped me out."

"With my number?" (Ruley years later being talked about. Two numbers.) "A *terrible* person," Daley said lightly. His wife's words, *Let him have it,* earthquake night years ago, Ruley's name on her *lips*, her *lips*, it was hope, her hand giving her husband whom she liked best of all one little last grip sitting up. "First-generation Dutch, but not pure Dutch; bizarre Dutch if it's all true. Slippery."

"Well he spoke of you."

"It wasn't me he was friends with."

"That's why." The smartness was young, it touched him in his shoulders, his face, he supposed it showed. "You and your wife. It's been a few years."

"You don't say what you don't know."

"You don't?" said the woman. She was superior, ready for news. A sudden opening in him, air rushing in at a certain height. If he could only find that exit and get out onto the street, wave water running up the sand, why hadn't he gone for the lobby? "'Knew more than I knew,'" she joked, "'knew more than I knew.'" It was nothing to her, and this nothing-to-her mood change was just the workplace, physical. Her grasp of things was expertly young. "What *would* you speak of then?"

"What I'm learning?" Daley looked at his watch and she gave a little murmur of a laugh. In the unexplored near wing two cats came into focus walking about with their tails straight up, a marmalade and a hungry black under the lightbulb. "What would happen if I left that way?" he said.

"You'd find yourself in the street. See?—you're speaking of it and you've never been there."

Was Becca coming up? He was a fool. He had missed the second set at Waters where Sid Knox was playing. It was Cary Grant who had said "terrible" that way. Becca slapped the edge of the stage. "So I came here, it's why I'm here, where you speak of what you almost know, and find you did. One of your guys said that, or half anyway."

"That *was* you, and you weren't out there for a cigarette at the end of intermission," Daley said. Leander missing from his seat, she'd stepped outside for a second. He wasn't interested, he could be driving a van with a bunch of people seated behind him.

"You speak of what you *don't* know," she said, "that's the best."

Daley smelled smoke and put it together, the building, what was going on with these young people, did they make love like that? "I was coming back at intermission, I was concerned."

Becca's chin poked out. "You didn't make it, just as well, you were with someone."

"So were you, and who knows who else you were expecting." He was mixing times, intermission with after the show, Barry then Barry leaving.

"Expecting!"

And not Leander's age but Daley's, for Barry would make the point. "It was someone," Daley said. He smelled the smoke. He bent down near the lip of the stage and found dark spots. You wouldn't know quite where she'd be standing one night to the next, yet you would.

"Could be anyone," she said. "Family." She had family here? "They can be so negative."

"Wouldn't they ask you for tickets?"

"You didn't."

He felt for her, the face, its age, the cheeks bleak with a faint down. Looking around, poking around in the dressing room. Coffee containers in the trash, table with a slip of paper on it, an open script propped facedown on the floor like a toy roof, skirt, underwear. Someone she was braced to receive. He respected a job, and she probably didn't know that many people here.

"God it's never just visiting," she said; "you have to be ready."

"Especially now," he threw out.

"I know," she said. She sounded flat. "Changing jobs will do it to you," she said. She'd been slugged. She did it for a living. He said he was quite interested in all that. "I know," she said. People finding their work. He had an agency, she understood.

"Phasing out," he said. (Why would Ruley Duymens mention the agency? It didn't matter.)

"Sometimes I forget why I'm here," she said. "To talk of what you almost know and find you do."

Daley stood up. "Somebody gave you a job and look what happened."

"Yeah, look."

"Your picture in the paper."

"Somebody got me the job; so I owe them."

"You do. Someone gave you a start."

"Who do *you* owe? Probably no one." It was a young person changing the subject. And her co-workers, what about *them*, Daley suggested.

"It was a safe little play," said the woman.

"They wanted you."

"I changed it," she said.

Daley said he didn't know a thing about the theater.

Did he think that's what she wanted him for? she said then. Because it was all economics.

No, he had thought she wanted him to represent her.

If he wasn't a housing lawyer what *was* he doing here?

A surprise for his friend, he said.

"That you dumped her and came back?" Becca retorted.

"Maybe not," Daley said good-humoredly.

"Because that's what you did." Becca came up the steps now and Daley figured if she stayed in the play the eviction suit could go away. They had gotten to this. "What do you do afternoons?" she said. He was in the office. Eyes *at* him, quite black, innocently wicked eyes he had imagined over the phone, sloe-ish he saw now.

"You feared for me so you came back," she said.

"Well, so did you, you came back," he said.

"I thought I might find my brother." It sounded truthful and over-done.

Daley was thirsty. "If he was in the theater wouldn't you know it?"

"Oh God he could be a thousand miles away, you don't know my *brother*." She widened the whites of her eyes. "Maybe you do. Always on the run, maybe you would take him off my hands."

What did she make up, this person, upright, exposed? Daley was moved by her, no more than that. Clara's silver ring unloaded onto this girl's hand, heavy like pipe, a fitting threaded of some extra-heavy aluminum he had seen a long time ago.

Not a sound from Barry and it had to be the Italian woman if they were still in the building. The warehouse cats were gone away into the wing, the lightbulb's energy-saver element burned unholy, loop legged, alien. She was half Scandinavian now, not his type.

Becca's hand swept the stage. She was one woman doing something not in partnership with a soul. "Yeah, *dump* your friend. You clean forgot her *name*, old-timer—"

"Helen," Daley said.

"When was the last time you two got it on?"

He had to get a move on. He felt the exit near. He forgave her. "Well, she's been away."

"You don't even remember."

"Tonight," said Daley.

# 13

"TONIGHT!" SHE SAID. HE FELT, *WE'RE EVEN*. "WE'RE EVEN," SHE SAID, the young woman a little fazed by him. "Clara opens up for you, she knows you're someone 'n' you walk right out here like you dunno *what* you're doin'." Becca in some altered manner, Becca's speech true to somewhere American, but forced. The Southwest if you cared to place it, or the movies. She excluded you and wanted you here. "Girl needs a lawyer. She's been re*fer*red y'know." Becca looked at her hand discovering it in its act of distributing these accents "*It's* not a lawyer *she* needs it's some *fool* you're thinkin'. Nothing throws *you*, not somebody half a world away asking you how you are."

Daley absorbed the coincidence, which was what it was. And after all who hadn't been asked how he was over the phone? "Speak of what you know," Daley said.

"Ah," she said. One thing: she paid attention, picked things up in no order, gave them back her way. (The wing is near, the steps down from the stage nearer.)

"And you, it's not the law you need, mister; you were in your office till five—till six tonight, am I right? When did you get a chance at her? Nothing throws *you*, and now you gotta *roll*"—an uptown street-black sound quite passable kicked in, false almost but bothersome—"you looking into the dark there"—she meant the left wing; was it Mittel Europe now?—"not a bad plan at all, mister, you thought you would fuck *me* later—in the tub, in the kitchen (all *right!*)—when did you find time to fuck *her*, she came back from the airport this morning, poor thing, and went to work, did she know she was getting fucked *before* the show?"

"Check it out," said Daley, for she was abusing him in all honesty, this now quite strange person.

"Give me her number I'll call her."

Daley wasn't saying no to any of this, any more than he was taking her case.

"You put her in a cab?"

"Put her in a cab." Daley said he had to get a move on.

"I've got an hour or so," Becca said.

A tiny message like an overseas phone-call echo you could call it came to him as she spoke, the old half-second time-delay echo technologically almost before Daley's time but not quite: but it's not her speaking, it's him. He was thirsty the way you got when you were in physical danger, he and his brother, or him alone, tracking a countryside where you didn't really belong alert to people somewhere nearby, you got thirsty and muttered out of that squeezed dryness in your mouth and throat. "*I* have a brother," he said, just like that.

"I know you do," she didn't hesitate. It was a guess: she smiled with relief, he was embarrassed at her feeling. "Is he a fair-weather brother?" she said. He didn't find an answer, but it was no.

He had missed a chance to leave.

"Oh so we were *both* expecting our brothers," she said. "Oh God must I wait here all night for my kinsman?"

"Not me," he said, "not you either." She had stalked him he thought.

"You don't know my *brother*." (Stressing the word with pride, she had a childlike speech now he didn't like.) "If he needs to get into my hair . . . no matter where he is."

"Your hair?" Daley couldn't think what to say. "He phones?"

Her thought aimed, her sort of frizzed-out hair honoring her limbs, her T-shirt, her humor, Becca fired a derisive blast of breath with her lips. "Well, he's in business. You never know when he'll sneak down here."

She looked around the house. She felt good.

Could Daley buy Becca that drink? She peered at her watch. She had an hour or so. "I'll hold you to that," Daley said.

"Start the meter."

"*I'm* not your lawyer."

"But a brother," she said, "a brother, we know about that, Mr. Daley." She was telling something yet he didn't like it, what she did. He had come here to take Helen to a play. But to be an audience for this? To pick up a slip of purple paper with numbers on it. To see the young mystery woman work; yet nothing secret so long as you asked, it came to him. "Stick with your brother, he needs you"—her voice altered toward someone he didn't know—"take him to heart, he needs a helping hand."

"That's what my father said."

"Hey, that's what the father said at home—"

"The father?"

"—putting his foot down but busting out laughing the asshole," the actress went on, a slight personality change or even a guess about the man in front of her, but it was her and on the attack. But the instant of Becca's abrupt insight, its instant had been marked somewhere in the building by a voice singing. A woman's voice singing, and Becca was stopped by it, this foolish singing out of a well it had sounded like. A door opening had unlocked the song, which gave it something, a line or two, a careless force that it would have lacked sung clear through, a nothing quite giddy.

Daley knew where there was a pretty good trio playing if she was interested, a club on the river, nothing much but. A drummer, a client of Daley's. (Why did he do that? He could tell she was not taken with the idea. Why did he invite her like that and describe the place? Might as well be a bones solo in a back alley.)

"Do you hang out with clients?"

Clients! he thought, but ignored it.

"Don't you?" he said—she hated him saying it just like that. But wait, this was an original banger with an original sound, whatever it was, momentum, a way of thinking, shooting from this to that. Two bass players played together, you never knew what was on.

"Doesn't she like jazz?" Becca said, "the person you were with?"

"Sure. No. She's an old friend."

"She doesn't get jazz," said Becca. "What does she like?"

"She finds it . . ." Daley tried again.

Becca nodded, derisively he thought. "If it's boring for six minutes, try it for twelve," she said.

"Well, she knows the Cotton Club from Basin Street. Matter of fact she . . ." Daley caught some lie developing and shut it down whatever it was or almost did. Daley answered all interesting questions if he could. Though who gave this young person the right to ask? It turned him against her and he very nearly described Helen to her. Helen wasn't in love with much that Daley would call jazz. "*Jazz* wasn't it tonight."

"It goes on, maybe it's always different."

"Oh, right," Daley said. It was exactly what *Helen* said.

"What was it tonight?"

"The lights were going down."

"For years," Becca said dramatically, how did she say it? "And the person you were with . . ."

"—got in the last word as the lights went down and—"

Becca laughed harshly

"—we heard the cracked ice and there was the bar and the bartender in his white shirt, the stage lights coming up, snapping the cocktail shaker in front of the Brother and the Wife, and things got under way and after a while we heard *you*."

"Little sister."

"Big Brother"—a low laugh from the woman—"writing home," Daley said.

"Big brother never writes."

"From the lotus blossom lake, I wasn't paying attention."

"Of course you were."

"This little thing we had as the lights were going down. About that Clara."

"Clara." She made a motion with her head.

"Clara coming from Rome."

"This why you're here?" Was Becca disappointed? She might have caught him in a lie but she didn't know because she didn't want to catch him in a lie, and the steps about to come on stage from the wing Daley had entered by were without a doubt Barry, in a state probably. And now you knew the dressing room door back there had been opened by Barry, who had left Clara sitting up on the floor—tugging her *pants* on singing!

Barry appeared from the opposite wing, the stage a carpentered storage area now. She would make this man come back at her was all it was; these were kids.

You could understand Barry smashing her. "If you're leaving, leave." Barry looked at them. A stored-up sense Barry had tried to sweep away in this woman who knew Daley—some shitty feeling she could induce in Barry.

"This is an audition. We'll just be a minute."

"A few minutes of yours is all it takes, honey." Barry came across the stage. Becca had Daley by the sleeve drawing him into the dark wing. "She's smarter than us, man," Barry said.

"Smarter than me," Daley said.

"They wipe the floor with us," Barry called after them.

Concrete steps, a red EXIT sign over the side street door. Narrow new concrete steps rough to the soles of your shoes (not the wide old wood stairs he had thought he smelled).

Barry called after them, "I knew it was him."

"Well, so did I," Becca tossed back over her shoulder.

Barry now came after them, projected by the dirty light behind him, his brain outlined. "Clara said no, but I knew it was him. I'll see ya, Bec," Barry said. Clara was somewhere behind him talking.

"Yeah, see ya later," Becca said.

Barry was her roommate, Daley thought. The sidewalk reflecting, steadying, bare, a cool tide clear to the moon's forgiving cusp out over Long Island City somewhere, and again Daley thought she was in a spot and was gambling. "One-woman piece, one-woman star," he heard Barry offstage it seemed. "You might need us, y'know."

A rind curled on the table with the crimson-decorated Kleenex on the table. The skirt flung on the chair. Orange and sweat, the pale inside of peel, underwear on the deck, all absorbed into Daley's steps and, now, dealings with the girl and turned into what, or who? Becca sinking to the floor, her intelligent gaze upward, doing something, her nose the worse for wear, a constant. Or . . . her lips curling, she doesn't exactly look for punishment, it comes to Daley. The bartender in his unchanging shirt and pants, yet slipping out of his shirt, he's hot, comes along the hall, doesn't *need* the dressing room but might like to sit down at intermission, pushes open the door—no, turns the knob and hears without looking, and goes back down the hall to the women's dressing room to grab a cigarette from someone. The Secretary, who's not talking to the Wife. It's about the producer. Whatever happened between the acts none of Daley's business, though something terminal going around, and nothing he would need to be disabused of.

# 14

SHE HAD A WAY WITH HER HIPS, A CURIOUS BELL TOLLING JUST FOR YOU. "I don't care what you do," Daley said.

"You're not producing us," she said over her shoulder.

"Change jobs," Daley said following her, "call a lawyer recommended not as a lawyer much less as a housing lawyer but as a fool of some kind, and by a man who you don't know."

"Not the first," he heard the girl chime back and almost didn't care to overtake her, only to do his duty and offer the best professional advice he could think of. (It wasn't another paycheck job she was going to, he was pretty sure.) "Score some uptown money, Becca. Pay your lawyers." Daley couldn't imagine what she could be leaving the play *for*. "And where's your loyalty?"

"That's always an idea somebody else has for you." She turned in the middle of the street and looked at Daley's trouser legs, he thought, and at him and continued across the street. What was the rush? They passed the other side of the huge green Dumpster and what was in it, high-loaded nine-foot aluminum studs and superhumanly bent and knotted steel cable crowned haphazardly with brown paper deli bags horizoning the Dumpster's length, and Daley knew he was with her, not especially why, but felt raw and taking action without rational analysis, it had little to do with Ruley Duymens and years ago his part in Daley's wife's chaotic months of retrenchment (as Daley had seen it) or gear shifting into other vocations; nor had this evening to do with the efforts of many small-time managers apparently visited upon the girl, none in full control even of their own plans or subterfuges, checking accounts or desires and partnerships, stuck (though in motion) in networks of persuasion and habit, telephoning and not telling, the easily breakable and banal codes of their businesses, which were not worth feeling impeded by or finding the material intent of: but "it" did have to do with acting, Daley saw, if only a little, though not stage stuff or pretending to be what you were not: but doing something: and here he knew that he was touched by this woman who was below you or on the ascent, hovered and zoomed away, who tried to face you down and make dates and was on the run too, undoubtedly abused in some fashion but who is not?

Daley caught up as they reached an overturned trash can rolling back and forth in a small arc, and Becca stopped for him when it wasn't necessary anymore. He understood something, it was nothing at all, and couldn't speak but pointed at her chest, the T-shirt under the open, roughed-up suede jacket that said SAIGON, VIETNAM: "Paris, France," he said.

"Paris, Texas," she said.

Was there one?

"It's a movie."

Of course. Come to think of it, he knew that. Someone had mentioned it.

"Your friend."

Becca was just a smarty-pants. That was right, Daley said.

"What is she, forty, forty-two? Did it make her mad I bet?"

Why yes, he thought it had. That was the one about—That's the one—the kid being raised by his uncle and his—That's the one—who didn't have any kids of their own—They had him—and the real father, it came back to Daley who'd never seen it, who's been bummed out in the desert somewhere (something Daley regretted mysteriously, prophetically, stupidly).

The girl's hip touched him. "We'll see it."

"I would doubt that."

"The honeymoon is over, Mister D."

Was it a voice of hers? These other things around her, it came to Daley chillingly envisioned, that had little to do with her. People coming toward her, her willing self and thorny will. Little secrecy, strangely. You had to ask. You had this freedom to ask. The producer who'd put Becca in an apartment and in the play; the eviction case;

sleeping around; people coming in from Canada, here already, commuting back over the border. Plenty to speak of without those others. "What honeymoon?"

"Who knows? Going on for years, I bet."

Daley laughed.

"You were with someone," Becca said.

A horn on the river to the west, they crossed the street and felt underfoot the passing of a truck somewhere. "I'm sure you know I got stood up," the woman said. Why had she only an hour, then? he wanted to know, not that it mattered. Her roommate was expecting her. Her roommate.

A drink. A wild cuppa coffee. Business, her case probably. Maybe a little fight. He wouldn't let tonight go sour. He felt fine. The rain stayed within itself. Daley smelled a burn like welding coming from the distant waterfront.

"Listen, your work is fine. Hard to make ends meet."

They were out together. She didn't talk about herself. She wasn't secretive either somehow.

"What do you do to make ends meet?"

"I forget."

"You forget?"

"My family help."

"They do?"

"When I let them; and I don't."

"You don't."

"I'm worth it—you've had a load of privileges around here," said Becca in an older voice.

"Is that you?" he said.

She wanted to give something back. She what? Give something back. Sounded like a minority person. "No. Give back something different."

"Well, you were terrific . . ."

Could they not talk about the play?

Just economics anyway, Daley recalled.

That was her brother's view, one of them, but it was nothing to do with economics.

Well, it was what she had said. "I never remember what I say."

(One of her *brothers*?) Well, not recalling what you'd said was a sign of creative . . . To take not a whole lot of responsibility for outrageous things you'd said . . .

"Governments do it." The reply changed everything for a second.

Daley meant creative people. Who would say anything. He had known a number of them once upon a time. You know, women process information much faster than men. We're all going to live to be two hundred (in this corner of the globe, of course); and your gift belongs not to you but to the universe it comes from. You said things like that and they were behind you, in the keeping of other suckers in Daley's opinion. A cab cruised them, its wipers swinging. They'd been walking. "No jazz tonight," he said. She gave him a smile, unfathomable or sad, and the cab passed on. They turned into a dark, old commercial block. He took Becca's arm, approaching two landmark warehouses, 1860s.

"No …," said Daley reflectively, "no . . ."

"Don't say no like that."

Well, he didn't mean no to *her*.

She might as well not've been here. No, it was a habit, he said. A stupid one, said the woman—*there*: he'd said no *again*.

Just sounding the long view. "Yours?" said this person walking beside him. No, it was his mother's as a matter of fact—who listened.

Listened? Now, that's hard.

Daley thought he wouldn't point out the landmark warehouses after all; Becca might think him stuffy, though probably it wasn't.

Yes, he wouldn't take that away from his mother. But whatever he said, opinion or fact, she might cast doubt on it.

The girl laughed. Like what?

Daley backed off a little. Oh . . . why a hummingbird with that beak doesn't break its shell before hatching time?

That wasn't an opinion, said this person with strange persistence. Right; it was a question. Daley thought a moment.

"Then she would say… ?" she pushed him.

"She would say, '. . . No'; . . . not *No*, but '. . .no . . .' thoughtful, give her that; tentative."

"Of course."

"It was damned irritating at fourteen. And later, let me tell you"

The girl seemed to find it comical. She was a girl to him, too.

"Eighteen, nineteen, twenty. When you'd *been* there."

"Been there?" was the reply.

"*Because* you had."

"That wasn't doubt," said the woman.

"Maybe not. It was something."

"It was fear," said this person with her presumption, her youth, her angle.

"Well," he said, "it was blame. That it was true and you'd said it. No. Unh unh; the no meant—"

"Time," said Becca, then.

# 15

HE ALMOST GOT IT. IT WAS TOO SMART. BUT IT MEANT HIS MOTHER had felt everything against her. Understood or not, he knew he would recall Becca's insight later, months and years later, as he had marked other moments for future recovery. The girl at the petrol station pushing the door open half tripping on the step coming out after taking a phone call, who would doubtless materialize in New York someday. Or that very deposition after passing the bar exam on the second try, strangely successful without his knowing quite what he had managed in his questions. And now, described for Becca Lang, his teenage brother's rebuilt leg, the knee going out during a boxing practice one morning. It was months after a dirt-bike accident when Wolf had taken a curve wide and whipped his bike abruptly back to the right to avoid a car and the bike caved on him and their mother without the hint of an accusation seemed unable to accept any of the accounts of the event.

"Who was he boxing?" Becca asked.

"Me. He clobbered me almost—"

"And you clobbered him."

"I pushed him, and I saw the knee give but it was okay. At thirteen, fourteen, those no's, that disbelief from her, it was damn irritating, it—"

"It toughened you, you had to see you were right, no matter what."

"Sure. But her no's meant '*Time*' did you say?"

"It topples into you," the girl said.

"I don't quite follow," he said.

"Anyhow, it was *you* that was being doubted," she said.

He tried to keep up with her. She was distant, like a woman turning away.

"Maybe not." They stood on the far curb from the two warehouse buildings he thought he would mention, he didn't want to be stuffy.

"Family," she said.

He was talking. He was influenced by the woman. She made you feel intelligent, then suddenly it was over and you weren't—but yes you were, even then; it was a status she shared with you. Survival-tank dialogues, it came to him, that she had come through. It was her education, her studies, but it wasn't, it was some retreat she brought with her for credentials, she was free no matter who detained her and was here and there willing to be inspiring. "And later on, too?" she said. "You reported in for debriefing?" Why yes.

Where was this? Oh . . . South Euclid. Shaker, he started to say, but no—Becca *knew* South Euclid. She did? Sure, Lakewood, Sandusky (how would she know them?—pretty rough places), the islands, lakefront, the region along the border. So she knew the area.

"And you reported in . . ."

From his travels now and then. "For debriefing . . ."

The loitering of poor coyotes New-Age-evolved at the edge of the woods, hunting fallen, ground-rotten apples not by choice; hummingbirds observed revving north from Salvador like daytime fireflies; a woodpecker upside down, sapsuckerish, nearly hidden and anxious of face among orchard blooms; the mildly toxic pink dye the fish farm reportedly colors its salmon flesh with (incredible to the mother, eating a second club sandwich in the kitchen) . . . or some

Dutch jazz one night in the apartment of a drummer half an hour from Amsterdam, who sometimes made music out of anything he could get his hands on: *chairs.* ("No . . ." from Becca.) Oh political, real active against the war just a few years earlier those guys.

Information was just how Daley mentioned it in passing to this young woman looking the warehouses over, their columns, contrasts, perhaps the dark upper windows—but with him now, and this was how he happened to add, "One day it was Winter Soldiers"—the older son now older, reporting in, being dubiously debriefed by his lunchable, mainly nature-knowledgeable parent.

"Before my time," the woman nodded yet with a curious reserve, waiting to be asked.

Daley hadn't said the words in twenty years and wouldn't again in twenty, might have said *winter melon soup* once to his father who had a lean and gluttonous interest in Asian cooking even if you found it at Howard Johnson's (he wondered what she knew, she appeared to know a little history). "A miserable time, '71," he said—twenty-five years now to be digested, not much more to be rethought.

"Always," she said. Perhaps she had read about the atrocity investigations, he added. She was contemplating the two warehouses, and he didn't make anything of her silence. The old columned fronts, warehouses from the last century. The pillars, the simple facades, the shadows. "The trick is to tell the limestone from the iron," Daley said.

"The limestone's on the left, the pillars on the right are stained. They're oxidized. They're iron."

Daley made a sound. "Excellent."

He was interested in all that, was he? It was her phone voice again, or she was estimating his age, how many rings around his trunk. *She* seemed to be interested in all that, he said. It was all so disappointing, she replied. "Am I good raw material?" Becca stepped into the street. He followed, he had picked up the phone expecting Lotta Monday, and now here he was. Becca was quite happy, in the middle of the dark, partly cobbled street. What they called Renaissance.

"Look," Daley pointed, "this one on the left was his own warehouse. Those top windows, they might be broken, they're so dirty."

"I can see."

"Good. I'm glad you can."

A woman came running along the sidewalk with a dalmatian ahead of her on an extensible leash: a black woman in black sweats, out late, a picture; Daley and Becca stepped to the curb to give her room.

"You can see a figure at the top-floor window behind all that grime," Becca said, "or is it the dirt? See? A watchman with his arms stretched out."

"Why would a watchman be doing that?"

"Did you see that woman?" said Becca.

Daley thought Becca wanted to move on, yet they didn't move.

"He and his partner had a foundry down near the North River during Civil War times and after. And before."

"And before."

He didn't understand her. Had he said the wrong thing? "Business was good," Daley went on.

"James Buchanan?"

"James Buchanan."

"Franklin Pierce," said Becca; "not your top people. The perfect man for a time of 'unwanted quiet and harmony.'" Oh she knew the presidents. A time of which it was said—she was only quoting—the two virtually merged parties maintained their antagonism through their old organizations rather than because any great and radical principles were in dispute.

"Well, that's a bit off, no one from that time would see it that way."

She laughed at him, he thought. "I can't imagine what they thought of that in Virginia," Daley said. He wondered what kind of trouble-maker he had on his hands, and to think he had taken her call thinking it was Lotta.

"Everything comes from this plain five-story with the arched windows on the ground floor and the third: you could still see how he turned the facade into an expanse of glass by using the cast-iron columns that used to be decoration for support now in place of brick."

"Oh. Everything?" This Canadian woman stood apart from him. Tourist. Graduate. In her a-little-awkward hip lean, a foot turned inward, equal to what's going to happen, some history in *her* shoulders, her waist, busy turning into a life of passing through, a sisterly itinerant, not motherly person of all work, and nothing secret at all if you knew how to take her.

"Yes, everything. It's the iron columns; it's not like timber into beam or quarry into masonry: iron's practically there. Pour it into molds. It's light, easy to put up. See the panels? the arches? A new native style."

She was frowning at the warehouses. "I like a useless building once in a while."

He didn't know what she meant. Maybe she knew the builders' names. "They called this Renaissance," he said.

"Robert E. Lee," said Becca.

"Yes, Virginia's man of the hour, the South's great general," said Daley.

"Wasn't he superintendent of West Point?"

Daley didn't think so; he was perturbed. She was looking up at windows, facade, history.

"I seem to recall he lived in Brooklyn."

Lee? In New York City? Daley didn't think so. Not likely.

"First in war, first in peace. Whatever," said Becca.

The words were familiar. Daley thought she had misapplied them. "That's Washington."

"Spoken at his death by another Lee," came the surprising retort. A cab with its top light on paused and he pointed to his watch but the girl smiled the sad smile and they stepped back onto the curb and the cab passed, its wipers swinging. It had begun with stretching up in front of a theater full of empty seats and then her out front in the dark house feeling *happy* about an unconscious dive that wasn't his at all. As if her instinct (no more than that) had known it was more than a good stretch. And now, two cabs later that they had passed up, Robert E. Lee a Brooklynite? "He got close," said Daley suddenly recalling, "we were afraid he'd bring his army right up here to Jersey City and take New York."

They stopped to hear the distances of the city and the particular hour, they had walked north and away from the river and now back toward it. The woman and the dalmatian turned the corner and were upon them again. She pulled up and reined the dog in close, snapping its head around. "Excuse me," she said.

"But it was right after Gettysburg," Becca ignored the woman, "and he went the other way. The army was wounded. Think of what that was like."

"What it was like?" said Daley, her elder.

"Yes, think of what that was like."

"Excuse me," said the woman.

"Well, it wasn't 'combat refusal' or 'cover your ass.' Can you imagine his own men putting a bounty on Lee's head the way they did in Vietnam?" said Daley, turning to the woman with the dog, which looked up at her and continued sniffing the wet street without much enthusiasm.

"She doesn't know what you're talking about," said Becca.

"Not any old Civil War," Daley said.

"God you have to take on something difficult," said Becca, "I'd enlist if there was a war on." It was the dumb side of her. He was tired of women, and the street, and the times, the war absorbed for years, law too in certain pleasures of civil and financial fairness pursued for his clients privileged to be represented by him in the discreet justice of a regular life.

The black woman's hair was cut short and bronzed in the night shadows and she wore diamond studs in her earlobes. "You two looking for a roof over your head?" The three listened for a moment to the distant cupping clucks of horses' hooves. "If you're in the market," the woman said.

"Bogardus's *ware*house?" Daley said.

The real estate woman processed the information. "Were you looking to buy? You're not a developer." She stepped off the curb and her dog took the lead past Daley into the middle of the street and around behind him as she dug a card out of the pocket of her shiny, top-to-bottom-zippered sweatpants. "You never know," she said. "I don't know Bogardus, but if he's a developer . . . What goes around—"

"I ran into one last week," Becca told the woman.

"Maybe I know him. Bang!" said the woman—the dog had looped Daley and Becca with the paid-out leash. "Bang," said the woman, who was pulled off the sidewalk and into the street and now around the other two, the dog setting off in the direction they'd come from. "You got my number," she said. She had come back just for them. She and the dog had a spectacular stride down the street, together they were like a vehicle.

"Where are we?" Daley looked at his watch.

An intersection ahead with more activity, Daley smelled orange and the damp hide of her coat and the stony, light rain out in the city, and he saw her cheek close up not much the worse for wear reflecting minutes of this history you could actually talk about. She wanted to get a move on too, he thought; she turned politely, to receive from him a little pass perhaps that he decided should wait, and again they heard the cupping hoof-clips of a horse a little closer maybe, you couldn't tell. Between the limestone and the iron the impulse would have to do, some joint instinct carrying them back west.

"You met a developer?"

"In a vacant lot."

"They like vacant lots. They feel at home in vacant lots."

"He was sizing up both of us, the lot and me," said Becca, uncharacteristically volunteering information about herself. "They left a high-low by the fence."

"A backhoe?" said Daley.

"A high-low I call it; they'd broken ground, and he introduced himself and knew me, it could have been worse."

"He knew you?"

"We were meeting the same guy. Who was late. More than late. Who knew my brother and so did this man. Who with his cufflinks wasn't surprised to see me he looked a little like . . . I don't know what—not an India Indian, but a person of color."

"It sounds like Ruley Duymens," said Daley.

"That's him."

"A developer?" Daley asked.

"A friend of developers. He made you feel he was there because of you."

"Ah," said Daley.

"He wanted my number."

"He did?"

"Anyone can get your number."

"He got it from your mutual friend."

"Beck's no friend of mine."

"I thought Ruley was just a voice on the phone," Daley said.

"I never said that," said Becca. Ruley Duymens getting talked about again. Anyone can get your number, your history, your friends, your name. Name recognition lately the thing to overcome all else, even blame, the order in which things had once upon a time happened. Daley lost touch with his companion, he was telling about a new private company, a mid-1990s stand-alone making its first million this year supplying all that data to the U.S. Marshals Service and the F.B.I. Daley happened to know. But he had missed some point.

"Right. What do Einstein, Rock Hudson, and Henry Ford have in common?" said Becca.

"I'm sure I'm among them," said Daley, "if only as a stand-in." He heard himself say this however not as someone who almost certainly had a file but countering whatever she had meant, was it investigated by the F.B.I.?—he had to trust his lawyer's ear if nothing else. "Robert E. Lee: what do you know about that?" said Daley.

"Yes, he was a vestryman in a church over there before the war."

"You know more than I," said Daley. They would take the next cab.

"Oh, I grew up with it," she said. He took her arm. They had a good school system up there, Daley understood. Well, her brother was a history buff. Used to buy books. He was a Lincoln buff.

Well.

He was a New York City buff.

Way up there? Sounded like he was a Brooklyn buff.

A *buff,* she said. He'd made his peace with it.

Peace, eh?

"He's in business."

"He made his peace with that?"

"Maybe he didn't have to."

"And maybe he did."

"This is scrap metal. He fell into it years ago, my half brother. Construction materials, machines to process dumped machines, an all-over system—be surprised what's still made of metal."

"Plenty of turnover," said Daley. The woman pulled away a little.

"I'll tell you sometime." (There it was again, like that movie that according to her they would see.) "Everything you didn't know about ball bearings."

"Auto bodies?"

Tell her about it. Hendrix guitars. Boat hulls. Local compactors. She learned it all without meaning to. It was somewhat decentralized, how it all networked.

Becca slipped her arm through Daley's again. "Huron, Erie, all along the border. So near yet so far. That's where it developed. He's okay. He dresses well. He's not a terrible person. Been through the wars. He's been through it." She looked at Daley. She was hopeful. "I owe him."

"What?"

"He worked for the distillery in Windsor before I was born and worked in a garage and developed a homing instinct for junkyards." Daley didn't want to know about it at the moment. "He's done well. There's business in the family, but." Daley didn't follow. "And then there's his." Becca knew things immensely in her own right and some-how not in the slightest private. She'd give you what you might ask for if you asked. What did *she* ask?

"So near yet so far from what?"

"Oh, the States."

"Did he send you rent money?"

"They sent me two months' rent that I sent back."

"Like a landlord."

Becca squeezed his arm. "And a plane ticket. Twice a plane ticket."

"Oh yes." (The trips home the landlord's lawyers got her on.)

Daley wasn't representing her, this person sent like a message he'd picked up by mistake thinking it was his client Lotta on the phone and from a historically unworthy source (Duymens van Diamond who needed you/didn't need you) gone in time, here in the city like everything else off and on these dozen and more years, cufflinks and demeanor being yet again described unnecessarily as Daley and Becca approached a back-street intersection, headlights down the block bobbing this way—a man you found yourself calling by his first name who'd made an impression on Daley's late wife and who certainly wasn't responsible for her but only an impression, at the end, a presence that passed, Becca telling the woman with the dog about the vacant lot when she hadn't told Daley. It was impolite, immature, she doled it out. It didn't matter, or it was making a point. Daley stepped apart from Becca and she let him. The honeymoon over, she'd said: what did that mean?

It occurred to Daley if her case had gone to trial she would need to show that she spent most nights at her place (183 in a year, he believed, little as he knew primary residence law). Though what she did now should have no bearing on the landlord's action, which embraced a period ending well before the papers had been served.

"Cufflinks in a vacant lot," Daley said. "You met him in a vacant lot? Before he ever phoned you?"

Becca's laugh soft, insolent, dumb. "Dumb cufflinks," she said. "I ran into him. We were meeting the same person. Wouldn't you know, the person was late."

"'More than late,' you said."

"Well, yes. I couldn't wait. Van Diamond said he could help me."

"Why would he do that?"

"He'd seen me work."

"He'd seen you work?"

"The first time he left right after the first act. It was painful, he said. Or there was a problem with the person he was with, he just got up and left, but. No. He needed to know about a little theater piece he knew of mine I don't know how because it hardly exists."

"All right."

"He asked about it."

"He wanted your number. He didn't get it," said Daley.

"I'd been there long enough. It didn't look too good."

The woman's spirit swerved again, it embraced everyone, how did she do that?—or she could just go home—sleep with her intelligence or memory—her roommate waited perhaps. "He owed you," she said.

Daley made a sound. "What could he owe *me*?"

That wasn't the idea she had gotten from Ruley. What idea was that?

"That he 'owed' you."

"Let's see. Twenty-eight bucks?"

"Money?" said Becca.

"Years ago."

"Twenty-eight dollars?"

"A jai alai junket up to Connecticut. It was when he was supposedly coaching a little diving."

"Our *diving* coach!" She exclaimed.

"He wasn't a pro. I watched him. Well, once. Got himself hurt."

"Twenty-eight dollars?"

"Long ago forgiven."

"A banker," she said. Daley ascertained that she had learned nothing much from Ruley Duymens. A friend of Della's. The agency. Daley a lawyer. "But he did you, you said." She had remembered.

"Well, you see . . ."

"Ah, don't tell me."

"I gave him—"

"Don't."

"Freedom."

"No one can give that."

"It doesn't matter what I gave him." Daley was getting irritated. "Civility. Enough rope to hang himself."

"You think you gave him your wife," said Becca then. It sounded clever like her on the phone. "But it doesn't matter. You could afford it. That's the thing about you on short acquaintance. But what did he take?"

Daley smelled her face. She was irritated. "I couldn't put a name to it."

"What you gave him. I'm irritating you," she said.

"Oh it isn't for a man to get irritated by a woman."

"Where'd you hear that?"

"From a woman," Daley said. She was that close, like when she'd been standing on the floor below the stage. The flesh of her cheeks, the little intentions of her face.

"I gave him leverage," Daley joked. "A free gift."

"I know," said the woman, she got the joke.

"But he *took* it from me then," Daley said.

She found this funny and made a sound. "I get it," she said, "he just up and *stole* it, what you'd already given him . . ." Daley stood. "You're grumbling," she said.

"I didn't say a thing."

"'Cause if you're *doing* a favor," she went on, "if you don't do it right away . . ."

"Exactly."

"Exactly," she mimicked him.

"Went by his first name," Daley said, "he was your *friend*, you understand? He knew my brother, he *said*, and—"

"It checked out?"

"Of course," said Daley, but it was a little uncanny.

"Well you don't have the *right* to do favors for people," said the woman coldly.

"*You* don't maybe," said Daley.

She nodded, learning something. "I'm not crazy about first names either," she said.

"You're not?"

"That's right," she said, "if you want to take something, let it be given."

Daley was a little out of his depth.

"Well, you won't give *me* away, there's nothing *to* give." She swung her hip into him. Where were they? Walking. Where something was waiting to happen; or nothing; and it was up to him. The girl was smart all right: his mother's *No* meant *Time*, this kid who just said things had said. Why in hell did it mean Time? The *No* of someone Daley sometimes now hardly remembered. What is it that waits to happen and where does it wait? it came to Daley. You couldn't ask a question like that except to be silly or not very entertaining. "I didn't get that about Time and my mother saying No."

"No, it was pretentious of me," said Becca; "but it's true."

"Maybe it is."

"You've confused people too."

The blue shadow across her cheek and nose passed as she moved; not a bruise. He thought of the rest of her. She looked up and read the street signs at right angles.

"Listen," said Daley: without going into detail he told her about his first real deposition out of law school and that he had succeeded by—she seemed engrossed in the street sign—by improvising time-lines or chronologies as—

"What are you saying?" Becca asked irritably—as choices for the defendant under questioning but actually to blitz her into showing she was making things up.

"A man was lynched near here," said Becca. She was quite happy. "During the riots?" she said deferentially.

"Not to the best of my knowledge," said Daley.

Shel smiled. "The draft riots," she said.

"Yes."

"Eighteen sixty-three to the best of my knowledge."

He was with her again, barely. "Can't blame them. Lose an arm or a leg in those days."

"A mob of Irishmen. It was worth your life in the streets." Becca sounded a little husky, something about her voice. "They hanged a black man. Not the one they were looking for, not the one who shot into them. Another one. Another black man. It was a tree at Varick and Charlton."

"Nothing they could use there now except a streetlamp," Daley said. The young woman laughed. "What is it that waits to happen. Where does it wait?" he said feeling a happy fool.

"What are you *saying*?" She took his hand to lead him there. She was pretty.

"It was a bricklayer who got shot. They didn't want to serve," Daley told her.

"Some already had," said Becca.

"There you go," said Daley.

"Check it out," she said.

"Probably got whipped like a troop of Arabs," said Daley.

"First Bull Run, thirty miles from Washington," said the woman. She reached into her bag for some gum, and Daley saw the camisole and the script.

"You've read up on this," he said.

"Been briefed," she said. "I always go for somebody who's been there." She must know some pretty intense graybeards, he said. Daley was irritated. He smiled at her. Time to put her in a cab. He looked forward to finding out what his client Lotta had wanted, as an indirect result of which he was here. "So you know some history," Daley said, "Winter Soldiers, Bull Run."

"The night streets."

Night streets indeed. He would recall it months later, he looked forward to remembering this smart stranger slipping her arm through his, to somehow keep him on some subject she had decreed.

"I have a feel for them. I feel just thrown into New York, now that so much is changing, it's all right, it's okay."

She would walk anywhere at night, he could tell, tempting the doorways, holding her side of the street no matter what. More than a tourist.

It was 1996? he thought. Who was she reassuring in her American voice? "*What* is okay? *What* is changing?" Daley objected.

She drew him gently by the hand. "I did read part of a memoir."

"A memoir?"

"By a gambler's slave girl who saved him when the rotten old East River dock or was it the West, fell in with a ton of horsemeat on it he was shipping upriver and he was swept out by the current and couldn't swim and she saved him, a white girl from the islands."

"No, no, wait a minute," Daley said, and took a breath: "what are you doing getting slugged every night?" But she pulled him by the hand, not coming back at him, which she did habitually he already knew. It came back in his own question, that the producer had gotten Becca the part—and her apartment; and she was through being managed by him and by her older brother, who had set her up with Beck like a coincidence. Or *trying* to be through.

She put him in mind of so much.

It was what a walk was, it occurred to him like a thought.

Troublemaker, to be sure, and now we had a white slave girl from the islands of what vintage pray tell; and was the horsemeat made up?

Lincoln, Lee: yet Winter Soldiers: what had happened before her time was how she had put it. Before she was born, looping back with a difference. Winter Soldiers *just* before.

What history was that? The older brother's? A war buff. Either he came down to see her or he didn't. You could ask her; she would tell you.

It was her business. It irritated Daley, all that she'd absorbed for some purpose. Canada, it came to him, had had its part. It was like Varick and Charlton, a person flung down, hoisted, flung upward not to come back down until it was history; the bothered, drained face, scraped forehead and nose. He dried up. Somebody nameless down from Canada, some past and future force trying to hook up. Why *would* Daley trust her? But her case, her job. It would be waiting for him like the number of a year.

"And that gambler, did he set her free when she rescued him?" Daley said. "And when were *they* supposed to be? A *white* slave? "

"Oh, he told her she could go. Civil War time. She always stayed." Becca's brother had had the book.

She didn't care if Daley believed her, she was more learned than she let herself seem, he guessed. She detached herself from him and did an impression of him along the sidewalk, throwing her leg out before her, rocking at the shoulders, an uncanny walk in which he saw himself, that was all. He wasn't doing one of her.

"This litto pig . . ." she began in a child's voice, and stopped. They thought they heard a horse on the cobblestones, like a lantern to be followed, and they did hear one but at the corner they never found the horse—a mounted policeman doubtless, though they tended to travel in pairs.

He was telling her how some of the warehouses had been sweat-equitied "up" but then taken over by well-off family types. He had a pretty busy life. She liked him okay. He would always remember this moment, this hour. And then they heard the horse approaching behind them in this quiet commercial block.

# 16

THE BIG CHESTNUT HORSE AND ITS RIDER HAD AN UNDERSTANDING going that was like a conversation and when Becca stepped over onto the left-hand sidewalk so the cop in his white helmet could pass, Daley stopped where he was in the middle of the street.

Yet he could have been wrong and her reasonable action—which brought him actually closer to her—could have been an instinct as receptive and supple and no less unknowing than it not occurring to Daley to move out of the way; or as generous as the horse and its capacity to understand the encounter feeling it as fully and skeptically as its will was with the rider whose touch it knew in advance. Daley backed away toward the other sidewalk and the rider nodded, giving himself to both people. "What a way to travel," Daley said. The policeman moved easily in the saddle, his nightstick hanging from its leather loop attached to the saddle. Daley smelled the horse. And if it was all the talk, or some caress of guilt to be experiencing this on an evening that had begun with Helen, or it was the city deceivingly beautiful and elegant and at peace at night, and the harbor and the tides—a voyage and the horse the great sway of the gelding passing on bearing you where you were bound—Daley thought that for this moment (and no need for a moment more) he was at one with this woman who said something and the rider with an imperceptible signal halted, and she seemed to repeat what she had said: "Do you ride along the river?"

"Not tonight, ma'am," the mounted cop bowed his head forward and the horse went on and the moment had done something for the rider as well as this man and woman enjoying a walk on a Wednesday night.

What was in her head? The horse might know as well as Daley. To speak of the outer rim of the district might have bored the young woman Becca, except that it was true, what he felt. Hell's Hundred Acres, the firetrap warehouses of the nineteenth century now reclaimed, but the further history of that reclaiming not so happy. You walk these night sidewalks and put your feet down exactly where you walked with others years ago. Not always, of course, if the city has drilled the street to pieces, less apt to last than the sidewalks. The shot tower no longer on Centre Street (or anywhere else). Yet a landmark . . .

Made of members that you could take apart, he reminded Becca, and put back together in Hoboken or Panama if you wanted, after the laugh they'd had about his forgetting where the Centre Street shot (as in ammo) tower was—or *wasn't!*

Though she said quite suddenly,

> Towers he would stare at so
> they were startled from their shapes—

(Towers startled?)

> restoring them suddenly in a storm of stones!

It wasn't true. Though what did it mean?

What towers? he asked. (Were they still under the spell of the horse and rider?)

Think about it, was the reply.

"I don't know what's in your head," Daley said. She liked it.

The bliss of these working streets to the west the nineteenth-century builders gone, the old work that had gone on in these buildings so little the work of today. "Bliss?" the woman said. Odd, Daley had said it. (What bliss? an old system posed, setlike, to absorb some shock?) The light industry so local then, hour by hour—not that it wasn't noisy (for let's not bring back wagons and horses, but—"Let's," the woman said), the wholesale warerooms one never saw, shadowy, great, cool in summer's oven, walls of crates, shoe boxes like an inner layer of structure. In those days paper products, the long storage floors of textiles, dry goods, shirtwaists and trousers manufactured by a German Jew who had prepared as an itinerant peddler nationwide only to put up this Italianate building near the Franklin Street Elevated. Filtered ice water and toilet rooms on every floor. Not far to the south, cheese and eggs. "Commerce, why not?" said Daley.

"Didn't they march celebrating Lincoln's second inaugural?" said Becca.

"Displaying their wares."

"Criticized for it," said Becca.

"It was early March. Did you know we had elephants and camels marching with the fire companies. Banners. OIL IS KING NOW, NOT COTTON."

"The tailors and the piano makers," said Becca. Now how did she know a thing like that? It was in the names of the streets, Staple, Mercer. "Desbrosses: what kind of brushes?"

All kinds. He didn't know.

She proposed that they have a look at the docks at the end of Desbrosses Street. It was way out of their way now and at this hour, Daley said.

Another time, she said, disappointed. Did Daley know that Lincoln came ashore there on the twenty-first of April and right there at the foot of Desbrosses Street they put him in a glass hearse drawn by six grays, spring soldier Lincoln immersed in that war, exiled.

"At the center," Daley said, "I can't imagine what that was like."

Exactly.

How did she know about the piano makers? Daley asked, but it was some other question, what could it be? Oh she had an uncle in the shoe business. "Oh?" And the store was right next to—it didn't matter. She could eat something.

Great.

"No, you were saying . . ."

"No . . . you were saying . . ."

"Spring soldier Lincoln. Your brother knows New York history."

"That's me," said the girl. "Summer winter autumn with spring like a fourth season in a series of three, that April," she said like a saying. Was Daley in the driver's seat? She wanted him to hear, to understand. She had the thirst for it; and for walking, she let *it* take *her*, a solitude concealed in her bones, Canadian, her hand as near his as his wristwatch. "No, you were saying . . . all these warehouses . . ."

Till artists began to occupy them around Vietnam time. A *new* kind of work, Daley said. It wasn't leisure activity at all, art, Daley figured out; it produced a product. Becca listened. He wasn't explaining it well. He was a little euphoric or boring, and flattered. "'Pioneers,' they called themselves—a little to the south of here. Spring soldiers?"

"What is leisure?" the woman beside him said.

"Time to do something."

"What?"

Pioneers, Daley went on with his account. Succeeded by professional folk a few years later who could pay the new rents—who *set* them. Health-club types, leveraging each other, and family-money women buying a new elevator from Canada, and educated plumbers with accountants, and good cabinetmakers who had sold drawings once upon a time to MOMA and gave it up, and good public-interest attorneys for whom the real contingency was everyday justice. My, she said. She knew someone who used to swim the eight hundred meters, that was how he took care of himself insofar as he did.

Leander coming in about a job tomorrow, Thursday. The week. Helen having a drink with the bartender; or home in her kitchen staring at the chair left turned between the table and the fridge, Daley felt the beveled inner outline on him, or she was taking a hot bath, she knew how. Becca figured in it. Daley *saw* Leander in front of Donna's desk—the picture came at him and he gave Leander a push, he had to be a swimmer. Then it was Barry's life that came to Daley, the years not in a row; Ruley's, Sook's, Lotta's, Wolf's. Becca's, what he knew just from this week or from his own life.

"What pool's Leander go to? Do you happen to know?"

She didn't know exactly where it was. Midtown, near her. She took it for granted Daley knew of the pool. She was easy with her body. On the loose like some adolescent. She hadn't acknowledged the eight hundred-meter guy as Leander.

"Market people, family types who even bought the art." Daley sounded a little off. Though it's the work that matters, he added, though often not great work. And there are other people, architects, media, drinkers, musicians, amateurs, professional people scraping by.

"Good work," Becca said. "It must have been a shock when they saw what was happening."

"It takes a while, it's gradual."

"No, I think it was a shock."

Something riding on this, it occurred to him. "Well, these original buildings were minding their own business you understand. The owners . . ."

"Crocodiles dozing in the shallows," said the girl.

"Owners had it scoped. You couldn't ignore the money. The properties bid up. The product."

What product was that?

"It's commercial, or empty commercial, giving way to residential, you might think we needed to live," Daley said (she made him say things), "it's renovation."

"It's what Beck does. Our producer. And he *promotes* the arts," said Becca.

"It's neighborhood—"

"*These* fixed-up buildings?" she said with a wave of her hand.

"Let me finish."

"You've been talking for hours."

Yet evidently she didn't mind.

"Beck got you your part."

"Give him something and he thinks you have to get something in return, it's bizarre, his friend van Diamond's another story."

"What did you give Beck?" Daley asked, and wished a taxi would come.

"You know what I gave him. It's bizarre that he thinks I had to get something in return, it's . . ."

"Return for what?" Daley said, feeling the unsaid word. What was it?

"He put me up when I got here."

"He did that for you." Daley tried to understand.

"He did it for my brother," said Becca, "damn them both."

"Oh your brother knew him."

"Evidently."

"You weren't in on it?"

"Oh you don't need to be in on things," said Becca sharply, "to be in the driver's seat."

Daley saw the audience tonight, the theater, Barry swatting her and the terrible resilience and obliviousness or bitter love or acting strength in her. "But Beck got you the part—"

"Only the audition . . . well . . . ."

"—and an apartment at what a month?"

"A loft."

"In return for, you said . . . ?"

"For nothing. I need to go," said Becca.

"The guy with the hat."

"That's him." She was unsurprised—it was how things worked here, access everybody had, or executive license. "He got me my *job*."

"In return for some future success."

"Maybe that was it," Becca said.

"He got you your place?"

"That too, that I'm being screwed out of on some technicality but along comes—"

How much rent did she pay? Five hundred a month for a great space.

After the roommate chipped in?

"Oh no: five hundred is the rent."

They had walked some blocks north to a club she didn't like the look of (you couldn't see in)—it was not his real and true jazz place, dilapidated and distinguished—and she couldn't imagine what kind of food they could sandwich in with music she was too tired to listen to, and he was afraid to look at his watch or for a clock. Was she edgy? "Five hundred until they get me out. But along comes your friend Diamond and recommends you," said Becca.

"Not as a lawyer." Daley was getting used to the idea; he kind of liked it in this transition world. To be recommended as a fool.

"And he's in the middle of it."

"A vacant lot," Daley said. He took Becca's arm, but she lifted it and swept the block. "You've had practice talking about all these . . ."

"They've lasted a while."

". . . utilitarian monuments."

"No, I don't like monuments," Daley said.

Two lots Ruley Duymens had been partners in in the old days, what had happened to them? Daley wondered aloud. The partner had been paying the taxes. "That was where I met him, just after I got here," Becca said, "he asked what I'd seen."

"I've passed those lots a hundred times. I don't know why we're discussing him," Daley said.

"We're not."

"I brought him up," Daley said.

And he knew she would be going home, which would be a relief, though maybe he would brush up on primary residence.

She was hungry, he guessed he had that over her.

"Don't tell me you've not had housing cases," she said.

The movie-industry parking everywhere, Daley pointed vaguely toward lower Manhattan, and a glut of restaurants down here, "a stream of service jobs, young people like you coming and going."

"And *families*," Becca said, "as if they couldn't think of anything else."

So little of *her* in her talk. Her life.

Now she didn't care to interrogate him. "Postwar money running things. This glutted democracy," she said. But business back and forth across the border, little to choose between Canadian and U.S. Children recording the family's outgoing message.

They stopped at the long windows of a restored diner. "No . . . ," she said (where did Daley recall that women process information faster than—), "no . . ." (even when they bring it around to themselves?), and, a block farther on, an abbreviated bar menu looked as if it had been rained on that, he pointed out, served a "Dangerous Brains Salad."

"No," she said.

"Whadda ya mean, no?"

"'No' like your Winter Soldiers your hungry mother couldn't believe when you came home and told her," said this pretty remarkable young woman.

"Wow," he said.

Becca, though an actress, had emerged from a good school and university system with some history under her belt. Name everything as it comes. And what did you name this, he had to wonder. Winter Soldiers.

"Listen," Daley said, easing up deliberately, "I never got around to checking out the trust bank Ruley Duymens represented, Austro-Israeli." Becca laughed. "Wait: irrigation loan to the nation-state of Chad; you know about *that* one?"

Surprisingly, she did. "The way we often just *don't* check," he added.

"You're so wise," she said. "Well, he seemed to know me."

"That's him." Daley waited for more. "He wasn't my business in the beginning or at the end."

"At the end of the day," she said. She turned sullen.

"A business contact of my wife's, okay. Australia came up because

I was going there. His bank had loans out on agricultural irrigation somewhere near where I was going."

"Of course," said Becca.

So little of *her* in her talk during this hour or two finding their way almost nowhere zigzag in the grid of streets, the ladder, no star shape possible for fortification on this lengthwise island already twenty percent larger due to landfill than in the days of Lenape trails bisecting north and south, branching west to fishing and planting . . . near the spring soldier's landing . . . too much to begin telling again as if history could be rethought.

Way west to one last place Daley thought of near the river that had food. You could see lights on the Jersey side and lights moving that became a shadowy shape passing upriver. Bogardus's foundries always near a river for pig-iron deliveries and such. Becca noticed a smell. Tar, harbor water, chemicals, Daley told her.

"Why isn't it the West River?" she said.

"It is, *and* it's the Hudson, but the North River's what they called it, if you look at an old map."

"Do you have one?"

Somewhere. He should look it up. From the Battery *looking* north.

"It's where you're looking from," she said, irritated.

Daley pointed out the amber plate-glass window of a bar. "We can eat here. I can put you in a cab."

"Was she the diver? Was your wife the diver?" Becca said.

"She did some." A tall boy in an apron appeared in the doorway and looked out at them like a thug, and Becca said, Hey, and gave him a wave, younger than Becca. Hey, he said—he recognized her you might think; yes he did. This "old sailors' bar" Daley seemed to have brought them to ("the landmark survey book talking") now patronized by artists ("that's the tourist book"). The cook-dishwasher had gone back to work.

Daley looked both ways along the street, hearing a familiar crowd of voices inside. "But you're brave," said Becca; "who *knows* what you'd do?"

"How did you know that?" Daley said; he stood his ground.

"He told me. You gave him something; he wants to give it back," she said. She was guessing.

"He's welcome to it," Daley said. Why did he do what he did now, looking at the river? He asked her if she had seen these moldedplastic walls city people were climbing. Of course she had. Well, the idea had taken a few years to sell. That is, if what Daley had been aware of at the West River pier and in a two-story-high alcove near Lincoln Center was theirs, a decade later. Whose? Oh Duymens and a Swiss engineer who had done all the work. Ruley's input a few photos, seed money. It stuck in your *mind*, Daley said. Becca stared into his face. "He described it to me and it happened but he was lying somewhere in there. You had to believe him."

"You did?"

"This lying honesty. Called himself a coward. Where *was* the coward, the things he did?"

Becca took Daley's arm. The engineer had divided his time between the city and somewhere else—a house in Catskill, New York, it came back to Daley. She left him and went and put her face up against the amber soiled glass, tables back there somewhere behind the massed drinkers Daley figured three and four deep. Who would Daley run into? She had decided against it, he could tell, she'd almost shied from the fogged glass, soot streaked, gold lettered. She knew the place, he thought. Who had brought who here? She knew the city, the way new people do. "They've got the smallest kitchen in New York," Daley said, remembering the kid in the apron whom he didn't remember seeing on the premises before. Now he was hungry.

"You must be starved," Becca said, coming to him. Was it dangerous here?

He had been accosted one early morning running and repelled his attackers with an umbrella. He was running with an umbrella? No he found it. It was broken.

"I'm going to take that barge trip, you get on at Cincinnati and get off at New Orleans, that's the way." They looked across at New Jersey lights.

"You don't know a river," Daley began—but she laughed at him or he felt her intelligence.

"—until you've been on it," she said.

"In it," Daley said, feeling in new sprinkles of rain the distinct chance that she had seen someone she knew standing at the bar.

"No . . . ," she said doubting whatever he was going to tell her, not the facts of it.

Well, he had swum the Harlem one night on a dare, he told her. From the dangerously steep concrete embankment to the far side. It was not the same river he had sculled in a borrowed shell several early mornings, for now it was night and his body had stood under a cloud-quickened half-moon just at the turn of the tide, the harbor ocean miles away though in the motion and business of the waters across the north end of Manhattan Island fluctuant and seductive and with a drive to resist yet go with. And the slack tide within the still-subtle and rough-edged current near High Bridge bore neither toward the East River ebbing nor toward the Hudson at flood: he told it to this person with him not at all in a spirit of pride or his life, and was about to go on to something he wanted her to know, when she said, "You must have been with people you trusted."

He laughed.

"What if you'd become a channel swimmer? A swimmer of the great rivers."

"*Become* is too . . ."

But that was nothing. One Sunday in August probably ten years ago Daley had swum the Hudson just after dawn. From very near this bar, Pier 25 (which they had since developed). Wolf, his brother, came along close behind in a skiff the Port Authority police had lent him for some reason. Typical. He was from the West Coast. And in a red, nearly invisible kayak rocking 150 yards off the pier, a ten-year-old stranger accompanied them at risk to himself out into midchannel under the broad front end of an early barge, square and black and newly painted: it was one of those swims you don't think about once you're in it, there was some other struggle that wasn't energy or wind or keeping your face in the water or your body level whatever the surge and sway of the swell or your eye on the seaplane tied up where you were aiming and the in-fact-friendly current he continually diagonaled the way you paddle in wind to keep from slipping off.

What a madman, Becca said. But you've swum the Black Sea and that's *deep* deep. Thousands of years deep, he said. Seven thousand, she said. Yet it was dry land down there once.

And you've swum it, madman.

Only a short distance.

How deep was this river? How many dead men lay in the silt at the bottom? Becca went on—he'd parachuted, hadn't he? She just knew he had—there must be oil in the water.

Upon reaching the other side Wolf had bought Daley breakfast in a Jersey City wharfside café that's gone now. A breakfast of mackerel and clams and "rats' tails" (they called them) and a round loaf of hard Polish bread and peach-and-pecan griddle cakes. Daley's spouse asleep in bed somewhat alarmed the night before by his plan (the blind, oncoming tankers, the stern wheelhouse) but not interested in spending the time or experiencing the breakfast. Rats' *tails*? said Becca. Oh they were a long strip jerky of the gristliest steer sinew they used to process in Cape May near the old Coast Guard boot camp that never took off commercially but would certainly keep and you would drink a beer and chew on one, and in the late 1970s up into the Reagan years they had green turtle jerky, clandestinely *farmed* (Daley understood) down there at the seaswept tip of New Jersey: animals huge in scale, humped map or Acadian mountain, and once prolific, now receiving human encouragement, but hey you couldn't make a green turtle do it if it wouldn't.

Well, it was a way of preserving them, Becca said. (He liked it.) It was another nature, she said. He thought that was it, he knew some of this so well he had put it aside till now, what was it? Lipids, amino acids, in a bottled animal leaking into the preserving fluid, get this, so the tissues lose chemicals that molecular biologists might want to study in them, he understood? She seemed to ignore this. She thought they had to travel great distances—she was still thinking about the turtles—to work up the appetite. Would they spawn on demand?

It was actually an interest of Daley's: with the new recirculating-tank technology you could encourage striped bass, yellow perch and so forth to reproduce earlier. They could make the bream think they had made it all the way to the Med to spawn, and the hormones they inject into the back of the fish have a timed release so they don't get it all at once. Still only a niche player in the billion-dollar aquaculture industry, the technology was emerging (he felt the girl's hunger and humor next to him), and you would be able to set up a fish farm in an old barn that takes only two hours a day to look after. Great for depressed areas, if they didn't pink-dye the salmon, they were going to try it in Iowa City, Phoenix, Detroit, he understood. Detroit? she said. Oh and he had *not* parachuted, not exactly.

You either have or you haven't.

Well, he had seen someone step out of a plane without a chute.

Must have been on the ground she said. But why the boy in the red kayak?

Police boat hailed him, he ignored them. A ten-year-old small for his age, dreads, mixed yaller, he would not take up Wolf's breakfast invitation, and wouldn't leave his boat (maybe it wasn't his), but Wolf promised him a dollar for the Coke machine and he tied up to a pontoon strut of the seaplane that was missing half the wing skin on one side and came with them reluctantly, he was smart, afraid of thieves at that rotting dock behind his back, you could see them in his mighty eyes.

But when the boy couldn't get his can out he attacked the machine, he deserved that Coke, at least he had earned it. (Becca approved of something.) Daley liked that boy who wouldn't eat—a shade Asian in there with Afro-Rican. Meanwhile Wolf was at the far end enjoying a shouting, largely agreeable discussion about hundreds of marines killed in Lebanon and someone who was attacking Israel's position in this, the same professor who attacked America in Vietnam, because Wolf discussed his trick knee that had not *quite* prevented him from going to Vietnam, the injury at age eleven unforgettably connected to a sorry chapter in the war January '63, though it wasn't the whole truth.

Who was this Wolf again? asked Becca.

The swimmer's brother. Wolf was his brother, who was based generally on the West Coast. He had produced a towel for Daley to rub down and get the harbor out of his hair that cold gray morning and he changed on the dock. He smelled like a swineherd, a vagrant.

"Important to have a brother."

They kept in touch. Oh if he hadn't had him . . .

"You'd have been more like him," Becca said just like that.

"We couldn't be more different. And two parents," Daley found himself almost inspired or relieved to see, "are mysteriously one thing to one son, another to the other. Our mother never questioned brother Wolf, though she almost never spoke to him."

"How could she?" she laughed.

"No no, immensely protective of him as if he might not make it, that rascal, but not close to him, do you see? Whereas to me she said no in the vegetable garden, no from the backseat of the car when I drove her to the marina, no when we were sanding her boat, no when I was washing the windows; so that I almost came to believe that not finding the right people to tell things to didn't matter after all." Becca listened. "My older brother had me," she said. Daley felt odd. "There must be oil out there," she said.

Yes, they saw it one morning at five-thirty alight. A slick behind a barge, it didn't spread, it was gone before a fireboat could come, but none came.

What would relative silence have been like, walking?

"Glad you got stood up."

"Don't get any ideas," she said.

"A pretty long walk with someone. Little decisions what to do."

"That's it," she said.

A seaport-damp night, the breeze coming up, a November dog on its way to the pier, a winter dog alone. All her lurking twenty-year-old circumstances to be kept in their place, heady and predictable. *Her* business. Her *case*. And a little extortionate when he sized up his own mere stalking sentiment. Covert playgoer who had dumped his date, his friend, for this.

Something of an experience.

Insofar as it went beyond representing in law a possibly bad-news young woman (which he'd resolved not to do) or protecting her from what was represented by the blow she had taken to her face—this Canadian chickadee, this goldfinch fond of eating thistles who said now, at it must have been midnight, "We're off again." You come upon things just as you're departing, it came to Daley; yet what if you are departing *with* someone? But this was how, long after the hour she had said, they went home to Daley's house to the basement kitchen to eat.

# 17

YOU WOULDN'T HEAR FOR MONTHS—IT WAS NEW YORK—FOR YEARS it seemed, a year and a day; and then would come a call: she needed him, it was Lotta, a client like other clients. Her calls no different from other alarms going off in the office, legal emergencies. She wasn't so unusual, she wasn't important (*she* might say).

This was a woman with her own jewelry business. Four times a year she flew to Mexico where artisans custom-rendered for her into silver and semiprecious (if that) stones American Indian motifs she had appropriated for them to use. Plateau villagers glad of the work. With an instinct of memory. It had a droll side. Possibly they recognized the raven, the white dog, this long-tongued frog, kachina Mudman, gods. Politely their work did not resist whatever marginal culture questions lurked in Lotta's input. In her turn, she sold the stuff all over the United States, these Zuni, Hopi, Navajo, Tlingit, Handsome Lake Iroquois objects made in Mexico. One or two found their way into the Wednesday-afternoon Tuba City auctions and one was authenticated by a great pawnshop in Gallup and when it became dead pawn fetched a much higher price even though discounted.

Lotta had a collection of her own that was not for sale. You assumed its value yet you assumed nothing about what her apartment housed. Her current apartment in this midtown tower (though she was on the third floor) Daley had never seen. He was her lawyer. You knew it was full of choice things, yet it might not be; it was (weirdly, considering) petless—she was away so much. She might not have had a single real idea, though she had views. ("What do you *mean* 'No one's right'?") Women need a vocation to provide a roof over their head. Appropriation, like recycling, may prove as creative as Leonardo or Leonard Bernstein anyday.

Lotta's timetables tended to get updated and itemized for you. The subject got around to her. When you hire a lawyer, *you* tell *him*. There was a saddle horse she took in trade for four of her signature Zuni brooches (made in Mexico); she boarded him cheaply in Holmdel, New Jersey, where he could look up and smell the racetrack a few miles down the highway. A Pentecostal storefront you had to look hard for in its upper Manhattan block she attended once in a blue moon for the Jamaica-style singing. She was sitting at the back in a white-and-flower-painted bench when Daley of all people joined her one Sunday night just as a little cowbell clinked several times and she pointed from it, wherever it was, to him, standing up as he sat down, prayer—no problem, prayers. That night went on and on, listening to "Wade in the wa-a-tuh" and then joining in (though she feared water he learned later, the way a parachutist Daley had known hated heights) she slipped her arm through his and looked up at what he had become interested in, this lawyer she hardly knew, the bright blue-and-green-and-orange-painted beams crossing the whitewashed ceiling.

She was spending her adult life based in Manhattan sort of. But resisting it; traveling; an unmarried person, in fact divorced, more political than she quite knew, visiting India, Indonesia, the Middle East—quick trips, never came back the way she went—wherever she was, early to bed; early-morning walks all over the globe. Her father a Bar Harbor Presbyterian, member of the Sessions, good with all classes of people. Her faith was in no "real" god: more many than one: though nature interested her: she could argue as she did the night Daley took her for a Cuban meal after the service, that her atheism required more faith than all these myths. Her hopes might have been deep-down bland. A global politics developing in her business mind. Her Anglo voice on the board of the Barrio Museum. Something for everybody. More men than women friends. Had really grown up outside Syracuse, but had began in Maine where her father would live and die, the Bangor registered representative for a New York brokerage house. Lotta was attached to him, a naturalist and superb photographer, though she told the unvarnished truth about him.

It was other people's lives she talked about on the phone. Lotta's clients shading into friends. Not only clients with second houses, who bought from her. A mixed couple sanding a table outside, fitting legs to it, having a fight while carrying on independent conversations with Lotta, the guest standing around under a tree, a failing Berkshire elm, with her coffee mug. Daley tried to put his finger on it.

A dentist and her singer husband butchering an old ewe near Watch Hill, Rhode Island, bending its uncertain head back by the chin to smother the browsing mouth and tight, soft little nose to make it quicker for this old friend, the throat gushing after a second on one side. A whole family absorbed in prying out of a Vermont hillside stones for a new hearth. It was her clients' anecdotes, perhaps, that she complained *led* nowhere, what was the point of these stories? Was it their lives: even when she visited clients in the country, they had so little to report, to weigh . . . hard to give them feedback was her word for it. She complained bitterly of people who had seen a coyote in Cambridge (New York) with a totally denuded tail eating fallen apples, and that was the *story?*—or a New Mexico magpie standing on a ewe's back snapping maggots out of its hide then suddenly flapping across nightmarishly white and black to stab its bill into the sweet eye of a lamb standing a few feet off. So what? Maybe if she'd been a landowner but. Was this bird-watching? The point would save her, its absence destroy her.

Mexico? Daley's wife Della knew the type, dresses in bright colors, finds fault with—"Americans." Della had absorbed what little Daley had to say about his client. Della was uncanny. "Out all the time?" she guessed; "a ton of things to talk about—Taipei, you said? You were there, weren't you?—always with people, you might think." But it was Lotta's underlying . . .

"She a complainer?" Della said, her head on his shoulder, it was the night of the earthquake.

"Not exactly." There was an exception, Daley went on: a woman looking off at Mount Cardigan, remarkable woman (a soft 'Yay' from Della), her husband hunting mushrooms, who made a thing of it pouncing on them in the woods, a writer, probing the ground with dinosaur eyes, his mushroom "exper*tise*" a party-game catechism almost an affront to you, suspicious; the scribe, Lotta called him. "A country essayist—in fact, published—or a novelist, maybe, he left you with the facts, that was it." Someone Lotta had cultivated. Though when she cleared her mind, it was the wife who mattered. Lotta lacked not personality or goodness, or loyalty or force, but a degree of charm. Daley tried to put his finger on it. She was at long intervals in him a dormant intelligence like an equal.

Another of the world's rare *un*shallow people Lotta had met on a plane. (Give her a stranger any day.) A story she had drawn Daley into—her lawyer. A woman befriended on the plane to Baghdad—Chinese, Taiwanese—the woman had spoken first, you felt she might give you a gift. The niece of Lotta's "family doctor" had written a thesis on three child prostitutes in Taipei now married to American GIs, she knew a good deal about it, and by the time they'd talked the flight away, it turned out the woman knew many people Lotta knew in New York. A friendship. Iraq Air. They were breakfasting, however, the second morning at the hotel when the unthinkable occurred. The two of them booked into the suburban Baghdad hotel a dozen miles from the airport enjoying a second cup of coffee when, discovering that everyone had left the dining room apparently for a conference room, they were visited by two men in short-sleeved shirts arriving at their table. Her new friend almost knew them, this woman with a Taiwan passport all but graciously agreeing to accompany them. That was it: gone; detained. It was not the business of the U.S. authorities. At the breakfast table she never questioned the right of these clowns to take her away but went graciously. Extradited to China, apparently. Lotta on a business trip, there was nothing she could do, she was there to visit a famous craftsperson and his wife in virtual house arrest on the border to the northeast in the village of a playwright who had written three hundred plays for anyone to do: so Lotta's new friend who had seen so much and was so attentive had disappeared, passport and all. Yet not quite all, for she had opened Lotta's bag the night before and slipped into it for safekeeping against thievery two packages so tightly wrapped and string-bound you could see and feel the forms within.

Lotta wrote it down years later. Fairly surprising, though not. Action, reaction, eye for an eye.

One anger, one thought, led to another and another, what happened, what she wrote down, one to one. Her early years committed to paper before you knew it, printed out. With the aid of that client, that prizewinning New England writer who said she was a learner though he was not quoted. Nowhere did Daley in his quick read-through find the suit against Connecticut, this person who had phoned him years before in the middle of the night to ask if he had heard the news. To report damage to her collection. Rare bric-a-brac, gods, Daley understood. When two pre-Columbian pieces had fallen off a shelf during an obscure earthquake (if that), Lotta had hoped to sue the source. The thought was a tad deeper than the quake. But at three in the morning?

Minutes after Daley hung up the second time, Lotta had phoned Hartford with surprising results. The tirade or lecture she received Daley retailed to his old Korean comrade Sook who had a good laugh and took it seriously. An operator perhaps overqualified and with a nasal, Asian tone who never named herself and declined to pass Lotta along to a higher authority seemed to berate her with news of Tokyo, 143,000 lives lost in the '23 quake and a quake now in the right spot would cripple the world economy. L.A., Taipei, Manila, Tehran, New York. If it's a quake you want, I mean, come on, miss, New York is due. Two M5s from about the same spot in Rockaway 1737 and 1884, and dozens of little 1s and 2s and 3s the last twenty-five years along the Westchester-Connecticut-Long Island belt, the time is soon. The 1886 Charleston quake cracked walls in Harlem, and who says you're due for a 5? But a 5 in L.A. where you're on the edge of a plate, two of them rubbing together generating volcano-level heat that damps out your quake, that's not a 5 in New York where your *intra*plate waves travel like a 6 or a 7, you can forget the Met, MOMA, Lincoln Center, you've got a regular grid of faults, you've got bricks in the streets. Manhattan's on bedrock but what about the fill they pumped in to build the waterfront? That's soft; in a quake it liquefies. Know anybody who lives in Battery Park, that's a whole city ready to dissolve, so if you're going to sue, sue Africa for bumping into North America four hundred million years ago, swallowing the ocean between, and leaving a suture that runs under the mayor's house clear to South Carolina. Swing by the Palisades, the sandstone you find there is the same as Central Africa and we have the same east–west rifts that produce M7s and 7.5s there. But without those old plates moving, you get no heat release: no heat no life, no life no death. So thanks for blowing the whistle, your little 0.5 out of Windsor where they didn't even feel it it's nothing next to the big one from Newark next time . . .

Lotta could never decide after she was disconnected if this had been a recording. If so it was spontaneous and spoken to her.

Who *was* Lotta? An American question, easy to ask. Lotta's drive, her travel time, her being there in your way, perhaps a single woman's routines, no more, but a little eccentricity somewhere, gristle (?) and a persistence and belief that tracked that operator for weeks with inquiries and then random calls hoping to hear that voice again, irritated and informed and then with an odd complimentary loop at the end.

Della had an impression of her husband's client. A woman who made a living. Who turned out marketable material. The making of a living authenticates the work itself, a way of "being in the world." Sitting on the bed touching, he and Della could think they knew something together, the way you do sometimes, or think you do on parting. Leaning against him lightly, Della accepted Lotta, a woman in business; though she asked of you unknowingly a sense of humor. That earthquake phone call now. Why? Something you haven't told me, my dear? A mystery to him at that moment when Ruley Duymens must have been rising from his bed in the guest room and entering the hall barefoot.

Yet weeks previous a curious exchange had occurred between Lotta and Daley. The story of the mugging. A summer cloudburst in mid-Manhattan, a downpour at Fifth Avenue and Forty-ninth Street, you might think the rain recondensed into floods of humidity as it hit the street. She was hatless in some kind of bright elaborate woven poncho, and he stopped when he saw her, a survivor, her hair down her forehead, the weather wet upon her shoulders, that woven purple bag of hers darkly sodden. "I wouldn't own an umbrella," she burst out, "they take up one hand, two hands, they break, they're in the way . . . *you* know," she said. Daley had just run into her—odd words, considering. It was an impulse like propositioning an old acquaintance, someone you've known and liked for years when you meet by chance on the subway or in the afternoon street. But instead telling this awful city story that we would never know all of, how he had survived recently a mugging at dawn. So unlike him to tell anyone a thing like this. The reason would come to him, he said charmingly. They were under the Atlas statue, would he tell her standing out in the Rockefeller Center rain?—such a moment typically a bit happy or false, a New York quickie, entertaining a woman perhaps impress her with the danger, the bizarre outcome, be blinded, soothed, no more than that. Well, it wasn't funny, she herself made the point. He would tell her the umbrella part he had spared his wife.

Two buses rolled past down the avenue. Lotta had to see the arm. Daley pushed open a heavy old glass door—she wasn't even a friend, was she? Two messengers watched Daley slip out of his raincoat sleeve, just the left, and his jacket sleeve, and Lotta put down her sodden bag and rolled up his shirtsleeve to get a load of the ugly welt still healing, a boiled and silky scar looking at you. An elevator man and a woman in nurse's white came over to see what would happen.

Did Lotta hear him? She listened with her hand, her fingers, on the wound. His abbreviated tale of the riverfront at quarter to six in the morning might have been coming from his arm. Daley was putting in his three and a half miles. Out in front of him fifty, seventy-five yards down drifted these two all-nighters, this couple, they were a couple not badly dressed at all, and he went a little wide, and he came up with them not comprehending even now that they had drifted a pace or two farther to be in his way, not derelicts at all but.

Yes, said his listener, four fingers resting on Exhibit A; she knew.

So that Daley had found himself running in place when the woman asked for money. Not badly dressed, not derelicts.

Yes.

He could have outrun them any day, dodged them, run inside between bench and guardrail. "What? What are you saying?" said Lotta—Not that it was unreal until—she was glad of his attention but what did it mean? (She dabs at the trickle of makeup that had been crossing her cheekbone standing under the Atlas statue and now, inside, it may be tears on her listening, shrewd face, she's weighed down by standing still in her red-and-purple wool poncho, thick-woven sopping wet). Why had he—?—Wait, Lotta—waylaid her? she joked—Not even surprising they had knives —"Wait a second—" —can you imagine this white-collar couple with knives out both of them?—they'd been having a fight—Lotta had to laugh—Wait, Lotta, just a fight . . . the river surging past big as a wake and on the bench an umbrella, right?

"What do you mean, 'right'?"

Busted brolly, one strut pointing toward New Jersey, no trifling Taiwan collapsible. A real umbrella. Daley had reached for the dark-varnished crook handle feeling the man make contact with his arm and Daley had swung the wrecked structure flapping half opening in the air, he thought that was what he had done.

Well, you see, it upset the man, it was the umbrella that did it— thin guy, with a bad face like a pie cutter, quick. Daley was planted on his heels now, and he'd been cut he discovered, his two assailants looking at him, the man shaken, wanting the umbrella. For them the end of a perfect evening; for Daley . . . "For me the beginning of an interesting day." Lotta stroked the wound, frowning, waiting. "Didn't occur to me that I'd been cut for a second."

It was a little serious now, but Daley was close to home with a fresh white handkerchief folded in the hip pocket he had not reached for when the woman had spoken. And there was another runner south toward Chambers Street turning back this way, a friend. Daley held his arm up and with the other swiped the umbrella at the woman and struck her wristwatch off but she knew what she was doing, she found his same forearm but didn't evade his hand joined by his other hand now on her surprisingly resistant neck as the man, taking up the umbrella, caught Daley's running shoe in the temple, toe on; and should have died (which really would have made his day) but Daley tugged the umbrella away and flung it over the rail into the river before realizing that the knife lay on the pavement. Lotta resisted the whole thing.

It wasn't money, she said. It was serious, two slices in the same place, had Daley gone straight to the hospital?

Stopped home first. The umbrella . . . Daley shook his head, rolling down his shirtsleeve.

"Why did you risk stopping? Is it a joke I'm not getting about the umbrella? I think he would have killed for the umbrella. That's unbelievable."

So that when, not three months later and as if nothing had ever happened, Daley heard himself speculating as to the value of figurines hundreds of years old, jade, clay, one badly nicked, one terminally cracked, or you would say busted—it was his own mugging story he remembered. A blurred head and potent little torso once raised upon a four-legged pot, this anchorage now separated from its centaur. A god, given to her, Daley seemed to remember. The figure in pieces. (Could nothing be done?)

More, Lotta's emotion, the surprise emptiness where did it come from? Forget the calls, the quake, and Seattle and Australia at 3 A.M. The client had shown herself to Daley. He had tried to tell his wife. That was it, too, that he had tried, briefly; or hadn't.

Over the phone a spirit tonight—damaged (such as it was); "if only a collector's." Della cocked her eyes at this. His client "seeking . . . proof," he said.

"Proof of?"

"My presence," Daley shrugged. He couldn't say it almost. But Della's shoulder against his said she liked it. Or she needed sleep. She worked so hard, switching from one career to another, in both places still.

Yes, all Lotta had hoped for on the late-night telephone was his presence. A need almost a gift, if there'd been anyone in the world to say this unclear thing to, any friend he could think of (for friends mostly met your confusions with their own, which was mostly what friendship was). A damaged person might understand, but at what cost, it came to him; some fool from the war, fusing your muddle with some congruence of theirs; or a thinker, from what you heard about thinkers, much fussier yet entertaining any damn question. Della's lack of reaction was taken for subtlety or anguish or delight she could not express. It was how they had gotten together, that he was not to speak of certain things yet had a gift. Della didn't mind at all Lotta needing Daley during earthquake night and sympathized with her. Sitting on the bed hanging out, he and his wife, like this, which was nice, it was after three in the morning. (Proof of Daley's *presence* was what Lotta wished for on the phone—not even his body, or bodily presence, though Lotta probably liked him.) A client's wish like a gift complete as a history, as the clay torso itself. A vessel damaged, belonging to her home, a friend, he had understood. A blow to Lotta. "She was pretty attached to them," Della said.

"But she wants to bring an *action*."

"Ah."

"Against Connecticut."

"Ah." Della didn't smile. Where the quake had originated according to the radio; Lotta wouldn't let it go. (She had no TV.) Sue the builders, what they're throwing up lately? What goes up must come down, the first law of development (but not right here, one of the parallel laws of response).

A demand on Daley, a gift if you could only say the right thing. "Just as well," Della murmured, he heard her and then something in the street—or the hall. "Each to his own."

"If they even were," his wife had said.

He recalled the lady from Taipei, a city sweet to a soldier, always all business. "Wonder what she'll do with them," Daley said, the clay torso broken, you could say she was sore as hell about it, a shame. Her *things*, that she would never sell (maybe) . . . Daley and his wife spoke softly that night (though they always spoke softly in the bedroom), between the two of them knowingly, but what did they know, discussing the earthquake? The summons from his brother—a junket to southeast Australia; repairing the old sash frames (their next-door neighbor had someone good); recurring to Lotta (the troubles of such a single person honestly fascinating to a point), the ancient objects she had reported damaged if not destroyed. A timer waiting for life to go off, though she had a life already if the present is not quite enough.

Next day nothing in the papers; a month later, and this was '81 or '82, an item out of Colorado—hardly the first Connecticut Valley temblor on record: for Daley had become interested around that time partly because his brother was not; Daley an occasional weekend gardener who had been in fact consulted by a malpractice acquaintance on the issue of the immune system for his mere common sense— "prudence aforethought," Daley put it. Yet a certain unpredictability of seismic events, even their tie-ins with midspace orbitals had touched his interest, whatever.

This client Lotta making a noise about any damn thing that troubled her.

By now he and Della were lying down across the bed, which they did. Della had fallen in with this old coworker on her river walk (and run) tonight, a dance "tough," a black genius, his new company, and she was speaking of him.

It was only now, the discussion's soft vessel turning inside out into a breathing space of peace and promise, that Della's houseguest appeared in the doorway.

Ruley couldn't have materialized more unwanted yet more domestically. What kind of man protests, "*I* know, *I* know" on the threshold of your New York bedroom at quarter to four in the morning in foreign-looking sweatpants? Door open, to be sure; bedside light on. "Ruley!" said Della. Daley sat up like a gym person exercising.

A fool disarming you. Used to being liked. "Strange," he said, sinking cross-legged onto the bedroom carpet, half-p.j.'d banker on an overnight confessing he "slept with one eye asquint"; telling Daley, "*Go.* Definitely go," for he'd been listening. But Daley had been there and had no business going to Australia at the moment with three cases on calendar he'd be coming back to, a wife making an unsettling career move, and an absorbing L.A. pianist based in Amsterdam swinging in with his trio pushing the new release *Listen, South Africa*. The same bullshit smell in the European visitor's word *strange* (you began to hear people saying it around this time) or was it how he said it?

Ruley, remembering the earthquake news, jumped up now to look out the window—as if there might really have been one (though there really had). As if Daley hadn't lived here for years. How these people know the city, these foreigners with bone structure, half-naked banker here with you for the night, not at all hairy, but lean like a type you had seen somewhere, alert, not much of a handshake, not especially built, but looking about, aggressive, unique. "This *place*." A gesture of awe. "Is it yours? or yours?" the question opens the whole house, shrinks it to the room like some answer. Your visitor a fool, embarrassing, *trying* things on you, is back in his cross-legged spot on the rug between bed and doorway, sparkling, if you will. Looking at you, asking if you had a handgun, getting only a historical, generic answer. A banker? A slippery Dutchman.

At four in the morning they had included him. What else could they do? Tell him to go back to bed. An acquaintance of Della, a money friend like someone on the board who could help the money, banker, person on a stopover. He was new to Daley.

It was late and Daley was determined to get in his early run. What kind of talk was this? "You think she's precious, right?" Houseguest or not, messenger, walking you through whatever.

Ruley would talk about you. (The accent unusual; rounder, less pinched than Swiss English; like a Dutch jazz player Daley had known. Ruley had the accent down; and *was* Dutch. New Jersey though on his mother's side it turned out.) "Precious?" *Precious* was what Daley's mother called children; also women friends—over the phone.

A talker, this Ruley, no joke somehow. (Anyone who talked that much . . . yet he was not a liar about *fact*, as it turned out.) He had climbed the Vancouver antenna pylon—the very one brother Wolf with his suspect knee had contemplated and thought better of. Ruley had been there. Think of the risk. Daley had seen it for himself, returning from business in California and visiting his nieces in Seattle; because Wolf had mentioned it. And you admired British Columbia for the forest cover. It sealed things in down there, particularly from a helicopter observing, slipping sideways, bending homeward. A history of frontier travelers. The exceedingly long lakes that provide backwaters for great river dams and some suspicion that you were a North American first.

A week with RD, as Della once called him on the phone, and she could believe in an Austro-Israeli bank grant to the dance company ("the company") and in the same careless breath fergidabodit. For she was leaving the company. In principle had left. Daley stepped off the plane at J.F.K. eight, nine days later and counting; phoned home on impulse, his bag leaning against his leg, and Ruley picked up: the voice always belonging; serving you right.

Though Ruley was packed and outa there in less time than it took Daley's cab to get home. Smart. The cab pulled over, and Daley stepped out onto the curb not knowing anything and hardly hearing the trunk swing up, looking at his watch to see how long since his call. He remembered afterward being conscious of the brownstone steps, the facings on certain of the risers cracked, split. Good brownstone from the Connecticut River once upon a time, not the Hackensack. Soft, beautiful, subject to erosion. Chiseled here you might think by a mason who had left off work for a job across town (coincidentally the very thing another unexpected guest told Daley years later). Careful who you have under your roof.

Two new wall outlets in Della's workroom RD-installed. A box for an overhead track Daley was happy to purchase. Another change went unnoticed for months. One of two lengths of BX cable in the basement rerun through a pipe. Duymens about as unlicensed an electrician as a pioneer could want.

Where was Ruley to begin with? He wasn't like bankers Daley knew. Another animal. In the hunt, definitely. A prowler, not quite silent about it; swift yet not in any hurry, a detour impending (never mapped), personal financial planner, soft, *aquatic* (!) unmistakably or once upon a time. Part partyer, or just un-grown-*up*, though adolescents didn't do *this*. A con*temp*orary banker (with "products"), where operating principles precede numbers. If you ever get to the numbers in this perpetual city detoured by talk, by styles, by Ruley, the news, tour of duty, sex, spec. It could be his skin, honestly, a matte or faint dark wash. This just before, historically, a noticeable invasion of California-trained north India analysts hit the New York financial markets—Ruley not that dark skinned at all. Was it money? His bank had loans out for irrigation grids to the Saudis, late 1970s; similar business in southeastern Australia, eyeing the orange desert. Though the deal was: the new covered stadiums.

Della had become preoccupied with the balance sheet of "the company." Della consented to make another dance. A springtime "Detour" not to be confused with a more famous number of the same name, it was pointed out to Daley. This roughly when Ruley Duymens stopping off on a trip to L.A. had first seen her work. A few weeks later he had a matching-funds (and more) proposition. Government money drying up even without a war to go to. An associate development loan banker, he said he was hopeless with figures. Look out what people apologize for. Investing all the time, but in what?

Possibly a thief. Above crunching numbers. In some larger capital sense, an interesting thief, the package wrapped with a measure of entitlement, was it sexual?—mostly talk that you heard. He'd seen Della dance, he had come back in August with "something more concrete," he was in New York/New Jersey in September about a casino.

In November he crashed on the Daleys. They were friends. Della said he knew about dancers.

Later still he belittled Della's "not-for-profit" agency he called it, this interim man: She needed this business for what? Not the money. She had her "housbond." She did an impression of him Daley couldn't have imagined her doing, the in-and-out, slightly rich Dutch (apparently) accent. Was she not an artist or something? Her joints functioning, her hips still hers. Didn't she still make dances? His frankness you would feel the curve of more than believe. It was abuse, light and magnetic, irritating how he discussed you in your presence, it was like bluntness but slippery. And whose hips *would* they be?

He made Della do things—including get hysterical. Laughing, that is. Quite hysterically (for her) once when she came home to her husband, laughed and laughed—unlike her. Was it that she couldn't meet Ruley's challenge, some European standard? He gave her a string of things to take up. Advising her like a woman friend. Upsetting her just when she was starting this business. Daley wasn't bothered, just a trifle bemused. He had always loved her, and the way she looked. He respected how she saw him and he was sold on "the two of them." It worked. He kept his misgivings to himself. He admired her. She wasn't silly. She was still in terrific shape. She wasn't unbusinesslike; she had some office space and an assistant and had conquered the phone. Bought two IBM Selectric IIIs. Referrals came in. Daley looked on.

He and Ruley had run into each other the next day after Daley got back—from Australia, or, rather, Seattle. They were waiting for the light at a midtown corner, noon, what a coincidence (like truth). It was him. "I came and went like a thief in the night," he greeted Daley, neither of them surprised.

He had stayed a *week*, Daley replied agreeably. What a week, Ruley said. Nine days, I believe, said Daley. Ruley wore a jumpsuit suitable for an upscale gas station or dangerous job, some specialist function, come to your home; a vice—police-blue, slick, weather-repellent material, light. A weekend parachutist, his hands on the bar, about to go; not out of place here across the intersection from Carnegie Hall, he belonged, he came and went, it was the Dutch side of him, he didn't need to buy or rent in Manhattan. Working on a partnership to build cliffs people would pay to climb in the early 1980s right here in the city, it was confidential. Also, a chain of jai alai on the model of that Connecticut fronton that would be struggling someday soon.

"Well you were right to urge me to go," Daley said. "I'll give you that. I won't take that away from you. But I'm stacked solid this week."

"You were going, your *brother* wanted you along."

"Well, he gets himself into things."

"They want his *input*," said Ruley for some reason.

"That's right," Daley said.

"Didn't *you*?" Ruley said.

"That's right." Daley got "input," it was some kind of early-'80s talk he'd heard around. Out there they'd been rethinking a dam, the masonry and the angle, but they had a situation. The truth was they were farther along than they'd said. Wolf never prepared, so he hadn't known till he got to the front line.

"They'll hate him," said Ruley, he talked too easily, his quickness was the shadow of nothing at stake. "Glad it worked out," he said.

Why did you talk to this guy?

"We were out in the country in a company bar," Daley began—

"Wish I had a brother."

"Well he gets himself into things."

"He's your brother. It comes back to you."

Traffic cramming the broad midtown street with starts and stops, we're trying to get somewhere on a day between Thanksgiving and Christmas. Chatting Australia, telling this "flying Dutchman" they called him in Della's company (not totally Dutch, of course) little things not the whole story. (*It comes back to you*—what did that mean?) A trick turkey, a blond gas station girl showing you how to listen, looking ahead to nothing—"see you in a few years." A thing or two waiting when Daley came home from Sydney, that was all. Nothing.

Ah. (Ah? What did Ruley mean?)

Daley gave him an idea of what was happening this week. The right to fire a keeper at the zoo, where hiring practices and vacancies information were already an issue. A paint contractor suing a Canadian roofing concern for serious money. A contractor in Jersey still trying to get money out of an insurer for a waste construction job in Ypsilanti,

Michigan, that two young college entrepreneurs had aborted. Not to mention the jewelry woman (and Daley almost did not), the earthquake-from-Connecticut client. "But that wasn't for real," Ruley's accent European, controlling, perhaps stupid: "Can't sue a fault line, can't sue vibrations, can't sue magma; you just don't sue a shelf—sue a roofer but not a roof," Daley said, and Ruley, "Though there's a pot of money in Connecticut per se and if I said there wasn't, I'd be lying." Daley knew Connecticut pretty well, he wondered what was made up, the jai alai and so forth. Surely Duymens didn't want to be friends. He doubted that Daley could carry through the zoo case, it sounded like city business, a rights lawyer what they needed. (He was correct of course, though the employee knew Daley from the army years ago and wanted him whatever the jurisdiction.) What was this partnership in the very early 1980s to produce cliffs people would someday pay to climb? Also a gambling casino in Camden, not to be believed though truly of the tribal lineage of the Middle Atlantic Lenape if it came to it. Height precipitated thoughts of the experimental new navy plane that could behave like a chopper: Daley had had a thought about the rotor and phoned it on to one of the designers he knew in Seattle. Why mention such a thing to Ruley, who would go you one better or remember it. He seemed to know of the transport helicopters it would replace: Sea Knight, Sea Stallion.

Daley did not as a rule talk about his clients or his brother's and was glad he hadn't told Ruley about New South Wales, Wolf's dam, the bar out by the river, the knife, the ruined wrist. Experience, however, lured Daley to weigh this brainstorm of Ruley's and an Italian-Swiss engineer's to produce thirty-three-foot molded-plastic cliffs to haul yourself up toe after toe. The crotch and pulley harness tackle to go with it. The employee training package.

All obvious if not provable, an air of lying about what would be. And Daley had to be somewhere, had to run. Run? said Ruley, this friend of Daley's dear wife's who took you up like somebody trying to understand, yet provokingly, not really honestly, a little hired, instrumental. "A deposition," Daley said.

"Deposition?"

"Only hope the client sticks to the questions," Daley said to this man you could almost not get away from.

"*Only hope?*" said Ruley.

He wondered if the zookeeper weren't a federal case. A shrug is the reply to that one. What was Ruley getting at? Daley could have destroyed him, this dance fancier seed-moneying fantasy cliffs who didn't look as if he could scale a basic training wall. Slippery more than muscular. Daley could have swept him away. Where to? Trashy, in those days before recycling nights.

Ruley and height, though. The Vancouver pylon. What pretext to extricate himself from a mere conversation that had become awkward with another consultant on the scene and climb a 274-foot ladder. Ruley had claimed not to believe it was a new semi-conductor-type rectifier controlling one-way current flow at the top. Excusing himself he went right up that narrow, white-painted steel ladder. Where *was* this coward we heard about if he was to be believed?—so far up that from the ground the ladder had a scale-model distance, the receding climber exposed all the more by height which turned distance into the closeness of effort, folly, smashed legs, spine, shoulder, head, heart, all apparently to inspect the gadget partly governing the signal's output gain.

It was Helen, Daley's new sort of business friend in '82 who never met Ruley, who said Ruley Duymens had always had an experience like yours. In those days she was a good friend, she would mostly listen to Daley. She had a spare ticket for a five o'clock screening, a black-tie museum opening, a play, a science show in Washington.

Experience to top yours, Daley added.

Where did Ruley get all the time to ferry over to Staten Island and run for miles and miles? Training he had picked up from a world-class athlete, an Arab no less. Back and forth along the sands of the gray Richmond beaches and down steep, half-deserted streets of two-story homes, Hispanic families not doing well, not *too* poor. Daley for his part put in his three-plus miles along the river, no matter what.

"Puts you in touch with—" Ruley laughed. "—with—" Daley continued.

"With nothing!" Ruley exploded, this tiresome competitor (though what was the competition) in a jumpsuit at Seventh and Fifty-seventh holding Daley up; a thief, but of what? Della's ambition to leave engrossing work in favor of socially useful.

Why did Daley have to broach to Ruley the—recon*struct* the—
somewhat aborted mugging then? Did Ruley know this from Della?
Unlikely, considering. An unexpected addition to Daley's morning run:
the couple, the injury, the light rain that early morning abating, the rob-
bery gone by the boards, not to mention that Daley had had nothing for
the couple to rob him of but his running shoes, his keys, not even fifty
cents, his handkerchief, his life you assumed they were no more interested in than most people are, but—and feeling clear and alone the way
the early day strips you bare, buoyed by air. You feel—"Absolutely"—
river right next to you, big swells, furrowed deep like racetrack earth
close-up, and—"Exactly"—English maybe, German, Swedish—a
client of Daley's who really knew said the Dutch make a splendid
umbrella, large and manual, that will last you a lifetime, good in wind.
A Long Island currency trader, an odd wattle below his chin. Was it *his*
umbrella? Inwardly concentrated or lost, even a low-level politician
surprised behind closed doors, arbitrage analyst occurred to you.

What was it?

Well, Daley thought what this experience showed if anything was
someone who doesn't know you wants to cut you, you might never
know why. Possibly kill you for the moment.

Only an event you associate with prison, shut in with other mani-
acs with nothing to do, it doesn't prove much. Or orphaned in the
desert. Barroom man to man often a matter of words toeing the line
not to be crossed. A particular jungle, mined with waiting silence,
and no matter what your news or who you were or how much you'd
come to know about the body. But Death hanging around the bench
by the riverfront bike path not saying much but, quite personably, a
lender of last resort. Not exactly the umbrella, yet it lingered. Was it
the umbrella, that signal and odd dawn? His wife dreaming under the
covers at six in the morning after a late night when a potential backer
had introduced himself to the company. The wound, his old buddy
running back up the bike path, the towel he'd contributed. But the
umbrella. Broken but turned into a homely weapon. Whose was it?
Momentarily withheld from Daley's telling, from Ruley, it seemed
personal, dumb, only itself. Well, he had traveled the dawn by the
back door of impromptu weapons research recycling this gear that,

broken or brand new, his client Lotta wouldn't be caught dead carrying in a downpour; he described again how he had knocked that slut arb's wristwatch off—"Arb, eh?"—"Brokers, a guess," said Daley—yet precisely here Ruley with significant changes of his own, threw almost the very thing back at you presently (but after you'd told *him* after all!), the umbrella restructured from hand-to-hand to huge, global, not to mention prophetic as we expect of business. Think, though, of this random couple—suddenly armed with six-inch blades sniffing him out in the damp, brisk, white-collar early morning. "It wasn't you they were waiting for," Ruley said. Daley said, "You know more than I." That kind of knowing talk.

The light at the corner across from Carnegie Hall had changed several times while Daley had had this exchange with Ruley Duymens. "They'd been having a fight, or they were looking for one, I guess."

"Nothing you couldn't handle," said Ruley just like that.

Oh, a friend had been nearby.

"What luck."

No, it had been Daley's running friend, Sook.

What kind of name was that?

"Korean. I know Sook," Daley said.

Ruley might have felt his contempt. "How you go through your *life* . . . not knowing what you would do . . ." Ruley tried to be something to Daley—"it's a gift when it comes to you." Daley stepped down off the curb, he would not gainsay Duymens, but, "Plenty a knife-fight stories out there. You answer an attack, you feel free afterward."

Ruley picked up the contempt. "You defended yourself. You disarmed them."

"Not me. I picked up a busted umbrella where they'd been sitting."

"Better a busted one if you don't need it over your head."

"Sook helped."

"Well of course he did."

"Just someone I know a long time, a lawyer and a broker in there somewhere now too, two hats under the same . . . and a damn good one, comrade in arms."

"I'll give him a call."

"Not necessary," said Daley.

"They were trying to cut you."

"I might have bled, I did bleed, do you understand?"

"You did."

"I did."

"You suffered serious—"

"A gash."

"A deep gash." Ruley was smiling and grinning like a fool.

Nothing got to Daley, not this man anyway. "Yes, a deep gash that somehow didn't cut the ulnar, though I recall not one but two hits."

"I get it," said Ruley: "You're approaching them on your morning run, and the easiest thing would be to run through them but you you fool—you could have avoided the whole thing. But the umbrella now, there's a structure," Ruley seemed to take thought. "That must have struck you."

A momentary stirring under foot, another river down there deep in the stony earth below the street, deep below the Hudson and parallel (like a theory), expanding, overflowing banks that simultaneously stretched and widened, rolling, a dragon having a minor nightmare at six in the morning underfoot, a temblor you would swear way below you when you had been expecting some weather overhead. Another floor down there, or from another viewpoint a roof.

Daley could not believe the direction it was taking, he looked at his watch. It wouldn't go away, this guy. "Just what I was telling Della last week," the lithe and ready man standing now a little too close to Daley was describing a tent, a very large tent, largest on earth. They were putting it up. Ruley looked up and there was a guy perched in the vast roof-in-progress taut or billowing with massive waves and skies of fabric winching and reefing this material with the skill of a foretopman, but in Saudi Arabia strangely at not a third of the pay riggers command. "Of course, he was a world-class diver, three-meter only, not platform, which was unusual. He had an art, which made all the difference to his work. I might never have looked up, I might never have spoken to him. Supremely technical this tent-making." A springboard diver. At Jedda, near Mecca. An interest they had in common. This was a champion, though.

Ruley described a roof made out of fabric, a huge fabric roof do

you believe it sheltering hundreds of thousands of people at an airport, a downright . . . what would once have been assumed to be an
American project, four hundred thousand Muslim pilgrims, and
Ruley had (as he'd explain) been in on the stretching of it from multiple points, and in fact later had a piece of it. He broke off, "I get it
the second cut sliced into the gash already there. There's your one
gash, two cuts, lucky you've got a bone left. But who were they?"—
Daley's attackers—"wait. You *served* with Sook. I get it."

"You get nothing," Daley had said. They both laughed.

Ruley was impressed. "Glad I skipped that trip."

"But you're Dutch."

"Not only. But I'm a mercenary."

At this Fifty-seventh street crossing a tall foreigner got out of the
backseat of a low black BMW very slowly moving, pushed like an
arthritic—which he was anything but—from inside the car so his big
hat tilted half off. You knew he was going to ask directions. Daley had
known three Dutch "mercenaries" he guessed you would call them in
the war, one a former policeman in the East Indies. Was it money he
was fighting for? "Della's right," Ruley said smiling.

Daley didn't like smilers. "She's always right."

"About you, I mean," the ripe, somewhere native accent itself
knowing things you wouldn't want to know. "Half right about you—
the right *idea*, if you know what I mean," said Ruley.

"She's my wife," Daley said—and then after an instant it was
gone, why he had married Della; "she's a great artist."

"If she's a great artiste, what's she giving it up for? And why would
you marry a great artiste? What did you need done?"

It was getting done. Daley could have swept Ruley away, a trashy
mouth who had lived in his home—*artiste* wasn't what a European
would say but an American. A jazzy mercenary out, though, not for
money. Out for what?

What the man brought was the thing. Which was what had
brought the man, in hindsight. Or foresight, as Daley reflected on the
folly of being hurt as if then with his fellow runner and comrade-in-
arms Sook to go on home to his sleeping wife instead of to
Emergency where he belonged.

Through some sleeping switch whereby the tension of plain old knitting-needle, bent, broken, and sharp umbrella ribs introduced to Daley the man whom Daley would not meet until a few months later, in your own bedroom just before Australia, and now right after it, happening to run into this Ruley Duymens person between Australia and Christmas on Fifty-seventh Street, this curious 19 (in a jumpsuit) 81 addition to your *life*—to Della? to the house? God, to you. Though a one-time thing, foreseeably. Though what was Ruley regaling Della with giant fabric roofs for? She had a fifty-year-old treadle sewing machine up there on the third floor, but it wasn't fabric, it was something else, not Islam or tent structure or travel. Daley tried to recall the name of Ruley Duymens's young tent maker in Jedda. The diver in which Olympics?

The drummer Sid Knox, persistent head cold, the connoisseur of good umbrellas Chilean, English, Italian, Swedish (actually suspect), West German, and on special order from Chittagong, responded sharply to Daley's points re rain damage in hotel rooms (which Sid did not wish to include in his breach action against the hotel in question) and about umbrella struts, one day years later sitting in the office. Well, these struts, or ribs, were powerless without the curves, curvature was everything. Sid argued that Daley was not thinking of the particular umbrella but of something else. Daley distinctly heard a phone call coming, but in advance of the ring—ringing you might think in the outer office first, and regretted that they were drifting away from the nonlegal though fascinating, if not secretly tragic, matter of Sid's original drumming. Okay, he agreed and disagreed with Sid Knox. He told him of a huge fabric roof he had heard of and ultimately visited. Four and a half million square feet of pale fabric, Daley was explaining, drawn taut as a drumskin yet unlike a drum on an endless curve across dozens of masts and cables. Not just any curve worked. Daley unfolded his white handkerchief. Well, a man Daley used to know had been in on the construction of this airport roof was what it was in Jedda. Was in with a member of the staff assembling it anyway. Saudi Arabia.

The drummer was at last feathering his nest on Daley's advice and that of Daley's friend Sook, once an IBM market analyst with a law degree now practicing on his own in the jungle again. (New York, that is.) Sid was in middling or failing (depending) health, thinner during the late 1980s with an antipathy to the phone that got worse with the new portables. But he had on display now for a few who knew a composite drumming that Daley had never quite heard before in Amsterdam, Paris, rhythm sections in Brussels, even New York, or in fact Sweden, where Sid in the 1970s had begun to make it up fielding it or centering it in several gut snares passed over, returned to, awash in silken thunder-song and dissolving back into what could only be called body that could retreat into virtual breath more rapidly than you would afterward have been able to clock. You could hear it on a Swedish label of that time. (One Dutch horn player favored Charlie Parker's improv security of turning away from the audience.) This key to keeping the most inquiring "breath" from leaking away had come to hand when he was playing with an expatriate Asian trombonist in Holland. Like intervals within already existing silence, it was just suddenly there. This storklike, opinionated lone body sitting in the office had lost a brother in a strange fall, a tragic death doubtless, just as his revolutionary tap-dancing troupe in Chicago was getting off the ground. Which might have made some brothers less ready to go to court but you knew had made Sid greedy to sue this not coincidentally quite dilapidated country hotel for cutting short a date, though Sid's irritating voice containing his intelligence like the whispering splashes across his snares multiplied his thoughts and rolled them out toward thunder and back toward silence as if you'd never hear that sound again, and you knew that for all the tight-snapped, brown silk umbrella and the excellent double-breasted dark suits of mysterious origin and the logic and concentration and politeness to women, he took care only of his appearance and would complain of anything rather than his own approaching death. Though how to measure that speed or acceleration, if that is even what it was.

He rearranged himself in his chair as the phone now did ring rudely. Daley had had his handkerchief out for a demonstration when the voice proved to be not the one he'd expected, and it fluttered to the floor establishing itself there not flat but as if something lay hidden under it; and the next thing Sid had uncrossed his grasshopper legs in their creased black pin-striped trousers and was raising himself out of his chair already absorbed with his next stop of the late afternoon. Though ill or because he was, his hearing had become uncanny, and now he heard several things at once, Daley knew. But what? The uncanny tap of his brother's famous-in-Chicago shoes? A dove on the parapet on a Monday afternoon. A voice as remote as Daley's ear could make it saying two words that must have crystallized Sid's decision to go.

It was Ruley Duymens who had once upon a time tacked three corners of a handkerchief Daley had supplied to a table and asked Daley to pull the fourth as taut as it would stretch, a whole 'nother dimension (drum-taut): the surface like a saddle; the tensions like how rigged stays stabilize a boat's mast: anyway the greater the curvature the stiffer your fabric roof against wind and snow. This came to Daley tacking back along a dark downtown street the following Wednesday speaking to his actress companion of cast-iron structure pioneered by James Bogardus over on Centre Street that he had not yet shown her. Yet Daley was keeping something in reserve or from himself. He even picked this up from her, as if she knew at her age what it was.

Witness the largest roof in the world. Ruley had a piece of it. It provided shade for 105 acres of desert to shelter hundreds of thousands of pilgrims deplaning at the Haj terminal. These roofs—a wave of the future. Look for a skyline of fabric. Imagine coated fiberglass strands impervious to stress and weather and relays of concussion threatening to give the tent a major, major comeback in America, they were saying. The picture lingered long after Ruley Duymens was gone: giant roofs. New desert terminals. Mall earth. Stadiums indoors, retractable revolutionary lids. Roofs, though, like suspension bridges: Daley took it up with his brother Wolf, who didn't see the connection—these roofs actually display the stresses. Years later, a decade and counting, the big balloon roofs of the new stadiums had become quite flat. Easier for the architects. Curvature clung to Daley's puzzlement, his insight. Stretch and Strong, Helen's health club had named one of the daily classes. It had begun (come to think of it) almost with this thief in the night a dozen years ago, Ruley, but not quite. The saddle curves, the tensile strength of those vast roofs.

*Simple* laws, was that it? A formula for life. Simple as greed—computable, Daley had learned, on a multidimensional screen projection, fabric roofs against wind and weather—they had shadowed Daley perhaps. His prospects, one could call it. Whatever his mystery gift that his wife had apparently broached with of all people as new an acquaintance as Ruley (this well-hidden gift, subtle, nonexistent—atrophied by everyday responsibility let us say—and no *free* gift, or a real estate agent at heart) . . .

Potential, that was all, a future; or it was in the past long before.

How did Ruley know? Ruley knew the ropes, but how good was his information? How technical, how structural? A desert supertent. An airport for Mecca-bound travelers. A capital man, connected, capable, even dangerous, a self-styled mercenary but with what gain in mind? Said to have caused certain people grief in Saudi Arabia: this from a client of Daley's, a bit more than gossip (Daley barely knew her), such happenings to people you knew hardly unreal anymore in the global city, where you could disappear even if you didn't want to.

Often on the road, Ruley was partners in two lots in lower Manhattan. A district soon to be landmarked in those days. While they waited, the partner, a contractor, was paying the taxes on those parking lots, it was said. Ruley divided his time between the tristate area and abroad, Daley told his friend Sook, who laughed at an unwitting joke apparently, which was better than no joke to a Pusan Korean, an Asian laugh, formal, eruptive. The person in question perhaps did not divide his time at all.

Ruley was gone really in no time. He had installed some under-the-counter lights in the kitchen, wires coiled taking up space of course in one of the dish closets, which you could see when you went for the keys on the hook.

No man tells you what your wife thinks of you. But listen to the guy: "Della's right. She can't quite put her finger on it."

"Sure she can put her finger on it." Daley could have fixed that smile of Duymens's once and for all, a whole body smile of this whatever he was, who one day (though nothing surprised him anymore) Daley learned had called Bill Daley a visionary! That's what prudence aforethought will get you.

Daley knew what would happen. He always seemed to. What *was* happening was different. Why did Daley solicit Ruley's help in the case of the Taiwan businesswoman? She wasn't Daley's case. She was Lotta's mission. Why would he go to such a person as Ruley Duymens? Because Ruley might *know*. A true hunch of Daley's.

Never would he have consulted Ruley had it been Della who'd disappeared, detained (extradited was an interesting thought; where would they have extradited her to?) or Daley's sister-in-law, Wolf's wife, or the little girls, their baby pictures stuck in a book somewhere in the kitchen. He put Lotta's affairs lower, naturally—and the Taiwanese woman had been Lotta's friend for two days, the flight, the bus, breakfast next morning, points unseen on which life passed. Typical Lotta, plane, hotel (as if Daley even knew her). Though something had passed between the two women in Bagdad. A feeling? A thing. A relation that could become ideal. Trivial confidings. No matter, Ruley asked how long ago it had happened but then he turned the talk apparently to the Olympics, and Taiwan went no farther. "Your client, now, *she* has an interest in that part of the world. Lotta?" So Ruley had been speaking of the Taiwanese lady perhaps after all, Lotta's fleeting friend on the trip to Iraq, not Iraq not the world, but some brief friendship, though Daley would never mention a client to someone else, at least by name, least of all in Duymens's hearing, nor would the Taiwanese woman have come up when Ruley was approaching along the dark, carpeted hallway the night of the earthquake unknown to Daley and his wife. Though in the privacy of their bedroom they had wryly pondered Lotta's "way of being in the world," how she had asked Daley to find her a doctor to help her stop coughing, she'd coughed for three months, it was Mallorca, a sojourn with a New Jersey family, dust she'd breathed from certain Mallorcan stones that had a history of giving as good as they got.

And then years later she had brought out this book about herself, thrust it forward to be printed, surrendered it up to be perused. Her life, if anyone cared. Her name. Get it out there, everybody else is. Lotta, her grandmother's name second-generation German—but Lotta *Yvonne*, coupling her mother's childhood friend. Names said who you were, when it was really the namers.

Daley's late wife named in it, though surely they had never met.

He could just see Della walking the kitchen floor absorbed in it, cracking the spine, recalling earthquake night (though asking *why* Lotta would call), whooping here and there (hey, this woman should be certified). Della would have relished it. Long on fact, if not necessarily true fact, at least where you could imagine *checking* facts all one thousand and one of them. How Lotta got into the arts, her taste in people, her parentage, her struggles to resist exploitation. Her testimony and, folded in almost secretly, a brief history of abuse, call it. Touching, was it? A thought in there that didn't get out.

Who was this long-divorced husband? A man who lived out his life as a C.P.A. But maybe not *as anything*. She had never taken a cent from him, of course. News to Daley. Daley was her lawyer, he kept himself in his place. "How long can a divorce last?" the writer asked. It was not really Daley's branch of the law. The husband's *poems* had lasted. Poems? Of an accountant, "unmistakably his," written to a cleaning person who it turned out had no green card. Poems? Verses —now it made sense to Daley— in an ancient *Persian* form we were told—a C.P.A.?—discovered in a pouch at the bottom of a garment bag. A trip, that time, to Iran—you check the map for some reason— on business that got her into difficulties. This seismic-alert-giver-to-be, this earthquake phoner—but Baghdad, long before, and the attachment (really) to the ill-fated Taiwanese businesswoman. Lotta gave Daley a time-sensitive walk-on in the book. Her own lawyer for God's sake buying a small lakeside farmhouse he knew she was interested in buying, while she was away in Mexico. Allegedly snapping it up having heard about it from *her*, her dream retreat, stunned as she was over the loss of two near priceless pieces of pre-Columbian art: damaged in a slight earthquake, and the story didn't end there. Her lust for things she readily confessed. From her, not "tell-all" but tell-what-was-after-all-strangely-interesting, only the birds on the ledge could distract Daley once he began it. The damaged pieces later stolen. Yet frankly her relief. The thief had done her a mysterious favor, maybe the pieces wouldn't come back or would be fixed.

A taste for business she got from her father (fair enough), her rather correct speech too. The father now: he sounded true. "Like two peas in a pod," he would say of himself and his daughter, a great-hearted person he once called her, a little sister, a chum.

Her drive not to collect but to recycle "materials" was her own. As an artist. Almost everyone is one. Don't let teacher, lawyer, doctor, banker, Death, birth, loved ones tell you different. Yet it was Daley's own traveling that framed this defiance flowering in his client's tale for him, the ring of mountains where he had camped with his brother Wolf, unbelievably stupidly risky river swims Daley had taken.

Her husband's hidden depth came through. Did he sweep things under the carpet? Or was it Lotta? It was punishing, some of it. A cache of gewgaws, gifts from him she gave away in a rage, dispersed to people they both knew—a collection of collectibles, a jade bird, a tiny yellow plaster ostrich with those fore and aft bulbous thickenings underneath the creature done in maroon. And her cruelty to the cleaning woman, it was cut for cut in her quick-read narrative of coming awake. Did she call this recycling? Yet not so quick a read for Daley, who privately wanted to know the dates of those first Persian poems of the C.P.A., their inspiration. And the letters dumped in the wet garbage that afternoon before she left, something else entirely. (Didn't do the burning trip—where would you burn them? Close to a faucet.) The Russian cabdriver depositing her at South Ferry took her for a tourist, her rage absorbed into her nerves as she abandoned him (though charmingly), and he said he would meet the boat if she would tell him when she was coming back.

American tenderness, too, don't forget the admired mother in this book coming in for posthumous blame—excessive warmth, smother-ingly warm—which took us into territory Lotta's lawyer frankly was unfamiliar with though maternal behavior quite the reverse of this by his client Lotta might be produced, he sensed, by a very (roughly) sim-ilar cause in the home.

Reassembling these hard (but weirdly fun) *things*, she got it all down in nine months. *A woman who isn't a woman can usually write her autobiography in a third of that time,* Hemingway had said. Helen had read it when she was in Paris for a week, Daley recalled. Women could offer Lotta girlfriend support but were not in a position to give her justice. Maybe her lawyer could if they were still speaking.

Daley had been stirred by the idealized person the husband's poems touched into being, the cleaning woman Luz, who, to her cost, lacked the green card, part Colombian, part Guatemalan (where Lotta had gotten her from).

Long after this, long after Lotta failed to find those few missing letters in the garbage (stolen from herself) and had to recall them (and was able to), including her father's where he gave it six months, her marriage to Tim, not realizing as Daley did that she would virtually not know *how* to leave, thank you; and long after she rang up her lawyer Bill Daley when he was living alone again, a recent widower, and took an impromptu (going-nowhere) walk with him, telling him what he must do now, put it behind him, it was a blessing—the breath with which she uttered the first syllable said it was a blessing for both of them—Daley divined and forgot and that when there is no desire all things are at peace; and months and months after she wrote her book, struggling with an editor (she almost shook him once) who told people it was his book, he'd cut it here and there and helped her with the words but gave her a Japanese novel to read, gave it to her twice she told Daley perhaps with the kindness of a teacher who can't help repeating himself, but did not desire *her*; and quite a while after that Friday afternoon call (taken by Donna, the message was that Lotta's ex was thinking of suing over the Luz material after a decade of not being in touch—at least he'd read it!)—and someone else Lotta apparently didn't name had phoned to point out that *he* was not in the book!—Lotta was still peddling a product and herself, her habits, if anyone would see them beyond the jewelry she imagined she was the creator of and at peace with except your life seemed in conversation to come round to *her* day, *her* history, some reincarnation without death exactly, if Daley were ever to think it through, because you didn't change your six-month twelve-month outlook for Lotta.

# FIRST WEEK

# 1

NIGHTS, HE HASN'T SEEN THE LIKE OF IT. ARE THESE HER PEOPLE? SHE couldn't have made them up. Is it what was done in her family? Is it true? (Because you almost have to know.) Two nights to begin with of this rigmarole put on just for him sort of seedy, if you can believe it. Was she sort of singing for her supper? Hey, she does all the voices, hers too, out of Canada, a touch Irish?—"the bum's rush," you hear, is that Canadian or is it American?

She was just twenty-*four*. She had come to *him*, hadn't she? Could this still be unclear? When she left, he could make the point. Yes she had seen him in the audience, the man who'd absorbed her glance who turned *out* to be him; no, she didn't know who he was till later. This was where they wound up. She with the man who'd sat behind the guy she was dumping. (Hadn't the big guy Leander dumped *her*?)

Daley's existence was like his house of city-darkened brick near the river; it would last with or without this young woman. (In his thought he forgot her name once or twice, didn't give her another.) He had walked right into it, his own home with her on a Wednesday night; age-related, it was as "why-not" as it was imprudent or a fling, possibly dangerous. Though he could be of use to her. And what was she doing here? Was it the brother said to be in town she'd on impulse decided not to avoid Wednesday and so had ultimately returned to the dressing room thinking it was him that Barry meant? Did she really know who it was—was it just her eviction case in mind? Or a whim to crash on some old guy? No divorce lawyer, Daley made his living off such details as these, but not his life. It was her business. A land-lord; a roommate; a violent coworker in Barry; a brother; and the pro-ducer rumored to be in film who'd given her an unheard-of chance, Beck, apparently going into film, too: they were all elsewhere for Daley. They weren't what he had to give back. The big guy though stayed leashed to Daley's thoughts. Leander. His overweight existence young with habits, needing work, his life's work, he played you imag-ined stride piano out somewhere depressingly late at night; a father back there, an incorporated father's name, one dreamy discipline sav-ing the son, a swimmer, a champion Daley just now, a secret résumé of what would yet come, swimming his imaginings in a pool, existence given at every unforeseen instant, but, fair enough, you need a job.

Daley was sort of with a very young woman, that was all, almost a girl (let's see some I.D.) The days possessed him, friendly habits yet betrayers. A day or two or three at first, softly charged, actually aro-matic and near and waiting like a market in a city he might have vis-ited. (Had his body changed? Calm as a martial artist.) A day, two days, three. One day she starved herself for a few hours. Who cared? She talked to you. Days spreading forward out of a reservoir of years.

Prismed by a drug (not Leander's), crossing the bed of a once familiar lake, Daley felt slow, imbued with his body and touched by another hour, half unburied no more than that, underwater as a per-son, an American, he knew who'd spent years speaking French and another language in Southeast Asia had told him she felt upon her return to speaking English in New York.

He went to the office. He enjoyed Donna, whose teeth were *too* perfect. Her eyes, the down invisible above her lip, he wanted to touch her arm and did. Almost gave her a raise, told her nothing, got a lot done with her, nearly terminated the employment agency still housed as a separate square-foot entity under the roof of his law prac-tice. Assembled a stack of paperwork for a client: not a housing case but it came to his mind: an artist, a real artist, a difficult person in his honesty, who made his slim living custom-crating art and spoke so briefly on the phone that Daley, who hardly had time to start the meter running and wouldn't have had it on anyway, spent some min-utes in the analysis and expansion of these words to make full sense of them. The client's customer had walked out on him, a well-to-do downtown painter doing an end run around one of his galleries by sending work off independently. He had left the country without paying for six large crates whose depth and interior packing had been masterfully designed to see these trashy oils clear to Germany and a collector whose daughter was studying in New York. Two and a half weeks' work, those crates, almost a month's rent, which Daley's guy was behind on, which led Daley to send Donna to a nearby law school library to check on nonpayment of rent and while she was there the law on landlord not accepting timely rent checks. The absent offender had rented his house though not his barn near Big Indian, Daley knew a Swiss engineer inventor up there, that quiet Catskill area, and the widow of a developer there. Defendant in Daley's case, the painter, had left in a hurry, and Daley thought he knew why.

But what was happening to Daley? Nothing really. Daley's friends, two or three who knew, did not really glean anything better or worse of him, or didn't say. An early riser of robust constitution. What man cares whether or not his friend hooks up with someone or marries for that matter? Wish him well and trust that she proves good company, that they whatever, enjoy doing nothing together, hopefully missing nothing. There would probably always be Helen, just as there are always real women to tell you to get a life even if they know you already have one. Women will get into it. They'll get the wind up and point out that "she's half your age," and some will be oversensitive or blame their eating problems on a man. It's like real estate transactions, though, and politics and the puzzlingly constant speed of light no matter how fast you're going (Daley thought that was it) or which way—you keep your own counsel until you feel like talking.

Donna had fielded a call from Helen, the latest semiannual installment of the story about Helen's protégé on the Coast, the musician she had gotten to the States from Prince Edward Island, how mean he'd been to her this time, yet now more to it that she would tell *Daley*. Lotta about probate, for which Donna on behalf of Daley could only refer her to someone uptown, though Lotta wanted to know if he had the country place still. Over the fence, Becca had passed the time of day with Isabel, Daley's neighbor. A client was not paying

Isabel the last eighteen hundred he owed her because the twice-redone floor, the last item on the punch list, still wasn't perfect according to him though the unacceptable marks were his terrier's feet. What did they talk about? Safety of the neighborhood, the riverfront. Canada. Women freed up not too differently.

Daley would take a cab home at three in the afternoon, figuring Becca was there. Writing rapidly in a notebook page after page, or she was in the window watching the street and people saw her. Or he would take his time at the end of the day, like time for himself though it was business calls: a prospective client they'd called each other's machines; or an old soldier he was able to help sent by his Korean comrade Sook with a gripe about a city sewer main plugged up and seeping into the cellar of a small building in downtown Brooklyn, mostly offices; or Sid Knox about the hotel-damage suit but to ask in passing how Daley had found the daughter of a great Danish flugel-hornist as a table companion Monday night, she had not sought out Sid after the set, he regretted to say, and then the table was vacant; she asked if he had the country place still—she wondered why he hadn't called her back she had heard from her many-years-ago tour guide Ruley Duymens who had read her book and had the nerve to criticize what got in and what didn't. And for three job seekers in this late stage of the agency that he could not quite let go, Daley discovered their experience all over again, seeing what they would be like in the positions he had in mind for them. While telling them that for good writing they should read the Gettysburg Address, and for citizenship the Declaration of Independence, which for Lincoln was a whole other Constitution. This also to the young Caribbean woman, Courtney, fresh from a community college and possessed of a gift for people, for the new job-interview dry runs despite her age, she had interesting rings under her eyes, she ran on five hour's sleep like Daley, "Tell them just what they ask, and if they put you down, don't get mad, get funny but not too." And Daley did and didn't want to let her go, she was no good to him except with the agency. She'd been leaving early to get to her culinary course and had a special relation with her teacher who helped her after class. Perhaps Leander would be Daley's last agency client. Della's agency, who would have (he knew) listened in her way to his curious view—sighting, really—of Leander, no dream Thursday, not a daydream, more a trivial but true résumé of certain hours habitual and/or to come, they were so clear and corporeal, audible as someone in another room—inquiring, though, and hardly uncanny as he'd have at once granted to his listener who trusted him so many ways to help her, to love her, to take care of things, to live with her, like her; but would have, well, "heard him out," said little: and so, since he'd experienced this reaction already in the old days describing his conviction that a black man he'd met had gone back to a jungle and dug for his lost cornet and found a piece of it, and that the turkey girl, a frizzy blond adolescent Australian, was standing in front of a giant American painting that though a fore-telling had made him think of the war but later in exact detail a beach, a clock, two local boys in baseball gloves, that day she was bathing (down to a brilliant aquamarine bikini) in some Australasian sea, feeling around her waist—what?—her right to fly, and her turkey with the factory in his belly dead—Daley would not on a Thursday in November of '96 have retailed (or confessed) this foreknowledge of Leander, a person he'd had a seven- or eight-minute conversation with outside a theater the night before.

Perhaps it was the fugitive and passing young woman Becca who added curious concentration and fullness to the understanding or the picture, or what Leander had said about the agency, or that it came like sounds to Daley from a pool humming like the city or like space or emptiness or the past together with its occasional creak of a diving board. Daley looking at the final client of the agency as he could all but hear this still-young distance swimmer musicking, he could swear, to himself, or his brain in saline solution, Daley discounted it but as his wife had once upon a time criticized him, of all people, for not doing, he stuck with it, this accurate-feeling imagination of a stranger filled with experience like Daley's, and there was a piano there too, the hands of the swimmer always close to the keys, sinking into them, an old piano, somewhere not far from Chinatown, east of there near a huge shadowy bridge.

When he walked in the door Thursday afternoon, Becca was upstairs apparently calling *him* and rang off without a word to his "secretary." It gave him a start. It wasn't typical. She kept to herself. He said, "Donna's more than my secretary," but he didn't check later. He was glad to be home. Becca met him with a long hug, a kiss, another kiss; she kissed everyone when she met them, she said, because she felt like it, but being with him had changed her manners a little.

He let Becca's other life insinuate itself toward him as it would with curious independence and without encouragement from him, these people and enterprises all linked like street noises or evidence, *her* business (compared to what he felt): he didn't know what to make of her landlord's group, and this uptown (largely) producer Beck, and her family (at least by voice) flowing toward this house like a low tide, a brother, a father, two brothers, other increasingly distinct members of an impression that might not be *her* family at all. It was an idea he couldn't weigh very well. Wednesday night, Thursday night. Time as charming as it was silly, and recalled so exactly as to be so crowded he was free of it.

Daley took one uncomfortable call from Helen at the office that ended almost at once. Helen wasn't at her best and yet he didn't mind the inopportune moment. "Your play is moving uptown." She had had lunch with Betty—*he* knew Betty . . . the playwright?

"No." (Helen worked fast.)

"You remember I met her. She was on television," Helen said, "you remember I told you. The producer wants Lang. He must have her."

"I don't know much," Daley said.

"Well, I believe you . . . You mean to tell me you didn't know? She quits, the play folds," said Helen in a certain way.

"It's out of my hands," said Daley.

"What's in your hands, buster?"

Would Becca's friends descend upon Daley's house? Pull an all-nighter, an Eve of something, a clutch of actors? She's not popular with the cast though now. He does talk to her about leaving the play. He's not supposed to. Daley's not what you call entertaining, but okay in her view you guess. Nothing special.

She is an actress, he divines, and somehow more. He wouldn't have said this, as they had come into his basement kitchen from the street areaway Wednesday night. From the start, she seemed to find him funny—or frank. So much got said wending their way home, a lot of nothing Wednesday night. He found an unmailed letter in his coat pocket the next day and a slip of purple paper fluttering toward the bedroom carpet, which he slipped into his trouser pocket.

He couldn't stop her talking when they got home Wednesday and went in the basement entrance after she had seen the front of the house and the stoop, and he hauled out the burned waffle iron while she was telling him how she had come here from London (Ontario) on a bet. "Like a *kiss*," he said.

"No, no," she said (though he was right), "if you're wrong with a kiss, what have you lost? Not your plan," she said, this remarkable young woman his for a moment, with the lift and turn in her walk, and the experience in her shoulders, the history, but of what? Turning to him for help or to put him in his place. The Canadians he had known were men and were hearty, he told her . . . *somewhat* like Americans, sort of Chicago/Boston not at all New Yorkers, not up to absolutely anything but vigorous, but thoughtful and more formal as if there were a code surrounding not ethics so much as talk. A lot of heavy mustaches—an army of them advancing at a conference Daley had attended in Chicago, he could tell the accent, and going off a diving board like football players. She told him he was a racist. He laughed in a more serious vein, and said he could see why draft dodgers went up there.

"It was the law that let them."

"Yes, and the country makes sense full time."

"No, it was Trudeau that let them," she said. "What kind of law do you practice?"

Well, not the radical law you found all over, twenty-five years ago.

"Not in Canada."

No, all over America.

"You don't find it in Canada. But you don't need to." He could tell she knew some Americans.

Wednesday night it was so late and they were in the kitchen a long time. While actually she rambled between the kitchen table, the microwave he had bought on an impulse and the cabinets full of things he hadn't set eyes on in a year, and the window, the window. She peered up at the sidewalk absorbed expecting somebody, you'd think, and later he was convinced of it. She fingered the books in a floor-to-ceiling bookcase there, and she told him a little bit of everything. She would have *missed* the States if she hadn't come—like this.

She pulled out two or three books, looking at each in turn in the way that Canadians are readers, gazed at the rest in self-contemplation, books, the window, a framed photo of the trumpeter hanging by the window. (Does she know it's Miles?) "Of course, you could just decide to stick in *Canada*," Daley pointed out.

"That's right," she said, delayed then by his manners. Canada a continent untrekked to the north except by fugitive American corporates flown in to their guided canoes and out again—like somebody who'd invited Daley to fish an inaccessible lake located like an island in extreme northern Manitoba.

"Well, instead of all this, which is not so tempting." Daley swept his arm across the room.

"Liar." She came and sat down. Elbows on the kitchen table seemingly about to talk about her life (but too civilized), she *included* him in it all. She had a way of sitting down that said she had a purpose here.

"Mexicans don't like our calling the United States 'America.'"

"I've never been."

"There's experience anywhere," he said forgetting what he was doing. "That bio," he said.

"Pathetic, eh?" she said.

"Liar."

Yes, he was right, she said, it was show-offy. That's me.

It was quite a résumé, you were supposed to feel it was—

Truer than the others. Yes, she knew. The main things were there.

The real story almost came to Daley. (And presently she nearly told it.) She'd had no *experience* to speak of, acting. She was bragging, Daley told her gently. A one-minute part in a community production of *The Merchant*. A crowd scene at Stratford with her high school group when she was fourteen. A play about the Vandals and Roman soldiers written by her science teacher. Mime on the university steps. All kind of stupid. She was reading philosophy by then, living with her brother. She didn't talk about herself.

Daley fed her waffle-iron waffles and syrup from the country. The dusty blue bowl lifted down out of the closet. Waffle iron clanked out of the lower cupboard from among pans and a Waring blender. Daley clattered another old plate out of the cupboard, his knuckles and fingertips, his ribs reaching, thinking of nothing. She was almost embarrassed to ask if there was a toilet on this floor. Between the kitchen and the stairway to the cellar.

God she was still hungry. She was back at the window. Where did that old kettle come from? she asked. He grilled two cheese sandwiches in the oven and nearly forgot them unearthing high up in the cupboard a dusty jar of eggplant chutney homemade—by Helen—in the country. Kitchen's always open in this hotel, he said.

And then cornflakes, when Becca was hungry still, which were a favorite, and week-old tarnished green grapes received like a luxury and a hard Granny Smith apple mottled from long refrigeration with a minute wisely circular red sticker on it he noticed she ate. A small container of chocolate milk half full, three or four days old. What the hell was he doing cooking for her? he joked. It was so masculine, she said, he knew how to make it all so luxurious—her shoulders slumped, her hands at her sides, *do what he would*. He seemed to have no choice, had the time of his life and had to think a little, and looked at her—you might have thought he was in danger or something, she said.

Did she like him? She sure talked.

The man who came to serve the eviction papers, she sure got him talking, she had him in for cappuccino, he didn't know what to do, he was absorbing it all, the place she lived, his sister-in-law got evicted from her apartment in Astoria, she had an unsavory roommate but what it was, the landlord wanted it for his daughter. Daley had heard the city in the speech of this woman over the phone, she'd had the warmest experience of the paper server he could tell now face to face.

Becca's—it was a look—thick-frizzed, pale hair: her hair meant for a moment She will stay tonight. She seemed to draw you out, absorbing it without trying to remember it; four fingers held the book open while her thumb caught each page at the bottom. Curious person, she did such things—even to the sensitively a-little-pigeon-toed way she stood acquainting herself with whatever. A fantastic all-nighter. You find out everything about the other (forget bedtime, this is practically the point). Daley didn't know. Your life at last clear to you at last over coffee and a cab home. The nonunion (Daley would bet) doorman noting Becca's arrival time to report to the super, the landlord, the plaintiff's attorney. It was slower than that. There was no doorman, it came to Daley. But a super and a kinsman running a freight elevator.

Daley measuring out ingredients like a fool into the blue bowl, the first time she says, "Bill," it's a word like things she would tell him, his full name she's trying it out as he measured ingredients from a place in the country into a mixing bowl and who could tell if this girl would stay and he looked at her answering to his name. But that's it. The courses had continued.

So much she wanted to do. She would show him, she said, though she couldn't mean much by it. He put together the bare bones of her life in his mind. It thrilled him a little, he could see it. The seasons would come and go, and she would show him. She didn't talk much about herself. It was a skill not entirely civilized. Why, he asked, was *he* one of the people she wanted to show? She made a sound, like forget it. An odd, quite attractive young woman. She never ate like this, she said; forget she said it.

"The play," he said.

She knew he didn't love it: "Worth getting out of, right?"

"Well I know someone who thought you faked the blood."

"Think twice before you go to a play with her again."

Oh Daley wasn't burning any bridges. By the way, the brother had had reason to punish her.

"*Reason!*" The woman stood; "he *needed* to, '*by* the way.'"

Daley'd been expecting it. Tedious. Yet she had her hand on his shoulder, and his neck asked to be touched.

"Some nights *I* make my nose bleed."

"Like diving—scuba diving." Daley could feel the sinus spread, wiring his eye sockets as truly as someone's history sitting across from him in the office, for once upon a time he had felt his blood and detached the mask and saw the small greenish crimson trail like shit

rise before his eyes, it was a marine lab in San Diego, in Turkey, in—
he had let it happen through not inexperience but separation, in each
instance from his brother Wolf he'd taken a respite from, but—

"No no: like Bernhardt."

Well, he knew who she was.

"No no." Becca was impatient: "I mean blushing right down to
here on stage. At will."

Daley looked up at her. She sat down. He recalled a swami some years
ago at the gas station he actually liked—who acted like he could tell you
what you would do but. Good guesswork only. She agreed. Experience
is the gift. She listened politely. He was not one of the mad ones.

The thing was, her Winnipeg girlfriend had brought her home
from Kathmandu a dull painting on shiny cloth of gods. They must
have been eating, feeling great lying on their sides, head propped in
hand, or cavorting, you looked for erections. Kathmandu? "You've
probably been there, a New Yorker; or you were on the point of it"
(curious guess) "—now there's a religion—"

"Not for us," said Daley, "from what I know of it—"

"—if you ever wanted to calm down."

"Hopeless," Daley said, nodding, feeling hopeless and all over and
entertained.

"I would dream of it, monks exposing me to some noble person,
the king," Becca said, "that's about it for reincarnation." She inspired
Daley and he said a foolish thing or two: "People so similar that someone you run into ten years later seems to be same person different
body; same body you have to beware, right?"

"Exactly," said the woman, "you dreamed of going out there."

"Part of me."

"And so . . ."

"Exactly."

"In the play."

"You know where." Becca attributed something to him.

"Where?"

She frowned. "The voice-overs of course." That was what had
attracted her.

Kathmandu?

Becca smiled. That's right. He thought she didn't mean it. Well, the woman who co-wrote was never near Kathmandu but she wanted to put a child prostitute story into the voice-over. Daley guessed that we all know so little about so much—or was it the other?

"Nepal wasn't in it originally."

Did she mean that her dream —?

That's right.

"And you had no real acting experience?"

"A class for eight months."

"How did you live?"

"Moved into the place Beck lined up for me. The play was a good fit, that's what they say here. Employers. Except they say: it's not a good fit for us—always *us*." Daley recognized it. It was Helen talk.

"And your man Beck you met on the plane set it up?" Daley wanted to help. He got a kick out of her, his father would have put it, that generation. She was pretty interesting.

"Well, we got to talking at Toronto check-in."

"Oh you were in Toronto."

"We were in Toronto. Both of us." A man with a hat. Next thing she knew they were in the plane, it was warm, they were delayed. He was down the aisle. Next thing he was leaning in under the luggage compartment telling the woman next to Becca that he would exchange his seat with her so she could go back and sit with her husband. The woman seemed to draw a blank, looking up from her book. "What a crazy idea," she said, distracted, not to anybody, *nodding*. It was only upon landing, an hour and a half later, that Becca had learned the man knew one of her brothers. How had it come up? Daley in a deposing mood tried to get it straight. Yet he didn't especially want to know. A couple more hours it seemed of this downstairs in the kitchen, friendly and disconcerting, secret from the rest of the empty house. Was it leading back to her case and she thought she had to corner him? The house—he didn't want to scare her away. Mindful that walking home the last, direction-recovering lap this woman had stopped to kiss him at a green light of all moments, and on the cheek; and a few blocks farther on, equally lightly, at a storage mailbox that vanished from time to time and reappeared.

She took her black knapsack up off the long table he loved, its surfaces scored with dim writings, impressions upon impressions and overwritten drawings, knife marks: "Come on, the dishes can wait," she said. He felt brutally successful, simplified, and touched. Who did she think she was?—her legs, the swing of her that seemed taller, he wondered how many flights of stairs she had in mind; she hadn't seen the house. He might sell it, it came to him, what he could get for it now.

Or it could be her home, he thought, the trip done on himself in an instant of silly feeling.

She could have it for a time.

Must be around midnight—'round one, in fact: lone sounds damped by late neighborhood night, our destination. One flight first, narrow, uncarpeted steps. She made a sound. "We have stairs like these," she said. Funny, the pair of them on these boards. She climbed them.

"Back home?" he heard himself say.

Wow. She sizes up the first-floor living room, furniture, objects, the not-so-grand piano, which he sees afresh in two bars of street light across its box shaping the brink of its inward curve. "Ouch," he hears the young woman say softly, seeing a chandelier, recalling something.

Well, she pointed Daley to the old yellow velvet sofa darkened by memory past whatever stains you might think to inspect. She runs things. He sat back in it. Becca stood over him. Will she pile in here on top? Between here and the piano he locates her *hegemony*, is it? Becca hasn't wasted a second this evening, you feel, maybe not since Ontario; not in years, poor thing. Is it a Canadian business deal and she needs his help in playing Beck? It's all right. Daley reaches out to her.

She picked up a *Geographic* and dropped it smack on the table.

"Do you mean *you* added Nepal?"

"Suggested it."

It might be awful, this whole, high-ceilinged room—is that her mood? Or the room is familiar, or will do, and is nothing. Who does she think she is? Jaunty now, embarrassing possibly, she addresses him. "Dunno what you folks thought you were gettin' into tonight."

He smiles, faking it. "You'll find yourself here," she promises, "the father you'd just do anything for to stop him doing what he's doing, and he's not even a real drunk, he's definitely not but I'll do anything for him anyway." The mother. She lost a gold comb and holds your hand regaling little you with Dad's flirtations so we laugh and laugh in the dark bedroom and talk about nipples; letting it all hang in, a population of family, a quite-amusing-for-a-few-minutes mess, no privileged voice, no privacy, until your very body's spread on the floor roughhoused, traded back and forth, exhausted with little-girl giggles, tickled into extinction, ravished with play, and dimly irritated by adult bad breath or something; the foundling, remember the foundling sometimes seems like it's the five-year-old in the bathtub wanting to get out before the plug is pulled, found you on the steps of the train station, hey that's a lie, you weren't found at the train station the brother chips in, which brother? you came out of your mummy's tummy—Hey Bruce, that's getting pretty raw—and Uncle Otto and the brother, and the sisters somewhere will be heard. Who's Uncle Otto? Her voice opens a crowd suddenly, they are all headed here. *Folks.* An act at this hour. We.

# 2

IT HAPPENED BETWEEN THE PIANO FIFTEEN FEET AWAY AND THE SOFA. Daley guessed it was the one-woman thing, awful family material. This show of her own was what she had had in mind all along, this "one-woman piece" right there in the bio Helen had read (he might have been behind the wheel, she in the passenger's seat) and reread by Daley for a second at the end of intermission when he helped the boy pick up his program folded right to the place and held it to the light of the stage. Freckled, connected, a champion, checked by his mother, who's in the cast, with the uptown (hopefully) producer Beck.

Can he look at his watch under her gaze (it's his house). At work she's harder looking, ruthless, prophetic in the fine imperfect nose. Close up, bare (how does she do that?). Something is expected of him and maybe she's not staying.

Is it her family? If it is not a family extended into the whole world, he has a low tolerance for it, this sensation in the buttocks (and wishes she'd sit down by him). Is it that she trusts him? Is that all? What to make of it. To make of what he's absorbing: are these her people? She couldn't have made them up. Is it what was done in her family? Standing by the piano she becomes the father crashed in his easy chair; pigeon-toed she's the image of the mother blaming her for the gold comb. Is it true? They talk, probably shout at each other. The brother's so close to her he's not only a brother—but a half brother, if Daley's ears have it right, this isn't his mother. Much older, he lies down with her to help her get to sleep, he's got a belly, he's old. Sometimes it's him, sometimes it's the two of them against the others, the other rooms there. It does have the tawdry tack of indictment, revenge energy; yet this is them themselves, her apparent family, quite another thing than her. It's hardly rape or really violence, is it?

This awful family *material* settling into Daley's living room, his house (after all these years—*these*?)—and the voices, hers too. You resist actors: is courage letting it hang out? This girl was here because Daley had picked up thinking it was another woman Monday. What was Daley doing for *his* supper? Feeding Becca downstairs, repairing upstairs to play audience at one in the morning.

It's a *story*, the truth there, the mother's gold comb lost with grease and hairs stuck in it, curled on the child's bed, Mom manipulating the family story not telling you who it was who left the note for Dad under the front door till the point where we learn how angry he got when our little girl spilled marshmallow on her shoe and then the mother brings up the note; yet the suspense is when, when will she gather her little girl into her arms, the sweet smell on her breath, the sweat of her loins. A little girl who was found. And some angel named . . . Otto, who served on a Great Lakes tug (she just made up the name you get the feeling). And an older brother, name changed as we went along, or two or three brothers, fugitive, passing, garrulous, interested in her. The really older brother she was like *that* with. And a daddy who put his foot down, then busted out laughing, voices guffawing, the forest of family, a father with white hair that his Peggy whoever-she-was told him to dye (the only one who could do anything with him) who's proud of her (ten, eleven, twelve, getting on in hormones, still cute though, and scoring scholarships); Dad hitting on her, et cetera, badgers her on science till she cries, makes her recite the gravedigger's scene who didn't himself know *Hamlet* from "The Lady in the Lake" he also demanded with relish from "Vain as a leaf upon the stream" to "Fantastic as a woman's mood, / And fierce as Frenzy's fever'd blood," makes her play herself at five singing "Ob-la-di, Ob-la-da" in the tub, little mother, her legs out. How does she be all this? She's a—"I'm a product of my downbringing, a commodity": for who caresses her in the checkout line? Who tempts her to eat by bringing her a jam sandwich in from the kitchen by plane, that pauses over her—really a helicopter, *really* this *new* one that's a plane *and* a helicopter, Daley saw the fish hawk it's named for migrating once high above Ohio of all places, its black wrist, its crook'd wing—till the jam sandwich (chopper in the area!) suddenly descends straight for her plate—who is this osprey in the house? It's all for her, as she's for all, she's so feminine, she does all these people, not to mention others (tells part of a bedtime tale for grown-ups, a lot of Canadian slang that sounds closer to home, she has a cough, a sniffle, a dictionary in her head, there's an American in here somewhere feeding her American talk, it's not worth thinking about, how many brothers and sisters there are here). And some other male (Daley comes to with a start, was it Daley?)—her at the center, a child managing a group, at meals and before bedtime, could be the States, making them stop and watch her and how she can't get rid of them, pondering a droopy wedge of pizza at the table, then half asleep on you guess a couch (how's Becca do that standing?).

What happened to her was just awful if we knew what it was. Life, if true: people at each other, rude, that's all, home trashing center, but *Grace* said in there somewhere.

Exhibit: a half-full running bath, grouting roughly missing along the porcelain rim Daley can see for himself without Becca's help: she stand-up soaps the wall (fortunately a fun, droll, penetratingly quirky family-*ori*ented activity that cuts the risk). "This litto mountain," a child's voice taps her wet knee rising above the bathwater, an island, for now she's lying down on the Oriental rug that Daley received as a present from a client; "this litto downy," the voice maturing, is it the child now?—"this little nippo a jelly bean—"

"No, no."

"—squeeze it—"

"No"

"—squirt water down into my—"

"No, no, no," the giggles turn *something* into habitual fearlessness up on her two wide-planted feet again—you think, Don't slip: "No, look at *me*."

"Oh, a founting, a founting." Wet little one entertaining smelly elder—next thing she's under the covers. "Lay me down to sleep." And she had sisters, where were they?

All this not hard to get if it's not the truth you're after or where she's coming really from. She's bare faced, a body asking he knew for a bath, happy landing. Something is expected of him, maybe it's she's not going to stay. "Come to me," she dodges into a new turn, talks with a man's unseemly dirt: "Jes' fergive me, you know *how*," and in almost the same but is it Otto's voice, "You know who *I* am." Daley's a mature fool, a professional even at this hour who doesn't want it to seem to have been lost on him. "If you really cared about me," the mother's voice need go no farther—"No, I'm not going into that," she finishes or is it she, now?—do things said enable new . . . being?

"*I* know," Daley says, and, saying, almost does know this sister.

"Here just let me take a look at you," the voice ignores him, "a slice outa you, *you* know . . ."

There's hypothetically undeniably consensual love here and looking over your shoulder and romance pursued from room to room of a house someplace (Daley decides—could be Canada but . . .), family thing, argued, as American as other out-of-New-York scenes, a dust-up all yours in a space of fifteen feet, piano, sofa, round trip.

There's a tree in there happening to her, with initials, he's sure, it's Canada, early-spring mud in the yard, a happening nation she's brought with her onto his carpet yet reverted to in her speech, a history or secret he might have to ask the right question to hear from her. He won't ask what exactly is happening, it's her *work*. Is she a tree? He hopes not. It would be obvious. It would remind him of dance or symbolism; that's it, symbolism. People don't want that. They want it amazing and straight out. More a tree without branches.

Or roots. It's adrift (to be truthful) but kind of disturbing work—is it acting?—or potential that's it. It is the one-woman piece noted in the bio just hours ago, this rigmarole, this rash of habits, self-inter-rupting gab-attacks, about as seamless as—he resents it, there's an idea in her belly better than this. Just the person in front of you car-rying on and nobody to slap her this time. Is it the injustice done her, something like that?

Is *this* the case? "You get slugged like that every night?"

"Oh he's not always up to it."

"Tonight, though . . ."

"It's great when it feels . . ."

"Your teeth might been jarred loose."

"When it feels . . ."

"It's never that," said Daley abruptly.

"Unpremeditated," she said. She was surprised how wrong he had to be. She had attended to him for a moment completely, then drawn back and looked at his mouth and almost laughed. "I pity someone like you," she said.

"Then I pity you too," he said, meaning that her pity was wasted.

The man Beck she met on the plane—no, at check-in—sent her to Lex a week later, the director—"Oh I told you that." No, she had not; she just got on a plane? That was the trouble, they hadn't believed she was taking a couple of weeks in New York. Who hadn't? He had too much else on his mind to think about how she left family and brother and then the brother helped her move and got her an apart-ment and moved in, though he had a business by then that took him around the lakes, he wasn't in the uncle's shoe business anymore. Though Daley was jealous—curious about her apartment mate, the older brother.

Daley sat out here exposed in the softness of his settee, proud to have her here though what she's actually *doing* embarrasses him, it's not *his* fault. (Did Leander—whom he can see playing an old mildewed jazz piano on the floor of a swimming pool but you'd never say it in a court of law—get a dose of this?) Daley experiences the syrupy risk of drowsy night.

It was the hard, slight irregularities of her face his struggling trance fixed upon, her skin he wanted to uncover for himself, her hand on the piano top that told him she tolerated him to the point of needing his attention, and he wouldn't violate her privacy, was cool, wouldn't over-read her.

Of course her otherwise fine nose infinitesimally hopefully swerved at a point just below where its narrow bridge begins, not "fixed" except by the life it had encountered, not Barry's fault. But in its daydream to escape the very blow that had in the first place or in another life *caused* this skew and enticing break and initiative of the bone and dear individual cartilage. Her somewhat heartbreaking nose was "the way" at after one-thirty in the morning; or how she aimed you *and* her to a future not yet there, he could tell her presently. He had set out to help his wife, the creative one. While Becca performed this bill of particulars against whoever, absorbed by Daley in turn unsurely during what might have been a wisely eyes-narrowed doze before he was himself again, focusing between the eyes of this appeal-ing young woman or subtle person—it wasn't these monologue women on TV Helen watched, joke after joke and the little things they hated, you're dead if you can't keep 'em laughing, little scenes with boss, mother, married girlfriend, plumber woman. Did Becca make it up though? These weird sisters who spoke and were gone. Where were they? A much older brother who said: "I'm leaving but I'll be back" and "It was China that lost the war if you ask me" and "This land is my land."

"As if I was," the little girl muses, "my mama," and Daley can feel the window she imagines in the middle of the air.

The kid here got seduced or sexually loved in a way. Fondled, crit-ically tickled, it was probably bad and Daley can imagine it, an out-of-control adult adoring, snorting like a stoat. A child standing up in the bathtub at work, consensually washed, eyes closed, yet a child leaning forward (same bathtub?) to recover a slippery oval of peach soap under the water down near the drain where a little mat of hair, not hers, has gathered. (She expected to sell this one-woman show? Yet the drain, the dark hair, the soap you could smell like a sweet butt.) And suddenly Becca turns and pulls down her jeans, the works, her can, flashes butt complete with dimples, surprise rosette, a hint of forward fur, for it's done and over with in no time like a memory-attention test and she's turned this way zipping up her belly and dark blond.

The name *Peg* in there, not Baby Peggy and not Baby Becca but a woman showering, municipal honesty in Ontario, the mother's name you have to believe who lost the gold comb (but down the drain?). Daley takes it in like he doesn't *have* to get it all. He's sort of it, her feet sometimes planted in one place and her arms twisted upward a dancer, she had to grow the way someone has to sing, he sees she can grow large or small. That's what he sees. Or smells. She runs a hand down her outstretched arm to become another.

Been danced to before, by his wife once. It was for him. And Helen not here to tell him (lovingly) what's going on. This one, though, looking you in the eye in your own home, it's a man she brings not her whole family to but her, and a dark eye for a dark eye, let the penalty fit the crime. The brother's out there, it comes to Daley, what if she were just to say where he's coming from?

The oven was left on, you smell the old burn and crust even from here, for she is doing these voices, what else does she make him see? Who really are they, who are the *parties* to this rigmarole? Is it true? It has to be, she makes it up on the spot, is it what he pays for love? She dances almost out of her blue jeans, she turns this way and that. Something up to Daley. Enter it. Put a stop to it, it's not behind his back.

He gets it and doesn't get it. She points the finger at someone called Fred: "Why *do* you?"—the mother's tone—perhaps kills him with her hands and teeth like a lamb shank if you could tell, and Otto again, giving her a hilarious bath; there's an Anthony, too, because someone male shined her brown school shoes (she works her elbow back and forth), he cooked her a frozen pizza, older brother/father, and sat with her while she bit into it and pulled way back on the cheese and slowly sated her hunger her way, his hand around his glass or kissing her neck occasionally as she ate, not Bruce you thought but Anthony tall as a grasshopper. Does she *have* to? the little girl asks. (Eat? Rise to the occasion? Tell a joke?) He taps her cheek, he wanted her dirty clothing to put in the laundry bag, he was going out to the laundromat, and she took off whatever she was wearing so it could be a fresh start tonight. "Turn the other cheek," he orders. But that's the brother's voice. Heartbreaking. Pretty funny. *Nose*-breaking maybe no more than. "I'm comin' to getcha, if you can just getcha motor started, get in the driver's seat."

This is how Daley figures it: weekends the father had a few brews and put his daughter on his lap and fondled her legs in that order; one Christmas (because she was singing and Daley hummed along "It Came Upon a Midnight Clear") the mother's gold greasy comb fell down an unreasonably large drain and it was the child's fault; now she had four arms interestingly having had the experience of becoming a tree in her younger years, but she was putting out the laundry now so she wasn't indoors after all and was taller and would she have been hanging out laundry in Canadian December on a clothesline knotted to one small branch of the backyard tree? You don't want to think about these things. Whole show took place in one day then it was over, you might think, but not Daley. Someone tells someone else they should have loved Peg, Peg's the mother: because it's late and Daley's neighbors west and east must have heard her crying out. (What's that guy doing in there? These days it might not be all bad.) And singing, his living room windows reflect her, the unasking street and all his other life and habits gathering to make the glass opaque, and the neighborhood transient white man in a burlap serape and sometimes an undersized top hat was under a lamppost right now scribbling upon already scribbled-upon pages of a little book (another writer)—lights rising floor by floor in Daley's house, the kitchen dark now, old sobs gathering, this high parlor presently, too—like Daley, chosen, it's the whole package all perhaps due to Ruley Duymens's steer.

These are true sobs, or late response to Barry clobbering her, to anything, they convince you anyway (but of what?), exercising her hopes as if they could see the waist of her underwear divided by her spine (it comes to Daley, she kind of teaches him), he figures she's staying over, but maybe not. When will he know? He loved her mind, or some of her thinking, was drawn to this disorder in her that took the shape of a troop of people she couldn't resist and here they were. Her shoulders shaking, get her upstairs—the piece is done—she had never behaved like *this* on stage, not when Barry crushed her one; and a put-upon parent or random citizen of whom charity is demanded as if all you need is love, Daley could shake her—like Stop it: was Daley taking advantage of her? He didn't care, he'd make it up to her, help her out. Is it hysteria? It isn't only voices she does, it's whole people—pretty good, really, people without a story. And now she was singing, accusingly, not Gospel, or Good Woman Blues, but: it comes out mean and cracked and the hell with everyone. Her father frightened her good, was he Bruce or Anthony? yet what he did was get away?—or somebody did. Just how did he? Into someone else's flesh right here and now.

It wasn't rape probably. She speaks for this "him," some leaning, male-oily voice, filthy games celebrated by gods, and like a craftsperson pulls on his *tongue* you might think: holds it slippery there, just an organ, ugly (Daley gave a mime twenty dollars during rush hour on the snowy steps of the public library, the day after a Swedish tourist had stepped from a cab at Fifty-seventh Street and asked him directions), and then she brings the tongue to her like an ice cream and puts it in her, overdone, is it that the man or loved one or molester or all three gave her his tongue?—it seems so, but then she couldn't speak, was that it?

Whoever did whatever to her you couldn't just blame someone. She can't say what happened, but she's got the hips for it, God knows. He hears his own voice, "Don't gimme the bum's rush," more his words impersonated from that fatal phone call, yet his father's words though here *her* father's or uncle's, "Okay heave-ho," also familiar like your business philosophy. Is he going to get his head handed to him?

He could ask her, Were you raped? Sounds wrong, that wasn't it; or she'll tell him, won't she? Many don't.

And it's late, is she here for the night? He hangs a leg over t'other, his own yawn comes up around his head, a sound, cottony, his quickness catches him. He resettles himself feeling uncomfortably snug in his pants and wants only to get out of these clothes or to touch her more than he is afraid to say so, and what's it matter, it's his experience against hers and he will just ask, it's his place.

Yet it's another thing he wants—and of her. Is it the apparent father saying now, "You've had a load of privileges around here, liberties, the lot, don't take advantage."

This show she's been working on, "one-woman" you say but a number of people, for she's also older, looking over her shoulder, on the run, male-ish, haggard, it's the father you're sure, and then puzzling over her, a laggard uncle half in the bag or intoxicated you could call it, or is all this not "fact" but what they're *really* like, these uncles two or three of them, mad, almost nice, brotherly, hawkalugueying phlegm up from their joint chest, she's had a long day, forced, *made* to love things that just kill her / want a piece of poor her.

And she's younger too, not so clean as Helen, as Della, thin compared to a person who'd sat down at his table Monday night after the set had begun. Did Daley do something? Are she and Daley not speaking? For a moment they don't get along. It's the way he's sitting, his older attention span, his hidden body, his faithful doubt, his house and then these foolish things are what she *finds* in him.

"What they get up to in Canada," Daley consulting his watch. She doesn't react, it and *he* are part of this one-woman, ongoing thing. "That's what the last guy said."

Laundry bowing the line, damp, warm, and weighty she needs three hands or has them, a bedspread brushing the grass that needs mowing, she'll pinch the clothespins open, underwear's evidently a cinch, a wet gravity in towels Daley remembers now. From her hair down, she's all body to be undressed from behind gently down over the shoulders, kneeling now *before* her but it won't happen.

She wheels at someone's approach, a nightgown on her arm, or jeans. She performs: with her hands, her palms, just does it, licks her upper lip, thinks a second.

"Right." Likes Daley again, almost loves him, what choice has he? (Walks *him* through it? Beckoning toward the piano, the stairs beyond, and, up the stairs, the landing, three bedrooms, the baths.) It gives way again to this rigmarole of men, crackling, ratchety, sort of awful brouhaha. She's got to obey what's said and done to her yet can't believe it, since she can't tell. She was not prey so much as used for another's experience and doesn't even need to be told not to tell, it's between us, or, now she's with Daley, none of their business. It wasn't *so* bad. She's here to turn it into something. Seedy in their approach to the landing. He's seeing her act for the first time.

The oven is on downstairs, smells pan-brown and crust-black and old, last month's exploded sweet potato or a drop of tonight's cheese, a rim of forgotten frozen potpie: but he would not move, not if he saw a flame's shadow reflected in the glass. She employs the furniture at hand, like a caterer, not quite moving in. For kneeling and falling, soft red-and-brown leather ottoman that had been his uncle's. A good table that had been his wife's stepmother's family's she bangs the meat end of her fist down on—she hates it—and pulls a wretched old ladder-back to her to sit down on backward facing him over the slats, the knees of her jeans frayed open, the chair giving sideways might not take it. "Who? me?" He's over his head and he nods on instinct, she seems to want a reply. "Because *I* did it, why did I do it?" asks a pure solo voice. "You were a foundling," a man's husky tenor obliges objectively, though Daley doesn't believe that really happened, though the woman cheerfully, "I'll just have to be philosophical about that one." Why's it give him a shiver in his belly (he's not-tired again). And a man, "Oh *I'm right . . . I'm*," it's Daley to the very life with that frank generosity.

But now a man's flat "Hol' it, hol' it, don't get the wrong idea," a drinker beautiful and friendly as intercourse or as incoherence will permit dismounts the chair *she* sat in (but disappeared from) and comes over to Daley and the sofa. To spiel some shitty idea: "There *is* no wrong idea," the man speaking out of her hates Daley, this middle-age New Yorker who's with their Becca. Is it Canada or Britain he calls forth? "We are a great empire. We stand at once the wonder and admiration of the world for our prosperity that is due to one thing and only one, that every man can make himself." The words go back a ways even into your memory. Will they trash Daley's furniture? In and out in three hours, she gone, never see her again, someday she's famous in a small way. Well he doesn't *want* Becca talking in that voice, he won't have it, won't stand for too much of that, her lowdown coarseness isn't him—embarrassing—a failure of talent, a tiresome and unfeminine sound: "I hear you like a hole in the head, honey" (the man's voice Canadian? *American*, almost), "it's up to you, honey, do I have to do unto you as I would have you do me? I've known you these ten, twelve years." Awful as well, he's got to tell her the truth. He would never *hire* a woman who talked like that—makes a mental list of what her story comes down to, bottom line: what her family was, allowing for north-of-the-border differences; and is glad he hired for the doomed agency Courtney for minority as well as her dazzling secretarial skills and surprising gift or rhythm for a kind of theatrical encouragement in these new dry-run job interviews he described to Becca coming home tonight, the client preparing to face a personnel director, though agency closing down, closing down. Will Becca one day be doing an impression of Daley, not him but his sound, his ways?—what was he *doing* with her (Helen won't even ask, because "with" won't occur to her yet), maybe Becca wasn't looking at him in the audience in the first place. He's badly kidding himself, and this could be a damaged person, her growl now, dumping a successful play part for this one-woman thing—is that what's up?

"Just 'cause I caught your eye, you're the king of Sheba?" Becca's growl, it's affected, has to be, womanish, street, a mama with match-less experience, racial, do they have street in Canada? She's at home, it's where she is, she said he made her feel good, he can touch it, that's all, this woman and her work, at one-twenty in the morning, his eye sockets deepen and ache. The little girl wouldn't eat for three days, he gleans from the piece. He's a sounding board touched by her lim-its is all. Is something up to him? *Was* she a foundling? And now, oh the song her woman's true voice sings,

> You're everything I got to lose,
> Got nothing else except my Blues,

rhymes, and is to someone who let you down and did you and you unloaded and then needed, that's all, who maybe went off the deep end. Who was it played up there for ten years, late 1960 early '70s, I'll leave you breathing see if I don't.

> I'll leave you breathin'
> See if I don't.

She hangs near the pre-war piano, the box's inner curve and the return marked by two up-and-down bars of light from the street the song alone is between them, the one-woman piece makes sense now in the sentiment and load and some pubic bone to it and an imperative winding-downness of the moment, if he can come up with the missing chunk (if it's not him for the night). He'd plotted ahead swiftly, the next day or two or three, would he go see the play tomorrow? What would Friday hold? What would the end of Act One be like the next time? The theater dark Monday night he seemed to recall. She hits a chord after all, looking at him over the piano, hitting the second jazz chord standing, then the first, Daley shows he's with her 120 percent, he's honored, this isn't caroling, will he be all over her soon? What's she do with her legs? A dance put on just for him here years ago by his wife, a concluding get-down. Twelve years Becca hit on. There are no miracles. The voice, part American, of uncle or brother strikes up again: "We find a people on the Northeast, who have a different government from ours, being ruled by a queen. We see a people to the south who, while they boast of being free, keep their fellow beings in bondage." It's a slavery speech in that voice of empire a minute or two ago. She goes silent a few beats like a soloist. *She* won't stay tonight. But she will—it's nothing to her, her languid yawns. It's pussy, Helen will say, Becca's palms he could kiss.

So long, week.

She needed to give him a picture of what went on once. And still does, without her.

She stretched, like looking at her watch. Just using the place. Swung her elbows, pivoted losing her balance over him hands on those hips (*he* yawns), working-girl hands: "I'm going to tell the story of the breakfast," she begins mean as anything, he needs to stop her, her neck so near, enough is enough. She's a mountain, though frail. She covers her face, she's been hurt, her belly at him. She picks up his need for the truth (and some sleep), speaking in the hard voice of supposedly a man: "So you see through this mountain of trash. And who were *you* phoning at that hour?"—the voice Dad's now, or the uncle's who messed her up (who puts an arm around Becca, she's two people in one, brotherly). She acting? or about to strike the jerk sitting forward in the couch? "*I* saw you stop dialing when I came out the door, darling." She's herself, accusing.

"Dialing!" Daley burst out, playing along, "for cryin' out tears, you came in the door and I was—"

"Tell me!" she shrieks, and he wonders if the neighbors are up, the father with his kids to the east in particular, the mother Isabel to the west, her boys.

"—I was *waiting* for you."

"Tell me."

"Well I sure hope it's worth it," he says truthfully.

It was then that he could see her, haloed, streetlamped, irritated, knowing some damn loving thing about him (brace yourself) probably just Della when he went looking for her at night, he had seen that it would happen, the problem at a later time out on the street. It was just his prudent insight on duty and this was only Wednesday. "Nothing mysterious about it." He held out his hand to her. "I was calling an old friend from the corner, twelve *years* I've known her. She *works* for a living." Becca was going to do something if he didn't where he sat back in the old sofa looking up at her.

"Oh please!" Becca cries, falling on him straddling him curled upon him lightly hugging him superiorly, a little laugh inside her shaking. If it wasn't business as usual for her. He didn't like it entirely.

"Did you like it?" she asked; "you didn't—"

"No," he protested.

"—I can tell." Unconsciously rubbing the silky scar along his forearm.

He could only think or hold her—not give some opinion. *Had* she known him? She'd thought he was someone else tonight. There must be other explanations that Daley's indiscriminate fairness conceived. Had *she* watched *Daley* and known him from experience? The audience performed! Had she paired a phone voice with this face?

The head behind Leander's wagging one. Daley wouldn't scare her off.

Had she been living with Barry and was ready for a breather? He saw Barry, before she lost the loft, moving out himself. It was her business, Daley had always said. He heard Clara on the phone: *Yes she is in the cast.* He saw meeting his wife the first time. He wondered what had been expected of Leander. To sit through this?

She had included Daley just like that in her thing, the world required more sex and compassion.

He tries: "There are no miracles." It works, he can see. Yes, he had been hoping there were no miracles, she would go anywhere with him if he talked like that—up the stairs for starters, and he makes up (as a lawyer tries to believe what the client partly makes up), "Your brother, I was just calling your brother."

"When I came in the *door?*" Becca chuckles, this mere girl, an odor of scalp, of neck. She throbs, he's silly to go along; but he's not. The amazing Helen, what could he have protected her from?—independent as a doctor, executive waiting for that phone call; athlete he thought with this woman on top of him, a motorcycle revving down the street and past the window, which nearly distracted her.

"I didn't have to have you here," he went too far, "you're not the only wrinkle on the prune."

"I'm all of them," she breathed; "see?" She wanted him to look.

"Be glad of where you are," he tilted a face to her, he had become gifted, another person using her.

"You're right, it was my old brother," she said," (The brother picking up a phone somewhere in the Northeast Corridor, thickset, ordering a strike, getting an update. Calling the producer maybe, you can't be sure, some curious past coming instantly to bear.) "'We are a great empire. We are eighty years old. We stand at once the wonder and admiration of the whole world. Such a race of prosperity has been run nowhere else. And why? Because here every man can make himself.'" The girl laughed at herself or the words. *Eighty years old?* that almost American voice proclaimed. Did that make it the 1850s?

"You've had enough of the wrong people in your life shaking their fingers," she said, a young woman condescending.

"Not for years," he said. There's something afoot, a deal, real estate entertainment money, though a test of Daley maybe, and beyond this visitor. It's outside them and this house. It's even a war zone and a joke. "Flatterer," he said.

She held up her hand, her fingers—"Look at these guys." His heart cooled. "But I'll never kill you," she said, "I think I can guarantee I'll leave you breathing."

"One question," he ignored hers, "you weren't really a foundling."

"No. That's right, come to think of it; I just knew one, not even a girl. You . . ." she said from her mouth to his, looking at his mouth, "you understood; you got it," her teasing teeth a little uneven and quite large as if what he'd made up in the instinct of the moment was true and it *was* a room not a sidewalk. *What* had he gotten?

Did he know Ellen Terry? she asked him. He didn't. The English actress? Played Shakespeare when she was eight. No, he didn't.

He had had twelve years free of punishment, thinking for himself. He would leave for work in the morning, and would she be here? Spirit her away to the country. Stop at Wendy's. She had the play, though. (Becca dropped her clothes in the bedroom wherever she was standing.)

First night, when he still didn't know what was happening, she needed some feedback (they all said it), singing for her supper, that's what she said, though all he could think looking at her all over for signs of This or of That was, Did that really happen?—though he thought he wasn't supposed to ask (or she would disapprove or disappear), nor did he point out that "feedback" wasn't what she— *feedback* meant . . . never mind. Just twenty-four, tell her what she wanted to hear.

Helen: "Did she bleed Thursday?" Helen's clarity over a phone they together had made strangely unphonelike yet forgivingly utilitarian, calling with tickets for . . . Becca: I can get us anything you want.

Becca does all the voices, his in there, not the deeper, grating courtesy voice, but it's him. "Take it even if you're not totally qualified. Sink or swim." How'd she know his voice? But how could she have made up his very words to a client? Either you're creative or you're not. Did they help each other see one thing? He saw it coming.

Why would she come to him? He asked this dishonestly perhaps keeping it to himself (there were better words for it than *dishonestly* somewhere out of reach) when he was at work with Donna (or returning to a message from Leander!) or at lunch with a restaurant-owner friend who was having lung trouble or with Sook, his running friend, when he would field a question about Helen, and it seemed as if his condition wasn't noticeable, and maybe it wasn't, to his friends.

The young woman in succeeding days there in his house—he saw her in the long window and someone in the street noticing; and in the bathtub and on the phone and (as he actually did find her) talking to Isabel, his neighbor, over the backyard fence about a poet's café on the East Side staging her one-woman piece (news to Daley); and poking around the kitchen where he knew that in her researches she would find on a hook back inside the cupboard the labeled key to the third-floor studio. But nothing unremembered or to be exhumed, just done with.

If she could find the time Daley would get the car from the garage and sneak her away to the country. They would walk in the November woods, a wild turkey somewhere listening, a flash of yellow under a siskin's wing, shrikes doing their specialized work, a snow-throated sparrow all but invisible in the brush. He was thus even more ruthlessly unfaithful to his old friend Helen than in body. But he hadn't found a moment to take Becca there. She had done some winter camping with her brother once upon a time. All she said. Canadians. This was her older brother who was in scrap iron, who knew New York. She had once contemplated a forestry degree, a woman of parts. Before studying, as the bio had said, philosophy, she had read classics briefly, wrote a paper on a fifth-century Greek naval commander generous to the hungry inspired partly by a small Spartan lyric recited to him by his beloved but unmarried sister in Becca's opinion.

Her businesslike glimpses of sisters (hers? it wasn't clear how many siblings there were the second time she did her piece for Daley and he didn't think to ask) and her father and uncle, who were "in shoes" (!) in (was it?) London, Ontario, and her older brother of course whom she had lived with, and another uncle who had done okay in Guelph: she missed the old bricks, and a mathematician cello player she knew, and "the States, you know?"

"*Missed* the States? But you're here."

You can live many lives, look at Ellen Terry, eight years on the stage already and at sixteen she marries an old guy, a painter named Watts. No, Daley wouldn't know him. The theater is dark, she washes her husband's brushes and plays the piano for him. "'Not one single pang of regret for the theater,'" she said, a few years later she has two kids by another guy, another life in the Victorian country and one day the wheel comes off the ponycart and a horseman offers help and recognizes her. From years ago when she was a child learning the stage, smacked and cuffed, her ears boxed while between them she was being toughened up. And now back to the stage after two other lives!

That's right! Daley exclaimed, stimulated, confused, a vision at hand. "You know Ellen Terry?"

No, no, he was thinking of . . . (Daley paused and withheld the name.) He described a lost-soul young man with a coke habit and, former champion he'd guessed, a swimming habit; and a late-night interest in the piano; for it had come to Daley from how the guy crossed the *street*—and smoked a *cigarette*—but, sorry, why was Daley deceiving his beloved, he interrupted himself, but—Becca added, "A great laugher, what a laugher," knowing maybe who he meant, or just reacting. Laugh sooner than breathe, Daley said. Like Daley Becca wasn't surprised by what others knew. She under*stood* you could sense the piano player in how somebody walked . . . not uncanny at all. "He almost clobbered me Monday night, if it's the one I'm thinking of, I thought he was going to," she said, knowing it was Leander Daley meant or assuming other Leanders, any Leanders you had in mind (was this promiscuous, open, damaged in her?). "Let things go their own way. I had it up to here"—she tried to do something with her hands, point or speak or fend off, and failed—"letting things go their way at home I mean, then I left but I was probably at the controls when I was four or five like a little piece of cake, not knowing *why* stuff was happening of course."

"How could you? You were a kid."

"Not even," Becca laughed, and wiggled crazily.

He wanted to tell some friend, or Donna, what was going on at home, then imagined Donna knew. This was the morning of the day Leander actually showed at the office soon after noon but Mr. D. was gone. He told Becca how he'd sized up Leander. She seemed not to know so much after all about Leander. He let Leander go, and there he was, Leander in a pool. The pool. The loitering water gross. Daley had pretty much foreseen what he had foreseen—Leander's arrival, his checking in with Donna when Daley was out, wouldn't make much of it though he told Becca how it felt, a plunge into another person or maybe just guessing a résumé—and that it had happened several times in twenty-five years or so when he really knew the person, but.

"But you *don't* know Andy."

Just experience. Or he knew her. You know what people will do.

Becca did not agree, but her hands, thinking like shaping him, her history she liked dark or sort of causeless, unfathomably coming from you didn't know where. Cause was a superstition, he was certain she had said. Having her these days when he doesn't know her.

All day at his desk, at lunch, on the phone, eye to eye with Donna, he can't get the blow to the face Barry will strike at around nine o'clock off his mind; Barry's work, his whole life (for he needs a job—does he need a life?) took shape like Leander swimming laps: and a Dumpster established across from the theater and a sewer at the corner blocked by cement compound a workman at the end of the day had tossed and now it was hard as rock. What will Daley do when she's off to the theater? One afternoon she's out, the voice on the incoming tape at "three on the button" asking her to call the Long Island paper they needed that interview with her: wasn't the play moving uptown?

Hadn't she come to him for a reason Wednesday? Not secretive; say anything; humming for a moment on the stairs, then at the top scenting someone else (on Daley) and "I don't mean perfume" in a voice of hers so that he felt not a twinge about Helen, which became in that moment one more thing about Becca. Unsurprisable—he heard the ancient syllables. Common words were singing foolishly in him What did it matter, her life she seemed to know he could take or leave. Not all good things would come to him together with her. Friday he asked her if she had called *Newsday* back. Of course not.

Daley expected his call. There was something wrong, tracking her from a distance or carried by her to deliver. Did the brother do business here? He must, considering. Construction firms, Oklahoma, Shanghai had been mentioned, a stockholder who went to meetings. Hopewell? Tian An? Business took off.

And telling Daley Wednesday night—it was two in the morning, "Please don't *ask* me for things."

"You'll know without my asking?"

"You'll know."

She meant in bed, he thought. He didn't feel sorry. He didn't owe her a single thing except courtesy, love. He could forget her life. Time this week like a deposition—his first, years ago. He didn't need to know the producer's predictable presence in real estate development. The brother who must have told the producer what plane she would be on when she came here a year ago. Her absences back home, the landlord had served a complaint, who knew the producer, maybe well. Now this one-woman surprise she was preparing.

They watched her in the building—the super, and a relative of his on the payroll. Brother-in-law running the freight elevator, said Daley with a laugh, he could see it. Why yes, how did he know? she said, and that wasn't the half of it. (Daley "saw" the super, he was tall, in sneakers, came from some humid shore, and had his own letter of the law.) She accepted Daley's curious guess—not amazed at all; accepted it; was she just gifted, or too thoughtful to be distracted by—outlying materials; though secretly keeping an eye out, crossing a field with a bull in it or in the middle of a two-way street. How, though, had Daley known? It figured. New York, the crude ground of experience repeating, of the city, a banal astrology, types, like the petrol station girl in New South Wales reborn with imperfect white teeth who was coming to New York someday or had come. And if she would now have three or four years on Becca, they surely looked alike but looked toward New York as a home for their spirits that would make something of any raw materials at all.

Becca said she would take off her own clothes yet he had known already, it had occurred to him downstairs when he was asking her if anyone else had been entertained by her little masterpiece. He was getting the gist of it.

"The pith." Her breath comes back to him, her voice over it the first night, late late, two-thirty in the morning.

"Those people?" he said (those awful people who did whatever they did to you, he was privately convinced).

"I owe them everything. You been daydreaming right in my face. But you understood, you got it," she said. Walking, they had talked about subjects, the city, she was well informed about the draft riots, a lynching at Varick and Charleton, the Swedish engineer who became a Civil War hero by designing the *Monitor* and lived downtown near the river for decades, strange talk to be leading home to Daley's place. A terrible sinking, Becca had said.

Wednesday night she pulled things out of her bag to show him. Objects soft, hard, shared, teasing. Genuinely surprised to find this hunk of a ring she'd almost said no thanks to and would have to give back, Clara wanted to unload it, not to just anyone.

He had trod the carpeted stairs after her Wednesday night, her feet bare, across one pocket of her jeans a wavy stitched line. From behind he wouldn't have guessed the frayed holes in the knees. (On stage she wore a skirt for Barry.) "Did you believe it?" she said of her one-woman piece.

"Sure."

"What do you mean 'Sure'? Did you see? Did you get it?"

The work, if you could call it that, turned frankness and all emotions into family, he could swear, Canada, a living room—no tale really, only experience, but of what? She reached the second-floor landing, the hall, some center of resistance in her or both of them joined. "It was you I saw," he said. (He wanted not to say the wrong thing—the untrue thing.)

"Oh good! But is that all?"

"No, the family, the father, the bathtub, the comb, the little girl every inch of her"—her pink dark asshole—"the brother and all; right in the same room as me, and I thought . . . he might ring the bell at any time."

"So did I."

At the stairhead she looked both ways.

Which was *their* room?

# 3

LEANDER SWIMMING LAPS IT CAME TO DALEY KISSING BECCA GOOD-BYE Thursday morning, this was how Daley saw it, extremely alive and true—and loyal!—the sight itself, and heard it: Leander swimming laps hummed underwater. It set him off again laughing and he let some water in his nose. Laughter awash in his chest and yelping and spreading behind his expensively but defectively goggled eyes like the hummed words. *A-buse mee, you sweet a-bu-sable you. Re-use me, you inex-cu-sable you.* The song came and went underwater, gobbles of high, wired sound bubbled from his hum, his nose. Not him alone; someone largely absent he had the distinct impression. His sense of humor though. The feeling continued, channeled perhaps from the Lap God. *Re-use me, you inexhaust-ible you.* Long winds chilled the passage of sinus space through Leander's brain, and from outside and inside him came the concussion of a woman entering the pool he had the distinct impression, the perfect insertion acoustically swallowed up so neat it was a splash reversed, a thin stone spun into the pale green waters. *Re-marr-kabul you*, it inspired the swimmer: how to *yooze* your laughter: and he shouldered and motored to the far end, rolling some but with that famed kick from the butt to complete his twenty-ninth lap. He back-flipped the turn and surfaced like a breaststroker to check out the dark cap coming down the left lane at speed, someone to sing *with* if he wasn't already picking something up or she his hum. (Daley on his way to work was in there with Leander—what it was like.)

No ring on her hand in passing, the elbow just high enough to bring her precious bent wrist through, and a watery glance breathing on the left, blurred, busy as only women swimming laps can be. Did she smile? It was good of her. Older, a woman with memories to plug into in a sweet black bathing cap. Familiar at the club, but what the hell was her name? Leander took it up a couple of beats, and the November day was springlike exhaling through the vaulted skylight. The Lap God or someone up there. Ignorant of anyone awash down here.

The dream of the lap swimmer rolling easy like his old self, upping the beat now, not a race except to make the turn and be moving in the same direction as the woman, be on the same page, his laughter absorbed in all its terribleness into his easy, whole-body rhythm the long, dissolving midst of a friendly fuck here with a real woman, whatever. *No side to her*, Pap used to say, *always the same person, same remarkable woman*. Humming lap after lap, a machine with an alarm clean-chlorinating the collapsing neutron labyrinth of his sinuses, head forgetting her name. Give her one. Loss eased Leander's spirit. Laughter in the night, nothing better than a good joke.

Each lap, each stretch and dig, surplus slid off his middle, his chest, leaving core body mass material of Leander (Daley was physically certain, he could not help seeing Leander—or Leander him and though he had missed his appointment Thursday Leander had made some determination he would be there Friday, seen in advance, Daley was certain.) Leander felt longer, at last older. A lift across his chest, his tubes best they'd been of late, his breathing if you will. *But don't blame me,* slow chords play off Leander's fingers otherwise engaged in tight-together waterwork. *Whatever you do, whatever (you hear?), don'tcha dare, don'tcha dare, don'tcha dare blame me.* The seeming broken-up biology of laughing scattered in among these little head volts, he forgot all but the lap count. The most beautiful of the distances eight hundred meters came toward him but parallel today in some other lane, you have just enough distance to get into the dream.

He lifted his heavy arm and feathered his wrist, checking the time without breaking his stroke, and thought something over fifty laps would do it for today, his underwater melody called up all of what he had been expected to hear out. It's all Abuse now, but it's just their opinion, a two-way thruway, say what they will about spousal husband, mother-to-be with a black-and-blue (and red, too, as a matter of fact) cheekbone eye socket sleepwalking daddy-do, brother getting a lick in, the quiet you keep. A life came into being close around Leander, it no less than *materialized* from, you might think, a memory in the water itself, but a woman's perfume swimming her lane, smell entering you like sound. He's in her pool now.

End-of-lap out-of-body fellow-feeling call it with the woman now up ahead and with all those who use the water, who lose their lives as Leander's own favorite cousin in a sailboat spill in Mystic before he had ever had her in his clutches; or find team stardom as Gams, his grandmother, once had done in the Aquacade where her husband-to-be saw her perform in a one-piece bathing suit still hanging small as a World's Fair icon rotting in a closet in Nunquite, Massachusetts. A fellow-feeling, he suspected, a pool being one of the ideal venues to make a woman's acquaintance, protected, classic, flesh clean and trusting out there.

But here she was at the finish line giving him thoughts to think, recalling cannonball diving boards of his youth before he had become solely and truly a swimmer; for the woman was standing at the shallow end of this diving-board-less twenty-one-yard pool, up to her largely rounded tits, rubbing her black cap back off till it popped off her head and she grabbed for it in the air and smiled and he wanted her at that moment for all those reasons, including the memory in the water, which was not his reason but had been inserted into him.

"Leander, how are you?" she said shaking her hair out so she might have been about to swim naked.

"Better," he said, half in half out, hungry for the first time today. Women better at names, he had a fit of coughing. He found her burgeoning hair gray-and-green-streaked, that old fucking fellow-feeling telling you unlikely people were the message bearers because you could not see it in their face. "Long gone," he said; it came to him (and that he'd be used better where he was going) he would tell *her* this, glistening with experience tanned the middle of November, forty-one or -two, hell, meet some time. The whaddayagonnado words *long gone* the Daley guy had let slip who was bent on making trouble for himself whom Leander had definitely made an impression on (because you don't always know). The wife *long gone*; "Let me give you my . . ." everything up to Leander. For Leander had a card, too.

"Your what?" said the woman.

Drops of water and rivulets stood out on her tan. Leander hauled himself up rather than use the ladder. "My card . . . my dripping . . ."

The woman shook her head. "I know what you mean," she said.

Exactly his words to the Daley guy, a dark runner, potentially inspiring, and too honest a man to be honest when he said what Leander now replied to the woman: "More than *I* know."

She tossed her cap and it slapped his foot lightly. Leander had an appointment. "What are you doing for Thanksgiving?" she said and surprised herself and laughed.

"Fasting," he said—"just kidding. Going home."

He raised his hand to the woman who liked him. She was a complete product, story still unfinished, he'd buy her a smoothie or she'd buy him one sometime. The woman lay back in the lapping waters perfumed with her hair. "How'm I doin', Leander?" (Or did she call him Leander? Daley didn't think it came through like that.)

"*Remarkable* is the word for you," said Leander as his own patented "Ciao for now." "Anon, Leander." Two men entered, stretching and swinging their arms.

It was noon, and Leander was outa here, he could see himself trying sitting on a doorstep on a city street. Instead he was in an elevator.

"Leander?" the secretary said. It might have been a doctor's office. You said your surname, which she had on a white pad. "What kind of a name is that?"

"You mean Leander?" Donna looked up at him in wonder.

She was no bully, a dyed auburn redhead. A sturdy person, unmarried, experienced, Catholic it occurred to him, and thirty-four or -five, the future not quite absorbed by her powers. "My father's name," he said, "if push comes to shove." He had not sunk to an employment agency as if he were hiking in fresh out of college. Though here he was. "My résumé."

Daley was out to lunch. "We had you down for yesterday," the woman said.

Behind this desk three doorways betokened quite an office Daley had going as a sideline. It was the executive headhunting not the dry-run interview simulations Leander was curious about. "Well, I lose a day here and there."

"And probably a good thing," the woman said; "Mr. Daley was . . ." she nodded.

"Yeah, I couldn't get rid of him the other night."

The secretary frowned, smiling. "He'll be back."

"Today?" said Leander on an instinct.

"I'm pretty sure he will."

"Ah."

He gave her the penitent charm of a heavy young man acquainted with money.

"Here." She handed over to Leander two pages to fill out. The touch of her fingers letting go of it. Her name white on the brown nameplate tilted on its little stand. "*Now* I know what I'm doing here," he lied. He was to be processed. In someone else's hands. Or mind, you hoped.

"Mr. Daley I know wanted to . . ." She nodded, she was not in the slightest indecisive, and Leander got a chill in his gut habitual as a taste at the back of his throat, sharp, medicinal, but this time possibly fresh chlorine he'd snorted crooning underwater.

"I gave him my card, that was it. Couldn't get rid of him."

"Good," the woman before him said.

He coughed hard and he slipped the forms back onto Donna's desk and reached for his handkerchief. He sniffed twitching his cheek. "He'll find out," Leander said. She looked at him. Would she be unprofessional? *One of these big lugs; overweight*, Leander could hear her think, *likes a good time, has the heart for it; take you to a decent restaurant, some mileage in that heart.*

"What're you taking for that?" Donna asked.

"Drugs," Leander coughed again. She laughed then. "Anytime," Leander said. She put her hand on the forms.

"Donna," he said, because she liked him. He sounded a little off. "Tell Mr. Daley I'll see him."

"He knows."

She wasn't going to tell Leander to fill out the forms or take them with him. She wanted him to stick around, though; he could tell. "Oh I'll be back," Leander said. She was concerned, surprised, amused, none of the above. "Seeing some guy about a job who pursued me outa the theater onto the sidewalk 'cause o' something I said."

"Oh it was you," Donna said, to his amazement. He thought she was a little more than a secretary. "*You* wouldn't hit a woman."

"I've come close." So Daley had *told* her! But not much. Except that Daley was everywhere for a second. "You like jazz?"

"I think I do."

Leander didn't tell her she was remarkable. He couldn't say it. "Luv ya," was what he said. He had to get out of there—a driving range on the Long Island City side where you could hit a golf ball in the general direction of the Empire State Building and the East River and seagulls on the netting overhead never moved.

All the things he could speak to her of. In a way made up out of the city he knew. Put together, reassembled, and so forth, to entertain a woman.

"I want to do something," Leander said.

"Something great?" said the woman before him.

"'You don't brag,' my father said. 'You tell the truth and you keep your trap shut,' he used to say."

"How do you do that?"

Leander laughed. "He would say, 'You don't criticize a woman; they're a pleasure getting what they wanted out of you. You don't lie.'"

"Pure accident sometimes," said this fine person, a little brassy looking, true gentlewoman, standing up now behind her desk with the insurance-company nameplate.

"That you lie?"

"That you avoid it."

Why had she stood? Leander wondered.

And you don't marry beneath you. The mean truth and confusion and humor of your father's voice, never mind the smell of cigar and chocolate in the car after a meet.

You used your connections, it wasn't the pulverized crystals that saw all. He went walking, it was darker. Leander at the east end of Chinatown. The off-track betting at Confucius Plaza in the evening. Asian men in unzipped windbreakers standing around with newspapers spread wide to divine the winners.

Outside the theater, the man on crutches wearing the military hat was delivering his invective, which was usually for the intermission crowd at the end of the first act, when it in fact was ten minutes to ten, when Leander, arriving at the corner, checked his watch. Leander knew the play backward, a problem, or did he? Couples emerging, the cream of the crop, a chick her shoulders hunched, arms crossed, listening to another chick beside her, hands stuck into her pants pockets bless her heart, Friday night date night. Leander half hidden behind a city Dumpster as big as a boxcar. He'd come to see if those two had hooked up. Well, he had backed off, enough was enough. Had come for one more freebie Wednesday, why not, she knew where she could find him but he couldn't take any more of her future after the first act—no more, no more. *Place there is none; we go both backward and forward and there is no place,* her words leaving him once. It was good for jazz.

It was Daley in the row behind him Wednesday that partly did it. Traveler in a small-time minefield, midlife decent, the hardest to tell, whom you felt wanted to give you things to *do*, watching Leander step off the curb and walk away, *I'll look for you tomorrow*.

Leander behind the Dumpster, out onto the sidewalk came Daley now to wait. Not a smoker, out of his depth, hands in his jacket pockets. Looking everywhere but across the street and, as Clara Jane in a hurry tonight, came out to remove the easel with the poster review that they said would make all the difference, Daley ducked into a corner phone booth Leander had never noticed and dug in his pocket for change. Leander couldn't quite kid Daley off the woman. He would find out. At his age. Without eyes in the back of his head. And an interesting woman his age with him Wednesday—Helen, a real woman's name—they were long-timers, hard-core possibly, a woman efficient in most things though you forgot.

Becca gave the lobby door its full weight, kind of beautiful, leaning, expecting, alert right and left the way she entered a place, not knowing. It said, They wouldn't let her quit. They would do something. To her. She was approaching the pay phone where Daley, that decent fool, both master and man and like most men fit for abuse if he didn't look out, opened his mouth to breathe, the receiver to his ear, and he put his hand over it and reached to hit the cradle.

And that was when they met, you had to believe. But no, they knew each other in a former life, it's ringing off the hook, it could choke the snot out of you and laugh you to your knees, this great green Dumpster told Leander, with some legitimate scrap in it too and a 1-800 number in yellow, a barricade no more than biology you could shake with coughs like this or toss your plastic into, until looking up you spot a pool cue sticking up and a piece of white lighting track and the corner of a raw pine packing skid, and what's he doing hiding here to see what he can see?

No, he had fucked her already. Not her kissing him, even on the lips (come to Papa do). You could see it rather in how she strolled beside him, swaying, thinking, and uncapped a bottle of water and while she swigged watched Daley. You can't swim uphill, see how long he'd last with his experience. They were perhaps having a little difference of opinion. And they stopped and faced each other, almost aware in the corner of the eye of someone through the Dumpster and its potential, the things in it, who had at least for a day stood up Daley, a man who knew Leander better than he knew he did, swimmer underwater, chief executive officer and half-baked piano player, who could hear her voice objecting who had told him one thing about him that he named everything as it came.

This was how Daley had imagined the bulky young man and if he had not meant to miss him at lunchtime the next day, Donna was there to confirm that Leander had come from a pool and to fill Daley in on Monday as to Leander's sense of humor, employment history, driving-range habit, humming standards underwater (sure enough, though Daley didn't tell Donna it gave her employer a slight jolt), not to mention Leander's cousin who had drowned sailing in Mystic, Connecticut.

# 4

THEY'LL DO IT AS A REFLEX, A "SHOCK" GOBBLE IT'S CALLED. YOU HEAR it in the morning in the woods, at evening maybe. And if a hunter tries it when the woods are crowded with turkeys no telling what you'll see. There's a soft, walking-around *cluck,* with pauses. And there's your basic *yawk yawk* Dad called "love yelps"—hens mating—they gather their young with those yelps, too. Gobblers yelp but . . . *Kee kee,* on the other hand, is the whistle of a young turkey, nothing like a duck's whistle, but it means *hurry, hurry, hurry*, three to five whistles.

Daley *knew* this? Becca asked.

Well, you see them from the road. And you hear them.

He hunted them?

That was his brother's department. Mostly talk though, and didn't know half what Daley did. About hunters? Guns, though Daley didn't really own one. No? He had a pistol somewhere, he lied to her. (Not because he didn't but because it was close by.)

Where is this? The edge of the woods.

The slow, jerky amble of a turkey alert at the edge of the woods. Two slim hens, brown and heather with barred black-and-white if you look close, rusty tailed, stalking seeds; another morning there's a glint of bronze and purple back in the trees, a gobbler, his blue naked head back like a fat person big breasted, a wonk of a wattle, layers of feathers massed like armor, tail fanned stalking acorns, insects, slowly but he can run. We could go there.

Where was it? Well close to home it would be the Catskills, Delaware . . .

There was the phone.

She got down to look under the bed for something. They do it in the road? Becca said as if the phone were not ringing or she were living here.

He put his hand on the phone and laughed with relief and would tell her about the Beatle-like Ob-la-di heard up the river gorge in Australia. It should be your national bird, she said. She had a black-and-blue mark on her ribs he had not seen. The wild one, he said.

He picked up and a man's serious voice said, "Becca Lang, if she's there." Not her acting partner, Barry. Possibly too polite for the producer Beck; and historical, important, time-sensitive as if she'd soon be gone.

On her knees, reaching for the receiver, she looked him in the eyes. Daley handed it over. Phoenicia way, he said softly, between there and Woodstock; up Gilboa, it's nice. (It was Friday, he thought, but she worked Friday and Saturday—as long as the play's on and she's in it.) He could see she was receiving calls. Somebody knew she was here. He didn't have to know who it was. Someone from the theater, from anywhere. No it was someone else. How many people knew? Somebody would break her neck for her. Becca's entitled to her privacy. To be strangled if that's what it is. She listens to the phone, and watches Daley; very faintly, like a thought, she shakes her head—for him (yet lest the person hear her). Turns away. "Yes? Hell*oh*." (How does she say it?—*wake up and smell the coffee*; or, *who is it?*) It goes on. *Is* anyone there? "Hell*o*." She hands him back the receiver. It's none of Daley's business. Unless all she heard was silence. Then we had a situation. It came to Daley that the voice on the phone was Becca's brother, that was all, a shot in the dark, her business. "They just hung up."

What did Becca mean?

Oh and south of Seattle, he added. (Wild turkeys seen on the way to Rainier with Wolf's family.) And in Tennessee and all over the South.

You have the South, the girl said.

When they're eating or contented you could hear a purr. Subtle, not loud. It's really a *trrrrr*—which could be a gobbler getting ready to fight.

So she had received calls here.

Does it run in the family, hunting? (Does she mean it?) He knew a musician who went bowhunting. An Englishwoman. Hit a turkey and couldn't get the shaft out. It seemed to Daley that her brother was in town. He was pretty sure of it.

Never seen a really big wild tom in this country, say twenty-five pounds. Strutting and spitting, fanning, somewhere between an eccentric, grounded walker and a rooster in trees at a moment's notice, excellent creatures. But for *sounds* an Australian turkey double that took the cake. Rougher, gravelly yelps, low pitched. From somewhere else. In a yard behind a gas station. Raunchy. Listen to this, the girl pumping gas went and took the bird and lifted him onto an oil drum and invited you to put your ear up against his side. You wouldn't believe it, listen to what was going on inside him, his gizzard grinding up every damn thing, nuts and bolts inside him, gizzard gravel was what did it.

No, said Becca.

He was proud of it. A one-quarter-wild, supposedly originally American bird because they're indigenous after all though widespread now though not exactly a long-range flier. Brought there somehow and left there by the former Ampol petrol franchiser. Strutting and spitting in the yard still looking for a harem, putt-putting when he was nervous. The frizzy blond girl ran into the office to get the phone leaving the turkey up on the oil drum.

Brother Wolf yacked at the huge gobbler the two of them sounding off, the turkey winged it up into his frigging tree then. It wasn't the turkey, it was the girl Wolf had taken a passing interest in. All talk.

How old?

Taking her *along* with them. But she had a job. Exactly. Where were you going? Canberra, Sydney, and back to Seattle.

Where were you taking her—down the road? Brother talk was all it was. A painting Daley insisted they see because the girl was proud it was there you could tell—what did she with her modest education see in all those trails of American abstract paint? She was coming to the States someday. She was destined to.

How old was she?

Then?

Becca laughed, and Daley knew the phone voice was still in her ear. Hunting talk.

Sheldrakes Wolf said he'd seen being shot out of the sky by Turkish construction workers, yet hadn't they been extinct since the First World War?—though not the ruddy sheldrake perhaps. Shelduck they call it, the Turks've been breeding them in the waters of a waste disposal—the girl laughed—center, it's quite pretty there along the North Anatolian fault line. There's a lake in eastern Turkey where most of the world population of the white-headed stiff-tailed ducks winter. We went up to the Black Sea coast to look around.

Asia Minor, said the girl.

The phone went and Daley—yes, Asia Minor—picked up. It was Isabel next door. Sorry, she'd dialed the wrong number. He mouthed the name to Becca, who had met Isabel over the backyard fence when Daley was at the office. She was just leaving, what time was it? What Isabel meant, though, was that Daley was home. Daley looked at his watch and Becca murmured the time. Two o'clock on a Friday afternoon. Isabel would hang up and try again; sorry.

Probably calling for you, said Daley hanging up, seeing Isabel as if she were looking at the phone.

She just wants to know what's going on, said the girl. Kneeling on the floor she rested her chin on his bare leg. Asia Minor, yes . . .

Flamingoes in Turkey. Wonderful flamingoes that need not apologize to anyone in the state of Florida.

You're a visionary. Come on, how old was she?

The girl pumping gas? In that part of the world twelve maybe. Or fifteen. Who knows?

Brother talk, said Becca, but Daley can see Isabel, he's sure of it, she has taken her coffee into the backyard, just his age; or swinging up the street now, her hair cut in a dark brush, blonded-off-center. Her soft-leather briefcase contains a state-of-the-art clipboard, her measuring tape, a small level, and a phone, maybe her copy of *Seven Habits*.

You could get the wrong idea about Wolf, Daley said.

She lifted her chin off his knee. From you: a brother, she shook her head.

You certainly gave him your divided attention.

Daley smoothed her hair. Wolf almost didn't need it. The day he cracked up his knee on a dirt bike when we didn't have any business being out on an icy street, he never complained at the hospital, and their father all he could talk about for the next two, three days, apart from the damage to Wolf's bike, was a battle in Vietnam that the Diem people had lost in spite of the winning advice they had been given by the American colonel who had worked the whole thing out for them and flew over in an observation plane and it was a setup and still we lost, and Wolf kept his mouth shut through it all, the father ignoring a serious, potentially life-altering injury to his knee that they had to rebuild, he was just eleven, and the father quoted perhaps it was the American colonel himself, "These people may be the world's greatest lovers but they're not the world's greatest fighters," and his wife said, "Well maybe neither are we." (His father a member of a shock troop company during Korea, but.)

When would this have been? said the girl. 'Sixty-three in January, and Daley had been twelve. She pondered it. Before my time, she said.

It was true. Australia. Amsterdam. Japan. God, Many Mouth, though Wolf had had to get himself out of that one.

Many Mouth?

Many Mouth in Southeast Asia. How he lived through it . . . He asked for it.

Was that how?

Who knows?

What do you think?

It might have been the footage they shot of him that saved him.

Come on, said Becca.

A veteran anyway.

Of Southeast Asia.

No, this was after the war. Suspension bridge in Burma. Paid for by the Chinese. There'd been a long-distance contractual dispute afterward that Daley, the older brother, the lawyer, had helped with at this end. He hadn't been present for that particular emergency.

A veteran, though, Becca persisted curiously.

Of risks, dirt bikes, high aftershock odds, ruffled feathers that he'd ruffled.

A veteran of dumb risks, said Becca, as if she didn't do likewise.

The dumbest.

Because he's your brother.

For him, it's one war zone after another, Daley said.

He didn't mean . . .

Oh unfit for military duty, had he said this uproarious brother had long been 4F?

Becca said she'd heard enough about this brother. She went to the closet and looked through the few clothes she had hanging there. She drew a hanger out and looked at both sides of a little dress he hadn't seen.

Okay, enough about Wolf. But it was nothing next to Osaka. Risks you could call criminal for a family man. Osaka was life-defying. An *under*water bridge you could call that one. We could care less about this brother, Becca said. It never seemed to weigh on Wolf, the work.

You could get the wrong idea about Wolf.

What did he say to you? the woman said. A woman's question. What does he say to you?

That I was the risk taker if you can believe it. He'll retreat; he'll be somewhere else, then he'll strike.

But she was smart and his next-door friend must have picked up on it. Always tell you what *he* thought, Daley went on. Not much of a thinker in some regards. On the job he had an incredible eye for structure. Clients didn't like what he told them. People would wait for the word from Wolf. He said you were the risk taker? she asked. And he got hurt, Daley said. He got blown out of the water.

Safety, she said. She told him the jobs Barry her acting partner had had. Daley didn't see her point. Safety, she said, that's what we talked about over the fence, Isabel and I.

Becca and Isabel.

Safety, you're not interested in safety, Daley said. Becca had apparently decided to get dressed. "Told me you got mugged."

"They didn't get a cent."

Suddenly she was working, she was on the bed taking notes. It's the green notebook she left on the piano. He wanted to say, *What're you writing?* She finished and looked up at him and he was dissolved by her offhanded way of including him, preoccupied but he's there. He's leaving the room tiptoeing, his hand finding in his pant pocket the slip of pink paper he'd torn off the little pad in the dressing room Wednesday night, but she wants to read to him from her notebook: "'Our moods do not know one another.'"

She left the room in her underwear and he heard bare feet on carpet. It was the hall, not the stairs. Why was she doing that? This morning he was making coffee and she had stumbled sweetly into the kitchen doorway in only her bra, had she been interrupted? He flipped open the green notebook on the bed: "No harm in looking," he read. "Just looking, looking good, look out, look here. Meisner: *would you say that again? What did I say?*" He heard a window slide up in the guest room. He flipped a page: "uneasy buildings veined with pipes attempt their work." He went after her.

Daley had never seen Isabel bemused, not in fifteen years. You might think her neighbor Daley had come home very early in the afternoon to a girlfriend; when the truth was that Becca, who received undoubtedly phone calls here, was off to the theater in a few hours and she and Daley hardly knew each other, though clothes had materialized in the closet Thursday and Daley was not inquiring about phone calls, friends, actors, producers, brothers, voices yesterday or today, it was her business, literally, and he'd heard actually only one voice and did not speculate, though Isabel had been a second voice calling surely for Becca on Thursday and then she tore herself away, she said—the edge in her voice had possessed him yesterday—and she left. He watched out the front window and stood at the top of the steps and looked up and down the street. He would be of help to her, but what help in the world? That was Thursday. This was Friday. She checked out other backyards, what they had growing there. It was her clear, curved back that he would remember, her bare ribs, the elastic low above the little downy hollow at the base of her spine, her hair, her absorbed profile half out the guest room window looking toward Isabel's yard, it was enough that she just did it. She turned around to him, her face an open question in shade with a reflection of its own against the afternoon light. A room should have light from two directions.

Look at you, she said.

What is happening to my afternoons? Daley said.

This is nothing, Becca said. She reached back to undo herself. She was contemplating the figures in motion carved into the maple headboard that he'd forgotten, whatever they were. Well, she was matter-of-fact. Thursday Friday, Friday Thursday. Had he missed an appointment.

He couldn't get enough of her. He slept swiftly, and unpredictably like an animal or a parent, it came to him, or a wanted terrorist in a basement he had known. He might hold her in the middle of the night and bring her to him. She could joke in her sleep, willing, then like a wit woken early in the morning, a soft lover, nosing around his growling stomach. She could be very nice with him in the middle of the night and go on partly sleeping if he didn't mind.

Was it Thursday?—he murmured before they slept, "I still don't know why you came to me like that. It's not your case surely." She had had a long day, she was already half dreaming in his body, touching him, but now she had decided something else: "I thought you were somebody I didn't know" was what he heard her say, half asleep. That was a good one.

"But you did."

She was asleep almost and she rolled over and gave him one kiss. "Your bones shall flourish like an herb."

"Some liars are special," he said.

Her back to him again, "This is a pretty fair mattress," she said distantly. She held his hand and slept. Had he "reached that age when one visits the heart merely as a courtesy"? Was that it? The words were worth more than the experience possibly. They came from Lotta, her book, her *ex* in fact, whose words she prized more than if he had said them to her. She'd been phoning the office. Her voice was not a caressing voice. It was her way of knowing you. She knew more about

Daley than the young woman at the sink would ever know, and Lotta was almost not even a friend but she had something invested in Daley. What was it?

Becca clattering at the sink, Helen's third call reached him in the kitchen. "She sings too," said Helen, for Becca was wordlessly rendering, "You're everything I got to lose," while she sponged soapy plates and racked them. "I thought you might be alone," Helen said. (What must she sound like to herself?) "Tell her to take care stacking the dishes."

"Just a sec," Daley folded the newspaper in front of him, Becca like an animal twisted around watching. "Hi," Daley said into the phone. Becca opened and shut the fridge. Becca stood over him. Her wet hand came up against his lips. Becca knelt at Daley's side, her head on his thigh, he looked to see if the water was running, but the sound was the hot water heater.

"They're moving it uptown maybe," Helen said.

It's a feeling he's never seen in Helen, she's forty-four, a great success. "They are?" said Daley, and switched hands. He stroked Becca's hair.

"The producer still doesn't know if she's in or out. He must need her. They knew each other. You probably knew that."

"It's all the same to me," Daley said. Becca poised her chin on his thigh contemplating him.

There's more, he senses. ". . . Daley?"

"Mm-hmm." Becca's cheek on his leg, her hand passing along the inside of his thigh.

"Don't let her break any of those plates we bought in Hudson. Two of them are chipped already."

"Well . . . ," he said. What was he doing to Helen? He just couldn't think of anything to say, his hand upon the only-a-little-frizzy, not-his-type sheaf of blond hair.

"I know she's there." Helen might have heard the scrape of a chair pushed back from the table.

"It's true," he said and did not stop what was happening or witness the years he had known Helen or experience an insult if there was any to her.

"You know you had no responsibility whatever for what happened to Della," came the familiar voice, gentle, pointed, cool, and out of control. Women working on him.

"Thank you," he said. The call came to an end.

Time so short, Daley could still enjoy doing nothing with Becca. He said so. Something to be found out. Maybe not.

They sat on the bleached old wooden bench outside the organic café that they'd postponed going into, they sat with their feet out and trusted nothing would interrupt whatever they were doing or not doing. And they had almost forgotten they'd been on the way to the supermarket. It was a nice long Friday. Two tall boys came by and Becca sort of waved and they coldly contemplated stopping but didn't. One was the cook-dishwasher at the sailors' bar who'd come out to have a look apparently at them Wednesday night. Street kids, eighteen, nineteen. Where had they come from? Employed, you felt. She wasn't just friendly, she knew them, they did sheetrocking and odd jobs. They'd worked for people she knew. They could help Daley out with the house, she said—these (he thought) sullen, maybe just socially awkward kids. He had been telling about the Osaka bay disaster but first things last. So they had to get up from the bench and go on down the street to get to it again, the actual job Wolf had let himself in for, and Becca broke in about safety. Look at her, though. *She* wasn't a safe person. He was sure of that. He told her so. He couldn't tell if she liked it. He wasn't supposed to know anything about her; yet she was grateful, too. He felt her power. It was amateur, it surprised her, an intellectual, a distinguished woman. He gathered that she had altered the play from maybe not her experience but what could happen in real life. A transient more than an independent, a thinker as she was subtly sexual and frontally antagonistic if not apparently to him, the older. Or as if he had never known a thinker. Or she was just a very bright person. And she was returning to the theater to that scene at the end of the first act tonight as she did Wednesday, Thursday.

Something was wrong with the Osaka story, she made you feel. Who's looking after who? she said—you could tell that years afterward. Something was obvious to her. She brushed her hand against his corduroy trousers. Nobody's fault, the day had gone dumb, she said. The day? he objected. She was moody, she was owlish, he told her.

She had given up being owlish when she came here. A police helicopter turned and hovered, he pointed it out.

You might think Becca needed to know. (He had described to her the Australian dam situation, because her mother had a cousin who was a mechanic in Australia. That was what Wolf would say to clients, *We got a situation*. They didn't know how to take it sometimes. Client *states* sometimes. Told her the trip, not what he had left behind.) No comment.

She passed through the electric eye and the supermarket double door jerked back and they found a shopping cart with a bad wheel that kept bearing to the right. He didn't forget why they were here, what they needed. He found his list. Cornflakes, bread, cheese, waffle mix, water, toilet paper, he thought of it all at once, like seeing what would happen to someone over her shoulder (imagining Leander's life, for example). What did he want, a medal? she asked over her shoulder. He expanded on the motorcycle segment, she was examining some apples, Israeli oranges, Quebec beets, but she was hearing him. The date on the yogurts, on every quart of milk, came under scrutiny, the strange dates on the orange juice cartons, the quarts and the half gallons that took you up into mid-December. The "Sell before" dates of the wrapped chickens came under scrutiny, the packaged shrimp, hamburger, leg of lamb. She had kept house and was a tourist.

She had found a big kosher bird and she held it up in her hands turning around toward Daley. They could roast a turkey! (When? he thought.) What was the matter? she demanded to know. Nothing was the matter. *When* could they? she asked. That was what *he* was wondering. (Was she planning to ask Barry? Clara? Ingrid? or whoever had phoned? the cast? Isabel next door of whom she seemed totally unjealous?) Forget it, she dumped the thing back into the bin, she had read his mind. We'll be coming back, he said. You think so? she retorted; to buy a turkey? somebody you were thinking of having Thanksgiving with?

Thanksgiving? When was that? "You and your friend. In the country."

"That's right, I forgot," said Daley.

The girl—his girlfriend?—smiled meanly. "Stuffing a bird," she hauled up another bird, "spooning corn bread and raisins and walnuts into the breast cavity."

"How did you know?"

"I didn't; it was just the prospect of getting out of here," said Becca looking above her. Her dark eyes and fair hair, his beloved abusing him for the moment, his friend (make haste); what time did she have to be at the theater? His heart sank a little. What was it? she asked.

She didn't like the supermarket perhaps. It was her, not the place. The place was like a refrigerator, did they get their months mixed up. She was welcome to leave. What was it?

Becca didn't know what they were doing here, she was ready to go. She was still thinking about Daley's brother. Why was she doing that? He had told her the Osaka story but. Weren't he and his wife on vacation? she asked at checkout. Oh yes; but caught by this emergency much, much nearer than Wolf's family in Seattle.

Where was she? Where was the wife? They'd been traveling in India? That's right, but now they were at the hotel in Osaka.

God, said this woman. Daley's wife had been curious as to the diagnosis and . . . but it was her vacation. She had seen some dancers in India.

Could have stayed in India. You're right. Probably went back to New York.

She probably did, said Daley; or back to India to catch the end of the performance.

Becca laughed. It was his business. Daley became aware of the surrounding music, a big-strings treatment of jazz standard "Embraceable You" and visible to one side of the discount stickers on the windows the two tall boys out on the sidewalk with a third. There was something going on and Becca had picked up on it indiscriminately, nothing to do with anything, Becca said. The Cuban woman computer-feeding prices into the register listened as Daley continued.

(Was she moving in? He didn't think so. She had studied philosophy and he thought she had said forestry.) Well, Daley had wristed the gas, winged out ahead, and leaned them into the right-hand lane, the blur of the concrete, the shock-absorber piston, and now in the back corner of his eye in the hand behind him the dark thing of tread swinging up out of sight and flying in the rapid air a whap sickeningly against some aspect of the truck Daley caught just a glimpse of in the left mirror. Sure enough it had smacked the driver's windshield and got hooked onto the wiper. In America you could get shot for serial recycling like that if the other guy had his weapon accessible. You could even be punished by the law.

That's not the end of it, Becca said, the tall boys following down the street (bringing up the rear) with a shopping cart taken from the supermarket. The end of them? No, the end of your biker story.

Did Becca *know* them, the boys?

Well, she'd been sitting on the steps thinking about things. The steps of our house? Yes, around noon. And they had come by and asked if she needed any work done. And what had been her answer? She had known one of them. Where on earth from? Not known, but recalled. From a bar where—A bar? He might be too young to work there but he helps out at the electrical supply down the street and he was washing dishes there one night. Dishes? They serve food at this bar.

Daley said that she got around. Oh it was the bar he'd wanted to stop at, she said. Our first night? Daley asked. Our first night. Daley looked back. The boys were gone, now that he knew what was what. He recalled her peering in the gold-lettered big window of that old bar Wednesday night, for she knew the place, twenty minutes from the theater, sailors' bar, he'd said like a guide, and now it was Friday afternoon, and he knew that electrical supply, knew the three-story brick building. It was in that block near the river north of here. You're thinking, she said. Just tell me about that hunk of tread. He took her arm with his free hand and she squeezed him close to her and he felt her breast under her sweatshirt against his knuckles.

He would feel them coming, questions asked on the offensive. Not the brother question yet in its purer form—behind you, distinct, absent. Why did Daley already remember her as if she had left? Though she would leave certainly, or he'd see that she did. Three, four days' living with Becca with never a word about his representing her. So early Thursday morning the wintry FM had ignorantly woken him for his run when she was already examining his entire body and the scar on his right forearm, silken, long, old, terrible wound, he told her suddenly awake as if he were not half asleep where it came from to make her smile at the story and kiss the length of the scar: you see what you get. When you go running. At dawn. She had thought it was some accident injury. Or a purple heart. Some uncanny ploy of hers he ignored. Well, you're pretty fit.

Her living with *him*. With practically nothing on, she was writing a thought down real quick like homework, is she copying it from the once slender, now thickened green volume lying open beside her notebook and couldn't be disturbed in the middle of the day? He can get around her, she likes being here, already the two of them coming and going, her ankles across the made bed.

It brought home to Daley what little he knew. You find disorder. If you can. Brother Wolf, your family firing pin detonating adventure and randomness. What kids bring too, or *their* order. Becca, in the bedroom and kitchen, was something of a kid. A sort of workday for both of them. Though he can get around her, she likes being here, her things on the rug. Comfortable enough on the bed writing, to let herself be irritated by him, when she's getting something down as fast as she can in the face of impending interruption. Time-sensitive, she's an actress working but she'll risk a little sexy politeness. Will he go back downstairs? He was gardening, cutting back. What was he doing up here anyway? Planning to seduce her. It was all there if he understood it blinds drawn against the midday November light. He wasn't home from the office; it was Saturday, amazingly—how was that? Or was it Friday? Why didn't she speak of her brother who apparently had been in town. A north light upon her narrowed shoulder blades, she's a kid, and the fortunate space between her bare thighs dimly green and shadowy that tracked him like her body's vector free as a mind to know just where you were moment to moment (they said like silly code) and still do her work, might be only her case. Now he was crossing the carpet on the way out yet then he went and looked in the closet. He unzipped the garment bag hanging in there. At the bottom, unknown to Della he had thought, he had placed a rather special pistol, a Joost, made in Korea. It was still there. Now the girl's reading out loud— she's such a thoughtful soul: Medea, Cassandra, Clytemnestra, Phaedra. We knew their names. What they got up to. How account for all those fierce women in tragedy? she relays the question (or it is her own), when women were "kept in almost Oriental suppression in Athena's city."

Ah, Athens? he replies, more than half ignorant pulling back out of the closet. "The list goes on."

"Of great women."

"All of them made up."

"Not anymore." Daley zipped up the garment bag. "And Nora wasn't just made up surely." (He and Helen had seen *A Doll's House* by Henrik Ibsen.) "It's a good time for women," he added.

"They still have that thing in the middle of them," Becca said, "but you're right, you're right. I knew you knew, you know it better than I do. The troubles come back to you if you have the faith and don't expect it one for one."

Ah, he said, uncomprehending, one for one. Something in chunk or liquid form and painful doesn't come back eye for eye. He was in the bathroom with the door open, maybe she didn't come through so clearly. He heard a drawer pulled out in the bureau he had cleared for her. He saw she hadn't flushed the toilet. A scrap of tissue on the floor. At the upward curve of the sink light hairs visible. After a moment he flushed down the old bowl. Did she find favor in his eyes? she had whispered at the stairway landing Wednesday night after her performance downstairs in the living room, though it was hardly that. She wrote in a hand legible from a distance, a beautiful belly of a hand. On the bed again she'd rolled over onto her side, her breasts touching. You didn't know what would happen, which was no surprise.

Get back into her coils. She whispered into his neck, Time for sexual *favors*. He couldn't believe she'd said it. Always make time, he said. Her old-fashioned or low-class words joking, vulgar, surely. Maybe Canadian? Did it seem all right? He didn't like it. He hated it.

# 5

YET HE WOULD FEEL THE QUESTIONS COMING ON THE OFFENSIVE. NOT the brother question except in a purer form—absent, behind you, distinct. Why did you already remember her gone? Though she would leave certainly, or (the awful truth) he'd see that she did.

Three, four, five days' living with Becca with never a word about his representing her though. Living with him.

He would not ask, but he occasionally wanted to know. What was it like? How old was she the first time? Was it in the house with others? Did she take the initiative? He wanted to ask. He looked in her notebook but it was more recent even than when she'd first come down here a year ago. Did it hurt her? Did the muscles of her vagina relax to receive him slowly, and what was going on in the house? Was she a wise child? The words came to him at the window and he put his hands to his face as if that would help him see and heard her coming up the stairs.

How she could converse without dwelling on herself. Yet here and there he learned. At fifteen, she had never stepped onto a stage, the theater embarrassed her, still did. (A gifted pilot who hated heights, Daley thought.) She wasn't the type, she told him, she'd been slow to react, people talking to each other in front of a bunch of others. She was a student, not that thinkers weren't dramatic, Socrates on the prowl (not that she had an interest in him), partying, staging his own death; Nietzsche banging away at the piano, stomach trouble, sinking suicidal into the sofa, hand over his eyebrows, only to jump up inspired by the thought of his friend. Those weren't good examples, Daley interrupted off the top of his head, and the young woman, this pretty unique person, was charmed by him (or acted it) not as a daughter but as he didn't know what, a fellow actor of the moment. Error more to the point than truth anyway, it came to Daley, upset or bothered, thrilled by her and taking refuge in plans. "Are you my long-lost other half, if so which?" She was being funny.

No surprises except in the infrastructure maybe. No surprises out in the city: theater guy who got her an apartment and a part; a much older, a parentlike brother north of the border who must have tried to set it up; and now that she was about to extremely imprudently quit the show the landlord apparently leaning on Becca to get her out. Quitting for this? A one-woman piece, a little girl big girl God knows, family voices wrangling partying per*haps* fucking af*fec*tionate, standing up in the bath, bath time, humorous soaping at the hands of blind hands, considerable kisses, kid star relied on for entertainment, for joy, love too, leaning-on, correcting apparently, and dirty laundry needing endless doing, a growing girl precociously even before she was a girl (hey, Baby), a tree in there almost indoors stretching its limbs, you name it, she can curl up into a hole inside mother inside a Ho Jo? (Howard Johnson in *Ca*nada? maybe within striking distance of, or *from,* Canada—near a hospital?) Carried like a kangaroo baby, confounded grown-up motives, abuse even before you're born probably or maybe no abuse at all to *speak* of, and she can dish it out too, this visiting sweetie. Why this distance between the sexes? Why this struggle? Why is the struggle hidden? Because they want to hide its meaning. Becca cared deeply about something Daley had not yet grasped. It was pretty much in this jumbled, cluttered piece she put on for him almost like a belly dance. No, not a belly dance. It was not her family exactly, she was just loose and more hot and take-it-or-leave-it smart in her one-woman or in that area. Forty-five minutes one night, and sweating; emotionally hot though, more than she actually cared about those fugitives who came to live in her show. He was still flattered, for the seedy, quirky passions, the broken-up, interrupted ongoingness of this duty-free import, seemed made up for him or driven by his presence. Blondes were deceptively less vivid for him or veiled in their simple, blanched exposure. He just doesn't like these solo offensives, he doesn't mind telling her.

A young girl, a Canadian Thanksgiving party: she came clearly across the room with a green bottle of ale for her brother, you could see it: it was her beloved brother she was speaking of, and the uncle who'd driven over from Guelph on Friday that he eventually went into partnership with, and as she handed her brother his ale and he touched her hand taking it, the two men holding their ales had turned on each other and were unrecognizable as if *she* had said something (let it out of the hat). And her uncle slid his beefy arm around her, his hand arriving just under her far arm, it was right then that she had thought of *acting*.

Why *then?* her audience of one asks just like that.

She didn't quite know—she was still in it a second later when her brother Tim could have clubbed her uncle down, the two men one dark and blue-eyed, the other you thought bald and very strong (how did you see them?)—pushers more than punchers. Becca's fair, without thank God that flaxen alien bluff invader tourist's simplicity, flaxen as cut off as darkest Africa, more so.

They both loved her, that's all there was to that, Daley said. She didn't like him when he talked like that, and would never feel comfortable with it. "No, it was building all that weekend," she said. Daley willingly irritated her; well, he needed facts in the midst of her stunts. Meanwhile, the humming of a woman trying to fix an umbrella, a man trying to find the jar of herring in the fridge, the smell of a lav, and how they all seemed to rely on the young girl—an impression only, some new material he thought. "That's good," she said (what had he said?); she picked up on you, had an ear. She was educated, and it was in the bio, un-NewYork mysterious and stripped down. Graduate work under her belt, he admired her education, achievement wanted or not, it's a promise she can't help making. Of help. Inherent, hidden, or with the sexiness of the intelligent, a bother, and she will do the corroborating or ignore your doubts. He hears her education in her breathing in the middle of the night. Knows that this carrying on downstairs can't be true true—it's just him—the voices always without a story except she's little-girl central, persuade you of less some outrage or low-level awfulness than . . . than this was life. Successful days approaching the weekend, a lot of talk, not that she's there every minute, but. The haunted house of the city communicates with Daley's place, the unfortunate phoning of landlord's secretary, of Beck the producer, and at the office the lawyer with the bow-tie and the legendary briefcase full of water and then a message at home lawyerly, laconic, distinct, then another call—a first name for Becca. She wouldn't play the machine so Daley . . . forgot what he said to her. Didn't get her one-woman, couldn't get it out of his head, it didn't get off the ground, it was groundwork.

Friday Thursday Wednesday Thursday Friday.

Which is when he can't believe he's sitting through it again, but it's not the same at the witching hour Friday. What are these changes, instinctive? Daley misses some familiar materials from Wednesday, what are they? Nothing you could call consensual rape albeit comfy this time but. The angel named Otto is back in harness but we need him like a giant a dollhouse, a grant for a dead artist, a dead Lincoln. It was better, or worse. Her eyes seem to feed upon him, or then she's looking beyond him so he would like to turn around and see what she sees. She's acting. For him. The voice taking "a slice outa you" tonight different, but Daddy not crashed in the armchair now, hasn't he been going through something other than change? And why do he and Mom blame on the little girl that goddamn *tortoise*shell (it is now, not gold) rattling round in the plumbing of the kitchen or bathroom drain, albeit in her voice or hers being his? And some man lying down, the voice damn familiar but unnamed, a man younger, with pitiable beating marks or a scar on his ribs the child can just make out before she was born and Daley has the name on the tip of his tongue reading off a list at the checkout line and Daley no random passerby about to *be* something (taken prisoner, entertained maybe—or to the point of shocked) but someone who understood, addressed not as "You folks gettin' into it," but "You there." The father crashed in his chair after all one of two male voices at it, with the girl in between or nothing. While the girl is reaching way, way down the drain to retrieve, feeling something at either end of her, she feels connected. A clever show of body, the young female turned into an instrument, a work you wanted to embrace, a history it didn't matter where true, it had something, but not worth quitting a job, while a mother pours a quart of Seagrams down the same drain. And if before, Dad and Mom getting it on in spite of everything, now with a note under the door Becca stoops to retrieve sort of prophetically it's Mom and the other (not Otto—and before the little girl came along), nothing about a foundling tonight, she's moving out. With her protector she stares at the ceiling's cracks and maps the hand that traces its poor will upon her breasts and belly for these are angles you can't get out of, she tells him: it's Daley the audience now, is it his interesting house in need of a minor face-lift, where she and her fellow fugitive from family sing like chilly carolers or bedded beloveds, "You're everything I got to lose." But the tree is acting out, banking in slowly to feed Daley, and a cracker from downstairs materializes in her hand for his mouth and only his, flown in yet hovering like your midair dance or lowered on a ladder but her set speech comes here: about the skill she has that might be misused, her daddy has taken care of it, reminding her of how he made these mistakes with his boyo years ago that were just nothing to what she could fall into, watch that stuff she had in her, it was juicy, it was talent, it was laundry, it was sweet as a kiss (you understand), roll your whole life up and slip it to somebody. Now some new power. She's sobbing embarrassingly that he must hold her, but she tosses him the cracker—what's she going to do with a real audience?—and dries her tears as if she were alone. It's beautiful how she does it. Was it not as good as the first time? she asked.

Saturday morning it was very early. He wasn't back to running. He spoke to Becca. She rolled over and backed into him. She should do both, he said, she should develop her own piece and she should stay in the play if they were moving it uptown. She groaned. Just a thought, he said. Not even, she murmured. She could dish it out but she couldn't take it, he said. Take it, she said. He rolled out of bed. Abuse of some sort. (He went to look in the garden.)

Yet this was how they would find their way to her *place* on Saturday. Dishing it out.

"She's articulate," he heard Isabel say abruptly seen to good advantage across their backyard fence, Daley kneeling by his November forsythia, Is cutting lilacs back with Daley's shears. They two half listening for their neighbor to the east safely in his house now to crank out a Saturday-morning rooster crow; a weekend habit, a giving thanks for eccentricity and Saturday. "Well, she's Canadian, how long is she here for?" Isabel said.

Daley heard the phone go. It was his house. "Here?" he said.

"Oh I know," said Isabel.

"She's got a job."

"Oh I know," said Isabel.

He thought, What does this struggling forsythia bush need? It was sort of one-sided. And did Isabel deserve a ticket to the show? It might close.

"She's not much older than Wheelock," Isabel said. Isabel's boys Wheelock and Bear were still at rest on the third floor. Daley looked up at his house. The 1870s black slate lintels above the almost double-height parlor windows became curved set into the brick above the smaller second-floor windows and flat across on the third.

"But she's a woman," Daley said. Why did this feel like the first real talk he had had in a week, when it wasn't? Was Wheelock still considering McGill? Applying first choice to Dartmouth, said his mother, who had managed well enough. That used to be a pretty heavy-drinking college, Daley said.

The phone rang again and rang just once and Daley stood and exchanged a look with Isabel that in other circumstances could have been about each other but supposedly said, Don't know how long she's going to be here. Presently, they heard voices in Daley's kitchen. Isabel looked at her watch and at her house. It's about time my guys got up, she said. The shared ailanthus tree stirred stiffly in the brisk November sun and was stark, familiar, raw, low-level prophetic like the jasmine scent of Isabel across the fence, flustered and powerful, as Daley turned from the forsythia bush, hearing a voice he recognized. It was the actor Barry.

"You didn't go to the country," Isabel said.

"Not yet," Daley said over his shoulder. Things he and Isabel didn't need to speak of. Were they understood? Hey did he remember it . . . ? she called to him, but Daley proceeded across the flagstones under a fresh, gray sky, a trowel in his hand. Becca and Barry were having a fight in Daley's kitchen to tell the truth with Barry uninvited, unlikable, and at home.

"She know Helen?" Isabel called after him almost trying to help.

"Helen's seen her work," Daley said over his shoulder.

Isabel laughed. "She told me about your scar, *she* told *me,* and I told her, I filled her in but not really," a note of reproach in his controlling, old-friend neighbor's voice, she had a problem client, couldn't collect or something according to Becca. Water dinning on the steel sink in Daley's kitchen and certain whiny or familiar or violent meanings in Barry's obscure tone. "Bear asked if you were taking them to the Rangers this year."

His brown and shadowy dining room, seldom if ever used except to get to the backyard. A rake against a mantelpiece; dusty glass candleholders in the form of figures in cumbersome motion, he knew where they came from; a bag of cement against a French door. From the other direction the close aroma of grease and eggs and more frying bore toward him from the next room sounds of Becca, the voice over the words, mystifyingly distinct and new again today, objective as her one-woman piece. He hesitated.

It was true, Daley needed to go get the car and drive to the country. But he couldn't leave Becca here. She drew it all to her.

"Why *do* you——?" he heard Becca say——

"Your laundry," Barry broke in.

"——ask for it," she finished, to the clatter of some implement and the awful unsticking of the fridge door. All day Daley would get ready for the blow, somebody striking his lover, he had in him the coming shape of it, the potential of it. It didn't matter. Yet she drew it to her. Him too, on a Saturday when suddenly his house is occupied by strangers as if never before that he could recall. Becoming now the heartsinkingly mere sight across the kitchen threshold of the bread knife on its board alongside a grainy loaf she had chosen and Barry staring over the open fridge door in Daley's general direction but not at him and Becca turning an omelet out onto the blue plate—her first actual cooking here? Of all the memories of Becca, this food memory could really stick, his lateness or nonexistence and the frame these young people in his house acted within, its moment of distance, his freedom to think, these strangers with their banal information, the young man grumbling that he had to get a laptop—what did they mean being here?

"Don't come telling me what's in my fridge," Becca said. "If you don't like it clean it out." She had a nerve, here only three days: the house needed a proper professional cleaning, she had felt obliged to go on the warpath and tell him, though she was a sultry, dutiful cleaner-up in the kitchen, thinking, purposeful (clattering a little when his friend Helen phoned).

"A foil container of asparagus with yellow sauce on it; a slice a pizza with a coupla bites out of it; blood sausage," said Barry.

"Blood sausage, of course."

"No, I recognized it from when I once went into a Spanish Harlem meat market by mistake to get some lunch," Barry said, "that's how I knew."

"That's how you knew about blood sausage," said Becca. She tipped pan grease over Barry's omelet and some went on the linoleum. Barry came out from behind the fridge door and slammed the door shut experimentally.

"I have no control over that," she said.

"Who gave him a key?" said Barry.

"Anyone might have." She ignored Daley, it was Becca's brother obviously, and her place, her fridge, she was talking about or Barry had been.

"Don't do that to the door," said Daley, gesturing with the trow, advancing on Barry who looked at him as if Daley were employed here, though a job's a job.

Barry stood a quart container of milk beside a cup of coffee. She always drew it to her, a shadow cast by herself. Last night he had been given to understand that Becca's Canadian brother had been in the theater apparently unannounced. Had she seen his eyes glittering in the packed house? It was her business, was always Daley's position, and she must make of it what she would. What had become of this person if he didn't appear backstage? She would want to see him, Daley had replied last night. How had he said it? for she didn't like it. Say too much, say too little, a woman'll get creative with it. Well, she'd spotted him back in the house somewhere, his eyes, a full Canadian mustache perhaps even faintly military.

"He got no key from me," said Becca, "it could have come from anywhere. I fixed Barry some breakfast," she said.

Barry pulled up a chair. "You got a nice place here," he said, you might think that Daley was renting the basement. He looked at his omelet and ran his finger around the edge of the plate. "He didn't make the bed or anything," Barry said, "I mean, give me some warning, a chocolate chip cookie on the edge of the tub?" He cut himself two slabs of the bread.

"But when did you . . . ?" Becca opened a cupboard and found the new jar of marmalade beside the blueberry preserves Helen had put up in August.

"This morning for God's sake," Barry said, his mouth full. He cut the flat omelet into four sections and cut each of these in half. Daley knew what Barry was going to say: *I gotta see about that job today.*

"What about Clara? She's loaded, she's got that place."

"It's what about you," said Barry, backing away from Daley's kitchen table. "And your place and your lawyer. And the show," he added.

"Yeah maybe you won't need that breakthrough day job," the woman said dryly.

"And your brother," he muttered.

"Isn't Clara loaded? Maybe not," said Becca.

Barry's shoulders could just rise up and sweep the old blue plate onto the floor, restructure the moment. He swung around and the chair scraped the floorboards, what was his mood? "I mean, what are *you* doing here?" he said to Daley, humorous almost.

"Well, I'm not Becca's lawyer." Daley looked at the chair legs and into the young man's squinting eyes, his reply okay but off. But would do for these people. Barry tilted his head at his breakfast, a little outnumbered, the milk carton, the omelet, the faintly familiar, frieze-decorated (where did it come from?) oversized, cup on its saucer, the blue plate Helen had found at a yard sale and then didn't want, the wide loaf, the serrated bread knife Becca had produced from her knapsack last night. Barry would be a fast eater for better or worse, Daley couldn't help feeling for him, get him outa here, give him the whole loaf to take, he ate the way he brushed his teeth, Daley actually saw Barry never quite at home, suffering through his energies that were not quite youthful, he'd had jobs as a light furniture mover and a contractor's sheetrocker and general laborer and assistant—did he know the marine supply warehouse in Far Rockaway? Why God how did Daley know? He'd worked there like a Seabee, he loved that job, horns and chalks and fire-main pipes for the big babies—and watch-man at a Japanese firm's warehouse in New Jersey (how did you do that job fast?), Daley had no pity for him, a grain of fellow-feeling here in the structure of the kitchen perhaps, because he was looking for his breakthrough day job at a moment when somehow he had scored a part in some play that had happened to give a lead to this untried foreign (basically) girl and got a surprising notice and now the play was turning into serious uptown money if Becca didn't pull out, a real job. Daley looked in the fridge at a bottle of Lebatt's Pale Ale at eleven in the morning, and wanted to go somewhere and call his brother Wolf if he was in Seattle: plain frame houses rising up the slopes, Pacific Rim ships in the inner harbor, slower frontier.

Becca scuffed to the sink and turned the tap off. Turned it right back on. What did she want? Her back to him, she had on Daley's slippers. Needing them to see ahead, though he was the one who always knew what was coming. She showed him her profile: "He called before he came over."

"Well, he must have been just around the corner then. Who was the other call?"

Barry was eating. "I just wanted her to know what's going on," he said; "you know what's going on here, you're right here. I thought *you* were her brother." Becca laughed, she knew how to enjoy Barry, abuse him, probably satisfy him. "She makes a great breakfast," Barry said, "some days I could kill for a good breakfast. I'd know what to do with this place, I'd rip out this low ceiling. Got a baseball bat?" Barry laughed. "Under my thumb once, she never quite jumped into the mosh pit, it's not your war, Mister Bill"—Barry hazarded a form of Daley's name.

Daley'd had enough. He knew something leaving the room—a woman behind; or at long last his long-lived, dishwasherless, valuable house on impulse abandoned though in the wrong direction for the garden wouldn't get him out of here onto the street, or on the road for that matter.

Isabel seemed, when he came out through the open French doors onto his muddy flagstones and in the familiar contact of her voice, never to have stopped talking to him. Or to have been waiting for him at the fence. Her strong, soiled hands, the shears dangling over onto his side, history in a small way. Remember the night when he brought the boys home from the Ranger game and the boys came in raving about the amazing seats—who was it he knew, some developer?—and she and Daley talked till two in the morning one on one? Did they talk the same language? He really thought so.

Many times, he said.

Remembered many times or talked like that many times?

Both, probably.

She didn't think so. Wheelock had wanted to drink some of Daley's beer at the game, pleading like a salesman you said, underage, and it was a little unpleasant until the third period exploded into their laps. A Ranger and a Black Hawk converging on the out-of-sight puck up against the boards hit the glass with elbows and heads like hammers shattering it into sudden visibility like an accident and drenching the boys in Daley's beer but more thrilling the spray of visible blood across the rough opened-up frame of sharded Plexiglas onto Bear the four-teen-year-old brother, his face, his blond ponytail, which by morning had crusted and was to be shown off at school, though which Canuck's blood in the penalty box was not definitely known (Lacroix, Savard, he didn't remember, someone yelling Dan*nee*, Dan*nee*, to get a player's attention when he was about to get killed)—"You said you liked to know whose blood you had on you when push came to shove, and of course you weren't kidding."The dark-haired, seasoned woman point-ed the shears at him. The trip to the Garden a Christmas tradition the last three or was it four years, Wheelock arguing like a pretty nasty salesman with Daley about Daley's beer last Christmas, an American boy was all but those days practically over.

How did that second tall cup of Bud *get* spilled? He had reached up to shield the boys, Wheelock interrupted by the violent double check, the supposedly unbreakable Plexiglas, Isabel waiting at home, always super appreciative of Daley taking the boys places and even just promising to.

None of this mattered, for behind him he felt along the walk the woman Becca Lang coming, who was nothing to him if there was a big picture, and very bare in her shift out here in the reality of abut-ting backyards, years of them, of ownership, West Side gardening and clutter, which she was already familiar with from Thursday or Friday, and with poignant, ruthless competition he now felt in her approach-ing, vulgar, juvenile will even to the death, that queer abuse, it came to Daley, feeling her so bare legged and backyard proprietary in his slippers and he was certain without her underwear on, and not accepting what he had just done which was just to leave the kitchen like that, though, slippers or not, she hardly needed this man who was, okay, slightly smitten by her.

Isabel was twice her age, elbows on the fence. Beautiful really (and Daley's type, no mystery about that). With a small business and two sons. It was Becca's cue, though: "The other call was my brother I'll bet, but you'll have to ask *him* why he rang off."

Daley nodded to Isabel, "That night Bear wouldn't wash the beer out of his hair, it was the blood."

"That's right," said Isabel.

"Anyhow," said the woman behind Daley, "you've got an answering machine."

"You should catch up with him and spend the day with him," Daley said over his shoulder.

"He's not my only brother."

Daley shrugged almost in sympathy at this lame retort and Isabel dropped the shears off her finger.

"It's not interesting," Becca said, "and there's nothing to discuss. Hi Isabel."

However, this was how Daley, who absently picked up the shears, ended by going uptown to Becca's. Minus Barry, who was seeing about a job and did the dishes before he silently went.

Daley had much to absorb. Was it going to be business, was that the size of it "at the end of the day"—as Wolf would say of how a job turned out? Becca had wanted Daley along. The eviction case was apparently in limbo if he didn't ask. The visit had an unfortunate even erotic scent of law, money, a seamy home, in the cab some interesting silence to do with affection, blame in the offing—Isabel. "She said some friend of yours scaled the back wall?"

"Friend of my wife's."

"Oh him." Daley laughed. "To get something she wanted from her workroom, I understand."

"You never asked what it was?"

"No I didn't; but it was a sketch of him in some shape or form all watery I understood, not quite there—stepping out of the shower for all I knew."

Acquainted with Beck, the producer, Daley recalled, this brother who hadn't yet a name must be aware of her decision to leave the play. Daley saw everything coming (always had): why he didn't react much, the way she might have liked him to. To events. She had just put into his head the prospect of asking some question of this brother. It came to Daley, who was eminently expendable, that it was their war. Imagine the brother turning up in the theater and not coming back to say hello. Only a mention from her Friday night and then the subject was closed. It was her business.

She would want to have dinner with her brother, Daley had suggested last night, they would have a lot to talk about. Talk about? Becca retorted. Maybe not, Daley said politely, and the subject was closed. (The transient street hopelessly sweet Friday night, even the weird, stinking Dumpster opposite the warehouse theater so full of mastlike rods and cable spools and sheets of cracked ribbed plastic from a building site that it looked rigged for a voyage through our city; the old Civil War commercial fronts they strolled past hand in hand had put a half thought in his head that he voiced: that the cast iron wasn't like timber and the beams it got made into, or stone and masonry, because here the material, whatever your distrust of its unnaturalness artificially manufactured, is in a different relation to what it's being used for. That wasn't it, that was almost it. The woman had laughed, her brother was in scrap metal now, he sneaked down here now and then, she had squeezed Daley's arm: Enough, it meant—had he ever heard of "Tears" (it sounded like), a premier of France who right about *this* time (she indicated a warehouse with her other hand), well in the 1840s, and a great historian of I almost forget what who would tell you a lot if you knew nothing, had gates put up everywhere in Paris at a moment when what was needed was railroads, which he thought were a dumb idea and would never work. Daley said he had had a North Jersey waste management client, aluminum cable scrap, nickel tubing as he recalled, but the issue was insurance on a job in Michigan that got aborted. She giggled, she rubbed his arm, which told him that he with his limitations couldn't help it. What was a historical moment? she giggled, like someone older. They did things together. Oh what *is* a walk? she was saying, so glad she didn't have to say. He had bought something at Galeries Lafayette once upon a time. God! she said.

Thus the subject of the brother had been closed Friday night yet left open as far as Daley was (not) concerned—and Saturday too. Something obvious there, what could it be? Well, he hadn't brought it up. Building materials, reworking of debris, Civil War somewhere else, business trips, stray kinsmen constant in their family feeling. The little girl taken to the theater once, or was it twice, Becca or not: she reminded Daley of this Ellen Terry actress at eight or nine years in the 1850s "stumbling home along the dark streets wrapped in her father's cloak" when other kids were sound asleep in bed—old streets that Daley (Wardour Street, Bentinck Street) had walked with his wife and later with Helen once when they went to London to see some Shakespeare. Why did the high, oratorical voice of Lincoln come back like things he didn't know he knew (and really didn't).

The brother took shape again, that was all there was to it. Traveled a lot. To Eastern Europe in the old days, he brought her things from Czechoslovakia, from Zagreb. He had visited her here of course; he must have. Erie region didn't have a monopoly on scrap. To see how she was doing. He must love Becca. He had known the producer, Beck, who had finagled the loft for her in a very large, turn-of-the-twentieth-century commercial building. She herself had said so.

She wanted him to see some value there, what he'd make of *her*. He went along with it, Isabel had seen it all. Around here, that is. It was Saturday. Not to have Becca spend what was left of their time away. And she wanted him along. To be between her and her brother, though Barry had only evidences of the brother's presence. It was not what Daley had planned to think about. He didn't charge. He hadn't been retained.

A great space, you said. Freedom too. Dollars potential as ideas. Real and choice space on Manhattan Island. It was hope and a future out there surrounding you, happening and skintight you could feel it. Rental is real estate, if you're protected; you just better not sell it, it's not the Brooklyn Bridge. A fortress against those who wanted success from Becca yet a thought encompassing them.

No one on the door downstairs, cigarette smoke so fresh the smoker might have vanished as he exhaled.

Management wanted her out. How was she acting about it? "You see?" she said, and explained that the super would come around and want to talk about Canada, and want to come in and take measurements.

# 6

A DESIRABLE LOFT YOU COULD TELL EVEN BEFORE YOU STEPPED OUT OF the elevator at twelve-thirty and saw the heavy metal security door, hearing mambo somewhere turn into a rapid-fire man's voice. They could hear a radio talking Spanish at them; "that's us," she said, she unlocked both locks.

"Someone left it on," Daley said.

"What?" said the tenant, pushing open the heavy metal door. A house call? Making him responsible, smelling burned toast and noting on the sink edge a shaving brush standing on its end.

The lease transferred from an abruptly departed tenant she had been given to understand, summoned home to Europe or somewhere, some transatlantic business though why a new lease bumping up the rent would not be the logical next step was a mystery if you wanted to make it one which Daley wouldn't and so it wasn't. It was evidently a deal with Beck, the producer. And now Beck had not gone to bat for her in the eviction case (or not so long as she was pigheaded enough to leave his play). Was Daley expected to stand between her and her brother, a much older brother, his eyes glittering out in the house feeling you wondered what at the end of the first act. Hearty Canadian mustache, a wide, reserved, citizen mouth, reserved eyes, melancholy with memory or resignation or north-of-the-border need—for Daley? Damn him, to depose whoever this man was, debrief him, catch up on things, your controlling older sib. Yet Daley had no interest in him or the dreary family, and this was the truth, for he liked the young woman. The landlord was a constant, you figured, he was in business and so he wanted her out. Yet hadn't before. A loft, she had said. Daley saw it, heard it in her voice on the phone, the curious fortune of their connecting Monday when he was expecting it to be Lotta, who had not called back.

Nothing to what Daley saw as he stepped in. A great space, she said. She could just let it go, she said. What's space?

A figure came to Daley. Well, everything, he said. This girl had maybe two thousand square feet in a midtown commercial but mixed-use building. Not a single partition except the L box of the bathroom breaking the pale, somewhat luminous expanse. She was contemplating from a distance the bed, a small double, a very beautiful cloak spread over basically a mattress on an inner spring on the floor. In another far corner under a window an olive futon was rolled up, and towels folded there and there was a duffel beside two dumbbells.

The space might have been an occasion for these great, industrial windows, three on each of three sides, but there was a thought at large in these interior lengths turned into potential or choice, or just the absence of clutter, a preparation for time, nothing to steal but not your residential setup though with a man on duty downstairs, not a doorman because you had to open the street door with your key while he watched, but he knew who came in and left and reported to the super, who reported to management. A largely commercial old building in midtown with high, steel-framed but old windows and views south, west, and north. The floor was of some cementish compound painted white to go with the high, raw light. She picked it up. They discussed it, the exposed electrical pipes on the ceiling, house finches on the ledges, the age of the building, and the landlord, who was a woman. Becca looked out a window. "Like a well staring up at the sky." Adjacent brick commercial structures and across the river the Jersey stacks.

"Lots of light here, Becca."

"Maybe we'll move in," she said.

"Come on," Daley said. Light raw, changing, falling from the sky, restored to the sky, light a material probably measurable by management like square footage.

Daley, a violent soul he recognized potentially, had looked for some force (absent, even) to be applied to Becca while they were there. For an hour and a half Saturday. What angered her later wasn't the super's visit, invisibly knocking soon after they came in, but that this event, vulgar, aimed, could cause the daylight, the bed, the timeless, hanging-out talk between Becca and Daley or some impressions, dear, irritable, opinionated, to slip away like a breath, drop away toward the darkness of a well before her super's sudden presence in the middle of Daley's visit.

They looked out a window toward the Jersey stacks, a helicopter stooped quite suddenly toward the river, and Becca said something, he thought. He would remember her. She was a tad self-destructive, maybe she made something of it. His presence here like this high-up loft meaningless and momentous, a thing passing through her hands. Changed by her, though. He liked it. Why would she surrender a grace like this? he asked.

Your guy Duymens wanted to see your house, she said, just a thought I had.

She flung off the brilliant spread and there was the unmade bed a fearful mess, the bottom sheet pulled off the mattress at the corner, the blankets pulled half around. She bent over and raised a pillow and her nostrils widened. Across one corner of the loft and transient and unshielded was the rudimentary kitchen. Becca cursed the sink and poked the radio button off. He hadn't heard her speak like that. She was young and she hated Daley being there now yet could make something of it. What foul thing had she found in the fridge? What male habit or foreign? "What are you looking at?" she said clear across the vast space.

"The bed obviously. No, we're looking at a nice four-figure rent, what did you say you were paying? Ah five hundred, I remember."

"You're talking about money," Becca said; "you." She drew out a plate with the sausage on it, and a foil container. A couple of dark green spears stuck up from congealed hollandaise. Becca tossed the asparagus and the sausage, the fridge door open still. "We lived together when I left the family thank God. When I was at university." She took a large bite off a curled edge of pizza wedge and found in the fridge a saucer for it, and put it back right in front. It was thirty feet back to the bed. She lifted a second pillow to see under it and bent her neck and smelled it. Daley didn't laugh. "Oh why did you come here?" she burst out.

"Me? God, the pruning shears!" He had picked them up on his side of the fence.

"You left them on the sack of cement in the dining room," the woman said to him.

"I came just in case," Daley said, "a buffer zone."

"Are you being my lawyer today?"

"No, just a zone."

"I don't need you," she was looking up out a window. On the floor near the bed a stack of books with something with Greek letters on top.

A knock turned the door into a door, then a pair of smart knocks. "I don't mind a scene. Kill me, I'll come out of it," said Becca, "I refuse myself nothing." Some question about the mysterious and disappointing (probably) brother, was it up to Daley to ask? Scrap-iron contracter, a phone call away from most of the business, older, devoted still, a helper once, with a story, some story you didn't want to hear. (What had she said? The brother thought he would be remembered for his scrap-metal achievements.) At the end of the day Daley was always right. She sat on the bed. "I was a character in my family," she said. The fondness between her and her brother. She got up and snatched up the other pillow by the corner of the pillowcase to see under it.

It was because of the one-woman piece that you wanted nothing to do with her family, Daley could still give her a push back into that play, the real job at hand. She would be mad, she was mad already. Something would have been achieved. She would have passed through his hands.

She had survived them, that family if they were the population in her one-woman thing or even if they weren't. Alcohol and sentiment north of the border. Fondling a child at bath time.

"I don't mind a scene. Kill me, I'll come out of it."

Daley stopped to watch.

"Experience," she said.

The one knock and then two knocks. Daley went to get it. "It's not your brother." Becca ignored the door. "Your brother was wild, isn't that what you said? A veteran you said he was?"

"Of risks, I said."

"I don't remember things that way; I have them here."

She palmed her belly.

"I had the idea he was in it too."

"In what?" said Daley, the door about to speak again.

"Your brother" She could delay him up to a point, was it something she'd been told and gotten wrong, guessing? "The war," she said.

The pair of knocks came again (backed up with a key or two, the hand extended to a pant pocket, a belt loop); the knocks still pretending to be half witty, said Ex*cuse* me.

She seemed to try to keep Daley from reaching the door, yet Daley was pushing her by being himself.

"'In it *too*'?" said Daley.

"So I understood," said Becca.

The pair of knocks came smartly again, determined, but hardly her brother, who wouldn't have needed to knock. Yet was Canadian, so you didn't know, Daley had his hand on the doorknob, which was loose, when it occurred to him to say, "Who is it?" thinking, Damn, it's *Duymens*! He's coming back for this place. *Ruley Duymens*! The slippery, half-Dutch developer (who had floated the idea of a soccer stadium to be built on a lake) who after all these decent years had met this strange woman in a waiting vacant lot and soon after given her Daley's number, though not for a lawyer necessarily: not bad; insult, joke, passed through the young woman as quick as a flush of history personal as a quirky "touch."

"Guy," the noble voice of a person of color, measured them in advance. "Super," he said to Daley, coming into view around the door, setting foot in just another space of a building he thought of at times as his. This loft of a woman sued for eviction who hadn't been seen in the building since Wednesday afternoon, Daley assumed, though this mattered not to the action brought against her to which only an earlier period of months was material. Yet a sweater, a dress, a shirt, new jeans had materialized in the other closet Thursday.

The Guyanan super had installed kinsmen of doubtful status but more or less openly nonunion as day and night doormen. They sat in a swivel chair in the lobby smoking and stayed there if someone had trouble getting in, the door locked after 6 P.M.

But no help to Becca's case.

He seemed in the deliberately rich voice bigger than the man in the sport jacket, blue jeans and sneakers who had opened the door of the great loft. Though before the visit was done Daley could have given Guy a push as soon as look at his grim grin and the serious little notebook and pen he took out of his shirt pocket seeming not to intrude on what passed between the loose-living girl and the older man discovered standing at a distance of thirty feet from one another. To measure her was also why he came. Guy thicker in the chest but no taller than Daley, his elaborate manner, his wondrous voice, were both black (to Daley's mind) and a rehearsed, self-satisfied compound of a process server's humility and the doomsday commission executed where the shock not for Daley but for your average citizen-tenant would strike you at the moment you had the envelope in your hand but before you saw the papers inside.

"Hi, stranger," the man hailed Becca. "Got a visitor from back home. I didn't expect to find you here." He addressed Daley with a curious respect. "My man said you left in a hurry. Must have stepped out to the deli?" The speaker met Daley's eyes and looked away.

Daley said that was someone else.

The big man chuckled and drew his pen and a notebook from his shirt pocket distinctly as if Daley had seen him do it before. "How's the weather up there? You celebrate Thanksgiving?"

"Thanksgiving's come and gone in Canada," said Daley.

Becca laughed and came to his arm. "No, this is not my brother."

"*All right,*" said Guy slowly. He pretended to survey the vast ceiling and the nobly exposed pipes. "Checking the paint job. They're coming in next week, getting the place ready."

"Ready for what?" said Daley.

"Piece o' cake." Guy paced off the length of the wall where Barry's futon and sleeping bag lay stowed.

Guy paced off the longer wall now.

"Ready for nothing," said Becca, her city light was bright and gray broken by the little sticky thud of the super's running shoes across this uninhibited space. She could take it or leave it, defend in court or walk away from. Were these choices?

"That's right, 'cause you're *gone,* dahlin'," murmured her super, eyeballing a distance between windows. "You been somewhere else. You can't be two places at once now can you." It was not a question, and it was his tactical error, but she said something now that the super flicked a mean eye at her for before Daley could raise his hand to counsel her not to answer, and Daley realized afterward that she had feared not that Daley would do something (which wasn't her kind of fear) but that her freedom would be subtly abused and she would find it gone; she had retreated to the fridge, the sink, the small breakfast table. At twenty paces Daley stood between the other man and the door. "Out," he said.

"I wouldn't let my niece carry on like this," said Guy, indicating the bed, the bedroll.

"That's my legal roommate," said Becca.

"Turn it into a flophouse, it's valuable property," said the man.

Daley held the door. "You won't be painting next week, you won't be painting till the place is vacant and who knows when that'll be. Not you."

"Got all I need."

"I guess you have." Daley let the door go.

The man had more to say at his own speed, he waved his little notebook. Daley shut the door on his heel just.

"You're the *lawyer* I been hearing about," the rich voice came back from the far side of the door. The messed-up bed stared at you. It looked like you didn't know what, a word for it, an installation. A set of shaving cream a dark hair on the sheet. Daley sat down on the dumb comfort of the unmade bed, cool as your own when left sometimes all day.

Becca was running across the loft and flung open the door. "So hard to know who's for you, right?" he said. Guy must have taken the stairs. She let the door swing shut. "That's why acting and the *law* work."

"It doesn't matter no one can trace where you're coming from, it's what you just do in acting, in answer on impulse or something I don't know; and law—well, you don't get friendly with your lawyer."

"Not with your acting partner either?" Daley nodded toward the bedroll in the far corner.

"That's Barry," she said.

But no real secrets with her. Ask her anything, girl, woman, actress. *Actor,* she said Robin the wife in the play called herself, it didn't sound right; whatever they wanted. Actor in your own one-woman thing. In answer, though, to who? He had a thought almost, and it passed like a connection he had once witnessed. Daley stared at the many-colored cloak flung on the floor, red, black, white, yellow, blue, he didn't know them all, flickering somehow. New world squares, quilt-clear, nice till you saw the reflections came from tiny mirrors Indian style. He looked at the bedclothes he was sitting on. He felt it in his legs, in the spaces of this place, it was history, no more. "George Washington slept here."

"He was just a brother to me when I needed him."

"He'll be back," said Daley.

"Well, we're not waiting around," said Becca.

He saw things from Guy's point of view. She must have eighteen hundred square feet, Daley said.

She needed very little to feel content, she said.

Oh no? He had an immigration client he had taken on against his better judgment in Queens, a relative of—it didn't matter—lived in a space perhaps a sixth the size of this along with his wife and his wife's kid sister and assorted children.

"Against your better judgment, that's what I like about you."

Becca came and sat beside him. If it was to secure Daley's services that she had been putting out so in the morning, waking even Daley so tenderly early, he would rather not know. He was touched by whatever she needed from him; but he was a fool—Ruley Duymens had had something, but what? "People crash, I know it's happened to you. Brothers show up."

"Wolf never had a key, though."

Americans crash, but like this?

It was one-thirty and Becca wanted to be gone, but they were speaking of brothers. "Real brothers you choose," she said.

"Oh yeah? You mean friends," Daley said. He didn't like her.

Yeah? How do you choose the *blood* of a brother he wanted to know. She thought about it. She had known how, he could tell. Half brother but he was her choice, she said. It was with him that she had left her family, Daley surely understood that. Went to live on her own when she was at university—at least when he was traveling on business. Incest was a term. What did it cover? Daley got up.

Brother and sister possessed of the same early mornings, humans long used to each other at home. Going to class and to work. Sound of the humid bathroom and interruption of the clock alarm, the fleshly total of home, humors, comings-in-the-door, steady. Scented habits, her puberty shared, he's entered the workforce a while ago, years, in a garage, a distillery, shoes, scrap ultimately. And still lived at home though he also didn't. He bonded with her. All that mess surely the material of her "piece." Was it that Daley didn't know a thing about Canadians? Protective jointly of some knowledge between them, Becca and this much older brother. Why did it touch Daley, a beckoning? It didn't; didn't disturb him as it came to him either. Experience was all it was. A stranger in that family like her. Was it polite not to push Becca to speak of it?

The brother done, it was the turn of others. They lined up.

"Your brother's all over the place."

But a worker, clever, a pretty good family man.

"Family's such an act."

"A real troublemaker, if you like."

"Like mine used to be."

"Creative, I think."

"Well."

"'Course, got himself pushed off a cliff almost."

"Something he said?"

"Hundreds of feet into a river. He'll be half in the conversation, which is not very grown-up, then he'll strike."

Asking for it." He was in the habit of coming to New York?

"Ruley was here," Daley said. The words were out before Daley had had the thought, it was foreknowledge practically.

"Oh *Duymens*," she said indifferently. "Not after I came, I can guarantee you that." She thought about it. "The place . . . it has so little in it. So you can't actually tell." A long time back Ruley had been here. A year and a half, Daley somehow figured, a long time these days.

Her brother was in the habit of coming to New York?

New York was how he knew Beck. "New York had been risky."

For a Canadian? Daley didn't understand something.

Did Daley do any international work?

Who for?

In the elevator Becca seemed closer again, her mouth pushed out, needing him. She lining Daley up to represent her brother? She wanted him out of her hair.

Lawyer, lover, prudent friend, date, he's out in the noise of the street of a Saturday afternoon heading for the movies.

A brother so close it's a phase. At the end of the day what's it matter? An important bond. What is a brother? Or what is a weekend or what is a walk?

She was saying his name. "Bill?"

Taking a walk to clear our head of that comedian, that incredible thug.

Not at all incredible, Becca.

"He wouldn't let his *niece* carry on like this," she hooted. "What? Do what I've done, bear my responsibilities? Carry on indeed, when he would be shocked out of his drawers if he knew what he was looking at even the few domestic furnishings he saw today."

"Maybe he wouldn't be. Listen, they'll put you out on the street. The court won't touch them."

She was startled he could tell. That he wasn't shocked. He could love that in her. Neither of them said it, and Daley suspected there was more of it than was commonly thought. Brother and sister hanging out. What did the girl feel in the morning? Pregnant, close, natural, family, not dirty or atrocious, secret though, and looking at the day. Daley told her to keep it tuned to what was important. "We know what's important," she said. Sex, he thought.

# 7

WHAT IS A WALK, HE SAID. AIMLESS? WE TOOK OVER*NIGHT* WALKS along Lake Huron, she said, did he know Delius? No, he was afraid he didn't. English who came here and wrote music about it. Florida. "If there isn't *time* you don't walk it. To get to the movie."

A walk had no aim but wasn't aimless, she said. "You ask yourself what exactly you like about this thing that's going on. Until you're not interested anymore."

What was there to be shocked by here? Daley thought. She entertained her family. She was a character. He asked if her brother took her to the movies much in the old days, which seem to be still going on?

When she had time. She was a good student. Daley'd see she was essentially a . . .

Something came back to Daley it was about the brother.

There was a sax player tomorrow night Daley hadn't seen in twenty years. If she felt like a little music.

A cab pulled over, and Becca gave in unsmiling at Daley's insistence. She wanted him to be stunned by her life and she wanted to serve him and serve him right by leaving him. The cab took them downtown and pulled over at the end of the ticket buyers' line. Again the thing half came back to him about Brother.

When he finally made it to the window, she was watching for him inside the lobby. She had spent twenty-three dollars on sandwiches and two containers of coffee she carried them on top of and something plastic-wrapped in each side pocket of her suede jacket. Daley saw a woman he remembered though not her name and he put from his mind like the messed bed and the smell Becca picked up on the pillows and the sneaky, mustached commuter the fact that she would be at work in four hours. What is a weekend? They were watching a movie in a narrow little theater, one of four the space had been turned into. The cheddar and avocado sandwich was unreal: she dripped coffee on his sneaker. "A rest from work, a change from the days," he whispered.

She was wiping his sneaker: "What?" she said.

His hand under her jacket ran up and down her back. "A weekend, if I go to the country away from the *phone*."

Isn't there a phone?

Didn't give out the number.

Except to?

He seemed absorbed by the film, the light upon his face in the narrow, old-style or European house the latest thing. Bill?

The lake, he whispered, his eyes on the screen, she would like it this time of year (the canoe on the cold, dark, late-afternoon water, slipping depthlessly through what was left of lily pads, one goose lingering that had lost its mate, the turkeys, a late-born fawn, a silver fox). He was lying, she whispered back. (Easy to say, *You're lying*—a New York buzzphrase. Why did he think she was, too?) She had slumped into the far corner of her seat and he leaned that way. "I came up with this idea for ice storms knocking out the power lines," he whispered.

"You didn't answer me," she said.

"County couldn't see it. Not last winter anyway." A sandwich in his lap, he felt someone pushing him from behind, settling in. He would miss these questions that were just for him.

After a while, she leaned against him. "What do you think?" she whispered.

He had forgotten they were going to the theater when they came out. Was she a tired actress? They walked two long blocks. She had experience, she could talk, walking was thinking, getting somewhere except he had a blinking, purged body he was attached to, no warehouses right now or Lincoln's eyelids covering now nothing.

She might have heard his thought, she took his arm. He needn't come tonight, she said.

"Well your run is closing one way or another." He remembered the brother now.

"Do what you like."

He thought, It *is* the brother.

"What is it?" she said, facing a cab with a black driver about to pull over but she wanted the cab right behind and she dived into the cramped backseat of a cab that had read her mind and pulled over. Do what he liked, she said and put her hand on him.

He caught his breath, to see her profile (but aware of him) made him dizzy and he lost the use of words except like an automaton he did speak to this creature who was no pet bird. They were aware of the woman in the driver's seat. "Seeing you get slugged," he said, "I know that part pretty well, it always did confuse me, but you're a damn fine actress—I'm going out with you, you picked me," he said.

"I did, I did," he heard beside him; "getting tired of me?" she said.

He didn't think so. The play maybe.

"Me too."

"Wait a minute."

"Yes, tired of your work is different. You don't get tired of that."

"What is a walk home?"

"Takes longer so you have less time when you get there."

"That is friendship?"

"I didn't pick you as a friend," she said.

He told her that was exactly what she had done and if you make a real choice you're lucky, and a walk home couldn't be anything apart from who's walking and what they're saying and what they're capable of saying and how they walk and are with you bodily. He almost didn't hear himself letting go or trying to impress her with an impulse inspired by her. "What is a weekend?" Daley sighed; "pick one, what is a garden, what is breakfast?"

Becca sat up and reached for the door handle, she was practiced and he was not. "Friendship is two people agreeing not to fuck with each other's congruent confusions and lies and being able to violate the other person's privacy and—" she was saying something; "that's why you can forget friendship because you're quite strong in your confusions, and I've enjoyed fucking with you."

They were aware of the driver. The person with him the last three nights he still saw half stripped on the floor of the dressing room at intermission Wednesday and striking up a conversation with Beck in the Toronto airport a year ago, and right now plotting the time left.

She didn't know, she didn't know, she said, as the cab took a turn badly. She let go of the door handle and gripped the inside of his thigh with the hand already there. It was about tonight probably. He said the wrong thing. He wanted to reimburse her for lunch, he hadn't meant—

That wouldn't be necessary. She knew how much she had to the penny most of the time; Ingrid, you know, didn't dare look at her A.T.M. receipts; Ingrid was acting out. His *friend* Ingrid, she said.

Daley let it pass. (His friend on account of a hug?) "Acting out," he said.

"Pretending you don't know what you do."

"It doesn't hurt anyone," said Daley, bored and on his guard, "most people have money problems."

"You mean you don't."

"I don't know how to spend it."

"That was true in my family except they didn't have any," said the woman. "And they were in the shoe business, some of them, so why didn't they have any?" she asked for the first time, it sounded like. "Nothing's secret from you," she said.

"What's the secret in scrap metal," Daley said, "when the business is just a phone call away?"

"I saw two thousand kilometers of insulated cable wasted once, so I'm all for recoup. He's been trying to deal in scrapped planes, helicopters."

"He's in with your Beck or trying to be."

"It was boats, because Beck's a sportsman; and development, and that warehouse—it was news to me—"

"They go back?" said Daley.

"—but it's no secret now," she rubbed Daley's thigh; "nothing is. The family, a brother old enough to be my dad protecting me in his own way, an outsider in the family practically—like me except my way of doing it was be the center of everything. Not that I had a choice, though I did. Performing for them in the bathroom, the kitchen, hand-to-mouth surviving, consulted by them when I was five about their *things* unbelievably, their loves and losses, caressed, made privy. It was a job, that's what it was. You don't ask about it. You wouldn't. And I'm not your walking résumé about an awful family. I've shown you—"

"In what you put on?" Daley had to ask.

"Just for you."

"Twice," Daley pinned it down.

"Really more than."

"You put it on for Leander."

"He's a kid; you couldn't imagine his life."

"More than twice?" said Daley.

"Tell me how you deal with ice storms in the country?" She rubbed his leg, fanning her fingers lightly.

"Use a helicopter; go low above the power line, downdraft it; follow along, it'll blow the ice right off."

"Any special helicopter?"

"Yes, of course."

"Could you do it?"

"Probably."

"See that's why I came down here," said the woman, Daley looking out the window.

"Said your brother worked in a distillery?"

"Long ago. In Windsor."

"Of course. Walkers."

"Sure, they have everything there."

"You could act in Canada."

"Beck was there."

"At the airport," Daley remembered.

"First time I'd ever seen him. His face was tanned with the wrong experience," she said. Now, who had said that? she wondered. Something wrong with it all, not what she'd actually said—the romance of history for a tourist or why New York was *risky*—the brother's view or the world's. "And the country?" she asked. "The fox, the geese, the turkeys?"

"Why yes. My father when he was on a defibrillator even looking up at the stewardess running through all the turkey sounds."

If he didn't go to the play. If he did. If he did go and didn't tell her. "Maybe you do want to see the show. It's up to you." Her breast against his arm, hand invading his shirt to rest on his heart. "Five-fifteen," she said.

The Asian driver was speeding, fleeing the people in the backseat. A memorable moment, Daley could foresee it already and that he was going to interfere only to tell Becca if it was the next to last thing he did to stay in the play, not ruin herself when Beck most required her to move with it uptown, two or three reviews, "raw talent." To say nothing of loyalty to the others. Ingrid. Robin. Barry. Fresh, other working people. Apart from this, he didn't get into her life. He was at home in the house she had been living in and he would be home probably when she got home, if she did, at eleven, twelve, one, or two. She could meet the brother, settle things with him. Something foreign about him, more foreign than Canadian. "I'll see it uptown," Daley said. "Why he comes here, lets you know he's here but doesn't come see you except to the theater or you see him and I don't know about it or want to. Why you smelled the pillow, it's family or it's all grist to your mill—it's nothing to me." Daley was just talking perhaps.

"I know everybody's smell," Becca said.

They slipped left then right in the backseat. The cabdriver incompetent, incomplete, the cab had screeched into their block and they saw Wheelock, Isabel's older son, nearer and nearer, in the middle of the street doing something familiar and now turning to sidestep the still-speeding cab so they saw Bear, when the driver made a sound you had never heard before, a whistling yet guttural sound threatened yet mellow and dangerous, a traditional sound that she had brought with her to these shores; for Isabel's younger boy had let fly the pigskin, Wheelock following its flight as it whacked the cab roof, you could feel it, "It's Bear and Wheelock," said Daley, the thing overhead denting off the roof skittering behind the car and into Wheelock's arms they could see out the back window close though they had been thrown forward by the brakes. "Good for Wheelock. Right here!"

Daley handed the woman a bill, the radio on Haitian. The rearview mirror a mask of two sharp eyes. The blond woman pulled the man around to give him a big kiss.

It meant they had an hour, an hour and a bit. The taxi had been the sex rush between the two passengers, late-afternoon, friendly, starkly successful, the end of the line.

A boy's voice shouted, "Screen pass!"

The driver said into the mirror, "You'll get your kids killed."

"Not by you, I hope," said the other woman.

"*My* kids are *home*."

"So are these kids." Becca pulled the door handle. The Asian woman being told by Daley leaning forward inside to keep whatever it was, a huge tip, and chugging water out of a bottle you expected her to chuck out the window, Wheelock, a responsible grin on his face, waited on the sidewalk.

"These your kids?" the driver said out the window to Becca, who heard Wheelock tell Daley someone had come by to see him, a woman.

"You're right," said Daley, "cab rushing the passer leaves the receiver free." Becca already up the steps had the note in her hand.

"Here's your receipt." The driver dropped the printout in the gut-ter. Wheelock picked it up and the cab lurched out into the street and was gone.

"But why was New York a problem for him?" Daley said climbing the steps. "If he's Canadian—"

"He's Canadian now."

"Ah, the mustache, he's Greek."

How did Daley know he had a mustache? Becca said. She handed over the slip of paper, her key in the vestibule-door lock, late afternoon.

Oh Canadian. Canadian male. Just a picture Daley had. Becca pushed the house door open, amused, irritated. "He was sounding almost American but nowadays . . ." Daley didn't finish. He got rid of the message slip.

"What sounds, if you know everything?"

"On the run but it's all right. It's you maybe."

"You thought he sounded a little American, what an ear, he's a businessman he could use you."

"He is already." Daley had spoken and it sounded pretty right. Becca took the message slip off the hall table by the umbrella rack and scrunched it and dropped it on the table but he had said something and it sounded in her thought more than *Who's Lotta? Why didn't you call her back?*—which she would never let him hear, though you didn't know with her. And Daley would find out soon enough, he supposed, if it was of any importance, the brother's somehow remote country of origin. There was no reason to ask.

Upstairs she pretended that he held her captive. She left it to him to be caught looking at the clock, and after an hour and a half, no ship in a bottle, she would make her tender escape. Nothing, no history Daley might learn of her would turn his attention from her herself, he prized her as momentarily his. He was excited by this performance that he wasn't going to tonight, no reason—this was closer to the living-together of Sunday time, a run in the park, a break from some perpetual, time-sensitive date.

Yet Becca had left for the theater in a mysterious female rush. "Police escort," she muttered looking at the time and then into her bag, her elbow pushing the door into the vestibule.

"That Mounty," said her lover, "that Mounty from the downtown stable," and she thought about that and was gone, he had to close the outside door and then called out after her, "You've got time," but into the empty house. The house needed him. Tomorrow too. But not five minutes later, the phone rang beside the bed—Becca he imagined wanting him to come, but—"The good news is I got through to you," said Lotta, it was Lotta.

"What is it about? Is it about your book?"

"The bad news is I'm right around the corner."

"What are you doing there?" Daley said, recalling how she'd treated him in her book.

"I'm at the last functioning pay phone in Manhattan."

# 8

A CLIENT, THAT'S ALL SHE WAS. SHE COULD HAVE REACHED HIM AT THE office. Was it over the line? Yet it was necessary curiously. A blow, finding things out, it happens. He remembered the time she had kept him on the line for twenty minutes with her hypothetical questions as if they weren't about her—whether it was wise to destroy certain letters, whether it was harder to sue a relative, whether he could possibly understand a bagful of pebbles treasured for years—careful what you toss—whether he could understand how great Tim was, her former husband now remembered in her book, once her friend she supposedly didn't make a move without, her absolute need to talk to him, maybe enjoying a late lunch somewhere. This before Lotta knew what was going on, though copies existed of those poems secretly accumulating at that time, folded in a pouch somewhere on the premises, patient, overflowing, Persian, exact in what they added up to, so personal in English in the hip pocket of her jeans underneath the smock-apron that this cleaning person, this girl, Luz, had not imagined them as copies.

Lookout what you throw away. The pebbly cove where her father instructed her in the fabric of rocks that had changed under pressure. In the preferred orientation of dark and light and sparkling grains within the rock that told you what you wanted to know, until they let you go—until she would break away and as if she were alone, stripped as swiftly as Superman, and take a quick, unselfconscious dip in the ocean. This was already long after what she had not known then.

What she would get around to telling, and did in her book.

What did they *have?* Long walks where nothing happened, nothing almost was said. Silent hand-in-hand passing around a wooded hill listening to a meadowlark on a post, along the edge of a midsummer cornfield startling a pair of ducks, which looked back at them whistling away over the birch trees toward the inlet.

Her selection of striped, speckled and ripe, dimly translucent stones; the funny verses they had written down together, a taste for words, for nature, she and her father, the piney woods behind them, the cold waters sliding up the pebbly shingles. Just what had happened.

The father, now: he would give her a special kiss, one to remember, try his tongue along her mouth at secret bedtime, understood between them, wordless, jocose, expected—until she must have outgrown it. Who knows? Until, years later, married, she learned of it, it woke up inside her a hum of moving things that shook her a little like a ride and had a taste of smoke and doughnut until she went to the mirror and admired her tongue and Daley noted that here you lost track of that special molester and would not soon forget the tongue tapering in the mirror, the taste at the corners, the throb in the tummy that goes free: but the thing was, her father had described "it" it seemed in detail to a new friend of his, his end of the kiss; and it got back to her. How? Her aptness at age five, her adroit and hearty appetite. How willing she had been he had demonstrated with gusto—paternal pride really— with wonder to this younger man, who was in real estate mumbling some morsel of supper you might think.

A blow, finding this out, she went into it at length. She had a great heart, he had told her himself. Had that old faithful habit lost her some later luck in love, access, ease, something that showed? Not that she'd noticed. Her first real boyfriend entered her from behind in the beginning. No problem. They could talk; they laughed. He was sweet and whispered *Fake it* once. According to her book *he* naturally did not.

Nothing the *matter* with her, her vagina demure. Her body in the mirror. Actually she had entertained a cosmetic option or two later on. Her expressive looks went from her and came back to be absorbed. Her eyes were quick and dark, she had extraordinary eyesight.

The Russian cabdriver humming. The helicopter overhead. The harbor under her. The ferry. It was like her first time: leaning at the far curve of the bow rail facing the Statue, the harbor swells briefly lensing then darkly absorbing the stones, those quite precious stones in sunlight and wind spray dumped into a harbor sea beyond even unforgiving on the way to Staten Island, stones she and her father had picked up years ago gone. Taking action. It's your life. Walk you through it. Unfolding "like a good lay," Lotta's book words were awkward enough—though who knows maybe true, an ear for men talking. She was tight and wanton. She knew some famous people. She knew Randy Newman apparently. Yellow woman, yellow man. Short people. Everyone has it in them, those old situations. Wrap your arms around a famous underground column in a village somewhere near Oaxaca where she did business, and the distance between your hands on the other side tells you how long you have left. Life expectancy on her mind, she took care of her arms, though, and face and belly. She was forty, women like her lived forever, though we were all going to.

At Staten Island she had turned around in the terminal without a glance at Saint George and come right back across the harbor on the next boat with the same family of brown and blue pigeons; watching inconsolably the Borough of Richmond Municipal Building recede, horrified at what she had done: it was the letters, not the stones (not then). She had a rush of anger, a vacuum in front pushing from no known place, stepping off the gangway and running for the train. It was the fastest, the old-fashioned, handmade, funhouse bend in the South Ferry station track looping back northward. So wired she couldn't look at her watch. She took the local to Chambers, burst across the platform to an express, and three excruciating slow stalled stops north found the same uptown local across the platform, her same *car,* her place next to a window washer now taken by a bristling man she was sure she'd known in school, a nice touch, Daley felt, if it was true—or in a quite other life and could not look at him. She reached her apartment house on the run to retrieve the letters in their white business envelopes. Some were gone, some still there among the orange peel and carrot pulp, coffee grounds and blue-green cottage cheese. She smelled the voice, measured, musical, near—it was what it was —what it was, her father, a habit she could taste, the poignant flare of his mouth. Lotta, never done, had been in a mood to appeal her case, please, but who to? Her brother not talking to her, par for the main family course; her sister with her totally different long, angular face, always distant from the father, content with her Ohio pilot's license and her strange adopted kids. Lotta had been out so early, the stones in the pouch in her bag, so mad, visited the post office box where she received her important mail, renewed her driver's license, decided to take the ferry, dive over the rail; had clean forgot today was Luz's day, the woman herself (hair all packed into a shower cap) never imagining that her mistress wasn't some-where—but where?—and for the first time, like second sight or sixth sense, the clairvoyance of unwarranted jealousy, Lotta looked upward unknowing from the basement garbage room dissolving the floors of the building, while on her hands and knees she hummed her songs cleaning the bathroom, and could not know Lotta's outrage—not at her father's kisses but the telling.

This emergency person with a complaint, when Daley came out onto his stoop and saw her approaching colorfully from the west he felt the old blame beachhead coming with her, a bone to pick with him. Yet how she carried herself, a country person on a visit, a purple and yellow woven poncho telling some story in itself, a foreign bag in her hand made of what looked to be orange plastic.

"I phoned and phoned," she said, coming up the steps, in her forties now.

Listen, Daley told her, holding the door, he'd picked up Monday afternoon *thinking* it was her, did she believe him? It was her, he had thought, but no, it wasn't. "I wasn't going anywhere," said Lotta; Daley could have said the same.

Lotta inside his house. After all these years. What years? Could he take her coat, her . . . ? She didn't hear him. Her poncho, he said. In the hallway she was upright, resistant. Looking for a thing she didn't even know she'd come for. She was looking at the heavy metal ring left on the hall table. The baseball gloves on the floor underneath. And then through the parlor door the piano. How she didn't take off this hairy, purple-and-sunshine-yellow poncho with the double-ended pocket in front. An uprightness in her determination not to strike a false note: though when the edge was in her voice (and Becca still almost here with Daley), it was the starts and stops in Lotta's very presence waiting for gusts of thought, of bodily feeling, to give them voice. For this man who did listen. Was that maddening? Or was it that she couldn't get through?

From the parlor you went either upstairs or downstairs, he explained, you rarely stayed, there was a thermostat in the parlor from years ago. "Never been here," Lotta said. Nothing wrong with that, Daley thought. He led the way downstairs. "Never had a client here," he said over his shoulder; it wasn't quite true. "I'm not here as one," said Lotta. "Wait a minute," she went back up and a moment later joined him in the kitchen.

What did the woman want? "You were in the neighborhood."

"Almost three hours," Lotta said like a question.

"Were you over by the river?"

What was it? They were sitting at the kitchen table. Daley felt her interest almost in him in the elbows spread on the table, her listening knuckles.

"That was it," Lotta said.

"Why you called?"

"I've called all week."

A little blue Q-tips box of Becca's stood on the table beside a breakfast mug. "Well, not *all* week. It's not business you said? I picked up once, but."

Did he remember the Middle East trip? Couldn't say he did. The tour? Ah, the tour. "The grave of Eve?" said Lotta.

It came back. "Of course she died, didn't she, it never occurred to me," Daley said, but he saw it was Ruley.

From the large orange bag with the handles Lotta produced a folder. In it were some chalk drawings bigger than the folder. "The

Middle East tour Ruley Duymens organized? Remember him?"

"Oh, Ruley. He had an interest in Jedda, the roof there, irrigation in the area, it was business," Daley said.

"Exactly." Lotta was looking at a drawing Daley couldn't make much of upside down, she was seeing it. Well, one night . . . it was a desert night and there were trees she'd never seen, she had told Ruley about Iraq and the hotel and the two art objects, the figurines, you could hold one in the palm of your hand; and how her friend had left the breakfast table with the two men and she had never seen her again.

"The woman you met on the plane," said Daley.

"Remember my Taiwan friend?"

Friend? She'd known her only a day or two, if Daley remembered right. Nineteen eighties, Lotta? —mid-1980s, earlier.

"Yes, because you didn't do much about her," said Lotta.

"I didn't do anything, and I regretted it." Daley got up to offer Lotta a drink.

"You regretted it," said Lotta.

Daley sat down again. Yes, he knew Taipei, he'd been there on leave.

"She's not in Taipei."

Probably so, but.

"No probably about it."

"And Ruley."

"He said he would see what he could do."

Well, said Daley.

What did that mean? said the woman across from him.

Nothing, Daley said.

"That's right," said the woman across the table. What on earth was it?

Daley got up and poured water into the kettle. Someone passed on the sidewalk outside bouncing a ball. Daley wasn't feeling polite. He knew Ruley in his sleep, Ruley was always a coincidence, and Daley remembered about the art, broken then stolen, taken, but unrepairable—what do you say? "Ruley always knew your business, it never failed that he had been there," Daley said. "She was extradited to Canton, wasn't she?"

Lotta put the empty folder up to her face. Daley knew what it was, or at least that Ruley had called her; he was sure of it. Lotta slapped the folder down on the table, she could hardly get it out, some awful sounds back in her lungs. "Do you know that he called me last week."

"Yes," said Daley.

"It was the book . . . the *book?*" The voice insinuated that Daley might do her the favor of making an effort to recall. "He upbraided me. Upbraided me."

"About the book," said Daley. (Uncertain terrain for Daley, this obscure book out for almost a year.) It was the *book* that Ruley had upbraided her for? Things in it that shouldn't be there?

"The opposite."

"Things that should." Did Lotta want Daley to understand something?

"He said I was . . ." Lotta took a deep breath and let it out, she had the Q-tip box in her hands. "He said you were . . ."

Daley heard it coming and he was not surprised except at the very words he had heard coming, they must be circulating because he had thought these words himself, the very ones.

"He said I made my living producing native knockoffs with cheap Third World labor."

Well, it was only a phone call, Daley said.

"It's my life we're talking about."

"Always," said Daley.

"I was a mercenary in the culture crusades."

"Always," said Daley.

"What do you mean always?" said Lotta.

"It's always your life we're talking about. I'm sure he won't sue," said Daley.

"Do you think that's why I tried you half a dozen times and came to see you twice on a Saturday?"

The possibility had occurred to Daley. "What was missing from the book?"

But the poor woman was looking at her lap, shaking her head.

What was the fuss? Daley said. It was true enough what Ruley had said. It was him.

What did he mean, it was true enough? Lotta retorted.

"Oh, materials," he said, "we all turned things into things."

"It's art," Lotta said. "That's what I'm about."

Well of *course,* Daley obliged, but he meant, *how.* Make a *car,* junk it, turn junk into *new* raw . . .

She must have felt Daley was getting them both into an explanation that would not help. "Cars, raw materials?" Lotta said impatiently of this footling, male detail, like *You're telling this to the wrong girl,* but.

"New raw *materials,* junkyard scrap okay, new fridge, scrap the fridge (separate the freon), make mailboxes. But no," Daley said, "listen to this: they make materials that think." He meant the material itself. Polymer sheets of infinitesimal units you can't even see that make decisions apparently. He wasn't saying it well. Because he didn't understand it probably. Yet he did. "Look at your book." (He had hardly looked at it himself.) He meant her, her appearance, which was fine; her character. He meant more than that.

Lotta leaned back and put a hand on the table edge, about to get up, having absorbed this news, this information, this grain of truth.

No wait. He knew people who . . .

Lotta reached to put the Q-tip box exactly where it had been. "*What* materials think?"

"Tiny chips decide when to turn your lights on."

"That's not thinking."

No, and Daley would never have such a system here but—his brother had a client, well, a city—a dam he had worked on. And in the future, a metal alloy itself will know when too much stress is torquing down from upstream and without any intervention it will decide that a valve a hundred feet away should kick open—to save the dam. But we were also talking about the most particular and extensive, even historical—

What if there wouldn't be time, Lotta said.

—a virtually historical you understand memory of something going on with nothing to stop it—a spin, say; an immense force.

"What if it's a midair collision, a shock to the system?"—Lotta's eyes by turns averted, then uncoolly glomming onto Daley as he had fallen away from her life into materials: brought on by hers, mind you, her business idea, yet her book where she had made something of herself even if it was one-to-one payback for the most part.

Lotta had stood up. It upset her. She was just another uncanny denizen of the city. She could learn to dislike him. That he had someone; or that he didn't. Or it was just her business, a value she put on it that he didn't. What was he to her? "What am *I* turned into?"

"But those art objects she gave you," Daley said; "those fragments, that little earthquake we had "—hadn't she *let* Duymens take them? The broken figurines? Or did Daley have that wrong? "Maybe it's in your . . ."

"Memoir," Lotta said. "But not his name."

"Good."

"No. That's why he was furious."

"He wanted his name in it?"

"As a thief."

"All right. What did you do about it?"

Lotta shook her head bitterly. "I told him . . ." What was the woman here for? "That's what you get writing a book," Lotta said.

"I was walking along the river and I remembered that umbrella and your wife. You know how you think about things."

"My wife?" Lotta was done with her complaint apparently, yet what she was asking of Daley was unclear. Maybe that was exactly it. He didn't mind, he had opened his door to her by picking up the phone.

"And your wife died. No more than that."

"No more than that?"

"I just thought about it. What can one say?"

"A lot or nothing," said Daley.

Lotta sat down again. "And that you went home after that slashing. What a shock it must have been for her."

"Sure," said Daley; "I guess it was." What could Daley tell her?

Lotta had tried to go to China; they wouldn't give her a visa. Well, that was interesting.

"The grave of Eve," Daley said. "So you made some pictures, you made something of it."

"That's a while ago."

Yet now Lotta tacked on a perplexing story of how people she met up with on the *road* insulted and abused her. A priest at a reservation who put down her product, whose own life was not above reproach. Lotta, however, a woman with, now that she was here under Daley's roof, the low ceiling of his basement kitchen, some erudition in there, she *spoke* succinctly you could say for her and still it had taken some time, God hadn't it. He would have to think about that story.

Yet it was the blue Q-tips box forgotten in Lotta's hand his client of the earthquake night that moved Daley to start, but only start, to tell her, and someone he didn't deeply trust, a thing or two about the old days with Ruley and Della. It was only things, not a story, though his own in a way. Yet not familiar to him. Della's drawings in a stack upstairs of water in a pool and awkward figures of swimmers, a dance theater floor with a fat child from the audience spinning on it, drawn into the performance; the nape of her neck bowing; a rocky cove pictured in a brochure—but he broke off. Should he speak of the subway? One evening on the way to meet someone at the Garden when he had met Della instead? And no one to remember all this—to confirm it or even, and this was a weird idea, to tell *Daley*—except Helen, or his brother, or, come to think of it, Ruley Duymens (some impoverished version of it all). Daley would regret what little he had told Lotta in a weak moment, but it wasn't a weak moment. Tonight and tomorrow he would regret it, he would be thinking, What did I tell her?

Why did you need someone to tell your stuff to? Or to tell *you* your stuff.

It was embarrassing here tonight but it wasn't, for who was Lotta? Why do we tell the people we tell? He would have to think about it.

There was a point. Even for Lotta.

What could all this explain?

The Q-tip box?

The sheer time Della had once spent with Ruley Duymens. The bank grant that helped the dance company she'd withdrawn from virtually, while the banker belittled her employment agency maddeningly on occasion. Daley didn't want to hold Lotta up. Lotta seemed spellbound. Daley felt cramped, like he needed to stretch.

And now years later Ruley was hooked up through real estate with a producer whose play featured this unknown young actress Ruley had hooked up with a new lawyer. Daley tapped his chest.

"I hear you," said Lotta; "bigger than both of us. What's her name? What's she been in?"

"It's what it is," said Daley, aware of the time. He wasn't pushing her to go. They were of one mind but it was time for her to go. She was leaving, wasn't she?

Leaving let you see. Let possibly both of you for a moment see what happens elsewhere and next. Was that how he'd seen Leander swimming, seen his day so exactly—framed by the next thing, by fluid, by departure? "I've gone on," Daley said looking at his watch.

Lotta was going now; but not before she told him what she had come to tell but forgotten to: that she was glad, really glad, that Duymens had pocketed the four pre-Columbian fragments wherever he had pocketed them in that infernal blue jumpsuit he looked so good in, taken them out of her house."

"I wish you had told me then," said Daley, but the mistake had meaning, if it was a mistake, two things side by side, maybe him and Lotta, no more than that. "And he thought I would be interested to see the inside of this place. But honestly I don't see much here."

Though if it was early for a Saturday night, at that instant Daley was certain Becca at the theater recalled him as she reenacted all over again seeing ahead not seeing anything ahead her own perilous way into what she was about to stun the brother with: her interview with his wife, her sister-in-law, the electric exchange between the two women abusive, unforgivable (whatever that means), tattletale and the blow to come. They were about halfway done there. Here in this house, however, lay something it occurred to Daley that Ruley Duymens wanted "back." Something of his. Sounded like he might have made it. Or a memento.

Well, he couldn't have the bookcase, Daley joked, seeing Lotta out the basement door.

"The time just flew," she said.

He couldn't recall what he'd said—the order of it, the past. He sat and stared at the kitchen cupboard for a time. Keys hanging up there looked gone. They were someplace. A car's prolonged horn as it passed the house couldn't be about to strike Lotta, she must be well away by now, he couldn't imagine her hit by a fender, a bumper, but why that arcing, lengthened note? He hardly knew what he'd told her all jumbled together. Helicopter paused overhead picking up, depositing, almost miraculously maneuverable but not quite. Imagine the projected Osprey lifting like a copter only to flip its two experimental wing engines forward and pass on at speed like a plane. To lift straight up. To hover. To flip the motors and take off in midair. Was this what they had been talking about? Sometimes you don't care if you ever see someone again.

# 9

DALEY TURNED LEFT OR WEST, TOWARD THE RIVER, AT THE FOOT OF his steps. But at the avenue a cab stopped for him as cars sometimes stop for a perfectly contented walker on a country road, and he got in and then the light changed, which Daley confirmed with the driver was not the main reason she had stopped because she'd had the light, she'd just thought she'd make up his mind for him, and now they began waiting for the light to change again, a woman quite fine or strong in profile with a thick braid down her back. He remembered a musician from years ago was playing with Sid Knox tonight and he thought tomorrow. He would go there, it would be good for him, he told the driver about the woman, unknown, tall, strong, ample, youngish—*Ample?* the perhaps Russian driver repeated—the woman had sat down at his dark table last Monday night at the very club he was now going to. The driver said that Daley was bragging— but not bragging. He liked her for this. Last Monday? she said. He gave the briefest idea of that evening, letting things take their course, but no less decidedly. It was a case of getting what you asked for. How they had left together and he had stopped a taxi outside the club and she'd said let's share it, her name was Anna (why did he single that out?), when he had turned to her for whatever she would say she did not turn to him, gave their driver the address (hers), and resumed a story of a Serbian jazz player who had been her father who said, "If the trumpet give an uncertain sound, who shall prepare himself for battle?"

Daley's driver asked for the address of this club again, for the light

had changed, her braid was thick and tightly arranged like a Puerto
Rican woman's though not dark, the profile full of the grandest equality to be equal to. He liked the driver. But two blocks ahead, there
was Lotta—whaddya know—Lotta waving and then not waving, they
stopped for her; and her mixed feelings like mixed times getting in,
she said she was reeling from what Daley had told her. This surprised
him, he supposed she meant the Ruley Duymens chapter, his first
(and only) marriage, or—

They would drop the *lady* off first, Daley told the driver.
Whatever you say, was the driver's reply. What did that mean? Lotta
asked, felt she'd interrupted something. Great circle route, said the
driver. Two early prostitutes in red and gold stood tall and pigeon-
toed outside a gigantic and famous glass-and-brick warehouse with
rounded-corner streamlining one block by two blocks extending
monumentally almost to the river. Look at them, said Lotta. Daley
said that he knew them to speak to, it was his neighborhood. One of
them had shown him a partly Asian invented calculator thing in her
hand not on the market yet called a Palm Pilot, not ready till '98
apparently. The woman in the driver's seat appreciated this, he could
tell, she slowed down. Are you in free fall or something? Lotta said,
or did I interrupt something? What was evidently somehow mystifyingly wrong with all Daley had told Lotta tonight threatened to carry
them in relative silence twenty minutes north and through Saturday-
night traffic east to drop her at her midtown tower. But then she
slipped her arm through Daley's and acted like a very old friend of his
when the driver with the braid struck up a conversation.

Lotta asked Daley in. He had to get out to let her out. It was a
chance to see her place after all these years. He held her hand and wondered if Ruley had fucked her the time he pocketed the broken art.

Hey, she could tell him some interesting news, Ruley was threatening to get into the film business.

Daley was sorry but he had the second half of someone's show to
see. Lotta folded a bill and stuck it in the upper pocket of Daley's sport
jacket. Great circle route, she said. Two women taking it all in. It was
in this way, along this curious and strangely uncomfortable or grateful
path, that he went to Becca's play after all, though with some premo-

nition he told the driver he might not stay more than a few minutes (now why would he say a thing like that?). Though, picking up the Monday-evening story they had dropped when they had picked up Lotta in the street, the "ample" woman. Oh yes, when they'd reached her building, a walk-up, she asked Daley in and seemed just fine. He had found her funny, warm, political, clear-headed . . . "Ample?" (Driver was flirting, more New York than Russian)—and hours later lying under her quilt and having a good laugh he discovered that—

"I know," the driver said, she was quick or bossy but just with balls and a tough humor in her bones, "she was pregnant."

"Four and a half months." Daley was paying the driver, whose routine extraordinariness matched the abruptness with which he burst now from the cab, noting the blown-up newspaper photo on the easel, Becca's finger pointed but really being shaken; you rush ahead then you pause and look down and almost take thought. The city itself following Daley. He had given the cabwoman two new twenties stuck together, he realized.

The freckled boy standing at the back. They were veterans. But the man Daley knew at once in the half dark coming up the aisle leaving midway through the second half had Beck the producer a pace or two behind him, and it was Becca's much older sibling, Daley had not the slightest doubt of it. The man passed with a sharp, absorbing, dismissive look, he could have been the several persons in his time that Daley had begun reluctantly to reckon him. A Canadian brother, a perhaps not terrible someway incestuous or loving protector against family abuse however interstitial (though at some level a user abuser himself, or guide to history, to business, a weekend soccer player). A history buff, an intelligent layman—the girl the first night had spoken of Algonquian Indians up along the border playing association football in 1865—though something concentratedly esoteric, which recalled certain watchful antiquarian dealer people a case had once brought Daley into contact with, arcane fact circling around a passionate bargain or reaching a hand toward clefts and softnesses marginally, clandestinely, quietly who knew what. Or here was a thought, suppose this guy with a substantial Canadian mustache and an executive ponytail behind the bald, commanding skull, had broken the law on this side of the border once upon a time, once right here in New York City, say, and kept a low profile when he flew in. Or he was just a businessman who didn't make his bed, scrap recycler, with an American curve in the equation somewhere. A universe of clients all privileged to be ignored or kept clear and separate if he wanted, by Daley. In the half-dark standing room where Daley, farsighted, watched the play with new interest tonight (for look at that actress, will you, independent, early ripe—fighting, though, for what? Her brother to stay and see her perform?), the at-least-twenty-years-older brother's quick eyes, liquid, familiar, staring even in a glance, found Daley in passing; both noteworthy for a second and insignificant; dismissed you and computed your importance as he passed like an officer Daley had known who was always on the run, restless at all times except in danger when he was not restless at all, a person of many minor deeds who somewhere in him hidden had a presence. And Daley, with his taxi driver's shoulder up against him, her braid, her smell, her almost black lipstick, Daley was absorbed still in the play he knew in his heart Becca must stay with, and all that education, her war and revolution facts, her trip to New Rochelle to see where Tom Paine had finally (though temporarily on this side) had his cemetery-less bones buried under his own tree; all Becca's history down strangely to the new Winter Soldiers protests just a year before she was born by Daley's reckoning, was her own, her knowledge, remembered, learned (and *used*—who knows? And "First in war, first in peace" wasn't Lee but Washington, first thing they'd learned, about Washington anyway, a school speech up on a stage; and hadn't she said Lee was not pro-slavery? and lived in Brooklyn?); yet for the rest about the brother, Daley did find it disquieting to know such things about anyone whose eyes he met, and therefore wondered if the other must know him. When as his attention instantly returned to the second, the later, scene between the sister and the secretary the turns and truth of which (if the words were exactly the same as Friday's) Daley was only now getting, Beck the producer came up out of the aisle only to see Daley and the boy and doubtless the cabdriver and whisper, "Hey, I saw you brought your friend again; wondered where *you* were," while simultaneously *sotto voce* waving Becca's impatient brother back from the lobby. To introduce Daley, whom the producer himself had never been introduced to. The sister's voice was all around them at that moment, the voice-over sounding its time-canceling closeness this time with the speaker on stage. "Bruce Lang. William Daley."

"Ah yes," the man said softly—this was Bruce! Didn't he recognize Daley from . . . knew his *name* from . . .

The secretary and Becca—no blood visible, was it a grain or two of powder pale and dry on her nose? The two women on stage transfixed by the voice-over, ever fresh or deeper than one had heard before or inflated junk or just not cleaving quite to the letter of the script, or not believably a letter but possibly something else: "I loved you too much. We learned from our love. From quiet walks we took between valleys and mountains, dividing the real war. We had a map between us showing real allegiances that you betrayed though I love you still."

While Daley, who knew exactly where we were, picked up the tone. This practiced vagueness not American exactly fading away, polite, thinking fast . . . "Detroit, Detroit area . . ." (The *I think* didn't fool you for a minute, but *Detroit area*—?) "We'll be back," Beck said to the boy. The boy looked blank; Bruce glanced at his watch. He was lobby-bound. It was the ponytail looking back at you that said, Get outa the way.

The boy is waiting for his mother to phone this office we are looking at on stage while the sister is talking to the secretary. A courage in him, a courage in Becca, a courage in her half brother succeeded by stinginess, scrap metal, car fenders flattened, it came to Daley—in the other man, gone thank God, like his name from the second (or umpteenth) version of Becca's one-woman. Something of Daley in that brother. Tracked by laws more serious than some love for a young woman. If desire like that had even entered Daley's life. Daley recognized himself and understood the play. Beck and the brother were not going out for a cigarette. It was business. The phone rang and the actress looked out into the audience. Daley thought she didn't see him. He thought this because so much had happened and most of it trivial in a few seconds. Was it his life? He touched the boy's shoulder and was gone.

Some equal necessity tediously detailed that you had nonetheless asked for followed Daley to the cab waiting outside. Why was she here? She thought she had seen a cop. No tickets at this hour, Daley said irritated. Well, she said, he had said he would only be ten *minutes*—True enough—and we had to complete this loop back to the jazz club, right?, and he had never finished the story about the woman who had invited him in Monday, so that's why she turned down a fare. He felt it in his lungs, not the old smoke cell in the cab but the weld burn from the river or trash incineration or some forthright poison dispensed by the time not the Port Authority or the Veterans of Foreign Wars. In his lungs it was as real as what came from the basement at home.

They drove in silence for a minute and Daley could not believe what he had heard Beck say but had to. *I saw you brought your friend again, I wondered where you were.*

Helen there tonight? To see about the blood. Alone, or sitting with somebody Beck didn't say, but absolutely not alone, it wasn't her. Was it the future or the past you were trying to grasp? (Tomorrow the house needed him. Sunday for years a day with Helen.) But when they got to the river and pulled up at Waters, Daley didn't go in after all and felt excited asking the driver to take him home. "That other fare wasn't going to the airport or anything?"

"Oh no, it was those guys, the bald guy and the one with the hat. They were going to report me. Just a little round trip, a particular route, over *here*. They weren't even going to stop except for a quick drink with somebody if I'd wait, then back where they came from." The woman laughed. In the light of the passing city blocks her braid was single, grand, admirable, old, temptingly in love, a woman at work, and he piloted them to the very corner where she had picked him up.

"So what do I think?" she said, looking in the mirror. "She was expecting, but that wasn't what she had to tell you."

# 10

Becca was very late unlocking the vestibule doors and Daley went up to greet her. Her cheek was cool and smoky, she put her face up to him, her pink and sallow cheeks, her personality, her parched lips, her mouth. What did he find? A narrow blur on the cheekbone under one eye, a bit of a tiny, fine crescent bruise stupid as could be. Like makeup applied by work itself (or the birthmark powdered over by the Korean lady at the laundry, if that wasn't a bruise but it was always there, month after month). His scrutiny was a kiss too. She might be just in danger it occurred to him. Or a genius.

"It's you after all," she said, she was hovering for a moment, with him or bound somewhere else, alive, quite glad to be home, needing to pee, simmering a bit, on her breath the message of a drink or two awash in her stomach, smiling. He followed her, aware of the chalk drawing on the hall table all by itself seen and magically ignored by her, some exchange he couldn't put his finger on, following her along the hall to the stairs down to the kitchen.

A moment later, when she could talk, she was present and doing things, sorting things from her bag onto the kitchen table, moving the Q-tip box out of the way, and leafing through her notebook. Here like a woman but distant like a woman. Thinking some new thing. If asked, she would always tell. Only that she came back at you. She needed to do some laundry, and he didn't have a washer-dryer. It was then it occurred to him that the heavy, ugly ring was missing from the foyer table upstairs, taken by his visitor he thought.

"Maybe they were angry," she said, sitting down at the table and reaching for the Q-tip box. "Lex, Phil, Dave, you know the rest."

The rest of *them*? he thought—and who was Phil? "You saw me standing at the back? I couldn't stay away but then I thought it was a night to give you your privacy."

"Thanks, brother," she said dryly.

They wanted to know her plans, those guys. Didn't they always?

he said. Why wouldn't they? "That's your part," it came to Daley. Listen, he had an idea for her. An idea? He became confused. *It's you after all,* she had greeted him. *After all.* Listen, all she needed to do was the play *and* the one-woman piece—let Beck produce her and in return she'll move with the play uptown.

It was also in Daley's scrutiny—what she interrupted then, getting up and reaching out and going to him to hug him where he stood at the stove, kiss him like an old hard-core wife. Presently bursting into a smile, had she divined the visitor he'd had? It was none of her business. Were they sensible in his breath, his warmth, his attention these things he'd heard a few hours ago and told? Bizarrely sacred things told to a visitor who had reached him the old way, a note stuck in the door snared by Becca turning with it on the top step as the angry cab had pulled away almost sideswiping the lanky blond boy Bear with the football in both hands, Becca's arm outstretched as if she hadn't read it. (Was the paperwork increasing? What had happened to Daley's life? Then imploding the note in her fist once she'd read it: wouldn't stay imploded, this it occurred to him feedback from Lotta, the unanswered calls, the week.) And then, hardly an hour and a half later when she had left the house (always for the last time maybe) bound for the theater (which she was also leaving) . . . "You came after all," she said, "but what happened?"

"Couldn't stay away."

"Ah, but . . . you left me to those guys."

Daley would remember that. "They left before I did."

"They were coming back."

"I guess they had to see someone," Daley said.

"Always, and you missed me at the end. Or were you sitting down somewhere?"

"Not tonight."

"What you missed. And they came back, and—"

"I left them to you. It's your business. You're very good."

"They saw you."

"*Saw* me! We *met.* We spoke. He's a bit of a . . . he's solid. We knew each other. He's all business."

"No he's not. You're wrong there." Becca was a woman, distracted, young and mature in her being, he smelled her face, nothing but the moment but he was in the presence of the future he could tell but that was almost all. God! he thought.

"What do you mean I'm very good?"

"Just formidable."

"Oh forget it," she said.

"What did I miss?" Daley was agreeable, stupid.

"Oh forget it. No one knows, " she said.

"No one knows what?"

"What I see looking out into the house at night."

"What do you see?"

"Oh you have no idea, Mister Lawyer," she said angrily. "I looked out there one night and I saw him I realize now with the man with the cufflinks, it's all the same to me, this is a month ago."

"With Duymens?"

"Isn't that what I said?"

"Man's been around," said Daley, "your brother. Something about him."

"He could use you," Becca said then lightly, the moment over, a blind spot of unpleasant responsibility between them, not getting less, not getting more. She had learned a thing or two, that was all. They were falling, not that a person of her experience needed to back out of whatever, for nothing was too much for her after being used as a trouble spot for her parents to clear their daily mess through. She was somehow easy on him then. Came to him but receded. It was late. Some long view you can't identify but have set foot in. He told her now in the kitchen about his first deposition after law school that he had wooed Della with, forgetting it was the middle of the night but she'd liked it. ("No. You knew.") He might have told it differently to the girl. He kept the Khmer shrines on the plateau, the archaeologist woman undescribed; kept the stations, the terrain, the alternative times he had thrown at her, the defendant, to show her up.

"Your heart wasn't in it," said Becca surprisingly.

"It's a story," he said; "I'll tell you sometime. What that archaeologist was probably looking for. Some other time."

But when? he thought.

"You met my brother, and then you left?"

"Something happened," Daley said.

"It was just your name."

"*Daley*? But surely he had it."

"Only the number here. He carries a lot around in his head. It might take a while but it comes to him sooner or later. You have a friend at Boeing?"

"That's in Washington. Washington State."

"Oh, you have family there." She was distant again. He felt the floor curve or roll, the ceiling very low and old here like the floor. Let her leave.

She was lying. It was unusual lying.

It was subtly honest lying. He heard it beginning.

When she would start in on him he didn't know but he was free and fairly ready. Late at night, she sat him down upstairs in the living room to hear some new material. It was getting there without becoming jokes or a rant. She hovered over him. He thought she would be gone by Monday. Yet she loved him a little and when they were in bed she wanted to know about his nieces and he told about taking them down to Tacoma and back, how Gemma the older one had spotted a pair of petrels—petrels?—the fork tails unmistakable if you paid the kind of attention she did, he'd been a thrilled uncle. But a shadow or only a squall on the horizon warned him of Becca beside him (how on earth?), and she felt it.

"You taught her?"

"I used to write to her. I probably mentioned . . ."

The middle of the night had come back to him in the theater, the theater back to him in the middle of the night. Was it interest flagging? Strange thought. It would be a whisper of teeth and lips and God knows what amplified along his body waking up a sound someplace in the dark house upstairs downstairs, Daley was pretty much without fear (which he would never confess), the voice thin, like a metal strip embedded in a shadowy panel: "You want the truth about it in so many words?—or *this*?" was what he recalled once. The truth about what? Still asleep, he threw out his arm to feel her there and he smote her and she objected but didn't much wake, he had hit her ear under her hair, cartilage eerie, maimable, and presently he slid over and gathered her in for she had said those words hadn't she?

In the middle of the late night waking on his side, swinging his arm like a backstroker, smacking her by mistake, contemplating her nose with the little bump on it, the shadow-softened, hair-shrouded forehead and cheek independently awake in the light across the ceiling of a passing vehicle in the street he had felt for her for sure; while it had occurred to him she might be damaged (just as she scratched herself). She licked her lip and laughed, it seemed, very softly awake behind her eyelids (was that it?). And he watched her until he had to let his eyelids drop, and only remembered in his seat in the theater the sound that awakened him upstairs downstairs you couldn't tell.

Was she sensitive? She might have heard him think so. When he was sweeping the walk and she was sitting on the steps in a skirt she said she didn't believe in it, in being "sensitive." She believed—not of herself but of her brother apparently (was there only one?)—that the strong needed to be protected against the sensitive. "Not you," she said to Daley when he stopped sweeping and looked at a neighbor arriving home across the street. A completely crazy craftsman, an early-middle-age white-haired specimen, distinguished, lean, and learned, who kept a framing shop on Broome Street and now spoke for the first time in recent memory: "Gotcha some company," he called, looking at Becca sitting on the stoop. It was to her he spoke, as if she were the neighbor.

She spoke up, "'Bout time, eh?"

"Oh it's always about that," said the man, climbing his steps all but oblivious to Daley, though no, absorbed in thoughts about Daley.

In the middle of the night hadn't she woken him and she was sitting upright, legs crossed, leaning over him going on about a business deal, a documentary or a waste disposal, it was blurred. And the man, it was two men, said she was not on the same page with them and would not quit persuading her, and she said it came home to her we were just written down or words and who was turning the pages. Daley's voice came out cracked, "No one, it's just lying open." She said something else that might have been irritating and he smelled her as she rolled and stretched out under the covers and was asleep at once. But Daley, a light sleeper, lay looking at her naked back, his hand on her shoulder, recalling when his brother had fallen in Australia and how in the barracks occupied by riggers and crane operators and just about everyone, he would lie awake listening to his brother snore, watching, understanding and loving his brother. *It's you, it's always you. It's you after all,* she had said coming tonight from her brother.

Late morning she took a laundry bag of his away and was away for several hours and came back with the laundry bag plus some other clothes he had never seen They had a date tonight and she seemed to be preparing for it. Serious all day long.

# 11

AND THEN IT WAS ONLY THE NEXT NIGHT, THE FIFTH NIGHT, SUNDAY. Was it a new take on him, some recoil coming home, felt behind him while he unlocked the gate of the basement areaway for them, some mutual expectation he didn't like, perhaps only a fight with her, the keyless woman behind him, though she did have the vestibule and front door keys. November, so private in the country and minor even here in the city if Thanksgiving could just be erased by secret proclamation, and this was 1996, he wondered if she was even coming in. She was wearing a plum-colored coat with dark fur around the neck he hadn't seen before tonight. She had left the house this morning with the laundry bag and two hangers of things, he had watched her reach them out of the closet and lay them over her arm and wondered if the hangers were going to the laundry too. She was pretty curt with him. Was it for he didn't know what? Visiting the play. Not telling her. And why did he not ask, hearing the metal hooks inside the packed closet coming off the pole. Thinking these were her clothes and never thinking to investigate till much later the closet she had shut before leaving the bedroom. The downstairs front door pulled heavily shut, the young woman in her suede jacket unwashed-looking because burdened with those hangers and the laundry bag looked both ways at the curb. She trudged east then to pick up a cab on the avenue. Daley had watched from the left corner of the basement window as long as he could see her. It was late afternoon when she came back. Over one of the hangers the plum-colored, fur-collared coat he saw later that evening.

That night Becca wore the fur-collared coat over a dress he hadn't seen. The coat so fine and smart, had she seemed out of place? Not in America, not in New York. Here at the entrance to his house, coerced or married? God forbid.

They had sat through a rare Sunday-night session at Waters, the club half out on a dilapidated dock past which he had been in the habit of taking his early-morning run. They'd been having a pretty nice time, surely. The amount of time in hours over five days they'd had together wasn't bad, it was glorious, it was nothing really. She was subdued. She knew something she had always known.

Right in the middle of a set, low-pitched barge horns out on the night river, two strangers had stood up and joined the band. A round-bellied little Turkish trombone player with a nimble slide and a tone even in dissonant collaboration that came from his large dark sleepy eyes; and a beat-up graybeard alto sax man more than twice his age who had added some surplus himself and whom Daley hadn't seen since the 1970s. It almost startled him when the pianist gave the eye to the Dutchman from Delft Daley had heard at even closer range with the legendary Benninck from post-Vietnam-concert days. For fifteen minutes the Dutchman and the Turk went their ways—how did they do it?—so separately jettisoning a succession of milling-around bop-like flights and halfway volcanic omnidirectional grinding that in self-defense against this no-man's-land of tonal *centers* (what the Free guys called them) you could feel oddly closer to the person you were with, barraged, instructed, not hardly borne along because what kind of vehicle *was* this? Instead intellected out, elasticked in a greater field than Daley could help being drawn toward yet unhappy and ignorant of the jazz sounds, the hopeful eyes, the plainer chords Daley didn't want to miss out on; *or* you could feel it was marvelously relative and/or pointless and deep going nowhere and wonder what you were doing here, singly *or* coupled, or curiously combat-ready. (Why was that? Was that the girl, who was pretty pumped, but by the music?) She whispered that he looked just like her dad's tugboat friend. It relieved Daley, he'd thought there was something a little wrong, nothing special, just—which was how Free Jazz hit on you, fleeing whatever: it was no Bird, not that far, no Trane—though the Modern that resumed now relaxed things when the Ottoman and the Hollander, whom Daley recalled playing with the legendary Benninck in that damp street with music like fire crackling upstairs, were done. Daley had brought Becca. You never knew what the drummer Sid Knox might say. In particular about Daley's visit a week ago and a stranger who had sat down at Daley's table in the half dark, the half daughter as it turned out of a Swedish flugelhorn player well known to Knox, yet she had not said a word to him and he had been perturbed, hurt, irritated, you didn't know what really. Knox a drummer whose hearing (as is sometimes true of the dying or predying) grew more acute as the rest of him broke down, his stomach, his eyesight, his balance walking even in those tailored suits, something in his throat too or swallowing he wouldn't get looked at; and his sensitivity and insensitivity to water on his skin in the shower (resistance, invasion?) and to financial slights in his current case against the hotel in Connecticut: while by the day, by the hour, he heard better and better from apparently simultaneously different directions, all the time, *and* not just music, horn, bass, keyboard, but people, individuals talking, "Could hear a ball bearing click at fifty paces," Knox had said more than once. Becca got all this, Daley was proud of her, she didn't bring anything in here with her; Sid recognized her, Daley could have sworn, though his *It's you* was maybe flirting around with her. Where was she staying, he must have taken her for a visitor, until the play came up and Sid knew *Phil*, the director: "strange he was here on Halloween, can you beat that?" Daley started in describing Becca's outstanding loft, but she kept it on the music. She asked real questions. If Sid felt it was all built on him (Yes to this), and was a drum solo a story? and was jazz lawless? (No to this), and did two drummers ever play duets and how did you tune drums—against what? Why would she ask? She was working up to some other question that didn't come. She was a prized possession of Daley's or was she distant now? She asked what cymbals felt like. Sid loved her. Funny she should ask about drum duet, Sid had proposed that very thing to Sonny Greer, who was built like him, meeting him in Quincy after Sonny left the Ellington church. Sid was only a boy listening to parade music and Dixie in Elkhart, Indiana, a scorpion of a boy, a tilt-bug his great-aunt called him. In those days drums kept time, drum solos unheard of, thank God that that had passed (he expanded, speaking to Becca), he'd been looking out for something—it was always obvious but you had to . . .

Daley was proud. "No harm in looking, just looking, look out, look here." Daley felt awkward. Coltrane had tried two drummers, Daley offered, hadn't he, now remembering the sax man who was packed up and on the way out when Daley flagged him. Sid pointed his finger at Becca and said he didn't think she was the one with Bill the last time. His eyesight was going, Daley who went over to the sax player heard Sid say behind him that he thought he had seen her before, wasn't that so? Or heard her. The Dutchman was a quiet soul, he saved it for his music, which had taken an unfortunate though brilliant turn (to Daley's ear): "The two brothers," he said slowly, recalling Wolf and some difficulty he had had with the police.

That was so.

"The one who didn't go but wanted to; and the one who did go," the Dutchman said and Daley held him by the arm and looked him in the eye, and then the man was gone.

Bent and thin and shaking his head, Sid Knox turned abruptly and Daley realized the *It's you* he'd greeted Becca with was what Sid had heard coming out of the phone from her to Daley Monday and why Sid had gotten up to go then, as if his disappearing out the back door onto the pier now, just as Daley had a dumb question to ask, were for some similar reason probably no more than mortal. "You really know some independent gals." Where would he go to get to the street? It reminded you the river was surging by. Leaving, "What does a drummer use from life?" Daley was able to get out, thinking more of Becca, but this flamingo of a man was gone. Forever, it felt like (because of Becca—*why?*).

The sax player who had played in a Sunday session over there in the late 1970s that Daley had attended was gone, and Daley wanted to talk to him. Daley was out the door looking along the pier, up and down the street and behind him—in the slip, adjoining raft-houses dimly lighted, apparently tied together, built of river logs and scrap metal, doubtless seagoing. The wind off the Hudson seemed to have taken the man, but Daley could get his phone number—the young woman herself had stirred a question in Daley for the Dutchman though she would hardly know it, yet the Dutch sax player had remembered Daley, he recalled Wolf.

On the walk home Daley had recounted the Amsterdam story, fiasco or good fortune really, the Haarlem part, where he had heard Sid Knox the first time on a Sunday in '76 probably, taking over for Benninck.

Harlem?

Haarlem, Holland. A session.

A session?

Why did Daley have a feeling she didn't like him. What was it? Why did he tell a story now?

# 12

A SUNDAY GET-DOWN AT A STUDIO, WELL-KNOWN LOCAL IMPROV teacher, white, a banger, though this was not early-1970s political Dutch that he used to hear about, but a little later, and they were kicking it around, the line shifting, curving, like going up to the first landing and then making up the next flight of stairs—was it Dutch?—and just jazz you could say, some horns, bass, bass clarinet, sax, guitar, remembered it well, some little Brazilian gourd cups tuned a fourth different, piano chords going by, it was jazz without the notorious crackle-box experiments—but then somebody brought one out, a small-is-better cigar box with metal strips, a people's electronic, an unstable oscillator, it stayed with Daley. And clear across Europe Wolf came looking for him who'd forgotten his brother was on his way home from a job of his own, from Istanbul and worse, and not traveling out-of-body thank God. On a

Sunday in '76 or '77 brother Wolf swinging back across Europe tracking Bill down as he said he would there in Benninck's place almost by accident—a twenty-five-minute drive in a borrowed car from Amsterdam. Only to pull one of his little stunts when he got there. Black cornetist, the story *he* told about losing his blow in the DMZ.

Was Daley's story falling flat? Why?

A flight Istanbul Paris, flight to the lowlands, and Wolf tracked his brother from fleshly, staid Amsterdam and barged in in the middle of the music finding him sitting cross-legged with this Sunday late crowd with another American a drummer he'd met. Daley had forgotten completely that his brother was on the way home. You never knew where he would break a trip. Wolf. He said he had sniffed the place out—he sniffed with his nose to show what he meant. The music pretty democratic, every one of those foot warmers had their chance, it was "Blame It on the Blues," no off-runs but going to each other the way piano and vibraphone will have a chat, and the host drummer kept this rough, wooden-shoe rhythm, and when they'd been at it for a while they subsided in a friendly going-to-pieces reverse improv you could call it. A man from Detroit who'd been in the war, a great staccato cornet man, had lost his horn somewhere up in the Demilitarized Zone but not his life (against the official numbers crunched for white versus black casualties) though how the horn came to be at risk and oh yes did for a platoon proved a story in itself. This he interrupted to tell how once in Brussels before he was born his aunt was in a place and there was Bechet. Her hero. Philadelphia, Chicago, Moline, she'd always needed to speak to him and she needed to now but her playing—she was a piano player—hadn't been going good. He saw her by the French doors and he was playing "Klooks Blues" out of that body of his with a tumbler of water on the floor and when he was done he came over and asked what was it? just like that, why she didn't come up and speak to him. He read her mind. Actually, she his!

And that was how she found the music again, what one musician does for another. He had his son with him and they all piled into a taxi and went and had dinner. Story faded out, but something to it. Horn lost in DMZ something else. Gross, a false note almost, can you *talk* like that about . . . Well, Wolf was glad to see his brother, and through all this anecdote about the aunt, Wolf in an undertone as if they were not at a session in somebody's flat at all, was telling Daley what had been going down in Turkey, pulled up his pant leg to show the welts on his calf. What rethinking a bridge and a parallel viaduct for reconstruction after a quake will get you. The work pretty well done when it had blown up in his face. Laid to dissidents, some part of the mess was a natural aftershock months late most curiously, and for one night he was extremely unpopular—that is, taken in for questioning, which he had never been any good at—trying to get himself killed if not taken apart—balls or stupidity post-Vietnam, where he hadn't served. A big, serious clarinetist took offense at Wolf's a cappella talking, and he was right for who knows what structure Wolf, an unpleasant talent, saw looking at our white South African and Daley said, Just shut up; yet Wolf seemed presently to have heard the Detroit man's story from start to finish and laughed and was heard to say clarinet was the wimpy blow, tenor was Bechet's instrument though Wolf claimed he didn't know what he was talking about, he'd heard his brother say all this—and where's your sense of humor? The big guy had laid his reed on the floor and wanted to stand up and had the aptitude to have thrown Wolf out that window he'd gone to look out of into the street to find a Dutch squad car and two cops checking on the car with the bikes still lashed to the luggage rack and looking up the block. It could have been trouble but the Detroit man said that happened to be his aunt's opinion too about the clarinet, but not about Sidney, a great piano composer you know. The Dutch drummer had been talking how he didn't do a thing when the students came for the improv class, just play a little Korean music sometimes. Everyone laughed and whatever Wolf had been trying to stir up didn't turn bad—not then. The American drummer Daley'd been talking with about the law before Wolf barged in took a turn and that was how Daley met Sid Knox who blew them all away if not Wolf, and tonight years later this woman who'd been five or six at the time.

Had his brother been medically discharged after serving in . . . no, she thought again. Daley laughed, yet the uncanny wrongness of her surmise; no, Wolf, who was seventeen, eighteen at the time of the draft did everything he could to get in the army—the air force, the Coast

Guard—to smuggle himself over. Was it Wolf or the war far away in the margins that got Becca going, for they were almost home. No reason to think so when the war is lost on people three times Becca's age. Though not her, we already knew. Some women would say, Shouldn't we talk about it? Wolf almost didn't buy the lost cornet, the DMZ, and the upshot. Or the princely paunchy black player with the heavy shoulders glad to have served his country the U.S.A., telling us about a Vietcong woman in an earth tunnel as it was pieced together later fingering the valves of the instrument, thumbing the trigger, the out-of-key and in those days still-Asian riff according to surviving witnesses who thought themselves a minute or so at least away from the congruent, familiar, distantly, shiningly but hardly bugle (or jazz) alert or however foreign correspondence until they were on top of it. And no choppers in the area, no air surveillance, though even hovering there was little to see from the air. It was in the earth, what was going on. Wolf spoke out: Didn't he have no respect for the war? That strange grammar Wolf put on depending who he's talking to. But in a room full of men who had (at least once) opposed the war, with the possible exception of the cornet player.

Here was where Daley had felt the girl lagging behind him, the streetlamp out, and cut the story short. One thing took you so far and then it was done. He knew the terrain but he had not spoken to the cornet player, a black jazz player, he told the story to not tell something else, that was all Daley knew, which might as well have been clairvoyant for all the good it did anyone.

The story fell flat. They approached the house. Becca's dress-up clothes formal for her, nice, special, forlorn, they excluded him, yet she was a professional. She might turn around and go home he was sure of it and a streetlamp out—what you get as a rule when you don't tell the whole story—yet there *is* none. Some imaginative circumstances she no longer gave herself to. The phone rang inside, he could hear it, and it stopped as if the house had answered.

Enough about his brother: the car that night not borrowed but taken, though proffered initially with make, year, and Am'dam plate number by the owner's friend (an engineer to whom Wolf had mentioned Vancouver where he was going two months hence possibly with his brother, whom they discussed, if he could pry him away from his life). And here in

Amsterdam at a number Wolf had miraculously (for him) fished out of his wallet bulging with drawings, rolling papers, gum, his own scribbled estimates of a 7 to 8 quake coming in north China in July, was the nameless Amsterdamer generously "proffering" (as he put it on the phone) his friend's car for the evening so the American consultant who unknown to him was phoning from across the street (and at first to the American) could drive over to Haarlem to meet his brother. Though in retrospect— which is always good for distance—the loan hadn't been quite definite. Why had the engineer now in Amsterdam in the lobby of the Park Hotel been so generous with the car of his friend who'd be back in a minute and the engineer went in search of him telling Wolf to call back in five minutes. But Wolf being Wolf went out into the street down the block from the red awnings and the black-and-white-checkerboard pavement outside the hotel and found the damn car.

More than you wanted to know, but something telling *Daley* it wasn't enough, the woman with attitude behind him at the basement door and then they were inside. It was Sunday late and it was him she started in on. He had expected it sometime, though do you say these things if you are really leaving? Maybe so.

# 13

W HO REALLY WAS THIS WOLF PERSON? AN ASSHOLE LOOKING FOR a scrap. *Good* to your brother, aren't you (her voice reached back onto some harsh palate performers hit at the right moment and a word that wasn't her). What was that junk *about?* Those jazz guys playing in somebody's flat in Holland? Telling stories about a horn getting mislaid in the DMZ. What was that, like, *about?* ("I didn't say they were all guys," Daley protested, the manner of speaking unlike her.) And your imbecile sibling getting you into things, provoking people who could take him apart ("You didn't know him," said Daley, "he would do anything"), people physically stronger who were dumb enough to imagine they were being good to him. Construction engineer flying about the world? She indicated the kitchen: "So blessed *helpful* here in this gloomy, stupid house, aren't you? Asking what I do to *make ends meet.*"

"That was Monday over the *phone*, that was *days* ago," he tried to say.

*Days,* she said. "Nice of you." When all she'd called for was a lawyer to take her case and look at him unlocking the gate asking how did she make ends meet: downright *uncanny* his ignorance: as if she had some *power*—well, she *did*—

Have your *own* key, Daley said; he'd get one made tomorrow, never occurred to him. *Fix* it, she hissed. She *had* keys for upstairs, he said. He meant the vestibule at the top of the front stoop. *You really know how to give 'em their independence,* your drummer friend said, she said; independence is easy to give, she said to him. It's a gift.

These *sounds* of hers not loud in the kitchen, cool and poisonous and just young. "Fix the sash, the floor, the stairs"—she ticked things off—"this dismal, cold house, fix *people.*"

"People," he said. *Me?* his face said.

"Cold in here." She flung open the fridge door, which cracked off its hinges it looked like.

"Look out," he said when he should have said more.

"And that drummer who said, 'It's you.' What was that?" she demanded.

Sid's hearing, Daley explained.

"Well it bothered the shit out of me."

The *shit?* The shit? he wanted to say. Because she didn't speak like that; was it un-Canadian? Daley had heard her say *fuck*; that was it; and, in her one-woman piece, *lay*. "*He* won't come bothering you."

"And telling him about my *place.*"

"Look here," Daley said like a line.

"He won't come sniffing around," she said. "Tagging along, see what you could see," she read her own mind.

"It was your idea," he said, and, "did you know you put down an Ontario address for a checking account, and a couple of rent checks didn't have your name on them?" He didn't know what she would do. It was not over. She had sniffed those pillows, she didn't forgive Daley for it and had done it if not for him with him. (They were close.) No surprise but it stuck with him, yes he had seen Becca's place now.

"I'm being evicted by people I at least *know*. They're all in it, even you get that."

Well, he'd learned that her landlord was a woman in Daytona, he retorted like a lawyer.

"Either way I'm being kept: up there—down here by somebody I *don't* know."

"Nothing keeping you"—Daley pointed to the basement hallway —"and wouldn't normally." (So this wasn't normal.) "You said we were of the same *blood* five days ago." His chuckle was mean, hard, put on, and convincing.

Hadn't he heard that before? she said.

Unfortunately he had.

She saw Daley in some complete way—to be shrugged off. It wasn't about finding things out; law failed there, it was good at it. The matter with him whatever it was he realized switching the light on over the kitchen table; seeing in a far cupboard not the unlabeled jar of chutney, as she flung at him *Isabel's* name now. "And that ugly wound you brought home like a fool," but an absence that was possibly his imagination, distracted by her raised voice, a key that he thought should have been hanging there, sampling the poison in her, "*Is*abel, your neighbor *Is*abel," how come he'd never screwed *her* all these years? "Who did you think you were?"

"Not an abuser of girls," Daley pointed at the west wall, to keep it *down* please but, "How do you *know*?" (He had to tease her.)

"I asked her; that's how. 'Who does he think he *is*?' I said to her—"

Daley laughed imagining Isabel's reaction, but the woman here was hopeless or on her way, getting ready to shove off.

"A person who can try a case and swim the river—fly a *heli*copter, give others what all," a hint of just-brash, the voice derisive, quick, but—it was Sunday—so loose-gun it was stupid and Daley shook his head "in despair," something was wrong with her but *con*templating him, "A man who is never shocked can't be . . ."

*What?* his face said.

"—expected—"

To what? Absorb this juvenile abuse?

*Grieve*, he thought.

But no one had said what she had said. And then it came to him she'd never had one single mention from him of helicopters—flying his nieces to Tacoma and back in a small executive borrowed from Boeing, or taking his hours before he went to law school and while he went, or inevitably using it as a diversion during a fortnight when he was supposed to be studying for the bar exam. Or any other mention, and he didn't know if it was a jump of intuition or some mercy in her to betray what she knew wherever it came from.

Out of the blue maybe with this kid, who thought she had caught him eyeing the cupboard. "Is that your wife all alone in a bottle up there where she belongs? You never learned to violate a person's privacy, did you." Yet it was upward into the house somewhere that Becca pointed, not the cupboard on the west wall, the voice itself, quite truthful, almost acting—but the third floor of this house, it came to him. "What *did* she do?—Duymens never got around to telling me—take a swan dive off the bridge? Get somebody so mad at her—" She saw it in his body, his hand on the edge of the oak table, and she went around the table playing tag too far and was closer than she meant to be.

But she wasn't a lover, Daley shook his head in despair at the cupboard behind her.

"No no, that wasn't how she died—"

"Why did I come here?" Becca cried.

"—that wasn't how," he said, for he thought he would tell her—he had told Leander—nothing to tell, an unlikely collapse in a dark and public place, breathing problems: lungs on either side of the heart a bit crowded with fiber; the misleading joint pains for weeks that she would try to jog her way through not joints but her lungs, where fibroids albeit benign were just getting a bit thick.

He was done with Becca, he wouldn't want a person who could talk like that (an early girlfriend of Wolf's came to mind who volunteered she wouldn't suck him off if he ate so much as a single forkful of steak and he blew her off the next week). "Two guys giving me your number, telling me to call you, and all." Becca had found the old bag of almonds, the muted drum-crush of her munching, she was talking in a fresh voice dryly like his or his nonaccent, which he now recognized he did have, and finding words in fact awkward for him: "Someone who's not very close to anyone, one shouldn't take it personally." Who was it had said them to her? No one. Common words? Accidental? Necessary? Not absolute perhaps.

"No surprise to *you*," she said, "I'll give you that, you don't pry, you're a good-guy conversationalist but you know what's coming."

"With you around," he said. Sorrow in it not un-nasty; intimate; damn showing off. House tries to hang on to our things. Upstairs growing up was intimate all around, the threat of surprise speech, interference, silent interference from the mother and her nagging, natural jokes that she had been denied a daughter; downstairs was public and guarded. How many floors had Becca's house, if it was she in the one-woman and the brother lying down with her when she was little and getting to like it?

It came from everywhere, it couldn't come from nowhere, yet it didn't matter where it came from, what was the difference? Was it her brother, was it Daley's unscheduled second-half visit Saturday night, bothering her? She was over by the basement window by the dance books now, ballet, painting he remembered, Indians cross-legged. Out on the sidewalk two pairs of legs passed briskly, a man and a woman in jeans. She was munching on the almonds and after all this drama it told him she might not be done but was thinking it over, and who were the *two* guys who'd told her to call him, Ruley was one. "You *been* married," she said, the answer supposedly there among the books she was looking at the spines of.

Escaping her, he heard her say in the kitchen, "You guys ever get pregnant?" On the stairs, she was following him up at his speed determined to control him here because she was out of control and had screwed up (hadn't she?). Past the door to the parlor (he made a gesture toward her little theater), up to the second-floor landing and the turn down the hall, she wasn't talking, she was assuming he was assuming she'd turn right into the bedroom when he did obediently. But it wasn't their bedroom, or then the guest room, but left and into the still-uncarpeted flight to the third floor. You turned left again along a wall of dusty posters. The key was in the door just where you needed it if you didn't have one. She caught him as he opened up. The working sink alcove, where they had torn down the sheetrock wall years ago of an unneeded bedroom like the guest room on the floor below. He knew Becca had been up here and seen the geometry on the walls, a few objects of Della's that hadn't been boxed, a couple of clean tables, and his own, with maps and surveys, forests and rivers, diagrams. There was something aimed and unpleasant and unguarded in the feeling of her arm up against his as they surveyed the double workroom, the narrow bathroom and the outside working sink for some prints Della had once embarked on. He wanted to send Becca away, ask her what it had been like with her brother and had she abused him and when had they been able to get together at home, when had they slept together. "When you slept with your brother—"

"We really slept," she said having a look around. "I think we did. I was very young at first."

Daley was sick and tired.

She was at a street window. "You know you've done some forestry. You know what this is supposed to look like," she said of the tables—"the two of you working up here."

He was on his own again.

"Well, this was her place. I can tell. You set up here much later on." They were in the kitchen again. "I mean I liked him, your friend Sid."

Sid was quite a lot older than Daley but Daley got her point. The anger pretending to be spent after all this drama, this one-woman trash. "You're a soldier; yay you." She peeled off, sort of, leaning on a chair not sadly now but impish.

Did Daley do international work? she asked, an older visitor, what a question, but when he said nothing she tried to stare him down till he looked away. But he thought, International work? Who for? he wondered. A trip or two protracted and temporarily interrupted he had once tried, that hide away in you just for twenty minutes, thirty, forty, and come back like a person in you, a being, half a forty-dollar mushroom he recalled from a reunion once upon a time—before law school? He was being used. She was the drug. What was the trip? Push comes to—

"Brothers, you bear with them," she said. "Yours might build dams, but wasn't he just angry about the war?"

And after all these minutes of abuse, she tried to sit him down with a sweet attention—this tell-all slight falseness, he knew if he put his fingers on her she would be wet—and, well, she had to deliver for him in their seldom-occupied living room upstairs her shorter and unrecognizably improved she said one-woman piece—

"Maybe so," he said (more all-at-once now, he foresaw). Though he wasn't having it. He looked at his watch.

"You're indicating," she said.

He would pass, he said; done for the night—as far as the product of her "researches" here and there amplified was concerned. He didn't know anything anymore. Which brought to mind her case. Tomorrow was Monday all day.

"You're a warrior," she said gently. "You don't toss your medals," she said.

How did she know that? he said; she knew more than he did. She wanted a night's sleep and she was giving the impression that the pretty convincing abuse he'd been treated to (though no surprise) would soon seem a prep essentially for any future getting-along. She could see him for herself passing up the stairs. He wanted to say *Juvenile*. Was *abuse* it? Do nothing, he had heard. So he had not gone to see her Saturday night as until then he had, but to see what he could see.

"It's not what you're used to these last few years," she said.

"It's what it is," he said. He disliked the phrase, it wasn't how he talked. She was below him, behind him, she was contemplating the stairs, and he told her to turn out the lights.

"We're quite equal," she said.

"We're even," he said.

"Can I sleep here?" she said.

They were at the landing and he turned to look at her.

"Ouch," he said.

# 14

"YOU PULL AWAY FROM HOME *SLOWLY*," SHE SAID, A BLONDE'S DARK EYES. She puts so much into the word *slowly*, what's it mean? And goes on as to a friend, "You don't take it with you, you don't leave it," she was saying, to him and him alone, "it's inside you." This at the landing! But

Daley was done. She padded barefoot after him down the hall. Where had she left her shoes? What was he thinking? she said.

He knew that one. Oh it was just Sunday, he said, looking across the bedroom at the loose and partly splintered sash. *Thinking?* he said, as she pushed by him. Thinking about a tree swallow nest he had seen in the country lined with goose feathers. Neat, she said. "An apple floating at the top of my tree that didn't get picked or pecked and didn't fall."

Would it still taste good?

The best.

It meant something to her. A comfort, that apple, for he had in reality recalled Helen chopping and simmering chutney, and sawing a poplar limb off and spreading antiseptic cement before spitting on the joint.

She'd seen too much to ever be like the girl.

What had she seen? She had that dress on.

Had it been the Holland story that he'd told coming home that had angered Becca tonight without any one single point? Meeting Sid Knox the first time. He would not ask. He would not give her that. The cornet player, the DMZ.

He came upon her in the bathroom a bunch of her hair grabbed in her hand and gleaming shears ready to slash off hunks of it. He ignored it. He brushed his teeth and thought of her on stage.

"That wasn't funny," she said, "that story."

No? he said, mouth full, holding on to it.

"No. Why woulda man go to a war like that, much less talk about it?" she said. But she was different again, amused. Something had come out. "Things I say nowadays."

Daley's mouth was full of everything but talk and glad of it. The mystery of a woman's power on stage: was it more future or more amplified than a man? He bent over the basin.

"Am I some odalisque?" the girl asked. He spat, and spat again, not quite knowing the word.

He needed to get out of the bathroom. She hummed something she had heard tonight. Who knew her mood? An inch of blue vein in her upper calf came closer and then you'd hear pass in the street outside a car playing the Hispanic station beat from Becca's place Saturday.

And now, half naked at the bathroom sink, she evidently thought some telling thing blown off in her words downstairs or the excitement of homecoming clung to the irritation of his wishes. She still hadn't mentioned his meeting her brother at the theater in passing, what the brother had said—to her, it came to Daley. Could it be Detroit '71? If it mattered, maybe she would speak of it. The request that took him on a quick round-trip "home" for a week to serve in an honor guard for someone whose home was in Saint Clair Shores—the frozen lake—a curious phrase to say for how did you "guard your honor" in those days or these? But Daley did not know this man from those three days, only two that Daley had shown up, of war testimony at a Ho Jo motel, curtains in high windows, one of the pickets outside he could have taken apart and Daley was there only to listen, eight degrees above, a couple of days free in a city he did not know, before flying back.

What was he feeling? she said, running water, turning it off, finding a toothbrush, staring at herself in the mirror. He was thinking about sleep. "What thought was that," she asked. Birds, he was thinking of birds, he said—You're lying, she cut in—birds wintering all over, less logic to it than apparently twenty years ago. And that first meeting with Sid Knox in Haarlem, he added—thinking about that—but didn't add missing the Dutch sax player at the end tonight because of you. Logic? She took him up on it though she was in the bathroom; he could count on her to disagree, to hang in there.

Pigeons picking up yellow crumbs off the yellow pavement. He had never thought about the color of the crumbs. Where were the new-hatched pigeons? Not only that. Rubythroats used to wintering in South Florida or the islands seen hovering over these unheard-of red flowers near the fault line in South Carolina in January! Partridge surprising you and you them. "You're a bird-watcher. What the hell do you watch for?" Partridge in a wet field flashing the rusty tail and the red tiny eye mark getting away at dawn into the woods, gray partridge where no partridge should be. "The world is changing, you mean . . ."

But geese wintering here now, feeding on the lush green common of a Jersey suburb by the fire station, small, footbridged river, the video store and sitting in his passenger's seat—Helen consulting her Filofax, freed her left hand to touch him.

Love one, think of another, we all do it, it's almost a compliment on occasion, who will know?—not the one who asked you home from a club, not the blond one fourteen, fifteen years ago pumped up from a passing gas station, a real kitchen chair not even a week ago, toilet seat, grassy slope, couch time, bed. Thinking things through mattered more than remembering even if without memory you had not much to think *about*. What she'd said in the kitchen, she was just uncomfortable with Daley. It was maybe sleeping with him. (He kind of doubted that.) What *did* she feel next to him? Something, being her. A woman with a thrifty bio, bless her. Good to talk to, a challenge to even just think with. Educated. Someone slightly abandoned who made a point of doing the leaving herself, you'd expect.

What was he *feeling*? she of course asked. A wish to be at large in the city, though he didn't say it as he turned from the threshold and went and sat on their unmade bed. Birds their habits of survival enduring as the silence of an old building, its ledges, its idea, its structure Daley now recognized fixed in stone, though mobile in its use and people.

Feeling? A longtime thought that he would buy himself a bike. What thought was that? she said again. A "brother thought" he hadn't shared, he said. A Honda. Get free of you, he said. She liked it. "You must find the right people to tell your things to." He was true to things if not her, he said off the top of his head. She came and sat down with him on the bed. It was a slippage or falsity he gave in to or a vague leverage. Then she got up and went back to the bathroom and he needed to tell her something, though what came out now wasn't it.

"I didn't tell about the car he borrowed."

"Is this your brother again?" Yes it was Wolf, who didn't know that the bicycles bungeed to the roof rack that night didn't exactly belong to the engineer's friend, nor the car it turned out later when it was picked up in Benninck's block while Wolf the second borrower was upstairs at a jazz session. "Who was the first?" The engineer, but never a word about the bikes on the roof that—"They were stolen?"—that the engineer's friend was exercised about: a special Dutch anger, citizen, honorable, quite eloquent, simultaneously on the edge of jolly—Becca on the bathroom threshold again, displaying herself, disappearing to the sound of water running—getting *married* in a couple of days to a ranking American mountain climber with a famous temper—planning to clear fifty dollars a bike on the street before dawn rose over flat Amsterdam, that was one way to see those bikes, at least they weren't wired for sound like crackle boxes.

"But the keys," said the woman in the bathroom, like a wife or a friend.

"On the floor underneath the seat."

So the car was open. That engineer, she said.

The engineer had left the car open, keys underneath the passenger seat.

The engineer?

Daley was being told something by her question, by memory or her herself, who acted as if nothing much had been said downstairs at this hour of an end-of-the-weekend night that had practically gone to pieces. When he had decided she was violent, asking for it. Had broken into his house. Had found a habit of using sex that now in later life swung her from situation to situation, every time a little different.

They were even.

Yes, who *was* this engineer who didn't think much of *Wolf* but had helped him get to the humdrum older brother in Haarlem that night? Something Wolf had said?

"You do international work?" Becca beside him changed the subject perhaps.

"What was I doing in Haarlem you mean?"

Her eyes preoccupied, she brushed her hair and the bed gave with her stroke. No, he could be in Holland or the Himalayas, she said.

It came to Daley that it was the brother the Ontario scrap magnate on her mind Daley could help out. You perceive such things at the end when they are only information.

She made a cluck of recognition, capable of being charming. "This was the tulip-bulb Haarlem?" said the person beside him taking interest again. Well, the engineer hadn't yet actually given the friend's car to Wolf, remember.

She did not.

Good old Wolf went out in the street a block from the hotel—
"Doesn't he boast a family?" Becca broke in; "oh you said —"

There it was, the car *and* the keys, and took for granted the bikes
strapped topside, which were in fact why the car was picked up later
while Wolf was upstairs at Benninck's making an American nuisance
of himself.

Back in the bathroom again, Becca he thought listened, and here
he was sitting on the bed, the whisper of nearness hair being brushed.
Her sounds as familiar as the street outside his house or the little pause
after Lotta got you on the phone or the tap of Sid Knox's foot in the
office or Donna's laugh of generous surprise, Becca clearing her throat
when she picked up the phone, sliding hangers in the close contain-
ment of her closet showing him like second sight her woman's eyes
examining that dark inside; or a clap of the hands when she thought of
something; but now, to Daley's acute sense of her her bare feet on tile.

"A family? Of course he has a family," Daley continued. He thought
he almost made Becca laugh out of sight in the bathroom now. Two kids.
Gifts from God, Daley's sister-in-law said like a joke though she meant it
and was entitled to. (Entitled to? said the philosopher in the bathroom.)

A wonder Roma didn't produce five or six more. If this big redhead originally from the Bay Area wanted, half born-again or in fun, to
call them a gift from God, so be it. Kids were kids, possibly. Seattleite
since the mid-1970s, she took the little girls camping up Rainier. That
was what she had to say about Wolf's absences. He was active, though,
knee and all. An hour and a half's drive to their preferred site below
Paradise Visitors Center. Daley knew exactly the number campsite at
the far turn coming around the loop. Here two Douglas firs six feet
thick lay at right angles almost by decree of the parks department for
the kids to clamber up on, find their way along one fallen giant to the
other. Making that sharp turn, they'd keep an eye out for new blood at
other tent sites. Never missed their footing. Mom could get the North
Face tent hung and staked all by herself in ten minutes. Roof over our
head. Don't pick the beadruby, find a trillium hiding dark red among
the ferns. Sniff the bark of that one over there, then smell the vanilla
leaf. We'll go down the mountain for ice cream after supper *maybe*.

Daley stopped. What had Wolf meant asking that en route to

Sydney? Not that he ever saw Della. It was a kind of faith. He had never liked her.

Was it children?

"How do you know the campsite number?"

At the bathroom threshold combing her hair out and down, tilting her head, reminding him if he needed reminding of her breasts, she knew him.

"I happened to be in Portland and I flew up for a day and camped there with them. Between two tongues of the glacier. Pay phone five-minute walk away."

The girl laughed. "Don't want to bury your horn in the ground," she said.

"Don't want to lose your horn in the DMZ, going back for it could be a problem," Daley said.

He didn't know what she would come up with.

Was Becca entertaining Daley?

Becca had spoken to her brother, she deferred to him, and Daley probably mattered very little, and yet she was light and curious to tell him things. Daley felt a little sad, though they were going to bed.

What law had he wanted to practice? Had he wanted to practice at all? she asked. "You're wasted on me," she said abruptly.

"You could call it public interest," Daley said. Plenty of people in his law school class went that way for a while. What way? Public interest? "When was that?" (It was law school she meant.) She listened grudgingly, he wanted to overcome her.

She picked up things you might take for granted. He had this out-of-sync premonition that she and her brother would find a use for him—degenerates, he smiled. He liked the way she thought. She was pretty funny too. She had a hopeless side, it was her eyes looking toward the window. Was she leaving? he wanted to ask her.

"Class of '77," Daley replied.

That figured, she said; wouldn't he say that figured? Public interest?

"The 1960s still leaking into the . . . whoever we were."

"And your war," she said.

# 15

S HE CAME AND SAT WITH HIM, AND THE MATTRESS GAVE GENTLY WITH her combing, and he trusted her to be this, no more. The box containing a new pair of shoes came into view on the floor of the closet, but it was his eyes moving. Who was it said don't get too friendly with your lawyer? Was that client privilege? she said cozily. Come on, she knew very well that wasn't client privilege.

Being not close to some clients he could think of offhand was a privilege, he said dryly. What was it to think offhand? she said. A longing invaded Daley, it was for an open door and the November wind bringing the busy noise of trees, or he was the one moving; it was not longing for Becca or even for her after she should have gone. (Tomorrow, he thought; could he ask her to go?) Lotta he had picked up thinking it was calling Monday and Sid Knox over his shoulder leaving the office had observed, *You don't call them, they call you,* and Daley expected Becca to say the name on the note left in the door yesterday when they had come back from the movie with an hour to get upstairs and lie down and forget everything.

"Giving me the push?" said Becca. "Which Daley are we getting now?"

"No, you're the mimic in this household."

She stopped combing.

"That family of yours"—he meant her one-woman "show."

"They're totally made up." She smiled radiantly into his head, really scornful and objective.

"They certainly came through," Daley said, not caring. He had her, but what was it? "What you must have done to them," he said. She liked it. "The center of it all," he said.

"At least they're a family," she said.

"'Specially that brother."

"Which one?"

"Maybe there's only one," it came to Daley to say, a thought beyond him.

"I owe him," Becca said.

"Not your bed."

"But not anymore. I'm not back home now, I'm here."

Daley didn't know where that was, though she was lying. Done with Daley; or would sleep with him and that was it. "Well they had you where they wanted you that family, to judge from—"

"From nothing." She was combing again, propelled.

"—your one-woman thing." She got up and went away. "To judge from what you put on for me."

"To judge," she said.

"And who knows where else," he said: "abuse in there if one could just gauge how far it went."

"One?"

"Yes, it wasn't clear what was done. But it's . . . good, your . . ." Becca laughed. "I mean it's not bad," he said.

"Yes, it could be soft and sweet, but nasty, interrupting," she said. "The piece or . . . ? Who flew that jam sandwich in; and did 'this litto nippo' get kissed on a regular basis?"

"I have to say you do the droopy triangle end of a pizza wedge very well, with (who was it?) Otto or once it was Bruce soaping you." An invasion. Of what he was less certain. Her privacy was secretly public, with its history, mainly evidence, events.

"If it fucks you up, it fucks you up; if you use it, maybe it was never whatever it was to begin with—abnormal . . ." she stuck her hairbrush between her thighs. She cupped a breast and chafed the undercurve and lifted it a little, her fingers into it. "Developing you, that's all." She wasn't much interested in the issue anymore, it was why she had come down to New York. But she'd *left* her (he began) . . . Let them stew in their own blood. (She didn't like him much.) "Nothing happening here," she sniffed fondly at the ceiling, "that's great," she was serious, she didn't mean New York, she was a little tragic or soft. Left her family but she was (he said awkwardly) living with—

What people could figure *out* to say, she ignored him. She exhaled from her throat—a danger she was in, he was convinced. "Smart people." (Oh that was what she meant.)

"In Canada?" he said; "down here that's all they do."

"New York," she said, "What *is* violence? Is shock so bad if we're not talking blood circulation and a heart rate of a hundred?"

"Over a hundred."

"Mister Chopper." She kept her eye on him meanly.

Something meant in this new name of his Mister Chopper? "You mean abuse?" he said. "If it's mental then it's a test how you fit in —"

"Fight, think, stand up, react, make it up, fuck," said the person who was on her way somewhere else.

"Abuse takes someone else," Daley said.

She didn't mind his just talking. "You mean abuse?" Becca said.

He didn't understand her. "Against your will," he said.

"Your will," she said with a look that passed over him.

The eye—its structure of interest to him once when he had had to read up quickly on displaced retinas—isn't anything apart from what it sees and where it . . . He was through. "It's force, right up against you, that's all I meant, you don't have the chance to . . ."

"Do nothing."

"A little abuse goes a long way," he said.

"You know more than I," she said, "but you get to where what you want . . ."

"Is to get smacked," Daley said.

"I'm not listening to this." She was up and across to the bureau and pulled out a drawer but somehow carefully and looked around her, alone, the very room opposing her, and found her bra curled on the rug, a little fence. "Anyway acting was all I meant and only for a while."

"I guess you're okay," she muttered moving a closet hanger where her few things were. Oh good, he said; when she'd been enjoying his home, kitchen, phone, his bed, privacy, his garden, his icebox.

Icebox?

"My aegis."

"Aegis you have to claim," she said.

"The opposite." She had angered him, he was tired of that estimate of him and angry; and he would have told her the chemical side of the Osaka Wolf story, the nontoxic new shock-*in*sensitive explosives yet sneaking up on you, like her bra dangling in one hand, as she sat down beside him, the point of the story would turn out to be something else.

He turned to look. Her nipples were plum colored and proud and prim, one stood out straight and the farther one turned very slightly toward him, minutely made.

Becca gave a low laugh, independent of him.

No, he said, violence had to be experienced—

"You would know," she said; "but you don't know; but you do. You're Mister Experience. Mister New York."

Like the odor of the neighbor-to-the-east's cigar out in the garden, remote, angelically acrid, he knew the brother to be near, purchasing an umbrella, striking a brownstone riser on the stoop, drinking to a done deal at some bar nearby; and still she had not mentioned Daley's meeting Bruce Saturday night. Daley was learning not something but how to do something. What? He could faint with the attention he gave her, her words, her shoulders, her thought.

They had theater up there, said Daley; in Canada. He didn't know what he was talking about. He was not happy. Not much of a theatergoer. "We're starting to shoot there on the cheap," he said. (Helen had said.)

Yeah, that's how she met Beck; "he's after some of that money."

"At the airport?" Daley recalled that Bruce had set it up, and he felt distinctly her half lie—in his neck (!)—yet she didn't hide whatever you later kind of wanted to know, and he struck her, damaged or whatever, as someone who could keep a secret, just a businesslike lawyer.

"Well, it was why he was up there," Becca said.

"He'll need a few bucks. He can hit your brother up, all that scrap he's scoring." Daley asked if she understood how deeply uninterested in all this he was. Rent a crew up there. Probably cheaper.

"Those boys at the bar, they're hoping to go along if he can get it together."

"The sheetrockers you're lining up to work here?" Daley said.

Downstairs she had gone too far she was aware, and she was inspired now, she could be flattering. (*We're not close at all*, her words downstairs like a kick in the nuts uncanny, unknowing, sounded like *him*, the accent, the words in fact Della's—but . . .)

"A person with your gift . . ." he said.

"It's not just mine," she said darkly. Somewhat painful, and then again laughable, damage to a child and the magic will, the joke of busted umbrellas, it is life that is the genius, forget all the universes out there, Daley decided, a whole lot of forces joined maybe by—

"Common . . ." she said, "a common mode of nutrition."

"Nonsense."

"No, it's all of ours."

She was confiding now, practical, an old love, live-in. Did she know something he should? he privately wondered.

"The trouble you've seen, the things you know," Becca said now, telling it straight, it even put him off, some badge she could see, an understanding man. "Things you've always known."

"Just don't waste it," Daley said, he yawned honestly, he was afraid of her and she got up and went into the bathroom trailing her bra and dropping it on the rug behind her, he couldn't imagine Della or Helen doing that. Yet now, vanished, every turn and sway in there was audible, the mirror, a cosmetic field of facial analysis and comfort contoured by gravity, despair, freedom: in the midst of which this idea for her came back, that if she stuck in the play she could get her one-woman piece produced by Beck himself and that would be best for her. Was this what he thought of? She was in front of the mirror, he was almost certain. Were these things he'd always known?

"Your super taking measurements, if you want an example of violence, entering your place like that. That's no good."

"He's a black guy with a fairly responsible job, he plays it up."

"It wasn't funny." The girl he thought turned from the basin, but came no farther. "I didn't know what you were going to do."

"Show him the door."

"Just don't bollix up my case."

"That's what you get hanging out with your lawyer."

Becca was at the bureau drawers for a moment, the Sunday-night sour expression passed across the fine wide mouth, she was no pet to tend, and yet, almost naked in white underpants you could see the pale and shadowy behind through. That is what she was. She herself in the cab going downtown to the movie yesterday had betrayed a certain knowledge of Dutch Guyana. The once and "former" Suriname the super hailed from.

"Let your brother defend you," Daley said.

"He's furious but he keeps it bottled up," she said returning to the bathroom—"at Beck and the building management; at me more. Dave's banking on the show. We'll see, won't we."

Lurking in her words—also that the brother had taken his knocks from her—Daley found his own position spoken to him, but what was it? Did it now depend on others? Yet he never had felt, or not for years, that the roof might fall in. She still hadn't mentioned last night. His meeting Bruce. Daley didn't care what was going on. The brother and Beck, then. Film, someone had said; Canada; these *people*. He had an idea for Beck and Becca so simple it had eluded them. His voice-under.

What she wanted of Daley. What she had in mind; nothing maybe. A pair of stockings she drew on, oblivious of him, Saturday before she left for the theater, thoughtful. These exhilarating days like hours of upstairs, downstairs, languid, quick, studious, quite airy, her clothes, this understanding room and about to really leave, he thought, but an uncanny and foolish time, no regrets. Her battery-pack presence in this house. He'd never seen her wear stockings. He thought she had met her brother and now she was back.

"Weekends are not for the likes of us," she observed from the bathroom. "I know, you used to have time for them."

"How did you know?"

He was a little over his head. What was she doing? Sitting on the toilet he thought but. "What a weekend," Daley sighed.

"We don't have time for weekends," Becca said.

"I used to."

"You will again." Who was she to promise? "Ordinary life, you topple into it," Becca said, "and all is lost and no one'll ever know."

"There isn't any, there's only . . ." He fell short because he wanted to impress the girl. Was she sitting on the edge of the tub, waiting for him to propose a bath?

She was thinking. "That's right," said Becca from in there. But she meant by ordinary some great thing you could do if you hung in there, if you could trust her.

She came and sat on the rug before him, cross-legged as she'd been one of these nights when she woke up at three or four in the morning and he opened his eyes and saw her belly a few inches from his mouth.

He would not find a thing sad in this moment. It was all quite new, it was a thrill, he could love her by letting the time elapse, processing the abuse if that's what it was. He could handle her case. He could go sleep in the guest room—which wouldn't be a bad idea.

She was speaking of those great Greek women. (Why was she?) She was cross-legged in front of him as if nothing had happened. Antigone, Cassandra, Clytemnestra, thought up by a man who didn't think much of women, she said, in a city where they—well, he knew what an Athenian wife's life was like, an odalisque. And that memoirist, Lucy Hutchinson, they objected to her writing down the sermon in church, even memorizing it, but what a woman. That's books, he said, not knowing any Hutchinson. (It sounded English though the Hutchinson River Parkway . . .)

"Now philosophy. That's something," he said.

"It's behind me, thank God. In this, you trust yourself," she flipped her hand. She meant here? Once it was done, that was okay, react to the next thing coming at you.

But her education. It was forestry she had read but she had bagged that. Well, really classics at first. Was she confiding? Now this, this chat, would have worked for her one-woman, and nowadays topless was nothing, but he hoped she would never.

"Thucydides?" she said. (Daley shook his head.) Virgil, Plutarch. Government. Wars. Who knows how it happened? A teacher she had wanted to please in high school. Who used to say in Homer you enter a foreign country and tell them your family history, genealogy, all that, but you look first for the right person to tell. The king, maybe.

"Someone in authority," Daley tried to make a contribution, a parental reining-in, a voice-under.

"Nowadays who knows? Here, anyone."

History. She began to think a bit, and got up and came and sat with him. Maybe that's what it is. (Daley wanted to ask What?) Then she read some Plato? The little rising accent half granting what he knew of—the writer she feared and loathed. What was behind these men talking? She had joined the discussion, and Plato, or Socrates behind him—the man sitting on the bed sensed some joke but didn't raise his hand—had sent her off like a messenger into a ree-surrch paper. Catapulted her. It was like an abduction.

Daley said he didn't really know Plato. That's terrific, Becca said softly. Daley could not agree. Well, neither could she.

Why catapulted?

That whole philosophy head trip, two years pretty near, at least she hadn't been living at home.

Her mentor at university had stripped to the waist in a lecture hall. (In Canada? Daley said.) Not Freedom Substance History but sentences, she half remembered, words. Everything hung on that, and skipping the newspaper twice a week.

Daley said he was ignorant. That was terrific, Becca said. Plato, Platonic, said Daley; philosophy was little *more* than a word to him. "What was the point in taking off his shirt?"

"His jacket, tie, shirt, and undershirt," she corrected him. "The body's a simple unity to begin with." But she got sick of it, literally sick, sick in the morning so she didn't go, for who knew what she might become, she wanted a job—in isolation, who knew what you were—hey, that's what the man said about words—she laughed with the delight of discovery. What man? It was late. He thought she was going to get up but do what then he didn't know. Sick? he asked.

Sick of diagnosing diseases in grammar. Language.

Grammar? Daley didn't get it. She didn't want him to. "It didn't help." She got up and came and sat down on the bed. She was healthy, her feet on the carpet, her absorption in things.

But Gibbon, now, he said. Gibbon? She laid her head on his shoulder. Yes, Gibbon years ago, when Daley was reading for the bar. That was about it. "Don't know what I was thinking of. Law, Gibbon, and flying. *Not* thinking, probably. Couldn't put it down, a regular speaker. The city, the land, you had the impression they got longer, the sentences, maybe it's the distances—it annihilated . . ."

It was very true, she said, the farther he got from Rome—was it Gibbon who said don't get too friendly with your lawyer? But not in the big book, she thought. Annihilated what? She was interested in what he said.

"Anything else but it; maybe Rome, but not Rome."

"If Cleopatra's nose had been longer or if she'd been crowned with a crown of asparagus, the history of the world would be totally different."

"It's just questions, isn't it?" said Daley, meaning a little more than he thought.

"Not like that," she said. "Easy to ask when you haven't been listening," she said.

He had meant hanging in there, but wouldn't say a thing that stupid.

"Hanging really in there," was the young woman's reply, "that's what it is, not agreeing; living. Maybe telling all before you're done but in the right order, and not *that* all. Because how does the other guy know?"

Daley was startled by her agreement, her garage-mechanic manner of speaking of it that enlarged and made easy, but . . .

But big questions, probably, yes.

Daley actually wanted to learn from her. His patient erection lay along one thigh. She refused to find it. "Like if you can't trust war, why not human nature, and if not human nature, why not have a dictatorship?"

"And trust *it*?"

"You're right," Becca said as if he'd surprised her.

"Who would be the führer?" Daley went on confidently.

"That's how you dump Plato," she said, getting up.

"It is?"

"No, of course not; you don't dump anyone for one slipup." Becca turned at the bathroom threshold. "But yes, that is how you dump Plato."

"You don't seem to know yourself," said Daley. Becca made a sound, and Daley said, "Human nature is Nature pretty much." (What was he talking like?)

"You can trust the hawk to go for the partridge," she said.

"What hawk is big enough?" he said wondering if she knew Canadian birds.

"Big questions," Becca said and he thought he heard contempt.

"The need," Daley heard him say, and hardly knew what he said.

She seemed not to hear. "Who is it just to get the better of? What love makes you better? Does everyone have one kind of work she should do?"

"She?" said Daley.

"You learned to fly a helicopter. Why did you learn to do that? You have a gift of foresight we haven't figured out what to do with yet."

Who was we? he stammered. "We what?" he said, she had gone too fast for him—skipped ahead, on the attack almost now. "Wait a second."

"What is violence? For example," it came to the woman like a teacher, but slow now *and* fast, slipping into something. (*Teach-er, teach-er*, he heard in his memory.) "They all say, the good ones, that the world welcomes the powers you possess. But it got to be little questions—"

Wait. What was the research paper?

So long ago. A statesman. You haven't heard of him. Who began life paying off a giant debt of his late father's and became a general, a naval commander, and though not a literary type gave Sophocles first prize in a play contest and was taught to sing by his sister—that was only Becca's opinion. They say he returned the bones of Theseus to Athens. (Theseus, Daley thought.) He thanked the gods and inspected the entrails of birds to divine the future. He maintained the balance of power—with Sparta (Becca nodded), but they thought he overreached and he was sent away for several years. "Once a thing's done, no one ever knows how it happened." She both lost Daley and came close to him, something about Thucydides exiled for twenty years the opposite of "your" Rip Van Winkle who slept . . . yet her paper, the reasons for Cimon's ostracism—the statesman was Cimon—*see*-mon, *see*-mon, she used to say it wrongly—were not the passions of his personal life . . . A paper on governing.

"His passions?" Daley kept up (recalling blankly the insides of the turkey girl's turkey and her own, so many years ago—the girl who looked like Becca).

Alleged incest. What else was new? Maybe not even abuse. A little abuse goes a long way. ("So does a lot," said Daley.) What had happened? It had happened before they went to Waters, and it was something about Daley. It was experience, whatever. Let her be unknown or mysterious. "His passions?" This study had sent Becca back to Plato, to government. But she wanted a job.

She meant at university, Daley guessed, a year ago or so, her brother possessive by now, was what Daley guessed, looking ahead.

He heard her peeing, thinking.

"Becca."

It was how he had said it. Daley heard the toilet paper plummet off the spool and bare heels unsticking from the tile.

"He got you away from that family and moved in with you."

"He was moved in my whole childhood," the voice from the bathroom replied, "it's no secret; he told me things Dad wouldn't listen to even when I was seven or eight; it's the trade-off for no privacy."

"What, for heaven's sake? Something inappropriate?" Daley saw a white basin and steel fixtures and a whirl of blades in the red air, how differently Della had used the bathroom.

"War stories he would come back to. Since you ask. And he wasn't in it, as you must know. But you need a fresh start. And he's so much older than me. For anyone else, it would be another generation." Some lie being told there in the bathroom.

Daley shed his clothes sitting on the bed. It made him mad. *For anyone else?* He got it. For anyone else but her. She was a Daddy's girl or old for her age, or felt comfortable with an older man. A comfort all around, accept it. She loved her brother, he guessed. She had lived with him off and on for years and in a home where Daley was assuming she had been used. He wasn't the father in her piece who even if it brought in other homes had manipulated her genitals in the bath beyond a doubt, and the mother had grown happier and warmer if not wiser under the touch of one of the brothers, the really old one for a while, if that was the same family. Bruised, damaged you could say or permanently coerced and altered, she was here to give not even "her side of it" and not an indictment but a conversion you might see before your eyes. A gig she'd made up. Out of a family not too odd by whatever standard you had, to judge by this gig. Daley had not been even really used, and it wasn't quite over. She was up and down.

"Why do you see me as a mystery woman? It's all so obvious."

He hit out: "You came down here for a fresh start but weren't you monitored every bit of the way, and didn't you go along with it?" He had sounded like a deposition.

"Plato's okay," he heard her say.

"He is?"

"You get the name you deserve."

Through with her tirade downstairs, she was going to crawl into a bed with familiar sheets and familiar sleep, in a room with street windows open with sashwork requiring a specialist.

Out of sight in the bathroom, surely in front of the mirror: "The best was what he was after."

"The best?"

"You have to keep talking."

"Talking! There's enough of that. No . . ."

"You're right"—her voice gave him a touch from the silent bath-room, unwonted agreement or humor—"p'raps that's why Socrates wouldn't let his friends spring him."

"Hey!"—that story told by a law professor Daley thought he remembered doubtless apocryphal—"I remember that one. But wasn't he worth more in exile?"

Was it the water off now or no click of toothbrush that was this girl's passing emotion, and was it despair? With time running out, they saw into each other's histories a little. Something she knew about Daley now. "It's what you're able to live with," Daley said.

"You see, you do know some Plato," Becca said abruptly.

"I meant, that I'll miss."

Water ran and she was rinsing her face. He liked talking to her. If he could keep her awake long enough. The water stopped running. "Change their view of what is just?" she said, understanding his senti-mental point about her leaving.

"No, he was stuck."

She thought he was right.

Daley had sounded pretty good; it was her. She brushed her teeth like Barry.

She said, "You don't know what that's like."

"I'm sorry you imagine that to be true," Daley said.

"Smug," he heard her say.

He could leave, he had places to go in this very house or in other houses, he didn't need to be used as she knew how to not only have the last word quite subtly in this making of her life, her way, but make you deliver it; or turn you into it, it came to him half (only half, thank God) retaining all those marital matters he had recalled last night keeping Lotta listening downstairs. Oh sleep on it.

Becca was thinking: "You have the event over here, and some name for it over here, you have to bring them together. Oh brother . . . I wish I hadn't been recommended to you."

"You to me?" Daley said. Not worth arguing, but what event was it she meant, what event was looking for a name? And who was this "we" of hers? He waited for her to come and stand in front of him. He could see her doing it. He was tired, too. Done with her, philosopher-actress. Her bare stomach. Matter of fact. Taking his hands she would place them on her hips where he would slip his fingers inside the waist. Turning and turning, wherever down and up were, getting a push, she liked to keep her eyes on his. Her fingertips presently in his scalp, a little hard scraping so it hurt a little getting into his head surviving her thankfully and hearing what was going on inside her *and* him, the belly of the beast she'd said of the theater (but the shortest distance between two points it came to Daley), but multidirectional he thought survival down the dregs of a dream and its *we* along a curve too local to track except as free fall.

Hell with her background she had come through it tough.

# FIRST LOVE

## 1

A LITTLE ABUSE WENT A LONG WAY. (SO DID A LOT.) TOGETHER WE could see it if we're speaking about the same thing: misuse of actual people. Mistaking what they could do for you. But there's abuse and abuse. How we're used. Unthinkable things, yet not if we will remember to ask or just repeat what we know; or dream of knowing. Events not at all unspeakable if we'll remember to speak if only to speak in order to remember them. But sleeping on it, history's thanks and shock absorber. Not the orphanage of orphans in orderly columns (quite famous, too) marching to cattle cars not quite halfway through the century. Not those others starved up and herded onward beyond pride, beyond their inner protests, smothered; and while death limits further prospects of unthinkable mistreatment, for those dead there is forgetting to look forward to if any can hear themselves remembered and at that distance call, *Hey that was it* (upgraded in hindsight like clairvoyance itself).

Not what we mean quite or are looking the other way about (for we don't want to run into something). And not a cover crop of former people plowed into earth. Or village men between all ages summarized, disposed of, and dispensed without the option of being recycled because they don't have that there (though to Vietnamize the Vietnamese proved more promising than to Surinamize the Surinamese, there being little there to work with but humidity and potential absence). And we don't quite mean our brother resisting either: because the brother who was two brothers, yours and mine, beaten about the ribs with truncheons priced for export and never a call to consulate or embassy, never endeared himself to governments but was to them your basic borderline.

Which brother was that? Mine. Ours. Your story told to me unknown to you. And these long before those nonevents of domestic November 1996 though inevitably pointing toward them or toward nothing, like health, rueful growth, or resignation taught by the ancient Greek Epictetus lame from slavery or birth whose book the director of a Swiss sanatorium put regularly into the hands of his neurasthenic and psychasthenic patients to cure them, none other than the *Enchiridion* or *Handbook* unpacked by an admiral in Vietnam for stoic navigation and citizenship of the world even while another high official himself on the lam stateside summoned men to die to preserve freedom those resister "misfits abuse."

No, there's abuse and abuse. Misuse of people standing in front of us who are used to waiting and hardly know it. Or to nonuse. For we had better be used, and to the hilt. Not even your garden-variety bruise is what we're speaking of, the closed eye. Spousal fear fumbling the wrong key into the lock of the car door, the trunk key darkly, as the hand that closed that pretty eye for her tilts open the blind in the upstairs window, half there, half hidden by the streetlamp reflection in the glass, and is gone. So though now the car door swings out successfully with the other key, the ignition feels obscure behind the wheel, feels insanely locked as only an object can be insane, for the Other sets foot on the porch, takes the four steps one by one and comes down the walk toward the car, which his wife really asking for it will never get moving before he reaches her they both think—and they are wrong, for she will escape kind of from him, who is in "no mood to" whatever, yet unknown to him he challenges her (she hears) to change her life. She must of course. He invades even when he doesn't, invades her time, Then into Now, Now into Then (he'll fix her as Present fixes Past). As we understand it his unconscious would dismember her to master her, whereas her intellect can manifoldly keep, just barely, him along another inlet/outlet and this could save her feelings, her consciousness, her history, if not her genes, from his temporal interpenetrations if we have it right, their hopes do not congrue.

Yet not this brand of politically correct abuse or war for that matter is what we are trying for so much, us licking each other into shape,
giving one another relief, forming even the relief *system* of another,
often manually manipulating the ties that bond, blindly siding with or
giving loved ones a push, gravitationally channeled exercising the right
to remain silent in the face of a deposing father, kids, grandkids, and
folks forming before our eyes in safe houses and households, partners
and others hinting, leaning, having their way with one another, angling
their perspective hook line and sinker, in a state, spinning Asian-made
toys, feeding our kids or other people's, raising them, adopting them,
or thinking about it, warning them like anchorwomen—stay with us—
attuned, pitching our Shelter Half tents, campsite paying guests, and
this was '96 we recall.

Studying this damp cave floor dripping thoughts onto its clayey
eras they who know the meaning of these long-lost figures may or
may not acknowledge the darkling child who looks up to recognize
animals painted across a site ceiling that will soon require legendary
humidity control: Lotta, who had met so many potential buyers, had
known a woman who had known a man who had known that child
who had first seen the drawings overhead like "a mere child's sky" (to
quote a specialist grown-up), a forest prime as a firmament, anciently
"*civil*" Lotta's Taipei plane friend for it was she on a rather different
subject would indelibly depose en route to Middle East describing
also the child prostitutes of her home city. Witness, or better reflect
on, the sheer attention a kid looking up and losing almost her balance
gives to an unearthed ceiling or an adult male before she is whisked
away to be told what she has seen in reply to questions she has not
asked like a parental kiss or who freed the slaves or what did Jesus
have in mind suffering the little children to come to him, did they
need a representative, an agent?

What had happened? When was that war about? Its beginnings?—
so easily lost—"the most mysterious of losses," it had been said, and
then mysteriously by Lotta Saturday night when Daley didn't go to
the theater, then did, Lotta spurred to such a phrase, by being with
Daley who had only heard the phrase not said it, originally referring
apparently to war's beginnings. Whereas by Lotta to two objects, art

objects we say, old pottery once lodged in a new friend's suitcase, then in a Baghdad hotel in hers, then back home in her apartment. What had happened to Lotta? Why, nothing. She'd made it happen she told Daley in his kitchen. Ask her jewelry clients. Ask the personal attention she gave them. That's what did it. One on one, Braintree to Hartford to Charleston, from Sweden to hopefully Hong Kong, a GAP limo waiting, it's all right, it's a market, the global courtesy shuttle, it's not ironic. (You caught the solitariness of her short hair-cut.) Lotta leaving his house but not leaving, looking around with the Q-tip box in her hand: "Can't put it down."

"Take it with you," Daley flashed on this basement kitchen as the half-dirt cellar below. Parts of the house. Clearing things out.

Lotta's new gripe brought home from a northern Indian pueblo. Just a young priest too big for his breeches was the gripe, no more than that, she will say, though thin, Hispanic, in brown robes. Unnecessarily smart he gained her trust. He saw how Lotta made her living. It was a week before Christmas in New Mexico, eclectic reli-gion meshing to a climax. Thinking of sticking around for the candles on the roofs, the Deer dance, New Year's business, potential clients in Santa Fe. She was passing through. An arguer, give him credit this priest. Alive with argument walking through the pueblo was what he was (but Daley was on the receiving end just now).

Saint Augustine, how ask God to come in to us when we couldn't exist unless he already was. In us? she said. Now, Thierry. Did she know Thierry? (Of *course* she didn't know whoever it was.) Not a local name, she said. Far from it: a minor church father who put the passion of Solomon's Song in context. Women were to be used. Used? Lotta asked. Used, the young priest told her. Nothing the matter with used. Used, if never enjoyed; for to enjoy a thing, which woman was, is to rest with satisfaction *in* it, the *church* taught.

Well, that didn't sound like the end of the world, said Daley, that was not *so* bad, checking his watch, alert to the owner of the blue Q-tip box who'd be getting home from work but when?

*Bad?* It was abuse. Abuse was what it was. Not serious abuse yet, but.

She'd stopped and thought, pulled out her notebook. She would put it right into her book though her publisher said it was at the printer.

Months later here they are at Daley's (at last), *Lotta* seeing the outer limit of the village, it's evening, a cellar being dug or who knew what it was, work that goes on in a strange or perhaps only poor place. She had never seen a cellar in an adobe structure much less at a pueblo. Maybe it wasn't a cellar. And music coming out of the pit, a tunnel or cave into one dirt wall, where work was going on. The priest was speaking of the church as the spouse of Christ, and Lotta guessed he was working his way around to the commercial purpose of her visit, a radiance or flush around his young nose. The music got louder and a fist holding a tape player planted itself outside the tunnel. A blondish woman like a plump albino Hopi you see five hundred miles from here emerged and stood up. The tape player in her hand, she contemplated the man beside Lotta. The situation wasn't in doubt. Nothing said, she left the tape player on the dirt floor and crawled back into the tunnel and they waited. But a dove, dropped down from an adobe wall and went pecking near the tape player, an earth-colored, long-tailed, speckled dove. The woman called out in another tongue, it was Hopi, a mellow, traveling sound she recognized, from inside the tunnel, and the priest answered with an intimacy flat and almost indescribable except something was about to happen to Lotta, he said something about time, and then, hands behind his back, he led her away to a little adobe apartment.

There a man was finishing a belt buckle like a dozen buckles Lotta had had made in a village outside Oaxaca, Mexico, a coral, jet, and turquoise image of a red-winged blackbird with legs transformed to luminous mother-of-pearl by some nocturnal iridescence. They were quite common, she told him, omitting the name of another pueblo up here where a few months previous she herself had sketched her original to take south. She liked him. Lithe he was and somewhat slippery. It didn't matter what was going on.

Why? It just didn't. Daley wondered where the cellar had come from. It he had foreseen, he realized. Minus only the tape player. Lotta had vowed to put it in her book as is.

And the attitude of the priest, who said she should kiss his hand. It had a smell of bread or horseflesh or cooking, or yeasty have-your-head-examined—and he took her into a space with an intimate shrine with morsels of food like she had seen in Asia or at an exit altar in a Chinatown restaurant and he sat down and took her on his lap.

His lap! Daley laughed. His living lap. No more than that.

No, go for it, Daley raised his hands. Lotta clasped her hands punctuating the early end of the evening with a practicality you felt. You took away from experience what was worth taking, the hinge swings and you are on your way, even if you are the hinge. Time was awake when all things slept, she said, this woman who had traveled; not bad—it had a ring to it or was true for Daley sitting at the kitchen table Saturday night, he had not accompanied Becca to the theater, the fourth night only of her stay. Lotta was leaving, and it occurred to Daley that a vision came sometimes when you were leaving—relief perhaps—Not that she was being thrown out, but she had a quality of it still, of having been implicitly or if you could see your way to it or bought *into* it thrown out.

Lotta got out and around. She looked at her watch. A friend of hers who designed bicycles belonged to a private-screening club. She had another who got ballet tickets. Unable to get through to Daley by phone, was Ruley Duymens why she'd come (his complaint about her omission of him in the book)? Only now an episode had come to mind, pieces not said in the right order, of Daley's life, Della, Dance, and Ruley Duymens. Lotta waited. A secret was anything not volunteered, was her philosophy. Gifts you hardly know you have. This was how he kept her a little longer when he wanted her to go. And she was gone soon enough.

# 2

DELLA LAWFUL, FREE, THE OUTLINE OF AN IDEAL; FAMOUSLY STILL, upstage, looking at you didn't know what; in performance irreducible, a sailing ship turned into its figurehead or seated twisted on the floor; or flying. Daley had married a modern dancer. It was to marry the unknown, didn't know where that came from. Daley was a learner. Daley was honored to be married to her. You could make things or you could be a thinker, she used to say. Quick and slight, she was really grounded he was told. Quick as you didn't know what, when she wanted—quick and slow as feeling. Some of this he wouldn't put into words for his guest who had to go. He thought she could stay in the air that split second longer like a small forward. He "got" the difference between ballet and this. He woke dreaming at daybreak like a ball bearing randomly riding around a basin finding the bottom or maybe central drain. And her fingertip was there, going around the dent in him, descending like finding it, pushing a little; yet no, she was asleep, he felt the hammocky breeze of her nostrils on his shoulder, in her breath smell the experience of sleep. She was strange to him only in his being with her. That he should think of marrying such a person. Or she had been "upheld" by a story he told her. His first deposition out of law school. Moved by it, she said.

Mystified a little by Della's interest in him, Daley could help her, it was true. But "uphold" her? He wondered if buying a house with her would do it. Spend his matter-of-fact mediocrity and upgrade himself. Her pale olive skin—not even olive—where did it come from? As close to the touch as the changing iridescence in the coverts of a bird. Her dusky ivory neck. Della was amused by his specific knowledge of things, of nature. Some pedantry of a nonartist? His brother Wolf testing your knowledge of the war, the visitors and historians knew more than the troops.

This man Della had been sleeping with, was he patient? Postponing some surprise he had in him. He could speak when he felt like it. She was very wet, sensitive about it in the bed, it was fine by him she knew. He didn't tell Lotta this bestowing on her in parting an idea of what it had been like, when she had to go—and he had to have her go (though the Ruley factor he spoke of because Lotta knew Ruley but).

There had arisen early some curious differences with Della. They were waiting for a crosstown bus and watched an argument between mother and a violent child whom the mother then left at the curb when she boarded the bus, a nine-year-old throwing a book after her striking the fare machine, a moment later yelling like a citizen at the driver, who surprisingly kicked the book out into the gutter and shut the door; the kid running down the block after the bus, crossing against a light in order to catch up with the bus apparently at the stop two blocks west. Della took issue with it, he didn't have a clue what was going on. She was upset (was it *him* she was against? Did she have a clue?—they were like newlyweds). She found herself attacking evidence as . . . eyewitness—she hardly knew, she did not believe in it much; and what was happening here, did you know?

No of course not, he insisted, but if you paid attention you could remember at least who said what.

*Did*, retorted Della, his new love.

The driver had blown *them* off—well, they were following the scene. They kind of pursued the child, who ran a red light and vanished into a little deli or a file of tourists outside a Radio Shack. Or did not vanish really. Did he catch the bus two blocks up? They never saw him again. Childhood. Della walked so lightly you forgot the speed. Nineteen seventy-seven. A math book.

Eyewitness, you can't get closer than that.

They argued because they were breathing hard. It was fighting. An accident on the ice Della recalled back home of a girl skating, falling from a height, it seemed, and picked up screaming by a darkish-skinned Pakistani man it turned out and carried off the rink, little more than a pond, her long, thin leg bloodied through her brown stocking and over one white figure skate, while the girl's father, a hardware store proprietor in that northern New Hampshire town, you didn't know what it was . . . did not react . . . Watching a performance? In shock?

Daley recalled a woman delivering her baby in the messed-up back of a cab before the driver had even made a note on his board of the hospital, the street; the driver ignoring what was happening, stalled in his nerves, his experience, but then excited, into it. Daley knew what to do in court. Eyewitness evidence was pretty hard to . . .

Suppose your witness can't imagine the other ways it could have gone? Della demanded.

He didn't believe a word of it. He had a story to tell her. Daley knew the grandnephew of a man who traveled twenty thousand miles out and back to see the seal Eskimos of arctic Canada and kept a log but fifty-five days of mist and storm missing, ice and mere going. Was that the story? No. Well, he was all wet about witnesses, she said.

If another form an event could have taken but didn't is something you can't imagine, you're even safer from making a mistake, he retorted, his learning curve paralleling her absolute conviction. Imagine? he thought. All the people telling you what they think, coming up to you. In Della's instinct here there was something. But not much. A thread. A curve. He dreamed of Della once—long gone, until he woke, discovering what he saw he had known to be the case, that when it was gone it might come back in a dream. How light she was, circling downward, slipping behind him, it was his ball-bearing dream, and someone had "just" said that the world was built on water. He woke in the dark forgiving chill and currents of the night, and they were in her place. And she woke, too, and he told her that thing he'd . . . that story she'd . . .

A gift discovered while deposing someone in an action. An archaeologist being sued by her nephew. An older person, engaging, glamorous, easy, good at it. A woman some nowadays might call elderly. A casually beautiful woman who in her *habit* (you decided) of slightly altering the order of events surrounding how and when she had used the moneys made available to her by her nephew for excavations along the southwestern rim of the Cambodian plateau—photos put into the record—and how his group's name had been damaged by publicity accorded her work, had so put young Daley to the test he had felt he couldn't think, or had *become* inexperienced or younger when he felt neither, his head turned by the photo of a twelfth-century Khmer head, a find of hers, eyes closed against the flame of flux, the wide full lips serene or smiling, the patterned skullcap and some *head-knot* he should have asked about, large, noble, question-mark ears ruddering this visible and private illumination—something wrong though. This not long after he had passed the bar the second try. "Understand you passed the bar; congrats," the other guy had said before the deposition; how this veteran counsel went at him was war or he was a novice fool functioning in some margin of it at first.

So he didn't grasp just how curiously well he'd done with the lady's resistance until—

*Resistance*, the dancer woman curled next to him in her little walk-up had added, only through resistance, Della said—it was the middle of the night.

Until three days later (feeling he'd told Lotta this already, like a mistake that is clairvoyant), Daley had had a look at the sworn transcript of his questions to the archaeologist (for he had been angry at her, too) and found there a command of events over the months addressed by the action more than equal to the subtly dislodging, dissolving layers and vibrations of whatever had obviously happened being recalled by the defendant coupled with her attorney's interruptions (twice Daley's age). And the reason was a flair practically unconscious for quick hypothesis discovered weirdly under this pressure in the young, cold-blooded lawyer Daley still in his late twenties.

He couldn't say it all to Lotta. Months later this independence he had not even granted in himself but discovered or was discovered accepting, cast a backward shadow over habits of mind surfacing or of what he didn't trouble to spell out—water or ground coming up to meet you. Absorbed then in learning to fly a helicopter. Through a friend at Boeing. His brother Wolf envious, for Daley took his license in Seattle and then back here again in New Jersey. Wolf could never have been bothered. A restricted but, with a waiver, normal *semi*-commercial license.

Idea came to him in law school during a class on the manifold differences between upholding and changing the laws. And someone he had gone out with. A whim, a stern whim. Going back, really. And Daley not a man to see the technology of the world through the everyday-rubbed-moderately-clean lens of your live-in relationship or any other with a woman, yet doing so with Wolf's Ecuadorian friend Virgilia Bomba, a fellow law student who had farmed altiplano grain in the Bolivian mountains, met Che McCarty the Chilean agronomist (and been dumped by him, she said: which was skipping a whole set of events she did not volunteer), an unpretentious person (with such hands—could make anything) and like Daley not sure the law was for her.

Women embarking on it coast to coast, costuming themselves, smart, sympathetic, and not only public-interest types; and Della and

Daley would imagine other lives, or she would for him, in the middle of the night, he could feel copiloted by the shaman in her. They were passing over terrain darkly arable with islands of hard ground for a landing, your enemy the shadow *you* cast, a two-armed paper hanger . . .

Wherever it came from, the gift for invention evident in deposing the archaeologist in the late mid-1970s, or suggesting sequences himself of events spun from *her* timelines in order to see what the woman would do now. For example, an evening, it seemed like an all-nighter, that she had spent with poor, much-interviewed Margaret Trudeau (though with a legitimate and jeans-rolled-up gripe) when she had left the elegant, cartwheeling prime minister's bed and board in Ottawa to pursue, to the south, an association with if not their world-class showman Mick Jagger's Rolling Stones, whose impact on the war (in the view of Daley's witness) both the physically androgynous bonding with huge assemblies of rock fans and the brain-blowing metal of the sound had come to so much less than the prime minister's long-standing position against the war for resisters both as a group and, as they mostly were, lone individual settlers.

This went without saying almost, never mind Trudeau's suspension of search and seizure to arrest three hundred Quebec separatists and as a result waste the life of one high-ranking hostage. Could anything afford to go without saying? If defendant had been where she'd said she'd been that month, then she could not have been present at a Monday colloquium in Cambridge after which she had allegedly received her nephew's word-of-mouth go-ahead to draw "moneys," funds (hey, it works just like a line of credit), for the further investigation of the Mon-Khmer shrines anciently secure on the plateau from waters of the delta and the lake—and to use the name of his group to raise more money.

Colloquium? Della asked.

A big critic of the war, Daley had explained to the low voice next to him, forgetting the name, remembering the name.

While this young Daley had hung in there grasping the line along which events had set up plaintiff nephew to be parted with a decent fraction of his income whom his number two counsel William (Bill) Daley who'd been hired on a hunch by his number one on the advice of a young

*Asian* lawyer, was deposing. In questions embracing hypothetical (border-line relevant) chronologies (given her premises) and "time" *travel*—chronologies and (the new word) "scenarios"—*he* had outinvented *her*: between the two excavation sites a full day of travel mainly on foot, a garden of English marigolds he didn't question, yet between each site and the village station where she had wired Boston, surely many more hours of dig for the two work teams than we saw in the sworn photos; in fact, one site hadn't visibly been touched, ground not broken, whereas the other (in terrain actually known apparently to this young number two lawyer) had produced thirty-nine pretty decomposed adult males and concussed to put it mildly children (mutilated "forms" of people was her word). These in two to three layers above the still-integral stonework of the shrine, the project for which, considering (or as it turned out, in spite of) her earlier work, the team had obtained funding and clearance. But the three routes possible between the Cambodian highland site that hadn't been worked and the site that was so far a modest Khmer Rouge or even American massacre cache, were far from congruent with the single round-trip route defendant claimed to have traversed (though with decreasing certainty). And these alternative (or trial!) options coupled with the journey to the village station (one-legged imps playing a slow-motion team tag dashing each other against the stones, children with goiter, a "strange" Vietnamese who wanted to give the visiting lady a haircut) agreed neither with the known topography of the land, nor the foliage as depicted by plaintiff's counsel (*recalled* really by him) providing the remarkable but overmatched defendant with so many stories (besides in fact his *witness* though not in the box) that she could only shake her head and smile (*this* was not the brief against her surely!) and try to shift gears adroitly toward the late Roman church wreck with which she had made her name, a not uncommon sunken cargo of building parts for a prefabricated basilica that she had helped to work out. Sixth century. But the Cambodian work was new for her. Her nephew loved her? Was that it?

The whole of which intrigued Daley, who proceeded nonetheless from far to near and by elimination had left defendant with a series of expense-account launderings (the dryer on Delicates, to say nothing of folding the results while still warm for transfer wherever) not only crystal clear but true. And to her surprise Daley had asked if the

Khmer head in the photo had come from either of the sites in question, and she had answered no; so that when she phoned this young number two lawyer for plaintiff the following week to speak of this and that, even try drawing him out about his own war, this lady who had been to Troy and Persia studying gems and bronzes with Gisella Richter and had in the space of five months he understood run a marathon, kissed Martin Luther King the day he called America "the greatest purveyor of violence in the world," and secured funding for another summer "church wreck" dive through her connection with the Council of Underwater Archaeology, couldn't disguise her happiness in this very fit and objectively grown-up lawyer's range of interest, his reach. So she was able to instruct him over the phone concerning that fourteen-hundred-year-old basilica of the watery world, the Corinthian capitals with acanthus leaves for the nave, and then in a hotel coffee shop, explaining the six-armed cross or Christogram upon the choir screen, the ambo pulpits—*how* they did it.

And she would not have guessed he'd only barely passed the New York State bar his second time, unless she sensed that law wasn't his first career pick (as she did later that afternoon), a not uncommon ordeal and lottery no matter how smart you were, the bar first time around. Daley had told her all about it in some flattered nerve knowing she thought well of him.

Yet that very night he told Della the deposition anecdote, this new unlikely person met on the subway: though if the cause of failing the bar first time out lay elsewhere than in brainpower or character, call it another Wolf emergency, his brother's professional career, which that subtle older lady embarked on questionable digs in early postwar Southeast Asia thought curious and worth a lunch invitation, attractive to Daley also in her account of the notorious M.I.T. professor's doubts as to massacre statistics voiced in a recent colloquium.

The strange soul who ran her finger around the rim of the neat dent blue-black between ribs three and four working up on his right side might have divined the exact shape of the rifle lead that had pierced him for all he could or would tell, because his wife's personal antiwar feelings interdicted accounts of it, which was fine with him though Della was evidently fond of the scar, like the head of his "dick" (her word surprisingly), and fond of him like a new friend. And of the version he had told her of the deposition story. Della had a touch and she knew what she knew.

How he had laid out for the dig-woman the consequences for her account in time and terrain of her movements in highland and delta, and between New York, the West Coast, Connecticut, apparently Boston, and someplace else. Yet Della proved no more interested in the remains than his tour of service, which the veteran counsel for defendant had warmly contrasted to his own survival in the Java Sea disaster of '42 and his Pacific Theater service in New Guinea, though Daley very nearly lost it arguing after the court recorder shut up shop that the two times had nothing in common.

It was his old comrade Sook, a year ahead finishing law school, who had passed the case on to Daley, recommended him to the well-to-do plaintiff's lead counsel. Sook could have handled it though his experience had been somewhat different from Daley's. Daley might have liked to see defendant win. Shrines, bodies—saturation of light in the woman's talk, she crossed her legs several times in the heat of explanation. Funds raised to exhume what was thought to be there.

For Della, this artist listening to him in her bed in an East Village walk-up, "Time and space." Well, he had nailed the defendant so she hardly knew it was happening by pinpointing the several timelines her side of it might lengthen or compact. How long it took on foot from Tin Hee through rocky woods to Long Sem, how far in kilometers from a temple to a church, from Loc Bue around an overgrown, mined, and thus not quite abandoned air strip through Sap and the area nicknamed Men Hu after the late bombing initiative to a station where there was a phone. Each time an alternative not parallel and thus confusing only because it threatened the female defendant with all the ways she could go, and he had seen them. Della never could have conceived of what he had done the afternoon of the night he'd told her the deposition story, it was accidental research, for the archaeologist after all this time had phoned him up to have lunch with her, she had been out of the country again, she was old, she was in a hotel lobby a cut above hotels Daley was familiar with. This story was what had done it, Daley was convinced.

# 3

SOMETHING (ABBREVIATED) OF THOSE DAYS WHEN HE WATCHED HIS WIFE perform he imparted to this safe person Lotta. It was the Q-tip box, or Lotta was single, or it was that she had heard the mugging part of the mugging story (which proved you can get blood out of a stone, though they didn't get a cent from him). He could sit in the bleacher stands at a dance theater workshop or on the floor and try to absorb what he saw or just enjoy it. He was content to say little. It was okay for him to. It hardly mattered what you said if you were vague or came up with one specific thing. Dancers wanted the attention. (Drank and smoked surprisingly.) So that once in a while maybe he would speak out, try and tell someone what it was. Path becoming path, coming out slightly beyond human in stillness and/or frenzy. Described, it came out dumb, like gravity. Yet he had been accepted. A person of substance, professional, a lawyer. A thoughtful "friend of the company."

Describing a dance like a power play coming down the Garden ice. Well, it was just what he had seen, a married outsider. And once, late at night talking with the black guy in the company, Daley had likened this man's work with Della to a helicopter maneuver where you let the main rotors "clockwise" you but don't pedal the tail-boom rotor quite enough to counter the fade, the leftward fall "really something" (bliss and experience itself he couldn't quite put into words). ("Right. That's the vertical one," said this polite athlete, a particular friend of Della's.)

Figures out on a polished floor, using just the floor. Rehearsing their joint desire. Plunging or "asking" themselves into parts of . . . a thing know what I'm—? A thing in itself that worked; a *living* thing possibly.

Daley thought, Didn't matter if some were gay men it was all material (more or less human), making more material. (Well, you know how lawyers always get paid whatever farce is playing out.) Insights like this. Loath to say them. So he hadn't come up with anything often, or couldn't. Yet what he had seen in his life made *into more material* upheld *him*. Things fall. They exist then.

His own brother coming back from a draft physical murderous unable, *almost* unable, to do violence to anyone in the house, raise the roof. A house made of wood and bricks, mortar and screws, a shelter too, it occurred to the elder brother who was afraid somebody would get killed.

Your eyewitness summoned even where you needed something even better than eyes—gray cells, a detective had said—and were to ask, not say. Nothing without eyes. Back of the head. The things he had seen and could not think about without seeing again. Could not see without thinking about; could not think.

A twelve-year-old giving birth holding on to a branch above her.

He didn't go on the road with Della but twice. He flew to Minneapolis for a show because he wanted to check out the Walker. And then she had agreed to fly up to Rainy Lake with him on the border opening upon the northern territory. And once to San Francisco, where they performed at a college. You could see they had a fine time, rambunctious, bingeing privately, worked so hard. It wasn't as if they didn't include him. They didn't take care of themselves. They were okay, boisterous, intense, or casually weird. One other trip; plus a drive to Connecticut, noisy hilarious—another company's rehearsal. That had been it for Daley out of town. The Alaska trip he was busy with a case.

Della was independently faithful.

Why "such a person" would hook up with him.

Nothing he would tell the banker contact who came into the equation in '81, potential arts grant—Lotta nodded, at the entrance of Ruley to this account; but every time for years then Daley would feel relief watching Dance, it was a medium: not water, not parachuting, not even air*space* in the small Kiowa-type helicopters he had learned to fly while he was in law school in the mid-1970s, your by no means miracle aircraft though subtle, multiple, and falling.

That is, he had never seen this *kind* of thing. He almost hadn't liked "Dance." (There was ballet and this, he knew; ballet was up in the air and with an orchestra and old stories or myths, which he'd until then seen once in Ohio and once in New York and it made him feel weird and male and subtle.) He saw what he saw: a person surprisingly long legged in motion, swinging and swiveling knowingly on the run, turning in the air dissolving the seconds, you lost how long, until it was done and these devoted people adjourned.

Then prone on the floor, rolling, pivoting, spinning like a pointer. They called it a language. He began to see the tricks repeated, like exercises. But was kind of blessed at long last, a gift to him in his existence. Or it was sex, bodies, it was almost his wife.

And what had it been given to him to say after half a dozen years, a layman cohabitant husband who was just supposed to show up and be there?

Yes, said Lotta on this Saturday night in November playing with a blue Q-tip box on the kitchen table.

Not even supposed. Who *liked* what he saw. (Who perhaps was liked.) The gliding around, very artistic; silly sometimes and embarrassing at first, though he would not say so, and then it could carry him away, music, a good movie, materials giving you hope. The stage rarely a raised stage in Dance, most often the floor shared with the audience, a group here in the city that knew one another. Or sitting in a grandstand. Sort of a loft. Though he did not applaud with the falsetto whoop that marked you as belonging. The stomping almost, but he didn't stomp; he admired what he had experienced. Was glad to be "exposed" to it. A kind of *thinking*, he found. Daley kept his views to himself. How they received each others' bodies in passing. Some even heavy experience not false that had been absorbed and changed utterly now in these almost speaking loops and judo entanglements. Made different. Silence and hope. And (though one didn't say it) honor.

Della evidently from what people said was a spiritual person, though Daley did not quite believe in it. He let it be.

Lotta concurred.

You didn't know. He believed in Della herself. And Daley knew that people who used this word *spiritual* didn't mean God only or God at all.

Della and the new black dancer steered close for a time. His name was Pwen. He talked about himself and didn't. He was a hurdler, a champion high school athlete, a one-act-play writer around Chicago. Dance had been pretty in the closet and inhibited and that was why it was opening toward show business, satire, shtick, he told Daley, sky was the limit. *Science*. Relativity, you know. Unknown, he had just walked in on a rehearsal in San Francisco, the company's West Coast trip; worked with them, came back east with them on the red-eye. Still a pretty traditional, not un-Graham company. Daley just as glad. It was only his opinion.

The company was periodically broke.

They brought in people with clout to serve on the board. A lesbian ad exec, and one with money. Board of directors for a little dance company. And suddenly this fellow Ruley. Who had swung into Della's life on a hinge of money prospects. It became a friendship. Was the guy gay? They were day-to-day, you might say.

# 4

TALK GAINING ENTRY INTO DANCE AT THIS TIME, AN ACCOMPANIMENT, IT changed things. The figure moved through its silence, its nature, turned into an alien or evolutionary freedom. Acts; comedy even in two or three companies, you name it. The figure less abstract up there; more a person. It was not Della's way but. Were these "guys" putting it down, these other dancers, these (he once or twice meant but did not say to his wife) *fruitcakes?* Why should he speak of what he didn't know? No one asked him. No, they were warm to him, women and men, devoted, brimming over and secretly he thought sometimes victims of this urge, yet objective practitioners, he couldn't express it. This at a time when Dance, which granted had brought in blacks, meant a little bit of everything.

Monologues in motion, funny lines, what you would call witty skits, "entertaining." Daley didn't like it. Not knowing where you were. The way some people, though this was hard to believe, had not liked Cassius Clay spoofing the ring, but he could do it all when he needed to.

Words. Words instead of silence which in its absence proved to have been hope. The new carrying-on didn't do away with the silences. It confused their hope. With cleverness. It was happening. It was not Della's way. A choreographer originally from Nebraska took off *Othello*. They went to see it.

*Othello!* said Lotta.

Sure. A pro football linebacker with the blond wife and a troop of business partners marching on like gangbusters (or "the musical"), their big hands in their left jacket pockets, you were supposed to imagine a gun prop in each, you didn't quite get the milling about, the quarterbacking. Which made Della laugh; her laughter went on; they had come home. Choreography quarterbacking! It had amused Della. Daley meant something besides. No matter. He couldn't quite identify it. *Unplanned. Singly. Managing.* With this fellow Ruley who had swung into Della's life on a hinge of money that had become an unpredictable friendship. It was shtick, was how Pwen put it. (Daley asked Della what shtick was exactly.) Pwen was sort of a purist, but a thug, Daley suspected. Arrested in Chicago when he was only fisting a victory sign, Pwen had been in the war but they oddly didn't think of discussing it. He and Della made a dance derived from the Vows section of the Sunday paper, which Della read avidly. It would have been susceptible to this new shtick, but they didn't need to speak. He would hear Della's end of a phone conversation with Pwen. "Trust it," he heard her say. He wondered what? "Movement's *confession?*" she said, to Daley too almost; the laugh was with Pwen. She was very serious. Once in a piece, as she swept by, arms reaching, fingers and palms in line like some athletic event he couldn't at the moment name, a fat little boy sitting on a floor cushion had jumped up, and she had come back and made up a step for the two of them on the spot, astounded the house, Daley had had it described to him. She in fact played follow-the-leader after *him*—

He wasn't there?

Not that night. The kid, somersaulting, he had a gift, six years old, skidding onto the seat of his pants, rolling over and goofing spread-eagled on the floor in front of all those people. This Daley thought was the evening the Dutch banker—

Ruley.

Yes. Had introduced himself. A wild night by Dance standards.

She would hold back a little. Stay within herself as Daley understood it. Not always.

They all drove up to Connecticut to see a rehearsal. A company up there of tumbling-about, reaching-for-things-unsuccessfully *children* really. What was Daley doing here? Some of them in their late thirties! Children in their style, but kids wouldn't . . .

Kids wouldn't do that, said Lotta.

Maybe going to get hurt; open to it. Babies on the floor, funny and disorderly, Daley certainly "got" the defenseless part. But the two companies loved each other. Going up, Della sat in back, Daley drove five in his car, listened to their housing and medical complaints, and parent stories and teaching stories—they did part-time teaching some of them.

But Ruley? said Lotta.

He had appeared out of nowhere, off the plane, coming from the West or the East. Expressly to see the company one night. He hadn't always been a banker. If ever, you could feel, or he let you. Felt. But it checked out. Liked Della's work. He wanted to get the company some funding. Daley hadn't been at the theater that night. Where had he been? A late night. In fact the night before that ill-fated (well, maybe not) morning run along the river, remember?

The couple. The umbrella.

That crum came back for it, Skip saw him.

Skip? Guy who runs. And you went home rather than—? We got to the hospital.

That said something, Lotta said. What?

Worth going home to have his wife with him.

She didn't need to go.

She didn't go?

Didn't go.

Why had he gone home then?

Gap in the tale.

Lotta actually remembered the agency—hadn't he mentioned it to her soon after the earthquake?—Della retiring for some reason from . . . Yeah, Lotta had a world-traveler friend out of work . . .

Daley was telling her how Helen couldn't seem to learn about doing things for others, for kids in fact, one reason she went to the West Coast two or three times a year on business but really to see a young protégé in San Francisco whom she had sponsored into the country when he was an adolescent, virtually adopted, how did she pull it off? She still had the stamina. But this was after Della's time. When she thought she would start phasing it out, the dancing, she wasn't suffering from arthritis in her toes and she could still bow so you saw the nape of her neck. Eighty-one, '82, he had known her for six or seven years by then, and she had been dancing for almost three times that. She conceived the idea of the employment agency. Mostly for women. Della secured that start-up loan from a women's bank (at too high a rate—Daley the last to hear of it); rented office space, bought two IBM typewriters; signed up an assistant, a woman, a former dancer, as it happened, ethnic Caribbean dancer from Saint Croix with a family. And they had some clients, mostly women—some educated immigrants. A battered woman who had become a photographer but was afraid to set up her own business and kept her portfolio of bruise shots, mostly women but not entirely, out of the house because of what her husband would do if he saw them.

Lotta could understand.

No . . . she was afraid she could not give him one more chance, Daley said, hearing the thought and flattered by Lotta's look. Della thought she could buck minimum-wage thinking, and she was amazing, it was as if she had *created* a job here and there, in arts organizations, at two of the botanical gardens, even some freelance projects she didn't take a commission on. (And *please don't chime in*—not that Daley ever would—because she could swing it. She had meditated this project of an agency all the preceding summer when she and Daley were traveling.)

Somewhat mysteriously she was phasing out what he had thought was her life when he'd met her. At one time before he knew her taking for the training alone two or three ballet classes a *day*; and a street mime group you could sometimes catch at the public library she ended by despising *for* their politics, which was one of agreement among themselves. (Though, granted, a family, she heard that one again elsewhere.) And to pay the bills, a pretty demanding job. A legendary one-on-one fitness system to pay the rent. She had lost her respect for the proprietor (legendary himself) over some matter of a co-worker who wouldn't blow the whistle.

And for a while a company with a two-week season and all the hassle of reaching the twenty-two-week minimum for unemployment but.

Massage by a member of the staff ("the family") that turned into holistic assault arguably, subtly, undeniably, deniably, "end of the day," it had been years before she told Daley, it hadn't seemed to him to diminish anything in her, her physical affection, her independence.

He felt Lotta's feeling but didn't know enough to ask what it was. She put her hands on the edge of the kitchen table.

Well, he hurried on, Della was friends with our Ruley. She had started swimming again. It could have been a kick in the teeth but it was a passing friendship with someone who knew a thing or two she wanted to know. Ruley knew the birds of Central Park almost as well as Daley—a coincidence. (Not Della's interest—though she was like a bird.) And probably the sewers—he and Daley both had an interest in water. What a quake would do to the water mains, the two sources north.

It has not been sufficiently thought through.

And he could tell you where the unfledged pigeons were. Pigeon habits. Why they were here in "Gotham" (he renamed the city, old style from the headless horseman man, and Mana-hatta): they liked cliffs and ledges, not *generally* trees though. Colors of pigeons; gulls, see them at night sometimes though they were not predators.

She and Ruley took the ferry. Why did they do *that*. Her agency just getting launched. Daley knew what Della was not. Silly. She wasn't especially gentle. Daley chaotic, wise, if she had known. Not startled or alarmed but. He bothered her. She would come home to her husband. "I don't *like* him," she said, stressing the word like a pathetic person. She valued him. Wasn't she an artist or something, Ruley would say, she didn't need the money from the agency, she had her husband, and the agency wasn't going to turn a profit to speak of. Della had taken an interest in a new dance company that did aerial stunts and violent falls as far as Daley could tell. With a spuriously boxing-gym atmosphere strong-woman generated breakthrough into some quick physics of physical and risk abstraction nothing at all to do with Della but the science of it or something else drew her but she wasn't in shape now to work with these people—that is, young enough—but Ruley urged her to try, which would have been dangerous.

Did Ruley tell the truth?

Lotta stood up.

He'd say he'd call and didn't. Then he'd call and say hi.

Daley thought, What was she doing with him? It wasn't a marital question. He kept his mouth shut "at the end of the day" (Ruley's end-of-a-job balance-sheet phrase foreign in his mouth). Daley felt like someone else: or his sympathy sealed the passing unimportance of it all. What did she expect?

Ruley spurred Della into work she did in her workroom upstairs. Reportedly scaled the back wall of the house one afternoon to retrieve a thing from Della's workroom, when they were supposedly gardening (not Della's preferred work—hubby in Australia).

Staten Island. Lotta was looking around the kitchen only in order not to say she was going.

This was the oddest thing and not to be believed.

I've *been* to Staten Island.

No, almost *because* it checked out.

The oddest thing? Know what you mean. Lotta remembered something was coming.

They took the ferry out there, got on a city bus, followed the old Lenape hunting grid; then on foot to Kill Van Kull. Know where that is? (Daley did now.) In the distant shadow, in fact, of Todt Hill someday to be surpassed by the largest landfill in the United States scheduled to be the highest point on the eastern seaboard by the year 2001, an old lady was putting out her garbage in her dull purple go-to-church hat and a red woollen poncho. (Della sitting on the edge of the bed late at night had described her.) Ruley talked German to her, sounded like German. She knew of him. New Jersey, Middle Atlantic; one-third Lenape, Lenape Indian if it was to be believed (not so uncommon anymore, when history replaces history, knowledge replaces memory, people coming out of the woodwork, Indian not the same as black).

How can you be a third something?

It was true if not quite straight but curved; for the truth wasn't the issue. Though he would not be around for long in Della's life.

Lotta had hold of the Q-tip box.

Daley said, "A friend of mine, a Canadian here who knows him slightly said when I happened to say that Ruley did not talk about himself, though he talked and talked—talked about you—she said, He's talking about himself."

Lotta rapped the blue box on the table. Now.

The Staten Island woman knew of Ruley from a family in Cape May. Lenape. Della attended a franchise setup conference with Ruley to get some business experience. Employee searches and treatment discussed, yet was this why they had gone? It was at the American Hotel in Freehold, within smelling distance of the track, and there Della met two of these (well, I will say) believers.

What?

Ruley plainly didn't encourage them. They were there for the harness racing as well. People down around Cape May thought he was a Roadman.

Roadman?

Yes, a covert Roadman whose work it was to carry on the ceremonies long outlawed. Outlawed? Daley said when Della told him. He doubted it. And now, though, look at what had happened since New Amsterdam wheeling and dealing; look at them, researching a state-of-the-art bingo package for a casino in Red Bank or Camden with the advice of this globe-girdling consultant whose father back in his lowland city maintained a landmark (we would say) home on the same street as the castle and the church.

Casino consultant? Lotta took the cynical view, yet "He had help from a real estate developer here in town, he was happy to make friends with him, he told me it was a working friendship, it was from him he learned of my book."

Though Ruley claimed Lenape Indian through his mother, who claimed it way back on her mother's side and knew her father's clan,

Lenape and Caddo Delaware. (Dreaming or researching, just looking at storks and vultures you'd never know they were kinfolk, it now turned out, or penguins and loons: the chemical evidence did it, he understood.) You could pick the warp of your timeline, your confession—your promotion as we think now in this lifelong nation. (What was Ruley *doing* with Della. Did her darkly unbound hair fall around *his* face when she leaned over him. Nothing of the sort, Daley had been certain.) So Ruley had with materials at hand helped them set up something on the model of an "operation" in Tesuque, New Mexico where they bussed people for an evening of filling multiple bingo cards at near-clairvoyant speed, junk-bingeing between calls, letting cigarettes burn perfect columns of smoke unless you were under the A/C. Raising money, taking it from Anglos not to mention Hispanics and their native selves. A brand-new red grand-prize pickup truck stood waiting in the middle of the room for all to think about.

Lotta nodded toward the door to the stairs.

Daley gestured toward the basement areaway door around the corner down the hall.

It was clear that the more Ruley denied any link whatever with the late peyote leader Willie Thomas and John Quapaw before him, the more this cluster of ethnically landless Middle Atlantic Caddo Delaware Lenape folk were convinced of Ruley's line. ("His line," said Daley; Della smiled; they were sitting side by side on the edge of the bed and life was no better than any other life—quality materials, some waste.) *Hereditary* line . . . confused sometimes with the Road line drawn across the altar, it was actually a peyote altar ("Come *on*, Della," Daley said, though the fact was she didn't think much of Ruley—was that it?—he had a gift of tongues, his own father spoke Russian with Quisling while plotting his abduction, and bottom line Ruley had dual citizenship through his mother though he spoke beautiful Dutch, you thought, listening to him once at a dance concert or he spoke beautiful English): this Road line some celebrity dynamic, though, to link Ruley with the Roadman Thomas.

Thomas had been dead for three days during a ceremony some time around the turn of the twentieth century only to come back to life. And to renewed belief in the all-night peyote and himself let us

face it. Ruley, give him credit, resisted this talk. He had more concrete projects to update with their own vision of solidarity and native
gain. And according to Della he felt the Great Spirit religion of our
indigenous people made more sense than the borrowed Christly
drama or the mumbo-jumbo in the patriarchal desert and the long-
running Holy Family cult, not to mention less-of-a-sacrifice medita-
tions on healthy Nothing then widespread in Gotham during a
Batman renaissance. Where his native blood had felt overblown if not
a hoax, now it was the two-thirds Dutch you wondered about but you
couldn't. His given name the family "Rulif."

A gambler, too, and with other people's money, maybe other
*people*, an *employer* of others. Half-considered pastimes. A jai alai fan, a
"player" at the Connecticut fronton. In the sense of "player" that got
out of hand—competitor participant, gambler innately cool,
American, hardball killer. Twelve years ago, more. Up in Connecticut.
A dinnertime drive to the Hartford fronton south of there . . .

Jai alai? Lotta wasn't interested, but she was. The long court, the
lethal rebound of the pelota caught for an instant with the shoehorn-
curved basket strapped to the forearm of the man you bet on, a one-
armed weight lifter, hurled back at the far wall in one straight-arm
arc. "I remember he sat in the backseat. Hooking up was the thing. He
would network a relay of frontons nationwide, Connecticut itself
generating a better idea, to build a city over Hartford, not Ruley's
idea, offered up the way he'd guess your life like your weight on a
handheld card, though where would the Hartford sky go? The tomb
of Eve, now." Lotta had described the tour. Middle East just outside
an actual town Duymens was doing business in.

Had Lotta stopped at Jedda? Of course she had, Daley answered
for her. Ruley had, of course, built or had been instrumental in con-
tracting the erection of the *roof*.

"I'm weak as a fig," said Ruley. It was a lie. Ruley flirted with
height, we know. They were in the garden the week Daley was away
in Australia, and Ruley had scaled the south side of the house without
a rope in the late-November sun. Why? Well, he would have gone to
the roof but he had disappeared through the third-floor window to
get something for Della she'd forgotten she'd asked for. He had cer-

tainly not looked like a banker. A soft handshake, Native American, with them custom and respect, not weakness. "A fig for virtue," was what she said. An encourager, possibly a liar.

He was not a bad carpenter, on the evidence only of the eight or nine days Daley was in Australia. Some pretty fine (not yet painted) shelving he came back to in the third-floor loft room with nice (standard stock) molding. Ruley could fix the sashes so the windows didn't threaten to suddenly fall and break the glass, but he didn't have time. He could build you a shrine in the backyard, bring him some rocks from the country. A fair tongue-and-groove carpenter, Daley would have granted, on the evidence of a bookcase.

Coward, climber, existentialist, thief, he told you. It dovetailed. Hey, capitalist wasn't quite it. Ruley picked up a couple of little things that didn't belong to him, yet who did they? He had earned them with his time. It came to Lotta that if he had pocketed these fragments of the pottery that had broken in the earthquake, he might also have been taking them off her mind.

"Banker, diving coach."

"Diving coach!"

"You might have thought he was out of work. If a thief is ever out of work. Personally he was a thief."

"But of what?" said Lotta, in the doorway dying to be gone. Yet this was what she had waited for: to ask this question.

"An appraiser of action and your value," Daley said.

"A good one?" Lotta friendly and intimate or lost now, wanting to be touched.

"Well, in those days it was okay to say you were a thief." What days? A while back; very early 1980s, earlier. "Oh." At least that was Daley's impression. Your thief was skilled; he was out there.

Well, he'd almost certainly taken some things off her bedroom credenza, and then they were gone.

"Not that you asked me to prove it, and I don't do criminal work."

"You do things you say you don't do."

Daley was done. Why had he told Lotta about Ruley and Della? Lotta passing out of Mexico had encountered a couple in Galveston who showed her their writing. A joint product, looking back on *his* career as a policeman and *their* shark-fishing franchise, the list of things they did not speak of, and the future of the nation, seeing it prove its case. They were all sitting in a park in Galveston Island and it was November in the upper Gulf and the next thing Lotta had been invited to a writing group that met once a week but she wasn't able to stay for her first meeting. All of them *memoirists!* Middle age. Elderly. Old.

Bought from her, too. Lotta had been amazed how interested she had been in their lives, their stressed-out lawns in late October, November, overwatered and infected with circular brown patches in the zoysia grass and Saint Augustine and their steady cheerful overcoming of the chinch bugs and white grubs, memories of the wars, resistance coffee shop right there in Texas the Oleo Strut up at Fort Hood where a nephew wrote for Fatigue Press and treated his family like—the same who in '71 April bivouacked just west of Capitol Hill, anecdotes of family that made you think That's history, though it occurred to Daley maybe story was exactly what history wasn't though he could not spell it out.

Lotta seemed to love Daley for a moment.

Why did this "confession" remind Daley of a gift Della had discovered. In herself. She saw *people* so that *they* felt remarkable. It was in them too. The wind, she called Daley once. So he was the wind. Oh. Well he remembered the wind whipping down from above. (The wind had been the beginning of it all, a January wind that his twelve-year-old brother could actually see looking out the window into the icy street that determined him to race his dirt bike that afternoon, his mother calling from the kitchen, Wolf eat one of those tangerines, you haven't had any fruit in days.)

The agency, during Della's brief, not-yet-lucrative career in it— she had found office space and an assistant, and the referrals began to come in. She was too private to be in this business, she said. She put her stamp on moments. Too nice? They would both have said no to that. She was often right—always right, people said; for she was uncanny, they said, and it was true, probably, if you believed. She said she was too private to be in this business. Della was his project, he fondly thought, yet then she had told him one night he was hers (a sluggish New Year's Eve party and they had drunk some champagne and decided to talk to each *other*). Just shrewd (and not very nice), people liked her severe. She was quite well known. How well known was she? she wanted to know. "I'm hopeless at all that," she said, sounding like someone; and he told her to get better at it, what did she expect him to do about it; this was lies, or half lies—he lied to help and, she said, think he helped, a poor sort of remark, a quarter true. He went with her on a shoestring (hers) to Stockholm where he cramped her style but she was overwhelmingly nice or grateful to him when he came back from ferrying around the city islands, though very busy with people after the show, and he was aggressive and likable with all the strangers until he forgot Della.

Now she was in business, a dancer starting a women's employment agency. What happens to dancers, they go on too long. No they don't. They think up dances for others. They teach. Pwen: "No greater work than that, no worse. Cartilage goes at thirty-five, as Dante says, joints ten years later." Maybe not always, but hips and knees and feet were just not constructed to take such a beating. He had heard all about it, he knew about it from a case of his in fact—not from Della much, but it was in her mind like a memory. In recent weeks trying to raise money for the dance company she would spend the whole day on the phone when she had always avoided it if she could; soliciting strangers was like eating raw meat. Della legendary for kindness to co-workers—to women. "She would stop at nothing," said an Estonian woman, whom she had helped obtain an apartment, an abortion, a visa, and of course a lawyer who was willing to learn a little immigration.

Ruley was a feminine man, it came to you. An athlete or instructor. Ruley and Della did things. He joked about it but it seemed to help. A breathing discipline: in deeply, then out so slowly, like this, making a specific wish; or bend down close to soy meal or lentils, inhale its spirit, no really. (When the land base is gone what was left but humor and capitalism?) It inspired the next-to-last dance Della made for the company, a benefit. The Lenape had borrowed breathing from the Pueblo ages ago, or it came to them across the continent somehow along with a subversive Hopi humor from the sacred mesas that helped propel several Delawares into good-paying NBC television studio jobs.

In six or seven years Daley rarely went backstage. Men and women receiving; Della visiting with an old friend Daley had never heard of; hugging somebody; or wanting to sit alone, busy, drained, sufficient, only a dancer. He understood. There wasn't much back-stage to go to. A place to dress—mirrored sometimes.

A scene, dance.

Tribal and devoted and narrowly exuberant. Basically he waited outside in a room with types he didn't always know and he thought of splitting to go hear some music. In Della's presence he would be sure to introduce himself to people.

No public to speak of, the celebrities over in ballet if you knew who they were, trying to stay up there. Literally.

# 5

ONE EVENING DURING THOSE FINAL MONTHS—
    Final?

When Della was about retired, she and Pwen (visiting) had made a springtime dance, story you knew was there, she and three men run-ning about with their hands up, closing but not able to reach and touch, carrying things, then lifting one another. Then carrying again precious beings, small from where to where? Daley would not have said so—not out loud—well, they *were* carrying things, then lifting one another, funny, deepish, had he ever been part of this? Carrying these precious organisms, he was sure they were doing that. Beings, from where to where? Then suddenly it was intermission, the "interval" he had heard Pwen call it more than once, and Ruley there unexpectedly.

He introduced Daley to the people he was standing with. A man cut Ruley short, he and his friend knew Daley. Two guys standing around munching brownies whom Della and her husband had includ-ed in an ambitious Thanksgiving dinner a year ago. (Peck, the short one with the weight of the world in his face, would not tolerate even being told news he hadn't heard and was sulky, it came to Daley later, because of his sidekick's comments on the show, his interpretation, that was it.) And a spectacular young woman Ruley was regaling with an improbable business trip (which in fact checked out) which bore somehow upon what they had just seen Della perform with the three men, you would give Ruley that.

Middle East material. The roof of the Jedda airport. Four and a half million square feet of fabric drawn taut as a drumskin to the endless curving across hundreds of masts and cables, the largest roof in the world providing shade for 105 acres of desert to shelter hundreds of thousands of deplaning pilgrims arriving at the Haj terminal and Ruley with a piece of it.

The radiant young person he addressed was Isobel Gramm (whom Daley as it happened had represented in a minor matter, written a letter on her behalf but had never met, a missionary). Had *Ruley* been a pilgrim? Well, Ruley was not there to walk fifty miles to Mecca. The men laughed. The spiritual brass had let him in. No threat, not Jew not Christian. No, he'd been there to see about the wadis, if these desert wadis could be developed into irrigation grids. "That's really interesting," the tall man, Johnson, said and looked at his friend. Ruley had rented a house made of coral. "Wow," said the tall young woman Isobel. His personal agenda had been, however, to find the tomb of Eve, which was outside of town. Not likely, said the young woman.

Said to have been razed or dug up half a century ago.

Yet it was really the roof. This big top. That's right. Several days he found himself at the airport staring up at hundreds of workers tightening it, trial-and-error pre-stressing this incredible—

"Tent," Daley said.

"Bill knows about this," said Ruley, who was more accurate than he knew. Ruley had recognized a laborer manning a winch way up high slowly luminously being tightened to its optimum strength this giant skin. ("No computers in those days," Daley told Lotta a dozen and more years later, wondering if she had had a thing with Ruley.) It was diving they had had in common—springboard, Ruley explained to the missionary woman blessed with rich and caring parents, grandparents, and friends—this world-class Olympian Ruley had recognized, airborne Arab, who had taken the time to explain from up there every cable, arch, mast, low point, and peak to Ruley of this stretching and drawing of the fabric, pulling, even pushing, these crests and slopes, these . . . "Just another Arab tent," Daley had said wondering when intermission was going to be over. The woman had turned her green-eyed gaze on Daley, she was a Roman Catholic lay worker, Darien money, "Wells Cathedral," she said, recalling from his name (uttered by Ruley), who he was (and that he knew her story). And Daley introduced himself and said he knew she didn't want to think about the letter he had written for her, but . . . "They're saddle shapes, that's all they are," Daley said; "they curve up in one direction and down in the other—an Arab tent."

A light blinked three times. Peck popped the last of his brownie, while his friend Johnson looked for a receptacle and said, "You know that's not so. You of all people." Remarkably, it was Daley he meant, addressing a trash basket but nonetheless direct and Daley heard. The woman touched Daley on the shoulder.

Ruley gripped Daley's arm. "Your umbrella!" Daley winced. "Same idea," Ruley was saying to Isobel. "You gotta hear his umbrella story, people coming at him with knives and he fights them off with an umbrella." The woman was somehow with Daley, approaching the doorway and the little passageway beyond it lined with black fabric.

"It was broken," he said and then very softly she said, "We think he sabotaged a couple of associates out there. I'll tell you the story." (She meant another time. Daley would keep it in mind perhaps only because a distant and late cousin of hers had been a radio commentator, Daley's father and mother, themselves third cousins, had listened to him as children and at least once together.) "He's right," Daley said, meaning Johnson; "tightening those roofs is everything at once, it made me see my house a little differently. Not only," Daley said thinking who was he talking to.

"You got slashed, you survived," Ruley broke in.

"Man came back for his umbrella," Daley gave in to a perhaps collective mood not his own.

"Where?" said the woman.

Della must have told him. The deep gash Daley had bound with a towel before he left the river path for home. They were in beside the grandstand now, and there were three children sitting very straight on cushions at the edge of the polished floor and Daley felt angrily for his program in his jacket pocket, the tall woman's eyes upon him so he felt it like a touch on his stomach.

"You read my mind," she murmured; she wanted *him* to bullshit her now. Bullshit cubed, but she was nice.

"We were thinking alike," Daley said.

Ruley said: "He had a deep gash in his arm, I know exactly where it is, I've heard all about it, life-threatening, practically ignored it, this is one tough guy, but he's a soft touch."

"You never sent me a bill," the tall woman said.

"You were Pwen's friend," Daley said.

"But you failed to con*vert* him," said Ruley, from the far side, knowing something Daley would as soon not know. He could have struck the man then, for knowing about the gash, as if he could explain why that couple had been waiting for him. "If I'd known you knew Isobel, I would have talked to her about you," Ruley said.

"You have been," Daley said grimly.

"Della's so modest," the tall woman said to Daley, her hand on his arm. "I don't think I like that kind of modesty. It's groundless modesty, isn't that the word for it?"

"Oh yes," said Ruley—"the roof they were holding up tonight running around trying to keep it from falling: pretty good idea, Daley, masts on the move? And I think it's falling in." Last name coming like that meant enemy.

"So it's about family," Peck said to Johnson coming up behind them and Daley thought perhaps he wouldn't make it through the shorter second half.

Khurma, though. The great Saudi three-meter champion.

Ruley had known him in Holland during the '73 gas crisis, Khurma a child, if that checked out; and then had met him again in '81 during the construction of the Jedda roof. Ruley offered to coach Della; he never lacked confidence. She had a neat figure, feet and hands, all of a piece. The coaching had touched her. How could that be?

Lotta, whom Daley wanted gone, had wanted to go herself. She had made him talk like drink, though he could talk or not talk. You loop out and back. Which was strangely what had happened after Lotta left, when Daley looked at the clock on this Saturday night, Becca must be at the end of the first act. And it never occurred to Lotta as she went out the kitchen door into the street alone, that this was only an intermission, and that nice taxi driver to come, and Daley beckoning her from the window, and her sensing the conversation she had interrupted with the Russian woman though then she told Daley she was "reeling" from all he'd told her, which even then persuaded him he would put off the trip to Waters until Sunday and go there with Becca.

She'd gotten a little shuteye one day at his place when she'd been tired, an hour's nap. Ruley called Daley's office one day by mistake. "Shall I give your best to Della? She's diving today, you probably know." Daley did not.

Her new agency project. Taken up it seemed mysteriously almost because it was open and frank yet without clear motive, so Daley thought it was his *fault*. And maybe so, considering the issue of Daley's gift never quite spelled out.

She made another dance and she was done, another after that.

Then had come the diving.

Now that the agency was under way.

Then Ruley gone, taking with him at the time it seemed almost the Daleys' own adventures. For in their travels, the time mixed up with way before and shortly before Ruley and necessarily only shortly after Ruley, they'd absorbed what could be reported and could have been shown to friends on slides if they had done that—experiences of Iceland and Morocco; Ceylon—the fume of magnolia, sweat, almond scent, and from a darkened house the faltering song of a boy perhaps; and India—a trip aborted on the northward leg by Wolf's injury in Japan so they never had their week in Kashmir but could see "the clouds advance like rutting elephants . . . like kings among armies," Della recited. Wolf had suffered a double in Japan. To his abdomen a suffocating shock from a hydraulic concussion when a tanker exploded while he was investigating underwater damage to an experimental dock, and on top of that a serious quake to his ear. Brother Wolf spent his life again and again and spent his long, tensile body, with plenty more left if you didn't ask his wife.

USE YOURSELF ILL, THE WIFE WILL SHARE IN IT. NO ONE SLEEPS THE sleep of the just unless the abuse of dreams rendering us powerfully helpless bottling up and unbottling renders a justice that restores us. That night asleep beside Becca Daley tried to wake up to tell her something, recalling all that he had had no business prolonging Lotta's visit with—*How did it start?* No, *How did it suddenly start?* Not much more of a dream than lawlike adjustments of words, stupidly getting it just right so it took gratefully a long time to be right before he would be in position to *answer* the question *being* adjusted, or wake from what?

Bill and Wolf had a little fight. Bill got him down, cracked his neck bones they thought. First aid not required. The day he was turned down by the draft no way they could blame it on that except indirectly and/or truly.

Wolf went to work. He had a gift, maybe not much more. It was for sizing up potential structures more than for existing buildings. A civilian construction project in Saigon (Vietnam), a hotel for GIs to replace hundreds of private billets. He had no business being involved. They didn't need him. An injury later on at a dam construction in Michigan, protesters far below him yelling up at him, some stunt; he had lost the use of his left hand, didn't respond to physiotherapy for months. Until it came back during a materials test one night in Malaysia. He left the belief or idea to his brother while living it himself with abandon: while muscle and tendon material have a recuperative elasticity incomparably greater than rubber (compare a pricked balloon and a torn bat wing), some human material (Wolf's in this case) apparently recalls origins in inanimate compounds currently synthetic but kin to the hard stuff like iron and traceable back to metal clays billions of "years" ago. The next morning Wolf had run along the skeleton of a bridge torquing its suspension in the East Asian wind like a just-decapitated eel and didn't make it back to where the cables (experimentally insulated) were anchored, but spun off howlingly two hundred feet into the river and survived the air crowded with strange potential, twists of aluminum and *steel* flying around him. Which Daley had had to be content with a report of. The next junket Australia, six months later was it?—just before Daley had met Helen and he had still obviously been married, and it was the wrong time to go just before Christmas; Della had said, *You will go,* and he had accepted his brother's invitation to join him on a job for a week. Just Band-Aid for a crisis in the materials planning for a dam in New South Wales. A week in the sun, yet they had almost come to grief. Wolf would kill himself one of these years.

Yet he pointed at his lawyer brother Bill as the one with more nerve in the family than anyone, a riddle Daley did not argue, it would have been self-involved to—he shook his cool head. He was thinking of an extortion case he had taken on, the city itself leaning over their shoulders, "a bunch of blockheads" he had called them in court defending his three outspoken women who'd been scared off their modest women's health center project in the garment district by a clutch of Russian-American furriers operating an entertainment real estate concern out of a building across the street from the Fur Synagogue. Wolf his brother wouldn't set foot in New York unless it was a connecting flight, and he saw his older brother the way Bill saw him, nerveless under pressure. Daley hadn't understood what risks Wolf meant. Maturity is accepting your reputation, good guy, bad guy, a character with some agreed-upon habit of being, or like accepting misunderstandings. But the north India Daley and his wife had missed, Ruley Duymens had been there and to Nepal on location with a low-budget documentary team he'd gotten work for the Arab diver with. A story Della didn't credit. Ruley had come upon things in his travels that they had never heard of. A book about Ceylon he loaned to Della, then told her to keep, many pages uncut. By an English official, *A Village in the Jungle.* Ordered to burn a peasant's hut so the colonists could take his land, the official had refused and been sent home. Daley could see Della carefully slitting the signatures so she would be able to read the book. She did it in the kitchen, and then she carried the book upstairs.

Ruley she took lightly at times, came home with the news that he was returning to Saudi Arabia on irrigation business. Distracted, she ran her fingers down her husband's cheek, looking for something, finding infinitesimal stubble. Yet it was true that Ruley had interested Daley's client in a group dig near Jedda promising considerable profits—to find the burial place of Eve, the lady (his client) who couldn't believe she had been worked up enough to challenge Connecticut and had lost those nicely insured pre-Columbian pieces to a burglar soon afterward.

Though it was Mexico Ruley left for when he left.

This a year or two before the great fiberglass-covered stadium seating sixty-five thousand was completed in Saudi Arabia.

Her olive skin as close to you as breath. First thing at breakfast she asked him the most interesting questions about his clients, had she been thinking business all night?—she understood he wanted to help them and especially at that hour, smooth and clean in the kitchen, tie knotted, ready to go: some ability of his *alluded* to in these twenty or thirty morning minutes of very direct talk about his work (and not just happily). Not law. It was expectation. "Something I wanted to talk to you about," just as he was leaving—a time when you got an idea between you—or she said she would tell him later, a dream of the house, each floor a—if she remembered—but it was a communicating dream, she was sure—a joint dream people had once in a while, maybe nothing to write home about but.

Her picture in the *Times* twice, once on her own. His wife. "A miracle," one review had called her. Pretty good for a girl from northern New Hampshire, well read of course. Modern dancers were better educated than your average theater person. A crisp salad plucked from the garbage of the past, was how she put it. Like the dry modesty, years later, of this young highly educated woman (to some extent) wanderer Becca, so sensitive to anything that looked like outside (not to say ulterior) control, had left Canada maybe because of that. Thank God Daley hadn't had to go to the ballet, yet later Helen came up with tickets a couple of times and he had honestly enjoyed it, while Helen sensed how Della's kind of Dance carried him away *and* embarrassed him, which he had never said so. "Well look where you were coming from," said Helen. She knew about arts funding. A little bit. Thinking of Martha Graham asking the NEA for a million. "You see?" Helen said, "Aim high. So you get turned down with $250,000."

(Was it the year of Della's death? Yes, it was '83.)

He took the steep brownstone steps slowly, for he would hear the piano and be happy. Della liked the neighborhood, the mercantile buildings—he and she had a long-haul residents' sense of the port, the North River piers, some permanent presence of materials. Kind of classical, the piano, he took the steps slow. Never the same piece; or *a* piece quite. He had taken her twice to a club up in the east Nineties to hear a pianist that reminded you how some skipping elaborate slow chordings can put you ahead before the destination is in place, beautiful or dissolving, as he had heard a great jazz (white) pianist was said to do with a vibrato that would then affect prior tones when vibrato in fact was impossible for the piano even a white jazz genius given work by Miles Davis. And then, standing on his step, Daley's key met the lock, and the free piano would stop like a person, a thing. To the right of the vacant music stand stood the old metronome, its arm an upside-down pendulum, trick furniture. Though she "didn't play." She was "just messing around," she was shy. By now standing at a distance from the instrument, its keys you might think still depressing chord upon chord. ("Shy" to him sounded gentle, hurt, superior, no return address, come to think of it.) "Shy" sounds very grand, Daley would say. "My Nietzsche manner." She meant the (she'd learned) improvisation playing of the notorious philosopher (a Hitler, you heard, philosopher) Daley would not really have read, a very young Keith Jarrett perhaps of his own day of hurricane force untrained. Sounded grand, he said, just in the door. *That's* a coincidence, she replied, I thought it sounded pretty bad. (*There* was an uncanny coincidence for you, her humor.) She could play six hours a day, she said. Why didn't she then?

Wrong thing to say, apparently. (No sheet music on the piano today.) She could have done anything. Some of the results were up on the third floor, junk she called it, objects locked away (he knew where she hung the key, he respected it all) some of it material you saw nowadays for sale. Small stuff. Not destroyed. He took a peek from time to time. Ruley must have gone in there once or twice.

Della's behavior to Daley, whom she loved, or objectivity or calmness in public, was taken as some sign of their sensual privacy—their relationship. Her friend had put it thus to Daley, actually a professor he had sat down next to arriving at the end of a rehearsal to take her out to dinner. "Sensual privacy," he'd said with gusto to Daley, a smell of cigar smoke and alcohol.

Until one evening it all seemed like a moving van filled up with other people or no one or suffocating with distance, and Daley looked ready to rough up a couple of her nice enough friends at intermission who had said something meaningless about her and Ruley and Daley had excused himself and gone off to hear some music and forgot to tell her. This was before Waters had come into existence basically taking a dilapidated structure and not honestly converting it.

Well, Della had a subtle, nasty, and do-anything habit in her too, when she delivered one of her judgments. "They should never have embarked on it." A couple they knew, and people remembered the remark. Daley heard the humor that maybe wasn't there. "Second guessing?" Long after the fact. She would say these things.

"She was right," said Helen, long before Della's death, glad of the independence between Daley and his wife.

"Wait," said Daley, "'it will kill them' was what she said. And meant it, and it did."

People remembered, because Della was the uncanny one. No one asked her to back it up except her husband once in a while. Della was as right as a ship out in the harbor, a red stoplight on the avenue late at night. Often of few words, she was in the habit of being right, and habit, instructed or not by us, becomes necessity, and in days long past Daley had joked about it—with Helen, who said it had made him mad because it was true. Yet her gift wasn't hers, she said; it was the universe's, that was all. Well, he didn't know about the universe. He *did* actually know a thing or two about it as he had a chance to point out later when Della entertained the notion of a return to a strange new company that played with midair motion and stunning, body-as-object falls and symmetrical collisions, good God. Time, space, and the rest, as if Einstein hadn't measured out these relatives to the atomic second. Yet was she prophetic? He knew he would hear someone else say it sometime. It was just before she died that they saw three Graham films with her voice-over explaining it all, though this wasn't the story of the wolves he later learned his late wife had modeled her life on. She had never told him.

He got confident and would say something and would learn that . . . ballet training and ballet extended into dance like an evolution that . . . well, Della or her friend might explain it.

She was an artist. She repeated herself. Someone said she had been raped by the unconscious. You guessed she meant it. They trudged across a rainy moor in Iceland, a pond desolate and leaden. A family of minks prowled the spongy shore, their backs arched like a raccoon's looking for garbage in the country at Thanksgiving time. Well, she said the same thing the day they left Morocco and arrived in a market town in northwest Algeria and were having a glass of tea in the shade: "I could just live here."

(Lotta knew that one. Daley sometimes forgot how big the house was.)

They had to get to Carthage, Della had to see the ruins; friends were on the beach in Tunisia like two dozen other New Yorkers, among them a restaurateur Daley had done some work for when he had delivery problems with some fairly nasty people in the Bronx. He gave Daley an interesting steer—he what?—and when Daley showed his wife the map, next thing they shipped on a little freighter to Sicily past the site of a famous late Roman "church wreck" sunk in eighty fathoms between Malta and Marsala; so they came to Trapani with a cargo of chemicals and explosives, where, between the dilapidated and the ugly postwar rebuilt, Della could have stayed a year for the snaky, impetuous dancers in an alley behind the port, three Arab maidens covered but for their eyes and a young half-naked sponge fisherman tracing the air with a great curved tail-docking knife: so careless their response to one another, so welcome after all that Spanish heel-clicking junk.

They had never been to Sicily.

Wolf on a consulting job down in the Toe. The Toe? Reggio, drank a little too much, Calabria, another near fiasco. She danced for him that first night in their room, the sounds down the hall never suspecting what *he* was viewing. A woman who was mortified to hear his brother assume Picasso was Italian.

# 7

IN *DELLA'S* SECOND CAREER, SO BRIEFLY EXPERIENCED YET WITH A HOST of new clients, she'd been the same person only more so. Manifoldly gifted and difficult. And patient now. Using the phone more. Difficult with her *husband*. Her friends wouldn't have imagined it. Marriage. Life. What was the gift she had gnomically ascribed to him? Given him? She slept better and longer. Daley slept worse. He tried to recall the breathing discipline Della had described. She was asleep. (He saw for a second the client's surprised eyes sitting in front of him when the client recognized the voice of a man he knew raising his voice to Daley's secretary Donna in the outer office.)

They went to a dance show. Daley if he was not drunk on two margaritas had seen something—witnessed it. The afterglow outline, he was certain. Where two "bodies" had passed an instant ago, it wasn't a trick of lighting. It was the environment, the era, an earlier one. They spoke of auras, the middle-class enlightened ones. Then next night, same thing—in his street, but the outline precedes the shape— of two figures running but seeming to fall forward. That was all. Was that it? he asked, maybe at this late date he had a feel for something. Della didn't know what to say. She said, Absolutely. She wasn't unkind. It was like a chair behind two performers, a prop very slightly lifting before your eyes. Guess it's all business, he said. Yet he could have rebuked her or if not that strangled her. Or hiked to work and back the next day or taken the car to the country overnight for they had heard of a place for sale that was better than it looked if you thought about it. He still liked her. Her hand on him, his chest, his neck, so light and original, quite Asian.

And that other company, the athletic, people said "amazing," troupe, that woman the director, she had brought science into Dance; matter anyway. An unusual show of gravity but with walls to slam themselves against, this wild, disciplined, rough-work straight-faced group who risked their limbs in feats that looked to Daley like the circus, though not as much fun, or an Eighth Avenue gym but you still called Dance. Della knew the woman and her friends. That was all. Transversely across this futuristic thoroughfare she marveled at the falls they took flat out, the body-after-body impacts against a white wall, a ramp wired for sound for the amped random rasps of a giant snare drum as they scrabbled slipping backward slowly up it; the struggles, the dives, the strange, resolute grounding of these gross experiments. Della by now was at a pool with Ruley two or three (or more) times a week. (She was talking like another Buddhist commuter.) The country, was it getting more democratic? Everyone an artist; one day to the next, no deciding among all these creatives. Why had he had told the tale of his marriage to Lotta (or of Della and Ruley Duymens)? For Lotta was unsympathetic enough to say she didn't see how they'd hooked up, it wasn't as if it had been one of those head-over-heels things of her father's. She had known of Della's death of course.

Lotta: "How did it start, though? I have to wonder about that," the words struck at him in his sleep Sunday night, almost woke him up.

It was that deposition. The story of it.

"No. I mean how did it suddenly start?" This didn't sound like Lotta. Though a demand; and pleading too, in the nicest, rather charming, cozy . . .

Suddenly start? He had been smitten. That was what *she* said, Della: sitting down next to him on the uptown local and he was reading a glossy brochure, he realized later how the photographs of Cape Breton and pictures of Nova Scotians with violins under their chins and apparently singing at the same time and a rocky cove, where you could feel the great swing of the cold sea near the rocks, had embraced this other thing, almost not the woman but some powerful movement of hers. Hardly aware of it, he still registered her two steps into the uptown car, the quick looks at the limited seating possibilities, her weight resting on her forward foot (that was it, a New York instant, no more, that you process), a powerful movement separating herself from the hands and backpacks and clothes and evening rush-hour irritation and resignation protecting herself (as he came to understand) aesthetically-or-something, angularly incomplete, against crowded standees who had chosen not to sit because they would be getting out (if that was the reason), and completing this powerful motion that embraced her sudden stillness looking around her, she slipped forward into the seat next to a man (not someone she wouldn't want to find herself sitting next to) reading a travel brochure.

So he caught her looking and she said it was a special place and when he said, You've been there, and she said, Oh no (a man's white coffee container swaying above them largely, angrily), Daley said he respected her opinion. The door opened at Penn Station in the crowded car and Daley had looked out the window behind him and stood up and an Asian woman tried to slip into his seat but he sat back down and he and Della laughed; first love revealed.

I suddenly saw us there, he had said. Which one was he? she wanted to know. Well she was the one with the violin and the one singing, he said. And he? He shook his head, stunned, he was meeting someone at the Garden, he'd missed his stop. He put his finger on the rocky cove. That's you? she laughed. This never used to be a good place to meet people, he said, meaning the subway. He tapped the picture and said he was afraid that he did see them there, look at the cliffs. She took the brochure. She was reckless then. He heard somehow his stomach rattle. I mean (he began)—No, you're right, his subway companion said, you oughta have your head examined. You're not a Bluebeard.

Though was that how they got married?

What she a performing artist valued in him.

Depose yourself.

For years after her death he would hear her when he cleared his throat or feel her eyes in his when he looked at a pomegranate (a useless fruit), an artichoke, or oatmeal or the wiring in the basement. He wouldn't hear her for months and then the sound of her tone would come to him unasked. Did he like her now she was gone? Maybe. Maybe not so much.

"Senseless repetition." The woman beside him, asleep—it was way after midnight, he heard the house hum tipping toward Monday, she was tired, her sleeping breath was real upon his shoulder. He'd woken just to hear the very blurred and sibillant syllables more than words, "Senseless repetition. Senseless repetition, I'll . . ." close to his lips, she said it again, in her sleep almost, "It'll go, it'll go."

# 8

AT AROUND A THOUSAND FEET YOU ARE BELOW THE OXYGEN LEVEL and you don't get woodworms eating the hull. The old structure turns out to be pretty well preserved, which is like striking gold for the archaeologist who can get down there in some form or other. This is the Black Sea a hundred miles or so out from the south coast, and the ancient wreck must be a thing of dreams. Not that a lay visitor would get to see it. A thing of dreams, this ancient hull, traveled in, lived in. No church wreck but anyway an early Roman ship the lady had told him years previous she hankered for but might never achieve. Others would.

Daley had been checking out certain ducks in south-central Turkey in a waste disposal center that doubled as a kind of preserve for them, he thought that was it. Brother Wolf on a job nearby. And then for a few days he left his brother and went to Sinop on the coast. The wreck dive way down below the oxygen level preparing, and nothing he would get to go on but just to look at the port. A fine harbor lacking adequate communications with the interior of the country (like New York, she had joked, the archaeologist, his friend so briefly known). Was he drawn to Sinop because of her? Yes. This was after her time. Army security base there now, a castle, a prison, the basics, on a peninsula that had been an island once. The air still sea air. He had swum off the rocks alone, the water not much. The archaeologist was still alive somewhere. Yes, the Cambodia work had been the high-water mark for her.

But the Black Sea (or Euxine) wrecks described beautifully by her and no doubt imagined one lazy, private, surprising, deserved afternoon in New York; what she might yet do; what she knew was out there—the old name for the sea between Russia and Asia Minor (her delicious Greek), "the inhospitable sea" because of the savage tribes around it, later changed to "Euxine," or "the hospitable sea"—an *opposite* and puzzling, or at least *"privative"* (she put it confidently) change

secluding the name now from the original *negative* so you get *well* +
*stranger* or *guest*, he remembered as well as he remembered her, she
had laughed about it with him that afternoon, these scholarly things
surprisingly intimate he guessed, mind and mouth—did he know any
Old French? she actually asked, they would read it together one day,
she had said. A charming woman, distinguished. And then strangely
the expense plaintiff had settled with her out of court after all for a
statement she had made, the plaintiff's aunt. Archaeologist of the late
1970s who'd not been digging for what she claimed in Cambodia, not
primarily though there was a Khmer head seven, eight hundred years
old—bust, that is—not at the Angkor Temple but . . . in any event she
found people under the ground, not shrines. "Cambodia?" Becca had said,
an hour, two hours ago: "they'd give her the bum's rush before she could
get a foot on her shovel, those people."

"You're right," Daley retorted so that she could not look him in
the face, "they would saw off her head with the teeth of a stiff old
palm leaf." But she had ridiculed him too. Cambridge, the meeting
the lady archaeologist alleged she had attended, the colloquium, it
had featured Chomsky, "a big critic of the war I think."

"I *know* who Chomsky is."

"He was someone, I believe."

"Mm-hmm."

"A critic of the war."

"Critic of the war? He's why I'm here," Becca had said. "How
could I hang out with somebody who . . . ?"

Daley in fact knew that this Chomsky, whose first name he didn't
recall, had opposed the U.S. engagement in Vietnam and was known
for his own war on official lying, necessary and dangerous, the war
and the lying. He was a professor of political economy Daley thought
but would not bet on it because he did not know for sure, and that
would be like assuming Picasso was Italian, as his own brother Wolf
navigating without a compass had done at a consulate reception after
a violent soccer game at Reggio di Calabria.

"I believe he was a brave man. A just man. With a bit of genius—
am I right?" said Daley. (Chomsky why she was *here*? Who had sent her
on a quest to New York? A philosopher? A Polish historian, this

Chomsky? A Russian émigré who had swung through western Ontario at a guess? But Harvard.)

Daley knew good things by hearsay. Underwater volcanoes out there the archaeologist had said. The Black Sea, which Daley remembered being told by her was actually what Homer was writing about whom you knew (like a movie) but hadn't read—the Dardanelles, the Bosphorus; Scylla, Charybdis, that those navigators had to sail for their lives between—all that sea dry *land* seven thousand years ago long before Homer, whenever he was. There was a flood, it was said, and the sea rose after the ice age and burst through the straits, turned the fresh water to salt, which is what we try to reverse with our processors nowadays, let the technology bombers blow up the saltwater converters if they want to and picket the manufacturers of the water-purifier kit we took into Canyonlands, we've got ours. That's why we're here almost.

They'd woken, he later thought, because—what repetition was senseless? He tried to understand her blurred words, he was between two thoughts of hers, or the circumstance, the circumstantial vise, of being with her—they'd woken because they remembered what they hadn't done. Daley slept soundly but was fresh after no matter how brief a doze, he was ready, but for what? He believed that a good night's sleep before your exam or your execution made more sense than even the deepest conversation in the wee hours. He stood at the window looking down through sycamore branches at the lighted street, the house heavy behind him, the girl, who had rolled over to face him, if she was really awake.

Who would not sympathize with her anger at the control that had been set up around her (though because she was powerful). The brother, the producer Beck, the once and future fondled child, the loft, the story it came to Daley that she'd been drawn into. Was it sympathy he should give for now? Shelter? Sleep? Maturity, for she might remember him as her primary residence lawyer. *Why did I come here?* she had said downstairs in the kitchen. Because she was hungry. Because of the river swim story with the breakfast on the far side. Because they had walked together and encountered a policeman, for all Daley knew. Or because Ruley Duymens had phoned her to recommend a lawyer. Someone else had directed her to Daley as well. Two people, she had said.

He was in bed and she didn't hate him; she felt trapped was all. It was after two o'clock and they were spirits. Was she half asleep? "What happened this week? Mmm, you be a good lawyer," she murmured, a bond with him, instinct's intimate pretense. "What?" she murmured, hearing herself or, he thought, him. She had something else to try on him maybe. He put his hand on her, she was tired. Becca moved her mouth. She could sound awake, she must be. She lay turned toward him breathing, his arm under her, her near arm on him. Everything was a risk, but they were as they were in the night, and he thought she was leaving "at the end of the day."

"When you were far away and came home . . ." Was she asking out of courtesy? "You'd hear that no?" she said.

"Oh, college, law school, and a binge for a year before law school . . ."

"But you'd hear that no." Becca laughed back in her throat, little dry gasps.

"The not-hearing," said Daley softly.

"And understand that it was her habit."

"You think it was no more than that?" he asked.

"The not-hearing." Becca put it as he had, the words close together; "oh well," she said.

Becca was here for the moment, tired in that let-me-catch-my-breath-before-I-embark-on-the-next-stage-of-my-life closeness. Yet she was trying to judge him. She might have woken up for that.

"From years of doing it to her husband," he said.

"No . . . ," she didn't see it that way.

A melancholy on her breath, her breasts awake while she leaned without apology toward rest again. "But no, you're right, you even mean well," she said wearily. Was she with him? "And take little credit for it." She was thinking. "And almost nothing surprises you . . . but we're tired of all that . . ." She made a sound in her throat, amused, not distant from him, and he saw why she had liked Leander, and saw her meeting him.

Oh this was after it got out that psychics were finding bones under trees with purple blossoms. (Well, he wasn't amazed anymore.)

But had he *seen* the hummingbird in the shell? But Daley knew what it was.

Oh she *really* went for the psychics, this woman, his mother, who would say no to your eyewitness news.

And finding eggshells in the forest and spinning them in a saucer to predict where you'd find a body.

"To spite my *father*."

"Why she got into the habit of saying no in the first place: resisting you was all it was."

"Yes, how did you . . . ?"—though to him it was just grown-up not-hearing.

"No more than that; and D.C.?" she asked. He'd mentioned D.C. The April '71 D.C.?

Oh, Daley hadn't been there, he was out of the country again, he sent a contribution.

Out of the country? An odd way of putting it. Long before he became a lawyer. The shrines and the war. And had he met her there? He had been asked by the girl, was he following up, was the archaeologist why he was there? And what was the contribution?

Money, folding money, not much.

"The April '71 D.C. you mean?" She wanted to make sure for some reason.

"In the form of possessing some blind eyewitness damn memory" (he ignored the question) "that called *you* into question, and if she— this mother—said no to you like that, it was a thought salvaged by her alone that contradicted you maybe but doubted you, your damn—"

"Your excitement, your—but she didn't mean it," the young Becca interrupted, "except—"

"Except she did; but it was you, not what you thought, whoever she was talking to, except it was—"

"It was only about what you thought," she told him. "She didn't need to know who you were." Becca attending irritatingly, wearily, and Daley felt it—lessoned in the middle of the night, he would take it. "Am I right?" she said. She knew some of the history and if she knew her Winter Soldiers who testified and the testimony though some of it discredited would always be history somewhere in the record, well, Canada had had its part, in fact historically its north-of-the-border ego booster in the 1960s and '70s, its modest national enhancement, and she was oddly proud.

"All she'd absorbed, you see."

"But you never knew how it would . . ."

"Come out of her?"

"Yes, it was *different* from what she'd . . ."

"Absorbed. And she wasn't what you would call . . ."

"Intelligent?"

"She could rile you."

"So people came back for more."

"No." Daley was a little drained. " . . . no."

Becca might have dozed off.

It was a while, and it was breathing, both of them, and then the breathing next to him turned to words again. Not without continuing to receive and register the events given somehow to her here in the middle of the night when she was tired. "You're quite up front," she said.

"What do you know about it?" he said.

She breathed beside him. She said, "Blood isn't thicker than mud, not when they're mixed."

"What do you know about it?"

"You were destined to meet her. Except someone arranged it."

"Well the friend from law school who recommended me."

"You didn't have to research it."

"Well. I knew what I knew."

"What is she doing there in '77—why would those butchers let her in."

"There was a reason."

"An American dig?"

"The bodies might have been our doing."

"You followed up." Years later. Years later? Daley wondered what he'd told her that she didn't know already. The shipwreck. Oh her shipwreck. God. Sinop.

You dog, are you a citizen of the world? she murmured. You met her somewhere.

Yes he had met her here once.

You dog.

In New York.

How did it turn out?

She was thirty years older than me.

How did it turn out?

Turn out? They settled.

"You don't know who Chomsky is?" she said.

Would she punish Daley for having to leave his house? For her half brother? For having experienced years of her brother on top of her?—though oral sex was tenderer, animal, she had said; less truthful. A little anthology of Becca remarks. Punish Daley for having joined her cast? If only as the understudy or legal adviser. For having doubts about her one-woman show? Doesn't know his Chomsky?

Tired of what?

"And you with your theater all economics then nothing to do with economics?" Daley said to her. And not recalling what she said, he went on, because she couldn't be bothered to. Some memorable creative freedom to take not a whole lot of responsibility for outrageous things said. Whole governments did it and that was what, as Daley understood it, your Chomsky had in mind.

A change had occurred in the conversation, and with the woman it was always conversation.

She was weary. What governments? she said.

Governments at war: Chiang Kai-shek—remember Chiang?—a modern-day equivalent of a . . . a founder of the church, a Christian gentleman who suffered for his faith in the eyes of the American secretary of state who was in fact before Daley's time almost who extolled this former Chinese premier for his adopted religion they both had plenty invested in, a whole new war for one thing.

Stalin supported him too, Becca said, for *his* church. But which government was Daley referring to?

The American government during the Cold War and getting ready for Indochina.

Had she dropped off? Yes and no.

What came next she couldn't have known. Slowly though:

"Except that the . . . whatchoocallit deposition . . . to your surprise . . . was how it came to it . . . how you got . . . something in the *times* that touched her . . ."

"The times?" he said.

". . . not your lawyering . . ."

"How the devil do you know?" Daley up on his elbow.

"Don't worry, I'll be gone before you know it," was the reply.

A bare hillside in the country came up close and he listened to a car motor slip past in the street.

"A woman . . . not the first to get pushed out the door," said the dull, concerned, why-so-slow voice for no one or him. Becca was not done. This person next to him. "Couple of hundred feet above the ground. When she got the heave-ho, the bum's rush you say here, no more than that. Less. We're not sure." Like falling it was not unexpected though coming from this woman a surprise if he understood her.

"And three men. Their names probably you don't recall either."

"*I* don't?"

They drifted, and yet presently he must have felt her voice had plotted its way.

"Isn't it you? It came up," she said. After the Sunday night they had had and after sleeping for a while, to wake grudgingly to his touch and the deposition probably an encapsulated *So long,* and to wrangle over words in the middle of the night like a longtime couple or professionals disputing exact terms, and despite all this physical familiarity with someone he'd learned too much about too fast yet nothing much (or all *changed* to what? . . . to her): learned too fast, it came to him smartly, in order to learn not too late and to head into sleep again and then this.

"I didn't get her name," said the person beside him, "if it was even known."

"And a girl, a teenage girl they needed where they were going, a fifth individual—in addition to the woman."

"In the main compartment," she went on, "of an old French helicopter. Do you call it a bay?"

"No."

# 9

SHE WAS POSSESSED OF SOME HEARSAY IT CAME TO HIM, FOR DALEY had had the foreglimpse, an impersonal voice awake then half asleep again but not now.

The woman had a name all right, his sheet anchor her life in the balance and he would wonder listening to the bizarre authority of this telling sprung on him how Becca could have known of her. The woman named Than. A thing repeating itself through this person with him for it could only have been reported to her. A report of a report. Yet that she had gotten around to it finally, through sleep even. It was no secret, it was public; but he had no call to hear such history from her, his in part. From this unknown person, and why would she tell him?

Telling so that over him came a chill of overtaking on its way elsewhere no doubt. The inside of an aircraft, a quite cumbersome in theory (and borrowed) but interesting aircraft: the overhead, an arched feeling standing, and furnishing it forward at sunset plain width and length; and receiving in all its plain design aft the cavernous space slightly upward tilted toward the tail summoning him to be in it like a building he was already in, loosely containing at *its* forward end persons being taken somewhere and others.

"They were to be questioned?"

Was it a question he was being asked so the tone of voice curved back inside *him*? She'd been doing this since that first Monday-afternoon *It's-you* phone call (some small danger from the get-go half question *You have someone with you?*).

"The teenage girl," Becca's voice so near to him went on, "*her* hands were *not* bound." (How did the voice know that?) "The pilot took you along. You were beside him . . ."

The controls were the wing commander's not his, of this (this time) not wing but cameo Alouette, old French copter that had been sitting somewhere near the border (though the wing commander was commanding semiunofficially, Daley was certainly not about to tell the girl, the voice that knew and didn't know, nor that Daley himself had ever even touched the controls before that day except in thought, that old French or the smaller helicopters (all pretty much the same) looking ahead in case or out of curiosity (as to driving a vehicle), as a boy watches a truck driver double clutch (though this was no truck, for you could go up or down or peel off, three-D and everything in between, though here what you had in the way of choice was necessity pretty much. The pedal, the pitch lever, gauges, this territory-in-motion of the cabin that was to be given him suddenly as a surprise act of territorial aggression (but it didn't work), by a wing commander without a wing tonight but commanding with some little wit or as even a risky dare who knew what Daley was capable of. A chill in the brain, semiconductor material with an on/off switch, but a quality still no colder than warm of premise or ground-breaking future conclusion spreading in Daley. Hearing now a naked woman telling it who had little right to it who hadn't been born then and had little right to it. Though things just like it anyone could know and by eyewitness testimony for it had been public once upon a time. Hardly even a statistic, twenty-five years later. Part of the good old-fashioned history.

"It was a little outrageous. The pilot took you along. Weren't you the one? We don't know why you were there except you knew the woman who was to be questioned with the three men . . . Vietcong: is that the right word?"

"Who is '*we*'?" Daley could kick her out for less than that. That "we." He had thought she was close to him. (It was in some round-about way the brother, Daley didn't trust either of them.) He felt her honesty beside him still.

"The woman was the important one"——Becca was awake, even aroused——"what was her name?"

"Her name was Than."

"Than?"

"That was her name."

"She sat on the floor."

"That's right." Daley could see her up against the bulkhead her hands behind her. Distinct in her features and demeanor from the three men who turned their heads this way and that to see. And from the eleven- or twelve-year-old girl her hands palm down on the floor long legged who seemed balanced in her midsection against the bulkhead, yes, her upper body, a child.

"She sat on the far side of the men against—I don't know how to refer to it." Becca meant the woman Than, not the girl.

But Daley, from her body up against him no less, believed she was adding quite exactly—where did it come from—to this curiously true account to which she had no right, Daley would have sworn this "bulkhead" (he said then) detail did not come quite from her source, which was not written down.

"The bulkheads, okay, if that is what you call them, of the converted multipurpose chopper—same word you use for watertight partitions in a lakes cutter belowdecks," said the speaker in bed beside him in a dry voice of obligation, even a message before she slept, before she left (well he would give her that). "The others, perhaps thrown around by the aircraft on the floor, they were guarded by automatic weapons, which doubled as clubs."

"I'm tired of hearing about automatic weapons," said Daley.

"And in . . . the cockpit?"

"Yes. The forward compartment . . ."

"Two men: a pilot; and another up there . . ."

"I wasn't remotely qualified."

"Kneeling."

Kneeling? Now how did she know this? She hadn't been holding out on Daley, he always knew that of her, convinced of it as he was offended, annoyed now, abused really in the night: yet dismayed for her, she might be in danger or he had made a choice of her.

"Armed of course," said the young woman, he could feel the hum of her voice through his skin. "Able to take over," she said.

"Believe me, I wasn't qualified."

"If you like. Observing, but able to take over."

"To take over?" Daley said. "An old Alouette?"

The young woman sighed with the same instinct.

He had not been qualified, whatever she thought she knew. A soldier on his knees, full of suspicion, watching the sunset through the windows and the prisoners, and anxious as to the questioning to come at the other end and one of the marines taking a look at two rifles on the floor taken from the people in custody, an AK and some old popper that was French if it was anything. "It was a ferry. I don't have to listen to this," Daley almost lied, hearing himself. "You're a fool," he said, at last, for he thought she was asleep.

When he was weary, too. Measuring the years and the person who came up off the bulkhead and fought with what she had. Her feet and head, shoulders, hips, teeth, eyes too, some of her, all of her. Moments, seconds, with all the terrible boringness of Time, registered in series by a somewhat out-of-place sergeant ordered along for the ride because he knew some of the people in custody.

And they him.

Or the woman Than at least, who the wing commander had taken pleasure in discovering was someone Daley valued. If only in a small frame.

"It's not true," he said. "People don't live in our memories. That's not what it is."

Becca chuckled. She didn't belittle anything. It was experience.

History by and large available to anyone. But she wanted to pass it on to him. Why did she? What was his already. Someone else's. Seemed like her brother. Yet always hers, you knew. But didn't know well enough.

"There was a scuffle," she said resuming after thought, after dozing off maybe.

History is not memory at all, it came to Daley. "Your brother told you this," he said to Becca. "Who the devil is he. Because you didn't read it."

"Him partly," the voice not unkind, not hurried next to him. "The men . . ." Becca at it again, ". . . kicking each other, angry about something, it was thought."

Had Becca phoned Daley with all this in mind? He did not think so.

"The woman you call Than crossing her legs and leaning forward. Maybe it wasn't Than but the child," Becca added. "It is known that he gave you the controls. The plane could have blown up, the helicopter I mean. Where was the door? I see it so plain but where is the door?"

"Near enough."

"But you. And the pilot. The woman was to be questioned on arrival. Where? The pilot from Ohio, the officer."

"Planning on getting home for a Thanksgiving football game,"
Daley said. "No Taiwan for him."

"The sun retrieving its last orange fire," the voice said beside him,
"and to the left darkness sinking in across triple-tier forest cover, like
a lake, a brilliant, late surface, you think of wind." He liked that. He
liked that wind very much. But how did Becca know? Knew more
about the forest than—of course she did.

"I had zero experience."

"He trusted you."

"He had another thing coming."

# 10

IT WAS BEGINNINGS THAT WERE LOST. HIS RESPECT FOR THAN. HE
wouldn't even begin to explain it to Becca, his apprehension of
what Than would say. What the wing commander had had in mind, or
just envy and lust. He remembered another man, a South Vietnamese
attack bomber pilot (former), who had been excused from the job at
the last moment, and that was why Daley came along.

Voices aft, abrupt movements of shod feet. A scuffle. The sounds
behind him now the pilot processed and cursed. The pilot pulled back
and they were upward of three hundred feet above the tree cover, the
sun lowering but the aircraft inhabits its own many-dimensional capa-
bility still . The pilot the soldier on his knees knew well perhaps, perhaps not. Yet respected because he was ready always. For what,
though? He was never unready for what he wanted to be ready for.

In the compartment where the woman Than has a leg out and gets
over onto one knee and one of the men kicks out and his foot is taken
by a marine and wrenched swiftly and you felt the wind pulling and
heard the huge rotor inside *and* out now. The wing commander
though is pointing at the pedals, he has picked his moment.

The four who were bound had twisted onto their knees and were on their feet backing toward the tail. They had the wild dignity available to those whose hands are bound. Orange plastic cord that tightened the more you loosened it. Struck in the chest with a rifle, one man went down onto his side, the other smashed in the knee knelt and was struck again in the ear, fell over and tripped the third man. They were trying to get up, silent, not a team, a soldier with a rifle butt standing over them. Daley was on his feet.

"The marine pilot Lon, or Hog as he was also known, stood up and said something, we would assume," she resumed.

The wing commander turned his face to you, his scalp shining through the thin, pale brush cut, the mustache, that mean Ohio intelligence risking ground fire, a broadness across the cheekbones and a sore on the upper lip, a short guy who had arranged a pass for Daley and was curiously informed about Daley. What was the pilot laughing for? He had made a joke at the expense of the man getting up next to him.

"Some small thing happened," Becca said with certainty. "That is, before he went aft to deal with the scuffle in the after compartment, which was an opportunity for him wasn't it."

"You don't know," Daley said, the girl was grotesquely sleepy, obliged almost to not think of what she would do.

"What did he say?"

"'Let's go,' he said," but to everyone, Daley said.

The pitch lever in his inexperienced hand, he had known at once how to feel the lift swung by the rotor disk overhead but coming up underneath, and dole it back like a tiller you won't swing too far across the wind. Yet as instantly with the cyclic stick an instinct to bring the chopper low, extremely close above the tree cover, the mobile, vulnerable ship, containing too many purposes, too low to insert insurgents, low enough to attract fire. Voices aft, when he turned to see what he saw the knowledge that the officer who'd stuck him with this in an impulse of violent intent long instinct in his readiness knew the loss of altitude was intended: though not the equally purposive-seeming roll to starboard that made the floor a sliding surface you could correct the other way if you had been able.

The rotor, Daley thought, tilting them away from the sunset and back, which the girl did not know, was perhaps all the chopper has since done for us: giant construction crane guidance, cattle and traffic control, air-sea rescue, firefighting, earthquake emergency removals, ice removal from power lines, crop sowing, crop dusting, basically whatever you want, freedom of multidimensional impulse if the wind doesn't flip you like a hang glider—main blades whirling clockwise, the chopper replies counter (sort of) he had known then by luck for that was all he had time for—equal and opposite thing, which is where the vertical rotor on the tail boom of a single-rotor machine comes in, push/pull, the whole thing can sound like a dump truck and feel like it's going to pieces.

"He knew you," she said.

"'Course. There we were."

"No. He knew you."

"Something."

"He made sure you were in his seat, holding course before he went back."

"I didn't qualify till long afterward. In law school was when I qualified!"

"*Law* school!" she exclaimed.

"A door slid."

"You heard a wind—"

"A wind."

"—or heard the engine now outside *and* inside," said the voice next to him. "Feet, scuffling, I don't know what."

"Why no copilot, if you know so much?"

"The woman Than knew what was happening. She could do little more. The men kicking each other. What did you see at the controls?" Daley swung out of bed, the carpet cool under his feet. The girl in bed said, "There must have been a copilot but he could have left at the last minute."

She was right. Though she had no right to be.

A bald dark hill ran under, and another, brown, and he didn't know what to do—to do, not how to fly this thing, which seemed secondary and second nature, but what to do. What did Than know, the woman sitting up against the bulkhead, her hands behind her? She knew what was happening. There was a moon beginning somewhere. Another hill came up and vanished under them, and tree cover took its place picked out like that burnished lake by the sun spreading its terrible color off to the right, to the left darkness sinking across the forest.

"I turned around and I saw her eyes. Who knows who they were on? And Lon pulling her forward."

Becca seemed passive for such a questioner; but she was outrageous, it was in all her talk he thought, her knowledge, her lack of it, she was outrageous, acting was outrageous, her history, her studies, her philosophy whatever *it* was. And something came to Daley, that she did have a right to know these things she mysteriously knew, or took the right. "We know what happened to them, the older ones," she said, disquieted in her own right, though her "we" was borderline criminal. "I'm sorry. The witness I understand wasn't sure about the girl, the young one, I mean exactly how it happened."

One of the three men backing against the power of two soldiers who had him by the arms like they were taking him somewhere, were Daley to describe it to her, which he would not. And the pilot talking to the woman as the hatch door slid again and someone shouted at Daley who could see nothing but glare and evening sky and tree cover, he had pushed the stick and aimed low, low as he dared, the landing gear like a snowplow on a dry street. He knew exactly what he had done and what he had done with the throttle for they had slowed but felt them slide and he had wondered if those were branches or leaves forgetting all he knew about those trees, which were not two hundred feet below, for the woman waited for him to do something.

The woman was prepared for anything, and nothing, she gave him nothing in her eyes yet it was Daley turned around in the seat whom she looked at, and when he had had to turn back to what he was doing —almost didn't have to tell the young Canadian woman now for she would with her superior mind probably hit upon it but he did not tell her, did not describe any of it—when he had had to turn back to what he was doing he realized that the three men were gone and he didn't know what Than was seeing and they were under two hundred feet he thought when he tried to go left with the stick, he didn't know why except to tilt the body of the aircraft away from the starboard hatchway having seen when he looked that Lon with some help was trying to hustle or shoulder the woman out and pry her fingers loose of him, Daley could have crashed them and saved nobody, which he imagined then and always recalled—no one had to remind him he had told Sook one day and his brother knew and who else? And when he stabilized the fuselage looking to hover with zero tilt overhead and could practically see, really see, the noseless ship clipping the tops of the trees, he was higher than he imagined, and he stood and he saw only the teenage girl a soldier was attempting to haul forward yet almost to the *left* side of the compartment (hard to tell) punch him when Lon grinning tried to sweep Daley aside with the French rifle and, failing, reached around Daley for the stick and lifted them abruptly into the terrible sky and slipped into the seat, as Daley reached again blindly for the stick seeing still with his own eyes what happened to the teenage girl in the little black shirt, gone into the bloody September twilight, and that made five.

"I don't have to listen to this," Daley said over her, the phone ringing at this hour. But he had been the one remembering, whether she could hear or just guessed. A kick in the head, a touch on the eardrum for he saw that hearing was touch, arresting vibration anyway. "Well, tell me what happened to them then. Tell me that?" he said.

"You almost crashed them," Becca said looking up at him in the dark, "but you were not incompetent, you knew what you were doing."

"That's a rumor."

"You had a purpose somewhere."

"Somewhere behind me."

Cold now, he didn't know what he could have done against the outrage and detail of Becca's talk, a charity in it unheard previously this week. What was the relief? Her purpose here? But knowledge wasn't power; thought was. The hatch clear—a marine and a soldier, one of them at least not enthusiastic to be defending against four comparatively small Asians who were bound, unlike the fifth, who was petrified. Joined by the skipper for a last-ditch gig, how the five did not arrive wherever they were going. Unless running down through the air they slipped through the waves of foliage, boughs giving, for they had been meant for the estuary, the shallows better still.

Becca's kind of information was common knowledge, common as her hand on his leg now. Where, still, did it come from? Where did common knowledge come from? No. Where did this girl's share of it come from? Born two years later almost, 1972, late August. A lynching post, a crystal casket, General Lee in Brooklyn.

But when did she come by this? In the past twenty-four hours? For if so, then we would know where she had come by it. Her brother, twice her age—it put the last week in question. Not even a week.

Daley was sitting down hunched on the bed. Why did she pull this in bed? It was a question. He let the phone ring and slipped back into bed and ran his arm under her head careful not to pull the hair. All this history of hers, education, commitment, superiority to all the alternatives he had not resisted for years.

"*I* don't need to get interrogated," he said, doubtless *being* someone; "I *know* about it."

"You're not being. You're being told. It's a relief passing it on," said Becca, "I'm the hinge."

"This is what I get," he grumbled. It was that brother of hers this all came from, wasn't it?

Her mother too.

Peggy in her piece?

No one's anyone there.

The mood had changed. Back to normal.

The gold comb became a tortoiseshell. There was a lot of drinking, I would say.

She got locked out a couple of times. She's got a mouth.

Peggy?

Mom.

She got locked out and then what did she do?

Went away for a few days.

Did Becca remember this?

Hardly.

Hardly, eh?

I wasn't thought of.

This wasn't *his* mother . . .

Daley thought she would change the subject.

It was Dad he wanted to join.

He followed his father.

Yes, he followed him.

I guess it didn't work out.

Why? said Becca.

He ended up with you.

That was years later. In the beginning Dad disapproved of him. He went away. Dad got him the job at the distillery.

Great. And Dad would lock your mother out? Where would she go, next door? When was this?

Nineteen seventy. 'Seventy-one. Can't hold on to it. Can't put it down.

That's true. Who can't?

Yeah, who? Becca laughed. He was glad. He was imagining the problems in her case. And managing her leaving. She had her near hand on him.

She went to Bruce, said Becca.

She went to Bruce. At the distillery?

The town where it was.

Which town was that?

The distillery was in Windsor.

She went clear to Windsor to see Bruce? Could that have been Seagrams? said Daley; or Walker? *Bruce! Bruce!* I speak of him as if I knew him or wanted to.

You'd have things to talk about.

The one-woman show with all the voices drifted into extreme clarity half of it gone leaving a foursome passing in the dark room, forming and crisscrossing and still. You should stay in the play no matter what he says, Daley said.

He says stay in it.

No matter what he says. No matter why he says it or who he is.

I'm through with you all. Daley had said something. He wanted the best for her. It was the middle of the night between Sunday and Monday, deeply awake yet touched by a freedom of rest and sleep.

Don't throw away that loft, that great space.

I will put aside what I wish.

Daley had given Becca the run of his house. Leaving the key on the hook in the kitchen meant she could use it, he realized. Or the garden. She didn't have to ask. He didn't take the house for granted with her in it. She was in it. How did it become more useful? Just that fixed structure with someone running around in it from place to place, why was a thermostat up in the parlor and why had he placed the furnace at the south end of the cellar almost under the garden flagstones?

You were not a sympathizer, Becca returned to Than. What were you?

With Than I was in a way.

With her.

I remember that she rebuilt a small, palm-roofed house, we had another word for it. Stones had been dropped on it from I don't know where. Like rain, she said. I didn't ask. She never described her family but they were nearby. The instances of this were widespread, what happened.

And the men, said Becca actually impatiently.

It was pretty common.

My mother told me about it. It wasn't you at all.

That your brother learned of.

It was the event. But data awaken in him like old dreams. All this history. He didn't go to college through all of that.

And your mother.

Who was with him when he first heard it.

They must have hung out together.

She went to see him. Later he didn't work at the distillery anymore. Dad accepted him, was the way it went.

Or the other way around, said Daley.

Drink wasn't his thing.

What was?

He worked in a garage. That was his . . . Well. (Becca was on her elbow looking at him.) The garage was his microscope, that was the hinge that turned him toward a new home. He discovered the compactor and the telephone. A mine of scrap all along the lakes border region as I understand it. (As she *understood* it? Daley thought—as if maybe she didn't, or it was Canadian/English objective, polite, distant.) An empire waiting for him, she went on. He lived at home for a long time. Surprising when he was so logical.

Daley didn't know for sure, though he could have put it in the form of a question. Though he didn't care enough. A brother with a much, much younger half sister and protecting her perhaps in a family like that.

And that close to his stepmother? Daley asked.

Sure. Let's go to sleep now. Who was that phoning?

It could be anyone. Daley heard the breeze off the river. I think it was my brother.

You would know.

Four or five people he could think of at this hour. A crank call. It could be for you.

True. Some crank.

A whole string of people I could name. Whom I never wanted to know. Your Beck, your brother, your landlord landlady, your lawyer, your play.

And me you never wanted to know?

You're plenty. Well I never wanted to know your business. Beck and your landlord—I found out it's a woman—and your brother and all . . .

He's a businessman, said Becca. And a good one. Let's go to sleep. A real head for detail. Terrifying.

Names.

Daley's a pretty common name. It was the incident he knew about.

The incident.

Only that.

A pretty common incident over there.

Well.

A statistic. So in the back of his mind he put one and one together.

My mother told me. He told me too.

Secondhand thirdhand, Daley said, puzzled. Doesn't matter. But these people, these people, he wondered if he knew what he meant by secondhand. A head for detail. A bald head, Daley thought. The brusque, self-important, guarded exit Saturday night, Becca far behind

Bruce standing in stage light, the voice-over transfixing her; this was the man, what had he said? *Detroit.*

*He* told you? said Daley. Why?

When I was young. And my mother once. It was her feeling for him. *And* Dad.

A family to stay clear of.

Daley didn't ask how they knew, or when they had identified him with the woman and the three others, the four others. He was damned if he would. Becca changed again.

She must have been a dangerous person.

I was standing beside her in the street, Daley said, flattering himself for the moment with "history" told authoritatively to a young woman, it was seductive and flattering. A funeral was passing. She gave me one of those quick nods. Not untypical but we didn't know one another.

What did she say?

# 11

*H*OW ARE YOU?
Like a learned phrase.

But then: *Who are you with?*

I didn't always know what she meant. She would say, *What happened?* It wasn't clear who she was working for. She said maybe they would build a better looking embassy. My brother came out there on a civilian construction project, residential housing to get the GIs out of this piecemeal billeting they had that had become a risk. Who knows how he worked that? Probably I do. Than asked about him. Three times we met. Once in a downpour that came out of nowhere on the wind. She said I was very strong. She was someone's daughter. She had survived that. I told her quite a lot. Not what she wanted maybe. We were seen walking. The captain thought I liked her, and when he saw me at a well-known café he tried to ask me about her. He counseled me. I saw through it. She was under observation. It was one of those friendly questionings.

What he did, Becca said.

Sex. Beauty. Though if there were an authority I'd wager he didn't think her beautiful. He said she had a brother and this brother had been seen at the Long Binh base in a warehouse and at the bowling alley. Pick him up, I said. Captain was trying to get home for a couple of weeks. (Which bowling alley anyhow?)

What he did.

I didn't get dumped out of an Alouette at three hundred feet. What you do with a chopper converted to observation.

You were driving it. The person beside Daley had changed again. Contempt can encourage sleep too.

Nowhere.

*Detroit*, the brother had said to Daley. Scrap metal. Metal scrap and residues. Beverage cans. Alu cable. Brass turnings. Propeller scrap. Ship propellers across the great glacier-gouged inland seas. Boiler tanks. Nickel tubing. Zinc blowings. Lead dross. Battery plates. Drained batteries. Old zinc carburetors. A small empire. Given to background checks. History. Perhaps a master of the phone.

No, a stepson once upon a time to a young Canadian woman who had made common cause with him when she had a row with her husband. Who was the young man's father, who had left him somewhere. Her husband's son, he showed up, left, and went to Windsor not far away, a job. There she visited him. And Windsor?

Well Windsor's not a particularly hot town, said Daley. It's changed, of course. Upscale gambling casino planned, restaurants, health club, probably chapel on the premises, maybe it's all in place. I don't follow Windsor.

This woman might as well be asleep.

You take the tunnel to get there from Detroit. I guess there's a bridge now.

She made those sounds like whispering laughter that were sounds of equality, inviting you to it.

Half hour drive.

Which way you going? Becca said drowsily.

He was sure her half brother, the stepson, wasn't Becca's real father, but it did occur to him. Enough closeness already without that. Canada a mixed bag like here more than a mystery. Her brother picking up on Daley's name was something.

What had happened since Wednesday? What had Daley done? Said no to Becca (though that was Monday on the phone). Pursued her, fair enough. Loved her. Talked at length and walked, definitely walked. He put the question: Did you know that I was the one?

Was she asleep?

On Monday when you . . . ?

Daley understood then that somehow she had not known. How did he understand this? Because she would have said. And now she was objectively asleep.

Daley did not sleep at once or see himself after a week's absence running the river path at dawn. Yet just possibly looking into the primary residence case not after all postponed indefinitely, and the action brought against Becca with materials mostly supplied by her, *her* records, *her* life, for in these rather special cases you provide the hatchet and even sharpen it for the landlord—land*lady* here, though living in Daytona—so that he/she can get rid of you while urging always a settlement, "to stop the bleeding" in our American way of speech. Circling this prospect, was the prospect of Daley too, it all stood waiting, somehow empty, for a voice to come and turn the statues into people or good solid furniture, table and chairs. And was he the circles downward, inward? He couldn't tell and wouldn't but would take stock in the morning when Becca was leaving, for this was the point of her telling his story to him, wasn't it?—or she would be leaving when she heard once more his advice to stick with this second-rate but fortunate play with the title somehow hard to say— *Blood Unwed*. It did not occupy him as he went to sleep, only a thought that action, of which he had supplied little, is always compensatory, but he couldn't work it out. Or ask her just when her brother had told her the story; and *why*, why tell a young *girl*—a little girl maybe?—and how he had learned of it, and, which might be the same thing, where.

# 12

THERE WAS A CELLAR BELOW THE KITCHEN OF DALEY'S CITY HOUSE, and it was cement floored yet yielding in small remote areas of interestingly packed rubble and dirt a look of manual improvisation. On certain afternoons and nights in his experience storm and tide raised the river not in floods upon the streets yet by some seeping and tidal and half-thoughtful but no less disturbing underhanded sweep eastward. Nonetheless through what layers of long-deposited sediment above and into clefts, unseen and unknown windows in the Manhattan metamorphic base rock and under the softish landfill that, barged, buried, and powered in during the 1950s and '60s to found new margins of a larger island, he had never for some reason checked out, the waters of the Hudson might make their way as far as the west wall of neighbor Isabel's cellar and five or six times into it when Daley went down there with Isabel and the boys to see if it was worth bailing into garbage bins, and another time down into his own still-dry cellar alone with a storm lamp to listen at the west wall for Isabel's boots sloshing (he might have been dreaming of her chest in a T-shirt), and in later years there would be her boys getting horsey and taking charge, and she was next door, her own hearing acute. Between these two houses a bond, no more; community distant as sleep, close and foolish as a connecting dream, the water, the known neighbors' life and quirks, Bear being yelled at for farting, something falling down, and the history of the city a wall away.

Natural forces greater than gravity had reasserted themselves in this last or next-to-last night beside this much-too-young person Becca who had summoned a story not hers out of a reverie of hers or fatigue or some peril or an obligation laid upon her by a brother.

Forces impersonally absorbing him like exigencies of a law practice in which people stand connected to you by these forces that may be as fixed as poured stone, as gusting and engulfing in their skeined, unyielding mobility as to guarantee our comradely hardship together linked by phone and memory more than by that experience of insight into other lives less swimmingly clairvoyant than experience itself (witness the corroborated vision of Leander's midday Friday), which is known case by case or in a variegated mass distinguished by the body not dual north and south but in many poles doing their work, holding up the roof or the floor for that matter. Daley had spoken of it to his brother once who, while thinking of abalone at that moment, had actually listened carefully before looking for a guard in the place where they were, to ask for the men's room, a museum in fact, not Wolf's favorite activity.

How swiftly on a project brother Wolf guessed the character of the bearing rock. Pebble-and-boulder conglomerates, sandstone, shales: forget the long-term history, the physics and chemistry let alone the forest habitat to be swamped with toxins and crushed into branchless trunks, you guard against the clefts. It's a little more than sticking a finger in the dike. Stratified rock, your enemy is leakage under the dam, to take an example: you bound the strata by drilling holes in the upstream face along the footing plane and just grout the mother. One job, Wolf saw at once a fault line had displaced strata eastward a hundred feet at least. You don't want them moving some more; but you design a jointed structure to limit your damage if they do.

Wolf had got himself on a civilian job in Saigon during the war, a residence "hotel" for American troops (not his type of thing at all, not raw *or* challenged in structure); and only six or seven years after this low-profile gig he was over in Burma on a dam, in his mid-twenties still. There he conceived a two-way curvature along the vertical and horizontal sections that was costly but ingenious—actually old-fashioned, back to the American 1930s, but the local government thought it was as new as venture capital. How he had come up with it so quickly, whatever the subsequent nuts-and-bolts problem with those who executed his plans and partly drew them, Wolf's idea provided resistance to bending in the vertical and horizontal planes not to forget bypassing lateral struts and face walls entirely. How had Wolf made it so quickly? Made what? Questions followed him. (Phone calls to be sometimes not answered.) Not much from Saigon, where his connections had materialized in a subforeman on-site drafting job that got him there. A word from their father, Daley understood, who had been on a heart fibrillator (or *de*fibrillator?) in Cleveland at the time; a *trip* for Wolf you could say; but not to see his older brother, it seemed, who though stuck at a fire support base near the western border with unknown day-to-day prospects, had traded a favor for a forty-eight-hour pass and even a lift to Saigon to see Wolf, though this had slipped Wolf's mind (back in Ohio *un*"draft"able because of his knee).

He had a lift to Hue in the north to insinuate himself by means of a correspondent from a Texas women's magazine into the DMZ, perhaps to get into trouble. He wasn't headed for Hanoi. Hanoi wasn't ready for him yet. He was fond of connecting his knee injury at eleven/twelve with the disastrous battle of Ap Bac near Saigon, which had occurred the same week and his father had talked about the catastrophic fiasco for days, the Diem people particularly Colonel Dam who would not take the advice of the U.S. adviser Colonel Vann who had had the position of the radically inferior Vietcong force nailed in advance like tracing paper to a drawing board.

"Always a mercenary," Della's take years later—"how's his knee holding up, by the way?" The man who gave us, *What are you doing with Della?* though Daley didn't bear messages of that kind, which was to him not her in any case. Wolf not a mercenary; it wasn't money.

Wolf's rebuilt knee on snowy days remembered beyond the bike smash to a scuffle with his brother at Thanksgiving: Wolf kidded by Bill for not knowing how to put a lighted match in his mouth. Wolf's daring had been challenged; and wrestling silently on the cement floor of the garage set off a thought, nothing to do with scraped elbows and ripped jeans, that continued like a capsule of resolve inertially for weeks to drive Wolf to try his dirt bike on a treacherous street in January. Bill joined him in the icy road but that was the extent of it, not a joint vision.

You wanted to kill him, you wanted to not kill him. Tried to stuff a tangerine in his mouth when you were six. Why had he approached an early-morning parked moving truck like a unknown gorge crossing? Why did he have to demolish his knee? To make everything harder? Not a draft dodger, we know that much. Daley dreamed of his brother. He found that he had dreamed Wolf's future. Materials turning into swaying, stretched spans and cities of population. Wolf loved his older brother but as in a dream had an odd way of showing it: to laud Daley for his "contribution" to a chopper mission that put down with five prisoners less than it had taken off with. It was the journey, not where you were going, the wing commander Lon (or Hog)'s in those days original-sounding quip, when Wolf before he left had met him and only partly antagonized him at the Clearing House café on a day when he expected, unknown to Wolf, to see Daley come walking by with a local friend.

After the war Wolf really found someone. "See?" he said to Daley. It was like his later question, What was Daley doing with Della? What kind of bro question was that? He just had never liked Della. Nowadays we trust our gut. (Daley would never have given his brother a full account of the riverfront slashing. There's not supposed to be one, but there is.)

What was *Ruley* doing with *Della*? was more like it. Nothing much. This Daley concluded on the way back from Australia. During a stopover on the Coast. In fact in a Boeing company helicopter he'd spectacularly borrowed to swing his nieces (though not quite solo) up over the sound and down to a park in Tacoma and back he gave his supposed banker guest some thought. (It was still to come, the day trips, the turmoil and awkwardness, the behavior of Ruley, and the diving.) The older girl identifying the petrels out the chopper window and then the curious coinciding of Ruley Duymens's intervention into the dance company's financial affairs with the slashing the next morning unleashed some doom of freedom in Daley's life that meant he had little to fear from Ruley. Here in Seattle, a special-events uncle was about it, three thousand miles away most of the year, but not only a pilot; for he would also sit for four hours in the TV room with the girls, as Roma and Wolf came and went, and brought him the phone when the veteran friend called from Boeing and both girls were on his lap. And when Daley punched off, he punched in his home number but then didn't put the call through, Roma had come in and was lecturing the girls, who, in his arms and no doubt processing everything, scarcely noticed.

They wanted to see the scar on his arm but screamed when he

rolled up his shirt sleeve. Wolf said it looked too fresh to be a war wound but . . . Bill had a way of not talking. (Wolf was planning a trip south into California to check on abalone research recently under way and wanted Bill along, they would visit a community of Southeast Asians, with an obscure disorder, hearing or seeing, not sure which.)

But time for Daley to get on a plane for New York. Lotta heard some of the story, Ruley who picked up on the umbrella got some more; Daley's closest neighbor acquired it initially with her own eyes within the hour of its happening, though this was the first part for her. Isabel had found a fine dusting of soot on her street windows one early morning—at a closer look a minute speckle of green (or blackened green) units seeming to multiply as she examined their sun-sheened sparkle around a quarter of seven. And wondering what her boys would ask to be paid for the job, she looked out through this delicate screen or field and saw Daley coming back from his run. A dark towel wrapped around his left forearm, blood thickening the terry cloth. His Asian friend Sook with him.

Her phone cord dragging the instrument off the table so she could keep an eye on next door, a few minutes later he came back down the steps, blood already soaking through a fresh towel, the Asian out in the middle of the street between parked cars trying to sight a taxi coming west, turning then to help Daley to the corner some fifty to sixty yards and an uptown cab, and he needed help now. Where was Della, the wife? Isabel wanted to know, hearing a distant alarm on the third floor go off onto snooze alert, five minutes more for her sons as she planned her day and was concerned for her neighbor and, wanting to run after the two men, she instinctively like a mistake dialed the Daleys only to hear Della's resigned voice and hang up.

Why did he tell Isabel? He dismissed the incident, it was like a dream honestly; yet he told her a full kind of story when she phoned him at the office, he took the time, she always remembered and so did he, they were contiguous neighbors, separate but near, even then. It was the exertion, this run he took at five forty-five or six in the morning, the self-reliant profiles of a fuel barge and tug stack making upriver at dawn, you could make your day then and there. Even with two six-inch steel blades sniffing him out. (My God, Bill, Isabel breathed, it's our neighborhood.) The canopy of the umbrella had collapsed, ribs bent; the black silky cotton material rent—all, though, into something else. This didn't come first.

A hundred yards south a couple sitting on a bench were carrying on about something and stood up suddenly. A wired vertical energy, looking at the water not to look at each other. Not derelicts. People extended, white collar up all night, Daley shifted to a passing lane without a thought. But they were there still.

Daley had felt springy, weightless, uniquely purposeless, the spirit of alert; enclosed happily in a final beginning. Airborne in the quads, bare, only half mortal, contained and empty the way the early day, or dawn with its memory of darkness touches you with—this contemptible two on one he would kick them to death and dump them into the river.

"Got 'ny money?" All-nighter lady, leather jacket, leather skirt, murderous black legs, she was quite green-eyed in the fine sallow and wear of her face. (Absolutely, breathed Isabel on the phone.) The woman. If it was letting blood he had felt, he experienced a lightness too, like time passing or thinking dissolved. What you remember is what you get, what you tell yourself you remember; a little dream of someone else, too, his wife gratefully asleep curled under the covers at home ("the hostile day," was her view of early morning). A dark slice of blood about to spill over along the forearm. The blood arriving slow not at all a thing deep in you or pushed by the heart, you remembered it could theoretically start squirting, it came now, cautious as an animal.

A man Sook he knew very well, extremely well, was running toward him, a black towel tucked into the neck of a red sweatshirt, a quick-stepping Korean in white sweatpants. Sook. (Absolutely, said Isabel.) How they got away, how Sook observed them from a distance and stayed with Daley. They negotiated the quiet blocks seriously. "It's okay buddy it's okay, I owe you one, I owe you two, you forget, hey we should be going to Saint Vincent's, you know what I mean?"—and rememberingly to Daley's house and sleeping wife, the black towel not tight enough upon the life and death of the cut, the two cuts congruently having somehow missed the ulnar artery that rises from the wrist on the other side from the thumb.

Lucky that Sook hadn't taken off after the knife people; not then. (Why home, Isabel wanted to know and not to the hospital?) Della dreaming under the covers at six-thirty, six forty-five after a late night when a potential backer had introduced himself to the company. (Yes, yes.)

Had this story had a point to satisfy Lotta without the going-home part, which he hadn't told her? For Della wasn't at the pier. (But . . . home . . . "I saw you pass my window with Sook and go up the steps.")

Here was what he had decided to tell Isabel. Up the carpeted stairs, then breathing for a moment at Della's emergency bedside half waking her without a word; a moment he forced on her—yet following him now, naked; and at the bathroom threshold, no farther, her reaction astounding or absent as imagination as he stood by the antique sink his bloodied free hand unwrapping the ruined towel. Yet she was startled then as a woman hearing Sook coming up from below calling out. Or registering danger out of the past when she had been chosen by Daley, an independent soul who had made it up out of nothing he knew about; persuading her with silence about a time she abhorred, and with a story of his first deposition after the second bar exam try. Not even reaching for a bathrobe, his wife had gone back to bed. The story in her head.

"No, you're right, let's go." He met Sook at the head of the stairs, the live gash hidden again but not from his chest, his house, the bedrock of his motion, his wife, his unshockable mind.

Odd, to say the least. A wake-up call. A snooze alert, no more than.

Did Sook reach the bedroom door from the landing? No he did not. What did he know? The basic facts upon which he did not build because he had to get his friend to the hospital, in fact walk west away from where they were actually going in order to get an early cab.

# 13

HIS HOUSEGUEST WAS LEAVING, HE FELT SURE, AND HE WAS UP EARLY. Not early enough to run but to be here in case something happened. It was what he understood he was doing, up betimes, dressed in trousers and shirt, in excellent new shoes, beautifully balanced shoes, springy, English, the new soles slippery on the bedroom carpet. Tiptoeing out, he saw she had changed position, flat out on her stomach, her arm flung across onto his side, a woman. Get out of there quietly, the pattern the now quite bare sycamore blurred through the bedroom shade. The purpose of these few days hadn't been the war, its remembering long done, or archaeological burial, or documenting abuse, though you could probably find against the brother and the family; nor, through Ruley Duymens, to remember Della. A doubling of Daley's horizons, faintly befuddling, emerged as a reason for whatever had happened he would gladly admit (extending even to a survey of this house, window sashes, front stoop risers, no dishwasher; a forgotten scrapbook in the kitchen bookcase by the window, an unearthing Becca had expected him to receive with ripeness and delight and fear in his face, and she was momentarily through with him. She had lifted the pages, the light and map and weight of snapshots, figure skater, speedboat, porched old folks in summer white, Della at the sawmill, Della singing on a stage between an American flag and another he didn't know.

Some training he had absorbed as purposeless as practical he was sure, leaving an emptiness to be filled promptly by the city, the motion of the river, thought, risk. He was not surprised that Becca existed, he was relieved, and he felt tender toward her future, it was in him, he would live with it. And he would like to make her a cup of coffee for the road, for the street he thought, descending the carpeted stairs. He heard the phone ring above him and below him and he now hastened to the basement and all that she knew, it seemed, and glad she had found something in a remark of his (a reply, really) that an architect took action and made something that joined what had already been made but that did not itself have knowledge of . . . he forgot the last part in his haste now, but it was waiting for him. He had a decent grasp of our limits. She saw him as an aid to navigating the housing courts he suspected, and on his own time he had availed himself of the witness list and made a phone call about a name that might have been a private detective testifying to Becca's occasional whereabouts but probably not a detective, and she hadn't been asked to produce airline ticket dates for when she was in Canada. Yet mysteriously wondering what he would do (and with the house, its undreaming floors that had come to mind in sleep, he knew that much), he was thinking as he caught the phone after three rings striding across the kitchen in his slippery new shoes that the hanging-out hadn't been aimless it just hadn't had much of a future over time or at least an aim over a number of days, six or seven, a thought somehow dragging along behind the primary residence case that must have been in his mind during the night.

"It's me," said Helen's voice at exactly seven-thirty, "you back from your run? Just kidding." No, he wasn't, he said at once. Daley saw the sharpness in her eyes, the dark expertly fluffed warmth of her hair, her body as he had given her a one-armed hug at the open door of the taxi Wednesday night. She liked it that he wasn't back from his run yet. Was this a good time to . . . ? Sure—she hadn't had a chance to talk . . . that nice young man the other night the bartender didn't know what he was in for, played it by ear, a lot of talk.

"Only way to go." Daley braced for what came next, for he knew Helen had returned to the theater Saturday, he could not imagine alone. (One thing, he did not have to answer, asked or not, about Becca, though he preferred to answer anything asked—the blow Wednesday and Thursday and Friday nights, the time spent, her nature, nothing volunteered, she had been apparently fucking Barry albeit briefly in the dressing room Wednesday night at intermission—the man who had just drawn blood from her nose; or Daley's possibly penultimate employment agency client the young man who had sat in front of them and of whose Friday Daley had had such a full and true if not, since he didn't believe in it (clairvoyant) vision that had paral-

leled in his experience a number of other like occurrences he would
have hesitated to mention to his late wife Della sometimes extending
into a case only of foresight (the name Daley would put to it), that he
would only tell Donna who, coincidentally confirming the truth of his
second sight this week, quite uncharacteristically did almost believe
in clairvoyance (a class matter? or that, Daley was almost certain, she
had had Leander on the phone late Friday afternoon?). And now
"their" breakfast guest Barry resigned to having to do something else
if he was to go on acting looking like the final such job client.

"San Francisco I meant." Yes. "Tom." Yes. "Are you by yourself?"
Yes and no, he said. "Doesn't matter, it was an awful trip." In Helen it
was no bad thing to get two or three jobs done at one go. Daley had
only the deepest respect for her. He knew her. Though she was sometimes misunderstood. "He was miserable to me. I shouldn't speak of
it, especially now." Daley heard two cars pass, one honking violently
behind the other. He had been keeping his voice down.

This was Tom, a boy now a man well into his twenties whom
Helen had taken under her wing. Years ago she had taken a vacation in
the Maritimes, in Prince Edward Island. Northern waters are
warmed there by the Gulf of Saint Lawrence, and the billowing sea-
side farmland reminded Daley of the south of England. Not that he
had flown up to P.E.I. *with* Helen. Yet she had phoned him from
Charlottetown to tell him of the remarkable harvesting she had witnessed on the west coast.

A dozen workhorses belly deep in the surf, up to their shoulders
some of them, she knew it would interest him, riders guiding the
ropes hauling huge loads of rock-growing Irish Moss off the sub-
merged sandstone ledges after a summer storm. "Storm toss" they
called it, the horses powering the harvest, the mossing, as no boat or
tractor could manage; bright and surging in the surf, dragging the
scoops of this special seaweed, holdfast algae more than real moss, to
the beach. An astonishing sight, out in the sea swells workhorses with
children riding them too. Whole families waiting on the beach to
gather the harvest and truck it to their driveways and fields to dry—
you could find it down back roads even.

And what was this Irish Moss? It was the spectacle that had moved

Helen, and she had "just" thought that the process if not the material itself would be really interesting to Daley, that was all. (She knew him.) But it was the boy she had met, a gifted delinquent, yet not really that at all, here in Charlottetown, P.E.I., eighty miles from the harvesting his own family were engaged in. She couldn't explain over the phone. Well she could but she couldn't. Yes, said Daley patiently from New York, a real moment, not that he felt sorry for Helen.

A small-for-his-age and thin fourteen-year-old boy playing the violin and singing on the street a block from the university; and dancing a jig. Pretty hard to do. I can imagine, said Daley to this woman who had tried the preceding week to persuade him to come with her, it was 1986, she was hopeful and busy and he had known her for three or four years. One thing had led to another, the boy had taken her to the coast ostensibly to see the mossing.

You should see it, Helen had told Daley. The horses, the two-wheeled wagons in the shallows, cash crop first come first served the morning after a blow. It was clear he didn't live there with his family, didn't care for the west coast or lobstering or mossing, where you could hardly earn a few dollars; even in P.E.I. period, though he played the local music.

Not that the money mattered, but it "didn't matter" to him in another way than it didn't matter to his family.

Though not his sister. She would do something maybe.

*Meanwhile* the mother and the aunt who were angry about Tom had gotten onto a social worker in Charlottetown fresh from Toronto to see what *he* could do to straighten out the boy, whose musical gift was unmistakable to almost everyone.

Daley packed a bag and caught a plane to Toronto connecting Halifax and Charlottetown. Why? That's where the boy was. Was it seeing Helen in another country? The horses arching their necks above the water at the other end of the island? Or a hundred black umbrellas one late, sticky afternoon in New York massed as one?

The boy declined to go back to the coast with them to show Daley what he had shown Helen. She phoned the family and there was nothing doing, but the next day there was. They drove across the far end of the island so he could see the mossing.

Was that the reason? A child turning her gray horse away from the lowering sun looking behind her at the heavy line they were dragging. Helen ready to get back to Charlottetown, as if it were home. Curving rows of potatoes in the fields.

They turned at a little harbor, past the fried-fish stand and the boat rental and a ranger and several people looking through telescopes at birds; and went up to the sea beach for a swim, a brown beach of the national park. They were together.

When they got back to Charlottetown she didn't find the boy for forty-eight hours. As if time were running down. The one thing he wanted was an acoustic guitar but it was not all he wanted, Helen explained it to Daley. A mystery to the mother, the boy's behavior, she didn't know who to blame, she'd told Helen. But it probably wasn't a mystery to her. Leave it to Helen.

A year later Tom was in New York under her roof, sponsored. When he went to California at sixteen, he had a place to stay in Santa Cruz with a friend of hers. Helen blamed herself. But he found work in a sound studio and stayed in touch and took her money, and she and Daley helped him get a green card. The word was that he wrote songs, he was gifted. He sang of course. Helen visited him when she could. He moved up to San Francisco, unwisely she thought, though he was happier there. He had a blues-singer kind of girlfriend. Then he was on a first-name basis with people written up in *Rolling Stone*. Helen introduced Tom, who was twenty-one by now, to a journalist, a celebrity biographer highly suspect Daley felt. This writer had moved from movies into jazz and referred to Billy Strayhorn as "Strays" and to "Red" (Norvo) and "Herbie" (Hancock) the way he had been wont to mention "Lauren" and "Shelly" and "Gore" and even "Duke" (Wayne) and "Marlon" himself (who had introduced himself graciously to this writer when they were occupying adjacent wheelchairs in a Los Angeles hospital one morning waiting for tests). Tom told the biographer he didn't have any time for those people.

Tom was twenty-five by now and very busy by San Francisco standards yet it was business that he blamed on Helen—that she came out only if she had another reason to come.

Abuse, Daley said, standing in his kitchen. That was the name for it. None of your finger shaking and no shouting. Cool, cruel, constantly brief-feeling: and mind reading, that's how some abuse gets started. Perhaps it was what drew her out to San Francisco. A subtle abuse Tom saved for when he put Helen into a cab for the airport, and this familiar indictment (could a woman not be nurturing, she wondered?) that she was complaining strangely to Daley of when their cab pulled over at the curb the following evening and he caught sight of the obscure theater and the review (which found *him*, the awkward, telling picture); and ignoring Helen's complaint and following her out of the cab, Daley found himself walking the open fault line of that time a decade gone when he had tried to make sense of his wife's more or less sudden disappearance from the scene. Tried not to. A decade plus almost two now. The house then around him like a shadow even when he was at the office. Not at all alone, to be honest. What was it? Grief? The future, it came to him staring at the phone on his office desk. The day Helen had phoned from Prince Edward Island and read him all the plane times.

Had nothing changed? Daley said he was sorry. Helen's voice became confidential, for a moment he could hardly hear her. "I don't know why I'm telling you how shitty he was to me in San Francisco." Daley was sorry. "I know you care," Helen said, "because," Helen's voice extremely confidential, "I'd really like to talk to you." Daley heard a click on the line, Becca awake.

"I could do with some of that," Daley said, "I don't know anything anymore except—"

"You should take—yes you do, Daley."

"—except what I know."

"—a trip was what I—"

A motorcycle barged past and there was something missing from its sound to Daley's ear. "I thought Barcelona," Helen said.

Daley chuckled. "Makes me sad." He heard the click again.

"He's in New York as of yesterday, do you believe it?"

"What did you do?" said Daley.

"He crashed on me. I think he wants to do this new singing . . . without words? I can't talk now. I don't know what next . . . Daley?"

"This is what's next," Daley said.

"The playwright was there Saturday, the future of that play, I had a little chat with her—well, a moment—she's got a hundred-year-old house up in Rockland County she's got some *real* problems with. I think I had company on the line," Helen said in that confidential voice again. She said good-bye.

But he had his eye on the doorway. He had heard feet on the stairs.

# 14

PRESENTLY BECCA APPEARED WEARING ONLY THE SKIMPY WHITE camisole that came down just below her navel, pigeon-toed in the doorway, sleepy girl was the impression, Her Highness or democracy fighter, hardly in traveling costume. Or she had transferred him into a scene. Nothing was understood. It was his kitchen, and he had come down here cheerfully.

Water in the kettle, fire on the range, he expected a surprise or two. She came and sat in a chair turned out from the table, her legs together for warmth, her belly there. She didn't speak of the phone; it was the new state of affairs, he thought (no doubt wrongly). "I didn't want you to leave," she said. He ground the coffee. He separated the filter and pressed it into the plastic cone on top of the pot, instinct homing on what would anger her. "Where did we get to?" she said. Daley said it was a new week and she would have to decide about the play, he was finished deciding.

She had already decided, he knew that.

There was a poet's café on the East Side that would be interested in her piece, she was wondering about costumes, a shawl, a towel. "You don't need to wear something, you make us believe it all." He was praising her partly to get rid of her, what she wanted obviously. "You're lying," she said; "you don't think it's anything." He waited for the water. He wouldn't speak of the Than story. How it arrived in bed with him got you into the brother and his history. The coffee steaming out of the wet cone was the proof of everything, of the future of his day. He would probably look into her case because he had said he would. Or had he said he wouldn't? And she would be gone, an argument at rest.

"I have to leave," Daley in his new shoes said pouring black coffee into the Charles and Diana mug 29 July 1981 that she enjoyed. The enclosing heart, a lot of hair, two strong noses, the lion with crown, the reared white unicorn with a chain from the hindquarters around to the right part of the message, THEIR MARRIAGE. Made in England but with ICH DIEN on the back. Daley took a step toward the table and slipped and a swash flew up over the rim of the cup.

She cried out and clutched her thigh, she had been scalded and she was rubbing the inside of her thigh down at her groin and the brownish hair, and then she struck at Daley backhanded and succeeded only in elbowing the cup and emptying it but not out of his hand and she tried to stand up but with her other hand she struck him in the face, his face downcast at what? The floor, the mess, her opened legs she tried to stand up on. He dropped the cup and took hold of her before she could stand upright.

"This isn't going anywhere; neither are you," she said pushing him away unsuccessfully so he tried to fling her around, he didn't know was it out of his way to get out of here and clean his shoe or dislodge her hands, her fists or hold her from further ripping his shirt which was open now? Swinging around, he fell into the chair, his thumbs under her armpits, her sideways on his lap until with her elbow she hit him again and he pulled her around, it wasn't just his doing too because she straddled him and he held her tight to keep her from fisting him in the chest.

She was sliding on his lap and gripping him with her arms around his neck and he held her wishing he could get to his belt and fuck her though she apparently was fucking him, her cheek against his ear. There was nothing for her to be up against, she wasn't straddling one leg like a little girl but his lap. Was it his belt buckle she was up against? There was nothing. She finished with him and he felt her face on his shoulder a moment. She lifted her leg off and he did not watch her go. He felt the wet under him.

She came back downstairs with the now not very big-looking backpack tight packed with what she must not leave behind when she went; and a laundry bag, was it his? She made it into a special trip for the keys because she extended her arm and dropped the two keys on the kitchen table. It was the sound of dumb, ringed keys, not money. She was irritated, chagrined; he knew her; it was probably sex. She hadn't washed. "Keep 'em," he said.

"For your next guest," she said, but she was amused: they might make a sentimental keepsake. She went back upstairs. He thought there was a suitcase left upstairs. He found a windbreaker in the dining room. He left in the windbreaker, the buttonless shirt, stained trousers. He went down the street.

He was at the corner by the grocery speaking with Isabel's cleaning person and he saw Becca come out with two suitcases and a shoulder bag and a laundry bag, it didn't matter if it was his: cab coming down the avenue, Daley flagged it and told the driver to turn into this block, there's a fare halfway down. He saw the trunk swing up and Becca load her bags and get out of the backpack and load that, too, and pull the trunk shut. He realized, then, that she was gone.

Her green class-size notebook hidden under a white towel in the bathroom linen closet. He took it downstairs. Its grainy, clothish surface was of some other educational system. Canadian or farther afield. Czech or Swedish. Not the plastic-covered elegant (*he* thought) notebooks seen in Mexico and Paris. More like a child's notebook *years* ago he had touched on a little desk in a village in Austria up in the mountains near the Yugoslav border. Setting the notebook down on the hall table, he felt the used thickness, the honest swell of the both-sides-written-on paper inside. He went back upstairs for some reason. In the linen closet he found the box of Tampax Regular Regulier gone. It was on the carpet on the window side of the bed. He picked it up. It had not succeeded in getting packed.

The phone rang and rang and stopped and he could hear the sound of a message and possibly female on the machine down in the kitchen. Immediately after, a call came in that was his brother, he knew the kidding sound, formal, expecting something, uncanny only as answering machines seem. Daley was perishingly sad not to have recognized the preceding message if it was Becca. Calling from where? A corner she had told the cab to wait for her at? It would be a relief of some kind, her going. He went back downstairs and saw the notebook dark gray-green in the glimmer from the glass street door glazed in arcs of decoration he had perhaps never noticed. The glass rattled when you slammed the door. He opened the green notebook carefully, the pages stiff and imprinted-feeling. He read some words—hers—"the independent activity must be difficult, truly difficult, and the reason why you do it has to have a consuming reality for you—"; "—a chain of events which shall be the formula for that *particular* emotion—" and another handwriting not round like hers and not in black ink but in blue:

> remember, he makes for his sleeping place
> in the shelter of a cave, and those children
> of the brine, the flippered seals, heave themselves
> up from the grey surf and go to sleep in herds
> around him, exhaling the pungent smell of the
> salt sea depths.

He shut the notebook as he had opened it, did not look. A rich, dirty old baseball mitt he hadn't traced the dust of in years—Graig Nettles's supposed signature on the left corner at the edge of the hollow—and a mitt beside it less used of similar vintage that had made a round trip to the stadium when the Tigers were in town in '79 or '80 or '81 lay under the hall table.

Daley took the green notebook and went to find a manila envelope for it in the kitchen, an offering for it, and, not finding one, found himself upstairs-bound again resisting by relishing the household's stunned peace; and he put the notebook back where he had found it. He refolded the white towel, the bedroom rug vacant behind him. Under the bed he found her heavily leafed paperback copy of an acting book, evidence of a struggle—to live, to be, to get the secret: Sanford Meisner, *On Acting*, on the creased, bent, stained cover the man himself in a coat with a fur collar, more ill than elegant, decisively large-rimmed glasses dark but pale like his beige color belying his terrible authority, wisdom, guidance, personal, lovable, chilly, distant, helpful, judging if you would take it. Sitting back down on his knees Daley fingered through the pages, a late chapter heading, INSTEAD OF *MERELY* THE TRUTH, and stage directions with the crossings-out all printed for some reason. Daley found himself in the garden and he took the taped hockey stick and smacked a tree and the end came off the way they make them now but when the phone rang he was inside in a moment but when it stopped returned upstairs and found a manila envelope but when he took the green notebook, aware of the empty carpet in the bedroom behind him, he leafed it open past several pages of crude drawings that he couldn't bear to see, and he read, *Will you do that for me? Will you do this for me? Will you just do it?* understanding again that the house could speak to him or communicate. In the kitchen, though, something was missing.

He couldn't focus his mind on what it was, the materials of the day around him, hard and soft, wet and dry, but during the day he remembered the thought she had approved of—he was stretching up to reach a file in a closet—that you made something and thus took action and made something that joined what had already been made but that did not itself have knowledge of you, for if it did you would be a god.

# 15

IT WAS TUESDAY EARLY, AND A BALD MAN DALEY RECOGNIZED SAT ON A stoop at this hour with a furled umbrella like a scepter before him. It was Bruce Lang. Becca had actually said she hoped Daley would take him off her hands. To be a means to some end had never confused Daley, to be of use even to this person, who held steady to a bond as well as some business. Yet Daley knew the bald man with the ponytail as much as he wanted to and wanted nothing from him and had nothing to say to him under this sky.

Daley came up the block. His legs ached with strength and possibility in long johns worn under his shorts. His first run in a week. The man on the steps looking with stoic familiarity in Daley's direction, Daley did not need to know, and he had no wish to discuss his sister's plans. Housing, theater, personal history. After Sunday night's third- or fourth-hand account of a painful event twenty-five years ago, he would not have cared if this man who must be the source of Becca's knowledge of it ever set foot in his home.

Daley had hit upon it Saturday at the top of his stoop. A naturalized Canadian, a draft dodger, this man who had turned his gifts to scrap-metal salvage along the lakes region years ago. Residues and reuseables and probably big-scale leavings, automobile and boiler and ocean brass and whatever sludge we have perfected in the making. And though the war was done it was so done with that it was done and discounted and was "history" in the new sense and you could say that "in the long run" the long-ago Communist enemy China had been the loser after all, the story of Than and her four fallen companions surfaces like a diver falling upward from the bottom; and a thorough review of the probabilities hardly ruled out this man knowing such a common method of disposal (not quite "termination with extreme prejudice" officially in that case because not official, but close enough to waste management on the human scale) or even knowing this event: one more in a late stage of a big Cambodian year, for coincidence if it was even that startled Daley no more than dear departed Becca, who assumed everyone knew everything and anyone could have anything if they would ask, history, her, you; and while a provoker, she was a secretly oiled hinge among men and had even said, Daley recalled now as he approached his own home, that she thought Daley could be of assistance to Bruce, and she had even thought that they would have a lot . . . but hadn't finished the vile phrase.

It came to Daley in the pale gray eyes, two skies not less violent or businesslike for being retreating in hue, it was schedule for Lang as it always had been. Yet not a matter of discovering something in him that had happened once, which anyone might know.

Daley stood before him, finding his keys in the hip pocket of his shorts, finding common cause in the other man's prepared look, the blunt, not especially hopeful, not at all unresisting, prizefighter-square, bluff figure asking of Daley some particular thing Daley later knew he had foreseen as jointly humbling. The Joost-Hoo automatic at the bottom of the clothes bag upstairs outlined itself in a quick, airport-departure-gate infra shot. The man must grudge this meeting.

"I know you," Daley said, beckoning Bruce up behind him.

A man to get right to the point, this man. In manner, if not really. "Thank you," Bruce Lang said introducing himself.

Daley said he was welcome, but for what?

"Good question. Damn," said the man. He turned toward the steps he had been sitting on, determined to be asked inside. But he was embarrassed. His fleshy, quick impatience took action. "Damn," he said, he kicked the brownstone step and a strip of facing fell off as big as a chocolate bar. Bruce picked it up. Had he rung the bell? Daley asked. No, it was early and he had expected Daley would be along soon. (Strange thing for him to know.) Heavy but not too heavy, bald with that Silicon (transplantable) intellectual and evilish ponytail happening at the back, light in some minute movement of his feet, well fed, and worn in the eyes and eyelids but a year or two younger than Daley at a guess. "Let's hope it won't be necessary to go back to court. You've had an extraordinary influence on her." Daley looked up to his front door and down into the basement areaway and started up the steps. "I mean," said the other, "urging her to stay on in the cast." Daley said he didn't much care what she did but he was not her lawyer. "I'm sure," said the other, "you'll know how to . . . you've extended a helping hand is all I mean."

Daley wondered if the other man believed him. He was leading the way again and again things behind him were out of control. That's what Becca testified to, Daley recalled, that things were out of control. "She's not here," Daley said, he opened the outer vestibule door, the old decorative beveling and now varnish-bare 1880s landmark look all he wanted to think about. Lang behind him, Daley could not bring himself to face him: "Why would you peddle that story now? Why would you do that? It happened, I'm the one not you who can vouch for that. Know why? I was there."

"She knew years ago," said Lang.

"—and it's done with," Daley said, surprised again. "It's public knowledge."

Some strain of excitement in the other man's voice, words between them, unknown next thing, roles. "*She* knew all those stories. She's a student of history, did you know that? A scholar. Gifted, if I do say so." Daley unlocked the inner door. "Her curiosity. My God. The States. Much she knows because of me," Bruce presented the slice of brownstone to Daley; it was surprisingly oblong.

"A history buff," said Daley.

"We've had amazing talks, it would be hard for you to imagine. Over the years. Over the miles. Since she was a child." (Who was this Bruce?)

"She's still a child," said Daley. It was his house. (*And she wants you to keep your hands off her life.*)

"She was never a child," said the brother. "The poise, the character, you can't imagine."

"I've seen her one-woman piece," said Daley.

It puzzled Bruce Lang, as if Daley had said something. "It's sort of her call," the brother said.

"You of all people," Daley said. What did he mean?

"She has extraordinary respect for you," said Bruce; "it's a professional decision; she'll make the best one she can. Eviction case aside, you have an influence here."

"I think you're mistaken," Daley said, "and we're not deciding her life." He laid the brownstone on the foyer table. He remembered the green notebook, the Tampax in the linen closet, a small cylindrical jar of some brown emollient left on the sink and still there beside his shaving soap.

In the dark hall, the man's presence questioned much, this house that he was looking over, everything and nothing, a place she had been. Daley heard a sort of snap, an energy change, from below and with it felt a seemingly structural, slightly shivering clunk in the house and asked Bruce to excuse him, there was a problem with the furnace. Bruce said he would come along. He stopped at the first-floor parlor doorway. "Look at that," he said.

"You can't imagine how strange that piece is," Daley found himself saying. "There's where she put it on for me."

"She's a thinker," said Bruce.

"I was a fool to get mixed up with you people," said Daley.

"Maybe you had no choice," said the other.

Daley excused himself: the furnace timer.

How did he heat this old place? Oil, Daley said over his shoulder. Daley wondered if Bruce expected to find the sister here, he was following Daley. They were descending the basement stairs. Daley indicated the kitchen saying that he would be right back. His uninvited visitor smelled of shaving cream. The cutoff had been switching on and off, he added, and Daley needed to call someone. How old was the furnace? the visitor asked, ignoring the kitchen and following Daley around to the cellar steps. Oil and wood furnace in the country, Daley said, though he didn't use that place much in the winter. Wood, said the other. Yes, it was fine but not that plentiful on the property if you were concerned about . . . Right. Daley had been sold the furnace in the country alternative oil and/or wood by a persuasive representative of an actually quite new company; Daley named it and Bruce knew the name of the Canadian partner. Daley didn't have a Kindred sink?

Daley didn't know what a Kindred sink was.

Canadian. They did a nice double sink.

Daley was quite happy with the kitchen as it was, but if he was throwing the kitchen sink out along with three or four lengths of waste pipe when he rerouted some of the plumbing, he would pass it on to Bruce if Bruce contracted for scrap this far south.

Why would you redo the plumbing? The man wanted to talk. He kept his black, rolled umbrella with him and here they were in the cellar. Well, he operated on a somewhat bigger scale than that, but he did try to make a difference. We save and we renew. It had not been terribly exciting, looking back, however. Except early on when the money came in and the business grew by itself almost independently, the empire as it had been called once in the press as it began to emerge along the lakes.

Bruce had not lost sight of his initial subject: "I meant only, when we were speaking before, that we expect a lot of you, considering. That is, to expedite her . . ."

"Her . . . ?" Daley peered along a line of exposed BX to remind himself where the power went, thinking, Who is this "we"? Thinking what questions about her he could ask if he were asking what exactly it had been like. Her curiosity.

"I have a couple of things of hers you can take with you," he said. Bruce Lang was at his elbow, the feeling was the man might know the answer to these electrical issues at a glance, though his business was scrap. He had other business with Daley, however. A deal to get done. Corners needed sweeping, the dusky cement odor, the house looking on largely. "What can I do for you?" Daley said, preoccupied.

"Ah," said the other. He didn't want to go. He didn't want to give up the house. "Do you get seepage down here?"

No, Daley had considered putting in a pump years ago, never got around to it. "Brickwork pretty sound," said the man standing before him listening maybe for silence.

Daley picked up the regular sound hardly even a hum signaling that the furnace was back to normal. Also now some rustle or steady recognition of light rain above him on the garden side reached Daley faint and bodily as memories of gray days when things got done if people would let you. He pulled back out of the place by the wall.

Why would not the *house* enable Daley to end this interview?

"I came here hoping she might continue in the play and that you could be prevailed upon to have the primary residence case dismissed, since Duymens told us you were handling it."

"The one outcome provides the other," Daley said, "stay with the play, case dismissed." (Ruley Duymens in his life again; another manager strangely independent of each other though not individual.)

Apparently not, was the surprising reply.

The furnace worked, who knew why? Daley would need to shower and leave for the office. He could feel the other man's focus like an opposite pole pushing Daley away from what? Would Lang like a cup of coffee? Thanks.

Indeed, the landlord, this woman in Florida, was bent on getting a market rent, and Beck's part in her operations seemed less clear than before. Becca sticks with the play, they get into the black, Beck sees his way to helping back the documentary next year or sooner. (Bruce using other people's money.) The men adjourned upstairs to the kitchen and Daley lifted a full kettle onto the front burner. He retrieved the paper from outside the basement areaway door and laid it on the kitchen table. He opened and pressed a filter into the hourglass. Bruce became a little hearty appreciating the old kitchen, the ancient custom cabinets, the "Miles" window, the dining room going toward the garden that didn't look as if there'd been many dinner parties lately. His mind was on this whatever-he-had-come-for; on the threshold of the backyard, "the garden," he came back to the kitchen just as Daley excused himself to see if the thermostat mercury was as it should be upstairs in the living room. "Why don't you . . . ?" Daley pointed to the *Times*, but Bruce Lang was following him, sociable, needing to talk, and suspicious here in the house as an entirety. "'Fraid I have things to do," Daley said on the stairs.

"So do I. As I said," said the other.

Daley said, "You didn't ring the bell this morning because it was too early; but you sat down to *wait* for me."

"I thought you might not be alone."

"Have you not understood your sister isn't here?"

In the living room, a floor through though half barricaded at the garden end by file cabinets and storage boxes, the visitor searched the street through the tall north windows. Daley needed to unscrew the thermostat to take it apart but this would wait until tonight. Bruce Lang was driving him crazy, but he wasn't. He tried to tighten the thermostat housing by hand. There was absolutely nothing he needed from this man who needed something from Daley. He came around the yellow sofa and sat down in it heavily. "Understand me, I've had a difficult life," said the brother; "mind you, I made something of it. You wouldn't believe what I went through after I went to Canada."

"It's true; I don't," said Daley, monkeying with the plastic housing, and realized that, apart from his reply being slightly off, it wasn't quite true; yet how *did* he know what Bruce had been through? Becca's words here in this room threatened to sift out from the thermostat and over the piano and along the rug—and Saturday night *It's you after all*— embodying her growing up in that family, screening it, transmitting, rethinking her history, her security at that time, the half brother helping her sleep in the beginning, telling her things as a child, she was a riot, a trip, which one was the sorcerer? *Him*, damn his trouble, his plans; damn even his poor mother who was visited by the F.B.I. twice a year and who died (though Bruce was friendly with the agent); and this American father of his, who drifted out of and into love with his Canada wife, Bruce's stepmother (for whom he had crossed the border a year before his son, as Daley was compelled to log the tedious history. "That's when——"); fisher-men killed, genitals plugged into a field telephone, Cong ears pickled for shipment to States, plastic explosive allegedly spread between crackers handed out to kids, but a marine colonel says answering these allegations is like "getting into a fistfight with a bucket of steam."——trouble? Her on top one private afternoon you only imagine, comfort, no more, except her life, the rest of——which has proved so far distinguished.

"No, that's not true I wouldn't believe whatever. I know you were a war resister," Daley said.

"It's nothing now."

"Probably so."

"That is why we want to create this record." Who was this "we" again? Daley would not ask; he wished for the kettle to whistle.

An old encroachment joined a new, and the vision was deeply uninteresting to Daley that was being offered, some past blurred or erasable. Some (the word that came to him through Becca) catastro-phe that was Bruce's business.

"Okay, you mean"——Daley would not pretend not to know—— "you mean a film. Small-scale, but with . . . pretensions."

A too-genial smile from the man: "Presenting that time."

"Draft evaders in Canada?" Daley said.

"War resisters. A selective record serving history."

"As if history existed prior to it," said Daley.

It puzzled the other man. "It was when she was talking about the States," he said.

"Pulling away from you."

Daley's visitor was up off the sofa his hand on the piano now. "Ottawa! We were in Ottawa the day after the vote of no confidence that Trudeau walked into the Commons and was presented with a daisy by the New Democratic leader and picked the petals off Yes No Yes No, will there be an election, will there not, and the answer was that there would be."

"Trudeau," Daley said.

"And I with a friend out there in the street, we could not know what a Conservative victory would do to our status in Canada. Can you understand that? Can you grasp it? In '74 with the amnesty hearings going on south of the border. All of us, though there was little contact, little solidarity among us once you made it into Canada, into the workforce. Little *hi*story you sometimes feared." But no, the film would be small, personal; *narrow* (Bruce said the word expressly, English, not American).

But no—Bruce looked around for a place to sit down again—not bitterly; with a sense rather of this house—did he still think Becca was in residence?—it was Daley's house. "It's about you, what you're saying," said Daley, and now he did hear the kettle downstairs and pointed to the door, and Bruce, raising and lowering his hand to the lid of the piano, said, "You play?"

His wife had played.

Ah, his wife; Becca played as a child.

Daley on the stairs to the kitchen, his visitor right behind him, saw again, in this swift sense, a little terrible, that he'd experienced before, at a piano with yellowed, here-and-there chipped-at-the-end real ivory keys, that disheveled overweight figure Leander a nicked and dilapidated baby grand in a club actually that Daley still didn't recognize with virtually no live music: stockbroker freed from the window of his monitor, that onetime competitive *swimmer*, Daley had been right—with mysteriously Becca's help or joint vision—hers elsewhere a happiness in the half gainer she imagined accurately he was stretching drily toward Wednesday onstage, and "Stick with the brother," mutual family words evoked by words or this swift sense (he was as certain of it as if he had made up a résumé for the prophetic young man who was a late-night pianist with troubled sinuses and lungs), those bearish shoulders hunched sensing the depth of the keyboard in the fingers inspired by the radiance of night, or *in advance* (!) by chords made up unknowing striding through a standard all by himself, it was that clear to Daley, convinced on instinct, not that it mattered. Daley had the wooden handle of the old kettle in his hand swinging it off the burner forgetting to just turn off the flame.

The steam came back at him burning his knuckle. He poured an ounce of water on the fresh ground Jamaican, let it soak in, filled up the cone halfway. "No," Bruce said, "we didn't know how it would go. I heard Trudeau in Windsor a week before the election, and then we heard him in Toronto that elegant man sharing the stage with Grease Ball Boogie, remember Marlboro Red in the rolled-up T-shirt sleeve, the Studebaker Hawk parked out at the curb, and he was going to win but for us it was uncertain, did you know that? And who would have thought Ford would give that brave speech to the V.F.W., except we didn't *want* 'earned reentry.' I have no idea where you were at that point, you were home by then."

Daley asked what Bruce Lang wanted of him—just so he knew. He had a few things of Becca's . . . He smelled the coffee. He had made it. Bruce took it black. So did Daley, who now found himself wondering, as perhaps Bruce did not, where Becca had spent Monday night, and most of all why she had not told him what she knew of him at once Wednesday night—Monday morning! Was there a reason?

Daley said he was going to shower now. He had a job. He paused at the door: "All this isn't it," he said. On the stairs he heard Bruce get up out of his chair. On the stairs he heard, "She didn't know who you were." Bruce doling out the truth to the girl who had left.

He smelled coffee following him like sound or the shape of the house, and at the bedroom threshold he stripped off his sweatshirt angry and sad but he left it by the bathroom door and came back out into the hall and went up the stairs to the third floor. Bruce turned off the landing slowly, balancing his coffee you assumed, intending to continue this conversation while Daley took his shower wherever that was.

But only Daley's shirt was there. Let the man find his sister's green notebook on the bed, her effects where he would; and Daley at the door to the third-floor workroom heard the steps seem to stop upon the carpet down there, and, finding a clean towel in the small bathroom here and a stained, milky old shower curtain, he stripped and ran the shower and stepped in and found an ancient sliver of soap on the tub edge and thought he had not seen the key in the door where it had been Sunday night and, in the defensive and abandoned and material and water-comforted instinct of the past few minutes and days, he believed that this young woman—her notebook with its lists of actions to take open on the unmade bed, its sayings, not your one-to-one confession (including another entry in that other hand in blue ink) even apparently illustrated with sketches of sex occasionally in some shape of memory, innocent instruction—had restored the key to its hook beside the amber jar of chutney homemade but not in this home, this kitchen, the unfolding aroma of coffee declaring the trouble and relief or silliness of this past week from Wednesday to Tuesday.

"So much is lost, what are you gonna do?" said Bruce in the doorway of this disused bathroom, for it was coffee Daley smelled. He peered around the shower curtain. Bruce Lang set Daley's full cup down on the toilet seat and retreated to the threshold, the street windows beyond, the privacy up here bearing once upon a time the weight of the house that bore in turn the creative motions of a marriage implicit and distantly tender and, it occurred to Daley, in some fashion "postwar." There was a table near the window that was Daley's and tables that had always been full of Della's materials, a stack of drawings still there of cliffs and beautiful ponds, Daley thought.

"A good thing," he said, and stepped out of the shower for a moment to drink.

"Your wife, now," said the visitor, his head outlined against the north light. He had managed now to see most of the house, and the question was unacceptable though not quite a question. Yes, she had worked up here.

"A dancer, though."

Daley soaped himself and could not fathom what this man wanted of him. Daley didn't find even an old rusty tube of Della's shampoo and he used what was left of the sliver to soap his head.

"She branched out. She retired. She ran an employment agency. She went in for diving."

"Was she any good?"

Well, she had a coach. It was Ruley Duymens, whom Bruce Lang knew.

The phone was ringing downstairs and then the machine came on. Daley rinsed his hair and turned down the hot and ran cold on his scalp and turned up the hot to warm his body, and turned the hot and cold off. The bathroom worked.

Daley brought his mug in and put it down on the tub edge inside the curtain and turned on the shower. He wanted to ask *What was it like?*

"To marry an artist," said the man in the room beyond.

"Yeah," said Daley. Daley found himself giving this Canadian businessman at seven-thirty on a Tuesday morning an account of Della's diving days abbreviated by time and discretion and ignorance. It was a medical center pool on the East Side down below the street level and it had a good one-meter diving board. Why was he doing this when Becca had known all along what she told him Sunday?

"It was a man's voice," Bruce reported, returning to the bathroom threshold.

"Della had access through the attendant, who was the sister of a client. It was the period of the agency, not long."

"But the agency still exists," said Bruce, it did not matter how he knew, Ruley or Becca, anyone or no one might know or care.

"They fought."

"Who fought?"

"He taught her what he could about diving. I'm not sure how he put it all together."

She must have told Daley about it, then, said Bruce just past the threshold.

Yes she told him, and once he went there.

Invited?

Why no.

Why had he done that?

And almost invisible. Della made her approach and took her high hop and landed and bent her legs, when Ruley screamed, "Too straight!" She didn't seem to hear. She went up off the board stretching for the ceiling for an instant before she fell into a full twist folding around not quite all the way into a tuck and opening out in a hurry to sneak in like an arrowhead, you weren't sure exactly what twisting and somersaulting she'd done in that second or two, yet Daley, absorbing it, was certain at the time that she had seen him.

"It doesn't sound very friendly."

It was private.

"It doesn't sound very—"

Though a public pool; and friendly wasn't the point; professional; or necessary.

"You're a widower," said Bruce. Daley said nothing. Bruce Lang lifted out of a stack of maps a geodetic survey inch-to-the-foot grid of an area Daley knew well. Daley was cold and wasn't putting his workout clothes on again; wrapped in a towel, he darted out the door into the hall. He turned to see Bruce let go of the map to float past the table edge onto the floor.

Daley was getting dressed when Bruce came into the second-floor bedroom holding both coffee mugs. The unmade bed, the green notebook fallen open, the round script in black, a sketch in the corner of a page. The bedroom. Daley opened a closet door. "At the bottom of this clothes bag there's a pistol. It's a Korean-Dutch-made automatic. A Joost-Hoo. I assume it's there. I thought I would throw it away when she died."

"You did?"

"Yes."

"You need protection over here near the river?"

"I couldn't say."

"And now?"

"Twelve and more years, it's still here."

Bruce went and sat on the unmade bed and rested his hand near the notebook. He seemed to take an interest in Daley. "A Russian poet shot himself—perhaps you know him—"

Daley shook his head, looking around for his shoes.

"—shot himself, a terrible thing to do—" Daley stood in the middle of the carpet nodding. "Shot himself with a pistol he had used as a prop years earlier in a movie. A revolver."

The man before him, no doubt already at work, showed some agitation. "That map. I've been back there," said Bruce, referring to the geodetic map he had left lying on the floor upstairs. "I've kayaked the sea caves at Ba Ham in November. You've probably been there, Tonkin Gulf, Halong Bay, those little little islands."

Daley said he had never made it up there; that was pretty close to Hanoi surely, when was this?

'Eighty-nine, it was in fact a business trip to the Fujian and

Shanghai area, a construction firm it was a good time to buy though he could have phoned his broker in Toronto but . . .

Daley had kayaked in Florida; they were unmatched for stealth fishing. Into sloughs—skimming across a mile-wide flat in six inches of water. Absolutely, said Bruce, trying to make a connection Daley could feel as he found a necktie and a ball of socks and drank his coffee—a sea kayak Bruce had tried in Galveston had rudder pedals, and the storage you need not worry about what with your low center of gravity. Daley said he had seen a ten-year-old kayaker out in the river at dawn rocking in the wake of a barge. "Who *was* that boy?" said Bruce strangely but seriously; you might think he knew of him. He would do better out there than in school, Daley said, knotting his tie; no, he didn't believe what he'd just said. He didn't want to make breakfast for this man.

"But you've been back," said Bruce.

Back? No. Not in that sense. Only once, still in the service.

Home on leave?

Honor guard. Daley unhung his jacket and took it by the collar loop and went and sat on the bed and drew on his socks. Daley saw Bruce's drift.

"So *that* was when." The man stood virtually over Daley as Daley thought where were his shoes, his shoes.

"What is it you want of me?" Daley took his jacket and left the room. His shoes must be in the kitchen. Even a lawyer could wear running sneakers nowadays with a business suit but.

"It is emerging," said the other man, patient now, unpleasant, not looking over the house anymore, a pathos in his blind thinking, the smell of him, on Daley's trail when knowing these things so easy to know might matter only to some personal project you really didn't want to hear about, sorry.

Daley outdistanced him. He heard Bruce say somewhere above him on the landing or the stairs, "It was *that* weekend."

"But you knew that," said Daley over his shoulder in his own house—the picket's placard BENEDICT ARNOLD SLEPT HERE you could see through the partly curtained motel window, eight degrees above; the Ho Jo New Center, a panel upstairs, coffee containers, the attention scary—a door gunner's testimony, and a helicopter gunner's from Philadelphia, more than one way to skin a Cong lady; rows of chairs on the second floor, a blond woman with a flag took over the podium briefly; and a few miles away the ceremony Daley had flown home for; and the rush of American news.

Daley turned the oven on. The strong, broad bald man with the ponytail arrived and put the two mugs on the counter next to the Melitta. He was a lion or a stubborn boxer or walrus or a slug here or manager looking a place over. He liked Daley, or needed him; it was in some decision come to on the stairs. "So your wife performed a full twist and a somersault or two and entered the water without a ripple," said Bruce surprisingly returning to the picture Daley'd . . . "How did she react to your presence?"

Daley cast an eye around the kitchen for his shoes. Bruce poured a half cup of coffee. It was the map and kayaking and back to this, and Daley's head was wet, and he wondered who Bruce and his stepmother had spoken to exactly at the Howard Johnson. He made you feel out of place but necessary.

"It was midmorning," Daley began again, as Becca's brother sat down—to find out the question; yes, and Daley guessed the side entrance, signed in at a desk and took the stairs down. His shoes on the cheap green carpet of the locker room, he heard the diving board recoil, the soft groan and wheeze of it, someone hitting the water like a soft sneeze. His shoes felt huge on the wet tiles—

Ah . . . uninvited.

—and in the shower room entrance he caught sight of the pool water truthful, comfortable, rough before he could bring himself to look down to the far end. Della stood dripping near the edge, her back to this guy in the black swimsuit Ruley, she was staring at the board, and her dark hair was slicked back like a pelt. She had on a black one-piece. She was a dancer, that was it—

"An athlete," said Daley's visitor who had a habit of looking like he was reaching a judgment, a brusque businessman on-site but taking his time. Some poignance or hope, what was it?

Daley sat down. "Well, in a way, and you don't know about the new work—"

"I'm sure I don't."

"—her friend, black artist named (it doesn't matter what his name was)—work with another company. Gym stunts you and I . . ." The new violence, trying to get out of a box, one end open to the audience, and crawling along high walls wired for sound so that you heard their nerves interrupting the . . . people who fall from great heights, young but . . . veteran.

Interrupting the . . . ?

Well, great paths, curves, inertial, intersecting.

Of course.

For this she wasn't spry enough anymore. She had virtually retired from *her* company yet hung around with these people who talked pretty loosely of Einstein. Daley listened to the cartoon physics worked up to explain what they were doing. Daley had predicted it, Della was a bird caged by not wire but chaos for the moment; got drawn into this inertial path falling bodies take, these extraordinary harnessed bodies, minds walking up walls so that the watcher's position itself shifted into a doubled midspace anchorage; and diving—

That must have been something, said Daley's guest.

Diving it came to Daley was her answer. To these bone-smacking experiments that extended Dance away from words again (thank goodness), yet from Dance up into the air. Daley wondered what he could do. For his wife. You get away with nothing, if you believe so. And elsewhere it seemed you could get away with anything.

"So there she was, dripping wet—" Bruce offered.

Daley got up and placed his mug in the sink. He hadn't *said* "dripping wet"—this woman beyond some protection or stage illusion. And he had said too much and would not go on. Ruley was talking to Della and she was looking away toward the board, the very peculiarity and bite of the instruction (or abuse, for it was both) kept the sound secret from the man in the blue blazer at the shower room threshold. Squinting in judgment, Ruley was still talking, and Della set off again but he went after her and as she noticed him—

Daley had edged back along the tile wall; it was just another rehearsal plus a little unpleasantness riveting for the uninvited and they could both die if he got his trivial wish, which he would never voice even to a visitor a dozen and more years later (who had a question for him Daley was about to elicit) and the woman attendant, auburn hair and a beautiful, a secretly courageous and focused chin, was waiting in the white-tiled entrance to the men's locker room not your typical lifesaver and Daley turned to look back at the board and they both watched the dive though the woman was watching him too, a new user, or somebody running the hospital, or a riddle, person visiting a patient who got into the wrong elevator, a salesman. But Daley might have to begin again.

Who was keeping who? Bruce Lang looked at his watch. "They say don't rehearse, these young people," Daley said, "did you know that? But you have to whatever they say."

"Absolutely," said Bruce Lang, "absolutely."

"Why I knew a man," said Daley, "who got a call from his wife telling him she was leaving him, she was sitting in the kitchen, and he must have gone cold, and he put down the phone in his office, and . . ." Daley made a gesture.

"You can't let them do that to you," said Bruce Lang, "in the office, in the pool, wherever; of course it's character."

"But if you never imagined it happening ...," said Daley.

"It's her character," said Bruce, "not yours—not mine."

"Do you know they had to bring in a defibrillator to revive him." Daley had to laugh. It was his own father.

"But what did he say?" Bruce asked.

"Say?"

Bruce got up to put his cup in the sink, and Daley heard steps on the sidewalk outside focusing the free disturbance of the city, its words breathed not for you yet not *not* for you. "There were three of you present in the pool?" Bruce said.

"I want you to know he cuffed her arm hard, it was kind of a shock to me—what do you do?—"

"And you're not supposed to be there." Becca's brother stood waiting.

"I was there," said Daley to Bruce, who didn't look away and the two men stared at each other, and Daley described two figures, two swimmers really, in a background of tile, neither seeming to register the fully dressed observer with an attaché case now several steps inside the humid light and chlorine ambiguity of the pool but then transfixed against the wall, afraid.

Bruce shook his head and looked around as if he had remembered something, he didn't register the footsteps ascending the stoop.

No, Della turned toward where she was going, and as she swung her arm out Ruley the rat man or otter, whatever he was, slammed her and she spun around at him, did Bruce get the picture?—bringing her other hand up to the place—

She died, didn't she? said the other man thinking of God knows what, maybe of his sister here with Daley for a few days.

—and Daley, still apparently invisible to these people, put down his case and thought Ruley would really hit her now, the attendant nowhere to be seen. "You deserve what you get," Ruley called to her, she had climbed onto the cocoa matting of the board running her fingers inside the seat of her bathing suit to pull it down over her buttock. She faced the board and still seemed not to see her husband who watched in amazement and knew what was going to happen and did not move as Ruley came too close now while the diver's concentration and split-second delay kept it all absorbed in her body—married or not—and jealousy was not the need to know what was in her body but to keep watch in it *with* her. Her eyes stared clear to this end of the pool. An arc surely, but did it touch the man in clothes?—who remained in question almost shockingly. The other man, the coach, whipped her thigh with a snap of the hand and she sidestepped and one foot slipped off the matting, her hands over her face though it was her leg that had been smacked. The man reached vainly for her arm, her wrist, destroying, now backing off cajoling, controlling, speaking low, what he had to offer, a gift probably not for absolutely top-drawer springboard diving instruction but for the plunge (other people's).

An obscenity from Della.

"Your wife died," said Bruce. Did he think . . . ?

"Not in a diving accident," said Daley.

"No, that automatic."

"The Korean—"

"The Joost-Hoo. I don't know that piece."

A Korean friend had given it to him.

So he had never . . . ?

Daley's friend Sook.

So this was . . .

"I had it the last year I was out there."

"So that in the incident, you were carrying it."

Daley continued with the diving. *Taking too much on yourself*, Ruley's harsh words to her insulting, while Della preparing to execute the dive and now stepping like a dancer along the cocoa toward the go-ahead hop mixed the man's sound into the lurking voice of the pool.

"Why didn't you speak at Detroit?" said Bruce Lang, looking here and there in the kitchen for something, so maybe this was what he had come to ask, what he had come for, or didn't care about diving or a woman smacked on the leg, or even what came next, though he had taken particular note of the full twist with a one-and-a-half? People take from what you give them something or other and you don't know what it might be.

"Why didn't I speak? Why didn't the guy?"

"He did. He spoke to us."

". . . because *he* wasn't afraid; he was the one who tried to pull the young one back."

"Why did he do that?" said Bruce.

"He must have told you that, didn't he tell you that or have you forgotten or didn't you think?—the others were pushed but he tried to pull her back, she had something in her head. And he was there, he was right there, he showed up that ugly day at Howard Johnson—they're out of business now."

"Right by the Ford Hospital," said Bruce.

"How did you get through the tunnel? They would have spotted you."

"Got m'feet wet," said the other man.

"You were a pretty busy guy. Fucking your stepmother, cruising the Winter Soldier hearing at the Ho Jo over the border—you were right to . . ." control going, things learned of necessity by accident, yet Daley had spoken.

"It's true," said this man with the broad face before him, Daley imagined a head of hair, this square face twenty-five years younger at one end of that second-floor conference room looking for a seat apparently. "He said it was *your* story. He said it wasn't clear, the issue of an unqualified man at the controls." Daley peered under the kitchen table. "God, man."

Daley had heard the front door above them. His visitor possibly had not. "But forgotten," was the reply, subdued; "we wondered why you were there."

The honor guard, Daley explained again, ignoring the "we," for a dead man he barely knew. Miscellaneous as the Ann Arbor pilot that morning or the previous morning rescued from the Lake Saint Clair ice field by a helicopter from Selfridge Air Force Base. Eight above.

"No no, not in Detroit! We know why you were there. Why were you—"

"At the controls you mean."

"Of that . . . Kiowa was it?" The false note historical, a scrap of information incorrect from the other incredible and banal man, no more, nothing that Daley, shaking his head almost imperceptibly, would want to make anything of. "No. In that aircraft in the *first* place," said Becca's brother.

"I told your sister why," Daley said.

Bruce became more sensitive; he was on the spot, persisting. "I heard about a court-martial that never happened. You were missing for three days?"

Daley felt across his stomach and his shoulder blades and the nape of his neck the impression of steps above them retreating, ascending he knew to the second floor, a carpeted stairwell, the bedroom, the unmade bed, the notebook open, and it dawned on Daley ending and extending a time-consuming session with a man who had now left his umbrella somewhere in the house, that the third person here had kept the front-door keys yesterday morning just in case and sure enough had recalled what she had forgotten; and a vaguer question not to do with deeds and effects that might be really why this dogged man before him who'd now heard what Daley had heard was here in the first place.

Bruce Lang in the doorway to the hall that led to the stairs in one direction, the basement areaway door in the other: "She must have come back for her things," he said. It was off, the way the brother said it.

"Why did you tell a kid a story like that?"

"It was what happened."

"Seven or eight years old?"

"It was what happened to me, a nightmare, everything and everyone in it."

"To you!"

"I never identified you."

"Why did you tell her now?"

"She knew that old story; now she knew you."

Daley didn't want to inquire because there was no bottom to get to. "When you told it, how could you not have named me if you knew my name?"

"As easy as anybody can find out these things, a name, somebody's history."

"It's not my credit history we're talking about." Daley had lost the question, which could not be more than the key to nothing important yet it was Becca, what had been told to her once and then now.

"Anybody at all," said the man with the ponytail. He hated Daley for a moment, having come here to look him over.

Daley played the message; he had to get on with his day. Wolf on the machine asking, "What does it take to get back to me?" He was swinging through with the younger girl; you couldn't tell when.

"Your friend van Diamond," Bruce Lang continued, on instinct, "he knew of the incident from way back."

"Those rows of folding chairs," Daley said.

"Yes we looked along the rows of folding chairs, up there in the second-floor ballroom."

"Did you think you'd see it in someone's face?"

"For years I knew the name."

"You have a head for business," said Daley.

"History," said the other.

"No, you saw me on your way out Saturday night and Beck introduced us and you remembered my face from twenty-five years ago because you never forget even a scrap of whatever."

There was more to know. At the Howard Johnson New Center Motor Lodge at West Grand and Third over the course of three days Bill and Bruce must have looked each other in the face at least once. Certainly they had narrowly missed each other on January 31 by an hour, no more, A.M., P.M., at 967 Emerson, the two-story brick house where names and testimony of a hundred supposed veterans covered the walls of one guarded room they kept locked some of the time for security. There was more to know. How Daley's name had come to be attached to him or to his face or to his work, trifling beyond the two people who had come into the house one after the other this morning. The brother lingered in the doorway, unsure what had been said or done to him: "Your friend van Diamond . . ."

"No friend of mine."

"When I told him to call my sister and give her the number of a certain lawyer . . ."

You overlooked this contemptible brag, though perhaps Becca did not. Yet Daley believed in Ruley. Ruley had wanted to make the call himself. He had been thinking about it for years.

The man was gone, leaving the smell of morning cologne, of coffee, of water, of earth below. But Daley said after him, "He had reasons of his own to give her my number."

Personal sounds somewhere in the house Daley couldn't identify except necessarily to feel invaded by these people.

And then it was Becca's voice: "How could you have come here?" she said, the reply obscure. "And what business did you come here for—to add yourself to *this*?"

The answer swung subtly away from Daley in some direction, he thought he heard the word *location* or *vacation* or *mistaken*. He saw on the kitchen table the absence he could not name yesterday morning. He could hear the keys come down on the table. These people were having a family argument, the point of it audible—maybe why Bruce had come here, after he and Daley had cleared away the other reasons.

Daley thought Becca had brought something, and then he saw she must have the notebook in her hands coming down the stairs from the second floor. It was his house telling him, or second sight that was experience of sound and distance and weight and air and experience. His house was being used at the moment. He needed his shoes. They were not here. He heard a distant something drop, and a cry from the man, it came from the second-floor bedroom, and presently Daley heard the front door, and from the kitchen doorway, uncertain where to go, he looked across the kitchen, and through the basement window he saw Bruce's legs hasten past.

# EXTEND

DALEY WAS UP THE LADDER STRETCHING TO HAMMER IN A BRACKET that had come loose strangely around a conduit along the beam near the furnace when Becca came down the steps and saw him and remembered. That was what had made her happy the first night on stage. That stretch. Nothing really that he did. He looked down from the ladder. The springboard's give, the swan dive flung upward arched instead with the whole upper body backward toward the quivering board while carrying forward, that was the genius of it, the whole body stretching, exposed, the compact legs-together, insteps-together, toes-pointed-like-a-tail body bringing its head back, the nose, the pubic horizon, this inertially forward back dive in toward the board on the way down clearing the end of the board just—the coarse matting folded under it—and always daring the cracked neck, scraped face, chest and thigh abrasions.

He told her, just as he had described the dive to Sook and how Ruley this time went in after Della and was talking to her treading water under the board following too close when she backstroked toward the ladder because suddenly she had drawn back a leg and stamped him in the face, gave him the heel of her foot hard enough to flatten his nose, and turned over and reached the ladder. The mark on Della's thigh was still there when she climbed up out of the water without further ado leaving Ruley in the pool until she looked over her shoulder and saw what she had done, curls of darkening blood there in the water. Did Ruley care for her?

And Daley up against the wall of the pool in his clothes. And Daley, after Ruley had struck Della on the leg, had known what would happen as he often wouldn't admit he did, this time sure that Ruley would upset Della or worse and qualify to be punished (for Daley could see him ten seconds before it happened diving in after Della though to be truthful his extreme brief but wrinkled European bathing suit could have been dry for years).

And for an instant in the air Daley thought it was him she really wanted to please, her husband, though not directly. If she even knew he was present.

Then, weeks after Ruley vanished, another half gainer damn near perfect.

"She looked down at you," said Becca. Daley looked down from the ladder.

"How did you know that? It had a great slow action that board," said Daley. "She was about to begin her approach and—it was funny—"

"Funny!" Becca said disappointed in him.

"I mean she took a deep breath as if she'd been holding it. She said, 'We're not really close at all.'"

He knew just how the diver up on the cocoa matting had picked that moment, taking her first step, it would be one-two-three almost to the end of the board and a dancer's toe-downward hop almost before he could think what to say. It was in Daley, whatever she meant, absorbed by him; she was right enough. A damn near perfect half gainer and his retort to the departing diver if he could only recall, an instant before, that this original young woman a dozen and more years later seemed to say was some mistake.

The mellow give of that long-ago slow board the diver knew how to wait for, flung upward then—that brief body above him chancing everything and ignoring it.

"Typical of you that you tried to answer her."
Della had had little splits in the sole of one foot, nothing serious. The phone rang.

Becca listened hard to hear anything she was missing. In the old days she would make an experience go away by talking over it. Out-

talking it. Until a thought came to her which she wrote down somewhere: you could make an experience go away the way when someone leaves you you go have a new experience of your own that you
haven't had with them. Though she had done most of the leaving up
to now. Damaged people did a lot of leaving or they did a lot of staying. She was far from damaged. Had it agreed with her?

He hadn't realized but he felt the infinitesimal alteration of pressure in the house with the opening and closure of doors a floor or two
floors away. The front door, the second-floor spare room door; the
door of the third-floor bathroom, which Becca used one morning
while he was shaving but then she came scampering down dripping
wet without a towel and wrapped herself around him, he had on his
running shorts and long johns and knew that she hadn't come dripping downstairs just to get a towel. Her hair flat and twinkling, her
shoulder humorous or young, her whole bareness and presence
reminded him of what he knew about the house. He asked her if she
had ever been pregnant? Yes, that was why she came down to New
York. What about the acting? That too; that was the main reason.
Did Bruce know?
No way.

They were out on the steps in the late afternoon and she listened
again to the account of his brother's mishap in Osaka, she had some
chemistry from her brief foray into forestry. Wolf's job originally an
underwater structure: to rebuild it of molybdenum-coated steel
trusses connected with diagonals and verticals and chords as if it were
a bridge. Trouble was, a pocket of a relatively new explosive (actually
environmentally friendly) had been deposited down there against an
existing bulkhead, an exploratory demolition that the design team
had simply abandoned. It was that simple.
"There's simplicity for you," said Becca.
"Not very Japanese."
The two jobs of demo and rebuilding had coincided by chance. As
the two explosions had seemed to. First, the Panamanian tanker of a new
wheelhouse design a quarter of a mile off, and then the cached experi-

mental compound practically next to the steel and aluminum trusses. The parent explosive was this cubane, which unlike gasoline sinks like a bullet.

"You bring things down to what you can understand," Becca said.

"Oh I always did."

"I don't mean you," said Becca. "Americans."

"Americans?"

"The old ways," she made a gesture.

"What old ways?" Daley said.

"They get them in the light of, not ancestral wisdom but . . . materials."

"Oh we just think we're judging for ourselves," he said to her. It carried him away, his willingness to know such things in the midst of his mysterious and acceptable ignorance.

"That's what the man said," Becca replied. She named an American thinker.

The car was parked in front of the house and as she went around to get in, something she had said, or perhaps it was him, brought his brother mysteriously close to him.

Wolf had several times traveled down the coast of California seeking cheap abalone. Their father had been told by a suburban (actually Lake Erie area) herbalist that this rock-dwelling shellfish, the best source of protein in the world but it would run you sixty to a hundred dollars a pound now in Cleveland or Seattle, might strengthen his prostate and his heart. At a beach north of Los Angeles Wolf and his older girl had watched a herring gull attacking an abalone. Not settling for what little of the flesh it could get at, the bird was trying to pry the stubbornly adhering abalone by its steely-mottled iridescent shell off the rock its home base from which with its "tongue" it had slowly month upon month licked nourishment and grown its "foot" beneath its roof. It was a big and determined herring gull and when at last it unstuck the shellfish, it had lifted it a few feet and lost it so it dropped with an unintended accuracy down onto the rock. When it hit on end, however, the abalone slid off into four feet of water.

Nearby was an Asian woman and she asked Gemma to help her retrieve the abalone. About the abalone the birds never learn, she said in a high, slightly breaking voice, smiling into the glitter of the afternoon. The girl waded in and soaked herself reaching to the bottom, and found the abalone, the edges definite against her fingertips. It was shaped like a steam iron without the handle or like an ear. She knew more about abalone than the woman perhaps realized. The girl came out, turning the abalone over to touch the tough flesh. She and the woman examined the breathing holes along one side of the shell. The shell was a roof, an unusual roof, as it turned out, for the living muscular material that you ate.

Gemma gave the abalone to the woman who put out her hand not quite asking but Gemma put the abalone in the woman's hand and looked into her face because there was always something to find in someone's face.

Thus it had happened that Wolf met, somewhat against his will, some members of a Cambodian community in a town nearby many of whom claimed they were blind. Yet no doctor would believe it.

Wolf had been thinking about abalone. The strength of the shell that could withstand extraordinary force. The Asian lady and the little girl, not so little anymore, walking up the beach ahead of him, Wolf imagined the material. Its composite nature. His instinct that you could hit this lightweight shell with a sledgehammer and it wouldn't break.

He spoke with his older brother by telephone. Did this lightweight shell material break as you increased the force upon it? Wolf didn't think so. All it was was the calcium deposited by seawater. How it hung in there, its own uncanny homemade cement binding its flesh to the rock. This mysterious inner structure of this composite material infinitesimally stacked. His brother in New York consulted someone with him in the room, probably the kitchen.

The name of a lab in fact not so many miles from Wolf's pay phone that Daley knew of was noted perfunctorily, but Wolf would figure this one out himself. He had even hoped to take the abalone off the lady's hands, this little slightly bowlegged Asian person of perhaps forty, it wasn't as if it was a cure for leprosy. What a crack it had taken, landing on end or partly on its back, on the rock it had been stuck to.

His daughter had read his mind. The lady wanted the abalone, knew exactly what it was, the extended muscular "*foot*" that you ate raw or steamed; and she wanted the iridescent shell, the creature's roof that was lined with mother-of-pearl. His daughter bent her head slightly to converse with the Asian lady.

This was near Arlight and Point Arguello, there were even safety areas left by the departed missile program that had preserved the coastline, and Wolf had phoned his brother several times and was angry at not getting through though at his daughter for making such good friends with the Cambodians; but glad as well as irritated, he recalled later when Daley filled him in on what an atomic force microscope had seen fit to measure.

Stuck into the infinitesimal stacked tablets of calcium carbonate, into really the glue, the cement, the matrix, the protein adhesive that the abalone secretes, the cantilever tip of the microscope pulls the material that stretches and stretches. Yet when it breaks . . .

The protein matrix breaks. But gradually. The abalone protein cement breaks little by little, like tiny knots or gatherings stuck together that pull out or break here and there along the length, as if this were a string. How to create materials like this in the lab. One by one the individual bonds in the abalone protein will break, but very slowly: and because, not to mention that they can re-form eventually, they break before the entire molecule does, they are called sacrificial bonds. It takes huge amounts of energy to break them. The abalone shell is three thousand times more fracture-resistant than a crystal of this very calcium carbonate it's made of.

Wolf's interest was not quite theoretical. His interest curiously had grown in his older daughter, her concentration, her learning, all that she knew. Wolf couldn't express it. Not birds exactly, or the river that passed through the valley; or only the people she seemed to meet and talk with, she was so grown-up. Was it everything? It was a mystery to him. Whatever it was, it was new.

They were in the car crossing the Tappan Zee Bridge. They had been speaking of Than, and now Becca was reading. "It was a shock," she said.

Daley said he had gotten himself into it.

"It was a shock."

"The whole thing—that they wanted me along for the questioning."

"It was a shock."

"You've said that. It was the young one more."

"My mother wondered about her."

"He tried to hold her back. He did all he could. God."

Becca was looking at him and he couldn't think.

"Who did?"

"The marine who told Bruce and your mother. She got free of him."

"She what?"

"Or he let her go, as the ship lifted, and she went out the starboard side sideways, and that makes five, okay? Put that in your film."

"Not mine."

"He acquired an old French rifle in the incident."

"And you? What did you get?"

They passed a gas station and a Wendy's. "It's history."

"If history were what happened," said Becca.

"It's what we think."

"Some of us," she said, always instructing him.

"Nothing is evidence except in respect to a question," said Daley somehow, but he said it. He had no idea if she would like the place he was taking her to.

"Does it all need to be held together?" Becca said reading her book.

"What we think about it is history," Daley said.

"Is that your contribution?"

"That's my contribution," Daley said.

"Plus a house," said Becca. "Two houses."

"See what you think."

One late afternoon it was unseasonably mild and they were sitting on the front stoop and aware of the neighbor watching them out his window across the street. Becca had a skirt on. She was still very much an actress. She would be leaving for the theater presently. Her shoulder was up against Daley. It was the future they were looking at. They were talking about earthquakes, though, and Daley told the late-night story of Lotta's Connecticut earthquake, how it had made more of an impression on him than he had realized then  and somehow he had acquired some knowledge about earthquakes in the next few months and years, he hardly knew where it had come from, and about the growing interest in the Northeast among seismologists.

Well, he had gone to look at the Armenian quake of '88, she recalled.

It was true, and the buildings there were not much weaker than here. New York is in the middle of a plate, not at the edge, so waves would travel faster than they do in California. They say a 7 quake is a two-thousand-year event. Two thousand years from when? From the Dutch and the Indians shaking hands? From 1492? From the time of Christ? Bricks in the street. Whole facades down. A guy up there above you sitting in his bathtub. Even a steel-frame high rise, which would be the most stable—think of what's going on at ground level, gas mains, fires, our two water tunnels from upstate built during World War I and at the beginning of World War II have never been shut down for maintenance. And one of them, which is actually leaking, is right next to a fault where there was once an earthquake in Wappingers Falls. And forget Manhattan bedrock, we've hydraulicked so much soft landfill in at the edges you can . . .

Was he passing this on to her, she wanted to know, for her to do something about it? Daley felt her shoulder against him and her thoughts. "Sleeping with you, I've learned a lot," he said.

"I've heard that one before." Becca took his hand and remembered and looked at his wristwatch. "I got a play to get to," she said.